"Bridie Chance! I know you are hiding nearby. I know you can hear me. Listen well now. If you do not come from hiding in three minutes, I will return to Chateau Valbrison. And with the help of my friends, I shall begin to make your sister wish that she had never been born! Do you understand, Bridie Chance?"

Bridie felt the blood drain from her face. She understood only too well. If she did not quickly offer herself up to the scoundrel who sought her, she would condemn her sister to a fate far worse than any death. There was nothing she could do but surrender—and gamble against all odds for her life...

The Capricorn Stone

**MADELEINE
BRENT**

FAWCETT CREST • NEW YORK

Library of Congress Catalog Card Number: 78-22807

ISBN 0-449-20149-X

Printed in the United States of America

First Fawcett Crest Edition: July 1983

10 9 8 7 6 5 4 3 2 1

⚡ *one* ⚡

Almost every week, for as long as I could remember, my mother had experienced a premonition and uttered a warning of disaster. Her forebodings were never specific, the calamity was always nameless, so it was strange that she did not speak of any premonition in the week before the two men came from London to Latchford Hall, for they brought with them sudden and terrible disaster which was to crush our family and change my life in a way unimaginable to me.

On that hot afternoon in July, when they came to our home on the low rise just outside the village of Wynford, I was two miles away on the edge of the heath, sitting in the sun outside old Tom Kettle's cottage, lazily penciling on my sketch pad while he worked with a great iron auger, boring out a log to make an elmwood pump.

Every now and then I would look up at the sky with a scowl of mock anger, pretending to myself that I felt annoyed because it was unblemished by a single cloud and too perfect for my liking. If Nannie Foster had been there, she would have chided me for the scowl, even though I was now twenty-one. "Exaggerated facial expressions are not ladylike, Miss Bridie." She had been saying those words to me ever since I was old enough to understand, but I had never broken myself of the habit. Surprise or puzzlement, pleasure or anxiety, whatever emotion I felt, my face would always want to show it much too emphatically.

Nannie Foster had tried hard. So had two governesses and my boarding-school teachers.

"Don't grin so, Miss Bridie."

"I'm sure your eyes will fall out if you raise your eyebrows any higher, young lady."

"For goodness' sake, child, don't laugh so heartily."

"Don't grimace as if you were in agony, dear. You're only writing a French translation."

Perhaps I did not try very hard myself. At school, and now at college, my friends seemed to find me amusing, and no doubt I played up to this. I was never going to be pretty enough to be admired for my looks or clever enough to be respected for my brains, so I had to be content with making people laugh, even if the laughter was not always entirely kind. But at least I could always make Bernard laugh with me rather than at me, and this was more important than anything else, for Bernard Page, from Lowestoft, a rising young architect, was my fiancé, and we were to be married next summer.

Looking up from my sketch pad, I studied the field of ripening corn beyond the cottage, wishing that I could show the heavy scattering of poppies. Scarlet on gold, they would give no pleasure to the tenant farmer when he came to reap the crop, but they were a joy to the eye. Field and cottage were no more than a background to my sketch. The central feature was Tom Kettle himself.

He had been born in the same year and on the same day as Queen Victoria, so both were now in their late seventies. Tom was a Fenman by birth, but after spending some time as a soldier and fighting in the Afghan War he had settled here in East Suffolk, two or three miles from the coast. For over half a century he had lived in this cottage alone, but the village folk still regarded him as something of a stranger, for the Fens lay a full fifty miles away to the west, in another world, where the farmers knew nothing of cows but thought only of beef animals and pigs.

Tom Kettle did no farmwork. He made kitchen furniture and elmwood pumps, and had been doing so all his life. The iron auger he was using now had a stem some four yards in length and as thick as my wrist. The T-piece at the end was as long as his outstretched arms. At this moment he was bracing himself to turn the huge instrument. Its stem was supported by a loop of rope attached to a stake driven into the ground, and the cutting screw was buried deep in the end of an elm log propped at an angle, slowly hollowing it out to make the body of the pump. Some of the farms had begun to use the new cast-iron pumps now, but these were not fully trusted. There were pumps Tom Kettle had made thirty years ago that still worked sweetly, and the iron pumps had yet to prove such endurance.

It was half an hour since we had spoken, half an hour since Tom had last taken a rest from his work. Now he released his grip on the massive handle, pushed his old hat back on his gray head, wiped his face with the neckcloth he wore winter and summer, and moved to sit with me on the oak bench. A tankard of ale stood in a canvas bucket, in a few inches of water, under the shade of the table beside the bench. Picking it up, he drank deeply, wiped his mouth, looked at my sketch for a while, then at last said, "T'ent bad."

"No, Mr. Kettle, it's not bad," I agreed, and laughed. "Most things I do aren't bad, but just occasionally I feel it would be nice to do something well for a change."

"Can't all be somethin' pertickler, Miss Bridie."

"Oh, I know." I hunched my shoulders and drew down the corners of my mouth. "I was just wishing."

He chuckled. "That don't do no good, wishin'. You fared lucky you got learnin', Miss Bridie. You wrought a good tidy time wi' schoolin'."

I nodded, and spoke with a heavy Suffolk accent. "Dew seem loike a duzzy long toime." Tom Kettle had known me all my life. He knew that in childhood there had been two governesses, then a boarding school for young ladies in Colchester, and now I was a student at Girton College, the handsome building of red brick three miles from Cambridge. To a man who had never been to school in his life, it would indeed seem that my education had been going on for "a good tidy time."

"Gettin' wed to that feller, then," he announced, and took another swallow of ale.

"Yes, we're to be married next June. It's very exciting, Tom."

He pondered. Then: "Going on wi' schoolin' after?"

"Oh, gracious, no. I shall leave Girton at Easter." I had been reading for my Tripos in Medieval with Modern Languages, but with no special purpose. I would be giving up nothing of importance.

After a little while Tom said, "Lucky feller, your Mister Page."

I turned to look at him with round-eyed surprise. "Bernard? Oh, I'm sure most folk think I'm the lucky one, Tom."

"Folk," he said with heavy contempt.

I laughed. Tom was a bachelor with a firm dislike of females. He had always made an exception of me, though I could never think why. Even so, it was a rare compliment he had just paid me, and I felt myself flush a little with pleasure. I had long ago resigned myself to the fact that I was a rather gangling, clumsy, plain girl, but there were sometimes moments when I could not help wishing that I looked more like my younger sister, Kate, who at eighteen was small and beautiful, with a way of moving that was like the swaying of a flower. She was also blessed with outstanding musical talent.

If I had not loved her dearly, I would have been jealous of Kate, for I lacked all her gifts. I even lacked ambition, for I always tended to drift comfortably along on whatever course the tides of fate carried me. I had barely scraped through the Little-Go, as it was called, the first of the examinations to be passed for acceptance at Girton. I was reading Languages because I enjoyed the subject, but knew I was a plodding student unlikely to do particularly well. The University of Cambridge did not confer degrees on ladies, which meant that we had to go in for honors, and as I did not expect to be successful I had probably been wasting my time.

This did not trouble me unduly, for I had felt no particular urge to use my time in any other way. I had a number of friends at college who liked me well enough, perhaps because I amused them—not by my wit, but because they found humor in the way I spoke, moved, and looked. If a girl jumped to her feet and exclaimed, "My goodness, I've left my notes somewhere in the Bottom Corridor!" other girls would take little notice. If Bridie Chance did it, everyone would laugh. I had been happy at Girton and looked forward to my last months there, but I looked forward very much more to becoming Bernard's wife and beginning a new life.

Beside me, Tom Kettle set down his tankard in the cool bucket, pushed it into the shade, then got to his feet. "I'll be goin' to hev me tea, come 'alf an hour. You'll stay for a dish o' frumenty, Miss Bridie?" This was wheat boiled in milk, with cinnamon and sugar, a much favored recipe in our parts.

I looked at the little gold watch my father had given to me at Christmas. "Thank you, Mr. Kettle, but I must go soon. This is the day Signor Peroni comes up from London for Kate's piano lesson every week. They're busy the whole afternoon, and then I have to be there to give him tea before he leaves to catch the train back to London. Mama is always so nervous about playing hostess to anybody, and she likes me to do it for her during vacation."

He shook his head, frowning. "Tes shame, your mam bein' so witched. Do she be born in the chime hours, them Pharisees keep her safe from witchin'."

I had heard this many times before. In old Suffolk lore, those born in the hours of three, six, nine, or twelve could not be bewitched. "Pharisees" were fairies, and Tom Kettle was far from being alone in his belief that the little folk were active among us. There were fairy loaves, so-called, on the brick hob of his cottage fireplace, and in many another fireplace throughout the county. In fact, they were fossilized sea urchins.

Tom stretched, spat on his hands, gripped the handle of the auger, and resumed his work. I studied him for a few moments, then decided to sketch his head and shoulders, trying to put into the bearded and weather-beaten old face some of the fierce strain imposed by the effort of turning the great auger in iron-hard elm.

As my pencil moved I realized that I had little hope of ever improving my very limited ability as an artist because I was never able to concentrate hard enough. While I sketched, or drew with pen and ink, or painted with water colors, my mind would always wander away. Now I was thinking about Kate, and how much my mother would miss her when she went away to London in September to be a student at the Prince Consort College of Music.

As Nannie Foster had said when we were children, and was still saying quite often, no two sisters could have been less alike. Kate did everything with passion, whether it was playing the piano or writing a letter, laughing or crying, loving or hating. She was a creature of strange moods, whims, and contradictions. I had often known her furiously angry with me one moment, contrite and full of affection the next. Compared with Kate I was a very prosaic girl, sharing none of the fervor and excitement that always seemed to be bubbling within her, and yet we got on well together. I did not even resent her being so obviously my father's favorite child, for this seemed only natural to me. I was deeply happy for her to be going to study at the Prince Consort College of Music, but I did not like to think of Latchford Hall without her. With my father abroad most of the time, Mama would only have old Nannie Foster for company.

My heart lifted as I thought of my father. He was coming home from Paris next week and would be remaining with us until mid-September. Papa was a tall man with thick brown hair curling over his temples and wide-set laughing eyes, a man who seemed to carry sunshine with him on the most wintry of days. Our home was a different place when he was with us, for he was quite unlike the rather stern and austere gentlemen I had occasionally met who were the fathers of some of my friends at college. Perhaps it was the Irish in him that made Roger Chance different, though he rarely spoke of his youth in Dublin, and his accent was slight. Certainly he had a gift for talk and a thousand stories to tell, many of them greatly exaggerated to make them the more amusing.

When my father was with us there was always a sense of excitement in Latchford Hall, and much laughter. Even Mama seemed at peace with the world instead of being in a state of constant anxiety and unease. Nannie Foster still sniffed and frowned in pretended disapproval of Papa's happy-go-lucky manner, as she had done from my earliest memories, but in her heart she was no less delighted than the rest of us to have him at home once more.

Nannie Foster had come to us late in her life, and when Kate joined me at boarding school, Nannie had stayed on at Latchford Hall to keep my mother company. She was now nearing seventy. "Lord bless us, are you still here, woman?" my father would cry in pretended amazement whenever he returned from abroad. "I thought some handsome fellow would have carried you off long since."

Nannie would bridle and purse her lips. "That's no way to speak in front of the young ladies, Mr. Chance. And besides, it's Black Shuck will carry me off, for it's too late for a man."

Black Shuck was the legendary creature of folklore in Norfolk, a monstrous black dog with a single flaming eye in the middle of his forehead. He wandered the fields and lanes on wild nights, howling in a way to freeze the blood, and to glimpse him was a sure sign that you would die within the year.

Nannie had been employed in two or three big houses in Norfolk for twenty years before coming to Latchford Hall, and although she had now been with us for almost as long, she still regarded herself, in true Norfolk fashion, as being somewhat superior to Suffolk people. This was in spite of the fact that she was not an East Anglian at all, but had been born in London.

In many ways Kate and I were more at home with her than with our mother, for it was Nannie Foster who in the main had brought us up until we went to boarding school. As a result, we did not speak with any particular accent. We could indeed use Suffolk talk if we wished, and sometimes did so for our own amusement. It was speech so broad and full of local words as to be almost like a foreign language to any stranger. Kate could do it better than I, for she had a quicker ear and a gift for mimicry. "Tes some crowd out abroad es' mornin', Bridie," she might say, "so dew yow luke out fer ice, don't yow'll slip an give yarself sich a julk."

A chuckle from old Tom Kettle broke my reverie. He had paused and was resting his elbows on the thick handle of the auger. "You luke right comical with your 'at loike that, Miss Bridie," he said. I had tipped my straw boater well forward over my nose to keep the sun from my eyes. Now, using both hands, I moved it back with a flourish that made him chuckle again, then closed my pad. I stood up and moved to where Daisy stood in the shafts of the gig, sleepily twitching her ears to discourage the flies. "I must be going along, Mr. Kettle," I said. "Thank you for letting me sketch you."

"Tes my pleasure, Miss Bridie." He handed me up into the gig, then led Daisy round the cottage and out into the little lane. She was a docile pony, and I enjoyed driving her. Kate preferred Saladin, a rather fiery animal who was too much for me.

"I be 'oping you find Mr. Chance pure well when he come 'ome," said Tom Kettle. "Tes real shame your mam be so very moderate in 'ealth."

Being "very moderate" was the local way of saying that a person was not at all well. I said, "Thank you, Mr. Kettle. I'll call to see you again next week."

He nodded. "Savin' trouble."

A shiver ran through me and I felt suddenly cold. When I looked up it was almost a surprise to see that the sun still shone and the sky was still without a speck of cloud.

"You all roight, miss?"

"Yes. Yes, thank you. It was just somebody walking over my grave."

"You put out a gift for them Pharisees come twilight. A piece o' silk, p'raps. Just in case, Miss Bridie."

"I'll try to remember. Good afternoon, Mr. Kettle."

A flick of the reins sent Daisy trotting away at a gentle pace. Unless we met something in the narrow lane I would have no more to do, for she knew her way home. A curious unease lay upon me now, and I could not shake it off. I was not given to such feelings. Sometimes they afflicted Kate, and I think Mama was troubled by them almost every day, but they were strange to me. To drive them away I began to think about my mother, and at once there came the usual twinge of guilt. To my shame, I loved my mother only because I knew her to be my mother, and I was lacking in the real and natural warmth of affection I should have felt. For most of my life I had been unable to help feeling sorry for her, and I was ashamed of that, too.

Mama had married above her and had found the burden too heavy. I think this had first dawned on me when I was twelve. Apart from the fact that my mother had been born in Oxfordshire, we knew nothing of her childhood, but it was clear to both Kate and me that she was different from other ladies of similar standing. Our family hardly mixed at all with the families of other gentry in the district, but we would see them about in the village, or in church, and though Mary Chance, our mother, was as well dressed as any of the ladies and more handsome than most, she might have come from another world.

She spoke correctly but with excessive care, as if afraid of making some error of speech. Her manner was equally anxious, as if she feared committing a breach of etiquette. We had good servants at Latchford Hall, but Mama was never quite at ease with them. Her whole bearing was touched by an air of apology. Constant premonitions of disaster made her highly nervous, and in recent years I had seen her begin to lose her fine looks as lines of worry became permanent and an unhealthy pallor stole the color from her cheeks.

I have no doubt she loved her daughters, but I am equally sure that the task of bringing us up had given her endless anxiety because she was poorly equipped for it. Truth to tell, the center of her existence and the sun that warmed her life was Papa, her husband. When he was at home she blossomed, seemed at ease, and was always smiling. She talked little, but would listen to his every word, watching him with something close to adoration.

The feeling between them was not one-sided. Often during his visits home I had seen my father look proudly down at her as they walked arm-in-arm in the grounds. "Am I not the luckiest of fellows to have married your beautiful mother?" he would say. "Eh, Bridie? Kate? Be honest, now, was there ever a luckier man?"

Once, during the summer holiday of my first year at boarding school, I had asked him where Mama had gone to school and why she had no family. We were standing on the platform at Halesworth at the time, waiting for the train that would take him to London. I had come to see him off, for my mother could never bear the strain of public parting when he returned to Paris. My question was more idle than concerned, for like most children I accepted my family situation with little curiosity. Others might find it strange that Roger Chance, the master of Latchford Hall, should spend so much of his life on the Continent. To me it was quite natural for it had always been so. I had learned, when I was old enough to understand, that my father's profession was that of an art dealer, and he was based in Paris because that city was the center of the world as far as art was concerned. Other children had fathers who were doctors or lawyers or land owners or simply gentlemen of private means. Mine was different, and I was rather proud of it.

When I asked about my mother, that day on the platform at Halesworth, he laughed in the full-hearted way I loved, throwing back his head and twirling his cane. "Why, Bridie dear, do you know I've never asked? It was Dublin University for me, but where your mama went I've no idea. I met her, wooed her, married her, and that's all that matters. As for family and background, I cut adrift from my own before I was twenty and never regretted it. A sober-sided lot they were, Bridie, with me the odd fellow out. I fancy they were as glad to see me cross the water from them as I was to leave them behind. And your mother, bless her, she'd long left her family when I met her, so we were two of a kind." He took one of my plaits and tickled my nose with it. "Learn a lesson, Bridie dear. Never look back and never look deep."

"But...I like to know about people, Papa."

He laughed again. "Lord bless you, Bridie, but that's a dangerous thing. Just take folk as you find them, don't try to change them, and don't ask what they've no wish to tell. Here's the train now, so give me a kiss and be sure to look after Mama while I'm away. I'll be back for a week or so in October, and then we'll have a month together at Christmas."

I was much older now than when I had asked that question, and had last seen my father only two or three months ago when he came home at Easter. It was then I asked him a question to which I had given more thought, for I was surprised that it was one which had not occurred to me until recently. "Papa, why have we never lived all together in Paris, since that is where your work is?"

He had looked at me with a hint of sorrow behind the twinkle of his eyes. "Ah now, Bridie, think what it would be like for your mama. It's a quiet life in the country she has need of."

"Yes, I suppose so. Oh, of course Paris would be bad for her, but she's only truly happy when you're here with us, and it seems such a shame."

"Does she really miss me, Bridie?" he said softly. I was in the library with him, sorting some books, and I looked up in surprise at his words.

"She's a different person, Papa."

He sighed. "She doesn't utter a word of complaint. Perhaps I've never quite realized..." He stood thinking for a moment, then gave one of his quick joyous laughs. "Never mind. Give me another year and I'll be ready to retire, Bridie. I've had to work away from home because my profession offered no other choice, but enough is enough. Come summer next year, and I'll not be going away any more."

My heart lifted. "You really mean it, Papa?"

"When did I ever break a promise to you, Bridie dear?

But don't speak of it yet to Mama. You'll make it a long year for her if you do, for she'll be wishing the days away."

I knew better perhaps than he did how anticipation of so wonderful a thing would work on my mother's nerves, and I nodded agreement.

"Promise, Bridie?" he said.

"Yes, of course, Papa."

I had kept that promise, counting the weeks as they passed and rejoicing in my heart that soon my father would come home to be with us always. I had no foreboding that before summer had felt the first hint of autumn's pursuit, there would come a day when my whole world would be destroyed in a matter of hours.

As Daisy trotted up the drive I saw that Dr. Carey's gig stood in front of the porch. Beside it was the cab which plied from the railway station. Kate was running toward me, her skirts flying, and some sort of dispute appeared to be going on between George Cooper, who drove the cab, and Henson, our butler and the only man among the indoor servants.

Kate's face was pale, her eyes very large. She began to speak while still running beside the gig. "Oh, it's awful, Bridie!" she gasped. "I—I don't know what's happening, but those two men came, and then Mama swooned, and Signor Peroni said he would leave early under the circumstances. Nannie sent Robert off in the governess cart to call Dr. Carey and then take Signor Peroni on to the station, and the men who came keep saying they must speak with somebody in authority here, and there's only you, Bridie, and we didn't know *where* you were—" She broke off, panting for breath, half crying. I had brought the gig to a halt, but in my haste to descend I tripped as my feet touched the ground and went sprawling.

Kate gave a hysterical laugh, and Henson hurried to help me up. As he did so the cab driver called after him angrily, "A tidy hour I been waitin' fer them Lunnon folk, so you tell 'em they best pay me. Do they don't, I'll set police on 'em."

"They *are* the police, you old fool!" snapped Henson, who had quite lost his usual calm manner. "Begging your pardon, Miss Bridie, but he's been carrying on ever since—"

"Police?" I broke in. "Did you say police?"

"Yes, miss." Henson drew a harassed breath and tried to compose himself. "An Inspector Browning and a sergeant. They're not in uniform, miss. From Scotland Yard, they say."

I straightened my hat, trying to collect myself.

"If they want fer I to wait," grumbled George Cooper, "then tes on'y roight they hev to pay. A tidy hour I been—"

"Will you be quiet, please?" I said sharply, and was surprised to find my voice so steady. "How much are you owed?"

He knuckled his forehead. "Fourpence a mile an' a shillin' an hour fer waitin', miss."

I opened my purse, took out a shilling and a sixpence with rather shaky fingers, and gave them to Henson to hand to him. "What time is the next train to London?"

Henson looked at the cabbie, who said, "Not till 'arparse six."

It was good to have to think, for it seemed to help in holding back the nameless fear that was pressing upon me. I said, "I shall inquire whether the gentlemen want you to wait till then. Come with me please, Kate."

We went up the steps and into the big oak-paneled hall. Henson followed, and closed the door. "I'm sorry, Miss Bridie," he said, "it's all been very confusing."

"All right, Henson." I was taking off my hat and coat. "Is Dr. Carey with my mother now?"

"Yes, miss. Nannie Foster and Ellen got her to bed, and Dr. Carey came just a few minutes ago. I expect I should have spoken to the gentlemen about the cab, but I didn't like to, miss, them being police and all."

"I'll speak to them myself. Are they in the drawing room?"

"Yes, Miss Bridie."

I moved to where the looking glass hung in its gilt-wood

frame and tried to push wisps of hair into place so that I would not look too untidy. I could not help my nose turning up at the end, or the spray of freckles across it, or my mouth being too wide, but whatever awaited me I wanted to meet it with some measure of dignity. Kate stood beside me, staring at me in the looking glass with a mixture of dread and excitement. "What do you think it's all about, Bridie?" she said breathlessly.

"I can't imagine. You go and sit with Mama while I find out."

"I tried to, but Nannie shooed me out."

"Well... go down to the servants' hall and ask Mrs. Ryland if you can sit with her and have a cup of tea. Henson, take Miss Kate with you, please. I'll ring if I need you for anything." Without waiting for an answer I turned from the looking glass, walked across the hall, and opened the door of the drawing room. Two men turned from the mullioned windows. One was of middle age, thickset, in a rather rumpled plain gray suit. He carried a short cape over one arm and held a brown bowler hat in the same hand. His face was square and his gaze placid. The other man was younger, more smartly dressed in a Norfolk jacket and knickerbockers, with a folded cap tucked in the belt of the jacket. He had a short moustache, quick eyes, and wore his hair in a quiff that curved up across his forehead.

I had intended to be very calm and composed as I asked them their business, but suddenly my mind went blank and then I heard myself saying, "I have paid your cab driver eighteen pence. If you want him to wait, it will be a shilling an hour."

The younger man blinked and looked taken aback. The older man studied me for a few moments, then nodded politely and said in a rather deep voice with a London accent, "I'm much obliged to you, miss. We shall be wanting him to take us to The Woodman later, where we've arranged lodgings for the night." He glanced at his companion. "Go and give him a florin. After that, we'll see."

"Right, sir. Excuse me, miss." The younger man went briskly out. The other took out a purse, opened it, shook some coins into his palm, counted them, then moved to place them on the mantelpiece. "Eighteen pence. Thank you, miss." He put the purse away, took out a notebook and pencil, and wrote something down. He slipped the notebook back into his pocket, took out something else, and came toward me, holding it displayed in his hand. "Inspector Browning of the Criminal Investigation Department," he said. "The young man is my colleague, Sergeant Dean. My warrant card, miss, as proof of identity."

I looked at what he was showing me without seeing it, and said, "Thank you. I think you will be more comfortable if you put down your hat and cape, Inspector." At any given moment I had no idea what words would come from me next, and I was thankful my second effort had been less stupid than my first.

"Thank you, miss." He looked about him, then laid his cape over the back of a chair and placed his bowler hat on it.

"I am Bridget Chance," I said. "I understand my mother is indisposed, following your arrival here."

"I fear so, miss."

The door opened to admit the sergeant. He gave me a little bow, looking embarrassed, darted a glance at the inspector, then went to stand beside him again.

I said, "Would you gentlemen care to sit down?"

"We prefer to stand, thank you, miss," said the inspector. "I understand from your butler that with your mother indisposed, you are the next in authority, as it were?"

"Yes. My father is abroad."

"We know that, miss," said the sergeant. Inspector Browning gave him a long stare, and he muttered an apology, looking uncomfortable.

"You have no brothers? No older relatives?" the inspector continued.

"No." I was struggling to keep my voice steady. "Whatever you have to say, Inspector, you had better say to me. There is nobody else."

He frowned and rubbed his chin. "It's very difficult, Miss Chance. I've already caused your mother great distress."

"My mother is a highly strung person. I am not." Since the sergeant had spoken, a dreadful suspicion was beginning to grow within me. "Does this concern my father?" I asked. "Has he been taken ill? Or suffered an accident?"

The inspector fidgeted with the silver watch-chain that hung across his waistcoat, then said simply, "It's very bad news concerning your father, Miss Chance. The worst possible news, I'm afraid."

I walked across the room and stared blindly out of the window. No tears came, but I was aching... aching with the most searing pain I had ever known. My father had always been so full of life that I had counted him immortal, but now he was dead. There could be no other meaning to the inspector's words.

I said, "My father is dead?"

"Yes, miss."

The last crumb of hope was gone. I do not know how long the silence lasted, but I was grateful that neither man uttered another word throughout that time. The pain came at me in waves, gnawing and tearing within my chest. My eyes stared into a gray wall. Somewhere far away I could hear the ponderous tick of the grandfather clock.

Slowly, slowly the numbness diminished and my mind began to stir again. I gathered my strength and turned. Both men stood with hands clasped behind them, staring down at the floor. It was a great effort to speak, and the words sounded slurred in my ears as I said, "I never knew my father to be ill. Was there an accident?"

"Well... in a manner of speaking, yes," said the inspector. "A sort of accident."

"What do you mean?"

"Your father had a fall, while he was a guest at a chatto."

"A what?"

"A chatto, miss. It's a French word for castle."

"Oh, a château. Yes?"

"I expect I said it wrong, not speaking the lingo. He fell from a balcony, and he died instantly."

The inspector stopped abruptly, as if he had been about to continue. Half a dozen questions were all tangled together in my dazed mind, but both men were looking at me strangely now, and I remembered that they were from Scotland Yard. "Is there something more you have to tell me?" I asked. "Is this a police matter because . . . because somebody harmed him?"

Sergeant Dean fingered his little moustache. The inspector looked at me steadily for a moment or two, then said, "You're a very intelligent young lady, if you don't mind my saying so, Miss Chance. Yes, it's quite true that this wouldn't be a police matter unless some form of crime was involved, but it wasn't a question of somebody harming your father."

"Then please explain."

"I do beg you to sit down, miss. It's bound to be a very nasty shock. I'm sorry we caused such an upset to your mother, but . . . well, with there not being a man of the family to talk to, I've had no choice." He ran a finger round his collar, tugging at it with an embarrassed air.

My face felt paper-white. My hands were clasped behind me, nails digging into the flesh. The inspector's words seemed strangely meaningless. My father was dead. How could I be shocked further?

"Please explain," I repeated dully.

He drew in a long breath, and took from his inside pocket a piece of stiff folded paper. "I regret to inform you," he said rapidly, "that we have received certain information from our colleagues, the French police. They claim that Roger Chance was engaged in an act of theft on the night he died; that he was caught in that act, and fell to his death while attempting to escape. Affidavits provided by eyewitnesses and evidence supplied by our French colleagues are so conclusive that the Assistant Commissioner has applied for and received this warrant, which I hereby show you, giving full authority for the police to search the residence of the deceased, namely Latchford Hall."

⟫ *two* ⟪

A full minute must have passed before the meaning of the words finally sank into my brain. For a moment I was swept by an almost overwhelming impulse to scream with laughter, but managed to check it with an effort that made my chest heave as if I had run a mile. Then came rage, a great black fury such as I had never known before. I think my face must have looked like the face of a gargoyle carved from white bone as I marched across the room to stand in front of Inspector Browning.

"How *dare* you!" I said in a trembling whisper. "How dare you say such a terrible thing about my father! He is— he was a gentleman of the highest reputation. His profession was that of an art dealer. He bought and sold pictures. He worked mainly from Paris, but traveled on the Continent a great deal in the course of his work. What you say is wicked! And ridiculous! And utterly *impossible!*"

Inspector Browning sighed. Sergeant Dean shook his head slowly and said, "He did a bit of dealing in pictures, miss, but that was just a smoke screen. The Frenchies reckon he'd been a professional jewel thief for twenty years and more, though he didn't come under suspicion until a couple of years ago, and it's taken since then to nobble him—"

"That will do," Inspector Browning broke in roughly. He looked at me. "But it's true. I'm very sorry, miss."

My mind had frozen. After a while I said, "Did you tell all this to my mother?"

"Yes. We had no option."

"The whole thing is a tissue of lies," I said slowly and distinctly. "For the moment I must attend to my mother, but I shall send a message to my father's solicitor at once. He is Mr. John Whitely, and his office is in Southwold. I . . . I hope he will find it possible to call here this evening, but if not I shall see him tomorrow morning and seek his advice."

"That's very sensible of you, miss," said the inspector. "I hope you'll believe I'm extremely sorry to have the job of bringing such tragic news to your family, but we'll try to be as unobtrusive as possible."

I looked at him blankly, uncomprehending. He lifted the paper he held and said, "The search warrant, Miss Chance. We have to search the house."

I still did not understand, and said, "What are you looking for?"

"We have orders to search for stolen property, miss. My own opinion is that we won't find any here. I think your father kept his business well away from Wynford—" He broke off as he saw the look on my face. "Well, never mind my opinion."

I felt sick, and there was a bitter taste in my mouth as I said, "This is a house of grief . . . of sudden grief. I have yet to tell my sister that our father has died. Surely you can leave us alone for a little while, Inspector?"

He bit his lip and looked unhappy. "There's the question that something might be removed, if you take my meaning, Miss Chance." He rubbed his chin. "Is there a safe in the house?"

I shook my head.

"I see. Well, your father's study and library are the most likely places for anything to be hidden. Upstairs? Bedroom? Most unlikely, him being away so much. Now, if we make a quick search of this drawing room, miss, so you can have the use of it, and if my sergeant puts a seal on the rest of the downstair rooms, then I'm willing to take a chance with my superiors by not executing this search warrant till tomorrow morning."

Before I could speak there was a tap on the door and Dr. Carey entered. He had brought me into the world over twenty years ago, and his thick hair was beginning to show gray now. He gave the two men a rather puzzled look, then came to me and took my hands. His touch seemed almost to burn, and I realized that my flesh was cold as winter.

"Have they told you, Bridie?" he said.

"About Papa's death? Yes. I know."

"I'm sorry. I was with your mother and only just learned that you were here. I would have come down to break it to you myself."

"Mama told you, Doctor?"

"Yes. I'm afraid she's suffering severely from shock."

"Did she tell you anything else?"

He stared in surprise. "What else could there be, of any importance?"

"Nothing. I mean . . . please excuse me, I'm rather confused."

"Of course. I've given your mother a sleeping draught, and she'll be asleep soon, but she wants to see you first, Bridie. Do you think you can avoid breaking down?"

I nodded. Somehow I had passed that point. I dwelt in a strange black limbo where pain laid siege to my every nerve, but I knew now that I would not break down.

"There's a good girl," said Dr. Carey, and held my arm as we moved to the door. "I'll come and see you tomorrow morning." He looked back at Inspector Browning and the sergeant. "Is there anything I can do for you before I go, Bridie?"

"No. No, thank you. The . . . presence of these two gentlemen is quite in order."

"Very well. Would you like me to stay until you have broken the news to Kate?"

"You're very kind, but I shall manage."

"I'll leave you some powders to help you sleep. Give Kate one in a little water, and see that you take one yourself."

"Thank you, Doctor." I was standing in the open doorway, and now I looked across the room at Inspector Browning and said, "Please proceed as arranged."

When I went into my mother's bedroom Nannie Foster was sitting beside the bed, holding her hand. My mother's face was like wax, the bones standing out to give her an almost skeletal appearance. I had expected her to look ill, but my nerves jumped in alarm at the sight of her. Nannie got to her feet, wincing with rheumatic twinges as usual, and took my hand. Her eyes were red-rimmed from weeping as she dabbed them with a handkerchief and said, "Do you know, Bridie dear? Do you know about your poor papa?"

"Yes, Nannie. Please help me by being brave and not making a fuss." My mother's eyes were closed but I saw the lids flicker. "Leave me alone with Mama for a few minutes," I went on, "but don't go away, Nannie. I shall want you to stay with her while I tell Kate and . . . and see to other things."

"Yes, dear. I'll be outside. Lord Jesus help us all in this time of sorrow."

She shuffled out, and I leaned over the bed. My mother looked up at me from a flushed, feverish face, her eyes haunted. "He is dead, Bridie," she whispered. "Your dear papa has been taken from us. I do not know what we shall do." Even in her distress she pronounced each word with all her usual care, as if afraid of making a mistake.

I said, "Try to sleep, Mama. Please try to sleep."

"They are saying terrible lies about him. You must understand that, Bridie. Those policemen are telling lies!"

"I know, Mama. But please try not to be ill. It's all so difficult. I have to tell Kate, and the servants . . . just about Papa having died, I mean. I'm going to send a note to Mr. Whitely as soon as I have a moment. I'll tell him about this dreadful mistake the police have made, and he'll know what to do about it."

"Yes, dear. You must do whatever you think best. I . . . I really can't manage." She put her hands over her face and began to sob. I patted her arm gently and said some stumbling words in a hopeless effort to comfort her. With growing despair I began to realize that whatever had to be done would rest upon my shoulders, and I was totally out of my depth. At this moment I would myself have been sobbing with shock and horror if there had been anybody else to do all that had to be done, but there was nobody.

After two or three minutes the crying faded and she lay with eyes closed, her breathing tremulous. I did not know if the sleeping draught had taken effect, but said in a whisper, "I must go and attend to everything, Mama. I'll come back as soon as I can."

Ellen, the housemaid, was waiting on the landing at the top of the stairs, looking upset. "Do there be somethin' I can do, Miss Bridie?" she said as I came along the passage. "I 'elped get Missus Chance to bed proper, then Nannie Foster told I to wait 'ere."

"Thank you, Ellen." When I touched my cheeks I found they were dry, so I had not wept yet, but my face felt like wood. "Go down to the kitchen now," I went on, "and tell Miss Kate to come at once to her room, please. I shall be waiting for her there."

She gave me an anxious look and went scuttling off down the stairs. I realized that Kate would need to have somebody with her after I had broken the news, and I could not remain with her myself, so I went back to fetch Nannie, who had taken up her post in my mother's room again. We had not been long in Kate's bedroom when she came hurrying in, and I think it had now dawned on her that such turmoil at Latchford Hall must in some way be connected with our father, for before I could speak she said, "Is Papa all right? Oh Bridie, has something happened?"

I made her sit down and drink a half glass of water in which I had dissolved one of the little sachets of powder Dr. Carey had left with Nannie. Then I told her that there had been an accident, and that Papa had died as a result. She sat with fists pressed to her cheeks, eyes closed, face twisted with grief as tears fell unheeded to her lap. I knelt by her, held her for a little while, and kissed her, then said that Nannie would get her to bed and stay with her until she slept.

It was a relief to close the door behind me, for I had dreaded that she might begin to ask questions about how Papa had died, and why this news had been brought by policemen from Scotland Yard. At the moment only my mother and I knew the horrifying accusation made against

Papa, and through all the numbing haze of grief that engulfed me I had clung desperately to the notion that this must be kept completely secret until Mr. Whitely, the solicitor, had made clear to the police how impossible the accusation was.

As I came down into the hall, Inspector Browning emerged from the drawing room, carrying his hat and cape. He waited for me to approach, then said in a low voice, "I've dealt with this room and with the breakfast room, Miss Chance, so you can have the use of both. Sergeant Dean is putting a seal on the doors of other rooms."

I said, "Very well, Inspector. I will see that the servants do not enter any of the sealed rooms." I wondered how I would explain this to them, but could not think. After a moment I went on, "There is something I must say to you. The charge against my father is completely false, but until this is shown to be the case I am anxious to prevent the dreadful situation my family will be placed in if this untrue story is given general currency. So I should be very grateful if you would refrain from speaking of it to anybody."

Inspector Browning stared down at his boots, then lifted his head to look directly at me with a troubled air. "I'm afraid you don't quite understand, miss," he said apologetically. "There have already been reports in some French newspapers. Some Austrian and Italian ones, too, I believe. And foreign correspondents for English newspapers would be bound to send in a story like this to their papers at home. With an Englishman being involved, it's quite a big piece of news here, you see. Well, I know your father came from Ireland really, but..."

I did not hear the end of the sentence, for there was a hammering in my head and I felt that my heart was trying to burst from my chest. When at last I could speak I said in a strained voice, "Do you mean that the newspapers will print what you have told me? They will name my father and say he is—he was a *thief*?"

"Well, they'll be a bit careful, miss, because there are laws of libel and suchlike, but there's nothing to stop them saying what's been alleged, and printing an official statement from the French police." He hesitated, then went on, "And the foreign papers have named your father, all right. Over on the Continent there's been a very high-class jewel thief working the big houses for years, but they could never nail him. The Frenchies even had a fancy name for him. Le sauce-ee-ay, that's what it sounds like, miss. It's a French word for magician—"

"But it was not my father!" I said in a trembling whisper, glancing behind me to make sure that nobody had entered the hall. "It's madness for them to say that my father was this thief, this man you call Le Sorcier!"

"Ah, I can tell you speak French yourself, miss. That's not surprising, with your father speaking it like a native, as you might say." He stopped, lifting an eyebrow at Sergeant Dean, who had appeared from the passage leading to the library.

The sergeant gave a doubtful nod. "I've done the doors on the downstair rooms like you said, sir, but it's not what you might call satisfactory. I mean, there's all the bedrooms, servants' hall, out-buildings, and so on."

"We've done sufficient for today." Inspector Browning's manner was abrupt. "Only a fool would hide that loot in his family house, where he's seldom present and where anyone might stumble on it. And Roger Chance was no fool, that's certain."

I bit hard on a knuckle to stop myself crying out with grief and anger, then said as steadily as I could, "How many more times must I tell you that a hideous mistake has been made? What you say about my father is utterly untrue!"

The inspector pursed his lips, swaying back and forth contemplatively. "I've no wish to cause you more distress than you've suffered already, miss," he said slowly, "but at the same time it's no kindness to leave you with false hopes. The fact is, there's no mistake. The French police had finally come round to suspecting Roger Chance was this sauce-ee-ay chap. They bided their time, laid a trap for him, and put out a nice bait. He took the bait, and they caught him red-handed. In the very act, miss. He'd come over the roof and into the bedroom of some Italian countess who'd been showing off a pendant that was supposed to be worth a fortune. Some high-up in the police had asked her to make a big display of it during this weekend party at the chatto, where your father was one of the guests. They were waiting for him, miss, and they caught him with the jewelry in his hand, a mask covering his face and head. Then he tried to bolt, and he fell. They found two skeleton keys and a miniature jimmy on him, and when they searched his room in the chatto they found a false compartment in one of his cases, with the finest set of burglar's tools the police had ever seen. I'm sorry, but there's been no mistake, miss."

I tried to wake up, knowing that I must be in the grip of a nightmare where truth was turned upside down and reason dead. After a few moments, when the world of horror in which I found myself remained solid and unchanging, I said, "You expect that all this will appear in the daily newspapers shortly?"

"I'm quite sure it will be in tomorrow's papers, miss. The Yard asked them to keep quiet until we'd searched Latchford Hall, but there's no need for further secrecy now, especially as it was in some foreign newspapers today."

I had never in my life wished that I were dead, but I wished it now. My mind simply could not cope with all the tumult of consequences that would follow when this dreadful story was told. The inspector was saying, "We'll take our leave of you now, miss, and call again tomorrow morning. I hope half past nine o'clock will be convenient?"

"Yes," I said vaguely, "yes, Inspector. And thank you for your courtesy."

I showed them out myself, rather than summon Henson to do so, then went into the drawing room, closed the door, and sat down in a chair by the window. Tomorrow the whole village, the whole county, would know the story the two detectives had just told me, and every eye would be upon the Chance family of Latchford Hall. My father was dead, my mother was ill and quite unable to deal with all that would have to be done. There was nobody in the house I could turn to for help, and soon I must say something to the servants. I wanted to lie down and weep myself into sleep, to wake and find that somebody had lifted all responsibility from my shoulders—

Bernard! I pressed my hands to the sides of my head, feeling almost sick with relief. The man I was to marry would give me the unstinting support and comfort I needed. He would know that the story told by the French police was hideously false, and he would find some way of showing it to be so. I saw his face in my mind's eye now, strong, assured, smiling, the eyes full of laughter beneath the thick fair hair. There was his father, too. Mr. Laurence Page was a man of influence in the county and had been most amiable toward me on the occasions when our two families had met. What was more, he had got on famously with my father.

I said very quietly and fervently, "Oh, thank God," for now I knew that I was not alone as I had at first thought. I had a capable man to turn to, one who loved me. Sitting at the bureau with a sheet of writing paper before me, I tried to think clearly. Robert, our groom, could catch a train to Lowestoft and deliver a letter from me by hand this evening. I knew that tonight both Bernard and his father would be out at a professional dinner in Norwich, but in any event nothing could be done until tomorrow now.

I picked up a pen and wrote hurriedly:

Dearest Bernard,

My father has died, and I am in great trouble which I will explain when I see you. Please come to me by the earliest train tomorrow. I am in desperate need of your help.

> With my love,
> Bridie

As I sealed and addressed the envelope it occurred to me that if Bernard paused to glance at the morning newspaper tomorrow, he would see at once how truly great was my need. With that thought came another. There was one thing which could be done this evening. It was very important for me to speak to Mr. Whitely, the solicitor, without delay.

Tomorrow morning he would doubtless read whatever *The Times* or *The Morning Post* chose to publish about Roger Chance, and it might well be that he would then refuse to act for our family. I did not know if the law allowed him to refuse, but the thought frightened me. I was desperate to have proper advice, and it seemed to me that once I was in Mr. Whitely's presence he could scarcely turn me out.

I rang for Henson, and when he came I stood by the fireplace and said, "I'm afraid I have bad news, Henson. My father has died in an accident in France. A wicked story is being told about him, which is why the police were here. They have sealed certain rooms, and nobody must enter them. I haven't time to explain any more now, because I intend driving to Southwold at once to see my father's solicitor. Will you have Robert harness Daisy again and bring the gig round for me? Then he must take the train to Lowestoft and deliver this letter to Mr. Bernard Page."

"I . . . I'm very sorry, miss." Henson looked bewildered and deeply shaken. "Your poor father. What on earth can the police be thinking of? And Mrs. Chance . . . oh dear, poor soul, she'll be hit that bad, I'm sure. But you're not fit to go out this evening, Miss Bridie. You'll make yourself ill."

"I have to go." My voice started to rise, and I struggled to keep it normal. "I have to, Henson. There are so many things to be done urgently. I don't think my mother or Miss Kate will want anything to eat tonight, they're probably asleep by now, but see Nannie Foster and do whatever she suggests. Some soup, perhaps, or beef tea . . . I don't know." Another thought came to me, making my heart lurch. "Oh, and speak to Ellen about clothes for mourning. She must talk to the dressmaker about them. Now please go and tell Robert I want the gig. I shall be ready in five minutes."

I reached the offices of Whitely and Whitely in Southwold soon after six o'clock. By the end of the long drive I had fallen into a kind of dream in which the grief, shock, and anger I felt were in some strange way set at a distance, perhaps because my inner self knew that without relief I would break under the burden.

The door was opened to me by an elderly man with a sheet of foolscap paper clipped round each cuff on his jacket for protection against rubbing. I recognized him as Mr. Bembridge, the solicitor's clerk, for I had waited in his office some years ago when my father had brought me into Southwold with him on an occasion when he had business to do with Mr. Whitely.

Mr. Bembridge did not remember me until I gave my name, but then told me that Mr. John and Mr. William, the two brothers who were partners in the firm, had gone home for the day. When I explained that my business was desperately urgent, he hesitated a little but at last suggested that I should call at the private residence of the Whitely brothers, where they lived with their spinster sister. The house was just beyond the church and less than a mile from the offices, so in another ten minutes I was tugging at the bellpull in the porch of a rather somber gray house set a little back from the main road.

A maid answered the door, took my card, and showed me into a study with a huge ornately carved desk, bookshelves covering a whole wall, and greatly enlarged photographs of cats occupying most of the rest of the walls. Five minutes later a tall man with thin gray hair entered the room. He wore spectacles, a frock coat with lapels faced in black silk, a high starched collar and gray tie. There was a slight stoop to his shoulders, and his face was wrinkled like a walnut. He held my card in his hand, and there was no expression either in his face or voice as he said, "Miss Bridget Chance? I am John Whitely."

I had risen as he entered, and now I gave him my hand and dropped a small curtsy. "I am most grateful to you for receiving me, Mr. Whitely, and I apologize for this intrusion."

He touched my hand, glanced at the back of the card, and said in a dry voice, "You have written, *Daughter of Mr. Roger Chance—on a matter of life-and-death*. In my experience few matters are quite as urgent as that."

"Please don't be angry with me, Mr. Whitely. It is already a matter of death, for we received news only a few hours ago that my father has died. But the accompanying news is so dreadful that unless something is done about it I truly fear for my mother's life."

No flicker of curiosity touched his face. He moved to a speaking tube on the wall, removed the whistle and blew down the tube, then put it to his ear. "Please accept my condolences," he said in the same dry tone as before, "and pray be seated. This has no doubt been a great shock to you. I am in some doubt as to the meaning of your last sentence, since the only thing that can be, as you put it, 'done about' news, however dreadful, is, in the first instance, to prove or disprove it." Without a pause in the flow of words, he said into the mouthpiece of the speaking tube, "Be so good as to bring a plate of wholemeal biscuits and a pot of tea to the study, Nelly. What? What? I don't give a tinker's curse what Miss Adelaide will say. She can mind her own confounded business." His voice and expression did not change to match his words, but remained as dispassionate as ever, and as he hung the mouthpiece in its cradle he went on speaking, but to me again now.

"I should have thought that you would wish to be with your mother at this moment, to comfort her in her loss, but one must not, of course, prejudge a situation such as this, or indeed any situation, and it may well be that whatever it is you have to tell me will show that it was more important for you to take the course of action you have in fact chosen to take. Pray excuse me, I believe I can hear my cat, Henrietta, at the door."

He moved with his stooping walk to the door, opened it, bent down, then turned back into the room with a large tortoise-shell cat purring in his arms. "I have a great affection for cats," he said without enthusiasm, "an affection shared, I may say, by my brother, William, rather strangely in my opinion, since he is not a man for whose tastes or intellect I have any great respect . . ." He went on talking in the same unvarying tone as he put the cat down in a leather armchair, moved to a cabinet, opened it, and took out a glass and a bottle of amber liquid.

". . . and now I am about to pour a small quantity of brandy for you, Miss Chance, and I shall be obliged if you will sip it a little at a time, very slowly. It is easy to perceive that your ordeal has left you in a state of exhaustion, and you have now to tax yourself further by relating some distressing news to me, so you are in need of some small sustenance, and by the time you have finished sipping this brandy," he handed me the glass, "there will be tea and biscuits to ensure that no untoward effect follows the consumption of alcohol, in no matter how small a quantity, upon an empty—ah—stomach."

He sat down in his swivel chair behind the desk, took the cat upon his lap, and began to stroke it, gazing absently at the ceiling. I thanked him, sipped the brandy obediently, gasping a little at the fiery touch of it in my throat, and drained the last drop a few minutes later, just as there came a tap on the door and a maid entered with a tray of tea. Mr. Whitely was still peering mistily into space, as if he were alone in the room.

As the maid set down the tray on the desk she said, "Mr. William says how much longer has he got to wait afore you come an' finish that game of dominoes, and Miss Adelaide says what time are you going to be wantin' dinner, an' they're both havin' a tidy ol' set to about whether it was your Henrietta that clawed the curtains or Mr. William's Jemima."

Mr. Whitely returned from his musing and said without heat, "You may tell Mr. William that he shall wait as long as I please, and Miss Adelaide that I shall decide the question as to the hour of dining when it is convenient for me to do so. That will be all, Nelly."

The maid went out. Mr. Whitely put down the cat, set out two cups and saucers, poured tea, leaving me to add milk and sugar for myself, placed a heaped plate of wholemeal biscuits within my convenient reach, and said, "It is important that you eat at least half a dozen biscuits to sustain you. I shall feel constrained to admonish you if you fall short." He settled back in his chair, drew a brass inkstand toward him, picked up a pen, examined the nib, opened the inkpot, and said, "Now. What is it that you wish to tell me, Miss Chance?"

At first my words were fumbling and confused. He did not interrupt, but waited patiently for me to continue in my own way. It was an effort for me to force the story from my lips, but I was helped by the realization that in his own curious way Mr. Whitely was a considerate and kindly man. Not for a moment did he show surprise or shock as my halting tale was told. His pen scratched steadily on the paper, and he paused only twice, to point sternly at the plate of biscuits.

By the time I had said all that was to be said I had managed to eat four biscuits. I had also drunk two cups of sweet tea, and was feeling less drained than when I first arrived. There was silence while Mr. Whitely read through what he had written, put down his pen, and took off his spectacles.

"You are of the opinion that what the French police have said concerning your late father, Roger Chance, is untrue?" he said.

"Yes, of course, Mr. Whitely!" I spoke a little hotly. "Surely you agree? After all, my father was your client."

"I have no opinion as yet, and in any event the truth is not a matter of opinion. I must tell you at once that the firm of Whitely and Whitely has never accepted cases involving criminal law—pray eat another biscuit, Miss Chance. However, as senior partner, I can also say that, in my view, to represent your mother and your good self would not in any way infringe our custom, and therefore if you wish to instruct me I shall do whatever I can to assist you in this very difficult time."

I felt a surge of gratitude toward this seemingly dry and unsympathetic man. When the report appeared in the newspapers there would be few if any of our neighbors and acquaintances who would speak to us. Some would avoid us as the family of a criminal, others from embarrassment. But Mr. John Whitely had declared that he would help, and I was more thankful than words could tell.

He said, "Do you know where the inspector from Scotland Yard is staying?"

"I'm afraid not—oh, wait. Yes, I remember now. The Woodman, in Wynford."

He put on his spectacles and wrote it down. "I shall call there this evening and speak with him, and I propose to catch an early train to London tomorrow in order to speak with whoever is in overall charge of the case at Scotland Yard. Meanwhile, I shall arrange for my brother, Mr. William, to speak with the branch manager of your father's bank, to ascertain what monies are available and if any documents are deposited there for safekeeping."

Mr. Whitely ran a finger down his nose several times, then seemed to come to a decision and continued, "I have no wish to add to your worries at such a time, but the financial matters are of some urgency. I have no idea of the extent of your father's substance. Doubtless there would be a bank account in Paris, and possibly elsewhere. It is almost certain that the French police will have gone into this aspect of his affairs and will have informed Scotland Yard. All this we must discover as soon as possible, so that you may know how best to arrange your family affairs henceforward. May I ask how the day-to-day expenditure of your household is managed, in view of the fact that your father was abroad for most of each year?"

"Yes." I paused to gather my thoughts, for I had begun to feel a little light-headed. "Yes, my father maintained a current account of a few hundred pounds with Goslings and Sharpe's Bank, at the branch here in Southwold. My mother is able to draw on that account as required for all expenses. I suppose my father arranged to replace those drawings at regular intervals by transferring money from abroad."

"The bank will be able to inform us on that point. You have mentioned a few hundred pounds. Are there any other accounts? Deposits? Reserves? Shareholdings? Funds of any nature?"

I found I was pulling a face, twisting my mouth up at one corner in an apologetic grimace. Hastily I stopped myself and said, "I really don't know, Mr. Whitely, but I suppose all that sort of thing would be set out in my father's will."

He sat back in his chair and said mildly, "Your father left no will, to the best of my knowledge. I urged him to do so on several occasions, but he merely laughed. He said he would make a point of leaving all his debts to *me* when the time came—he was speaking in jest of course—and that meanwhile he would thank me to avoid a topic he considered excessively morbid."

"Oh." I was disconcerted for a moment, but not really surprised. I could almost hear my father rallying this dry, precise solicitor, and brushing his advice aside with a laugh.

"I shall apply for Letters of Administration on behalf of your mother," said Mr. Whitely, "and I imagine there will be no problem as to her claim to be the sole and rightful inheritrix of your father's estate."

He shuffled together the sheets of paper on which he had been writing, placed a paperweight on top of them, and stood up, taking a gold hunter from his waistcoat pocket. Methodically he opened the cover, studied the dial, and said, "Two minutes past seven. We must see about getting you home, Miss Chance. It is too long a drive for you after such an exhausting day."

As I stood up, Henrietta jumped from the armchair and began to rub herself against Mr. Whitely's leg, purring loudly. I said, "Please don't disturb yourself. I shall manage very well, thank you, Mr. Whitely, and I cannot tell you how grateful I am to you for the way you have received me."

"Not at all," he said with seeming indifference, turning away as he spoke. "Your demeanor has earned my deep respect." I thought I had misheard his words, for they were so surprising. Next moment he blew down the speaking tube, listened for a few moments, then spoke into the mouthpiece. "Nelly, you will be so good as to tell Frederick to get out the gig at once. I am about to drive Miss Bridget Chance home, and he is to follow so that he may drive me back to Southwold. Pray do not interrupt me, Nelly. On our way home I shall be calling at The Woodman hostelry in Wynford, to speak with an inspector from Scotland Yard on a matter of some urgency. You may therefore inform Miss Adelaide that dinner is to be delayed until a quarter past nine o'clock. Is that understood?"

Mr. Whitely put the tube to his ear and listened. As he did so, the glimmer of a malicious smile stole over his face. After a few moments he spoke again. "Quite so, Nelly. But you may say to Mr. William that although Frederick is indeed our joint manservant, I expect from Mr. William the deference due to an elder brother and senior partner, and I require Frederick's services this evening. Therefore, Mr. William can brush and press his own confounded suit this evening, or leave it unbrushed and unpressed, as he pleases. You may also tell Miss Adelaide that pending my return she and Mr. William can sustain themselves with some cold meats, or other suitable provender, or they may go hungry, as they choose, but dinner is to be served at a quarter past nine o'clock. That will be all, Nelly."

He hung up the speaking tube and turned toward me, rubbing thin hands together, a glint of satisfaction in his eye. In another moment it was gone, and his remote, imperturbable manner had settled upon him again like a cloak.

I remember little of the drive through growing dusk from Southwold to Wynford, for though I was sitting bolt upright, and clutching tightly to the side of the carriage, I seemed to be in a kind of sleep, my mind dormant. To hold on securely was necessary because, astonishingly, Mr. Whitely drove like a young blood, feet spread and body leaning forward as he sent the gig rattling along the lanes at a fiery pace. Daisy had never been pushed so hard in her life, but she seemed to enjoy it, and in forty minutes we came to Latchford Hall, with Frederick, the manservant, following close behind in the Whitely gig.

Henson opened the door to me, Mr. Whitely raised his hat, bowed, and wished me good night. I thanked him and waited in the porch until he and Frederick had driven off, then said to Henson, "How are my mother and Miss Kate?"

"I understand from Nannie Foster that they are asleep, Miss Bridie."

"Thank goodness. When do you expect Robert back from Lowestoft?"

"That's hard to say, miss. There's only one train an hour each way. If he isn't back very shortly then I expect it will be after nine o'clock."

"All right. I'll see to Daisy myself."

"Oh, you mustn't do that, Miss Bridie. You just go to bed and leave her to me. You look so tired."

"Well...thank you, Henson." For a butler to do the work of a groom was unheard of, and I realized then how deeply troubled Henson must be. As I turned and began to loosen the bow beneath my chin where the ribbon of my boater was tied, he said diffidently, "The staff below stairs are wondering what their position is, Miss Bridie. I mean, do you think we shall be staying on at Latchford Hall, or might we all have to look for a new situation?"

The question caught me unprepared, and I was ashamed that it did so, for naturally the servants would be concerned about the possibility that we would move to a much smaller house. As usual when I was embarrassed I found myself responding in an exaggerated way, stretching my mouth and biting my lower lip in a troubled grimace of apology as I lifted my shoulders in a helpless shrug. "I'm sorry, Henson, but I just don't know what will happen yet." I ran fingers into my hair and felt tears suddenly flood my eyes, but managed to control my voice as I went on, "Everything is...very difficult and complicated, but I promise to let you and the rest of the servants know where you stand at the first possible moment."

"Thank you, Miss Bridie." He went down the steps to the gig, and I wondered what his thoughts would be when he read or heard the dreadful story that would soon be told about his master, Roger Chance. We might then find it impossible to employ anyone at all, for the reputation of the master was of high importance to the domestic staff of any household. To remain in service with the family of a master who had been named as a criminal was scarcely to be thought of.

Slowly I mounted the stairs, and as I reached my bedroom

Nannie Foster came along the passage in her dressing gown, a plain nightcap on her gray head. I knew that she would be much concerned about me, and beckoned her into my room so that we could talk without fear of disturbing my mother or Kate.

"They're both asleep, dear," she said rather tremulously as I pushed the door to. "I've been peeping first into one room, then the other." She peered at me from red-rimmed eyes. "Heavens, child, you look worn to a thread. You take the doctor's medicine and get to bed now. I'll keep an eye on your mama and Miss Kate, never fear. I don't sleep much at the best of times, so it won't hurt me to sit up tonight."

"Thank you, Nannie." I took her hands. She was like one of the family, and I felt I could not leave her to learn the cruel story from a newspaper or one of the servants. "Sit down, Nannie, here on the bed, just for a few moments while I explain something..."

It was hard to make myself speak the words I had to speak as I repeated to her what Inspector Browning had said to me. Through my weariness I was vaguely surprised that she understood on first telling, for I had thought she might be dazed by such a monstrous story and unable to take it in. When I finished her hands were trembling in mine, her mouth working. "Wicked devils!" she said in a fierce whisper. "Call themselves policemen and come telling lies about their betters. You should have let me deal with them, Miss Bridie. I'd have sent them about their business!"

"They're not the kind to be sent about their business, Nannie. I know it's all untrue, and there must be some dreadful mistake somewhere, but what I've just told you is what the chief man at Scotland Yard believes, and it's the story that will be published in the newspapers tomorrow, so we have to brace ourselves for a very hard ordeal."

She was silent for a long time, staring into space, and I saw horror growing within her as she slowly realized all that would follow from what I had now told her.

"Dear God, help us all," she whispered at last.

"Yes, Nannie. And we must help each other." I let her

hands go and began to take off my coat. "I wish I could send Kate away somewhere, but there's nowhere for her to go. I mean, no relatives. I've never quite realized before what a solitary family we are. But it's my mother who will be in greatest need of help, and you're the one who can do most for her, Nannie. In many ways you're closer to her than Kate and I."

The gray head nodded. "Yes, dear," Nannie Foster said in a faraway voice, as if thinking aloud. "It's the loneliness, you see, from being taken out of her station in life. Poor dear soul, she could always be at ease with me . . . and there was always the next homecoming to look forward to . . . she just lived for the times when Mr. Roger came home . . ."

Nannie Foster's voice faded to silence, then she came to herself with a start. "Oh, I beg your pardon, Miss Bridie. I hope I haven't spoken out of place. Now tell me, because I'm sure your mama will ask about it tomorrow, have you made arrangements for your poor dear papa to be brought home to Wynford to be buried?"

I stood gazing at her stupidly, realizing that this question had not occurred to me. Now it raised further questions. Would the French allow my father's body to be brought home? How was such a matter arranged? What would the vicar and church wardens at St. Mary's have to say about their churchyard being used for the burial of a man declared by the authorities to be a criminal?

After what seemed a long while I said, "I'll ask Mr. Whitely tomorrow. He's very kind, and I'm sure he will advise me what's best to do."

The room swayed, and I caught at the bedpost to steady myself. Then Nannie Foster was holding my arm, making me sit down, starting to unbutton my dress, and chattering briskly away as if I were a child again. "There. You've overdone it, Miss Bridie, haven't you? Never mind, Nannie will put you to bed and give you the nice medicine the doctor left, and you'll have a lovely sleep. Come along now, we must get this chemise over our head, mustn't we? Ready? Over we go. There we are. Come along now, dear, lift up a little. That's a good girl. Here's your nightie . . ."

The chatter became a blur. I was in bed, sitting up with Nannie holding a little glass to my lips. Somehow I swallowed the draught, then lay thankfully back on the pillows. The world swung away. Somewhere within me I tried to cling to consciousness, telling myself that I had left a host of things undone, that I must think, plan, decide . . . but I had been cast in the mold of those who can rise above their own frailties. My feeble struggle against waves of darkness was shamefully brief, and soon came the peace of oblivion.

I did not know the hour or the day, or whether the scene before me was dream or reality. I stood by the tall window of my bedroom, pushing one of the heavy curtains aside a little. I felt hot and stifled. The casement window stood half open, though I could not remember opening it. Even the night air seemed too warm and moist.

The moon and stars were bright, but a ground mist swirled across the lawns, flowerbeds, and shrubbery, a feeble wind drawing it into tendrils. My mind held no thought. My eyes rested on the dark line of trees that marked the beginning of the copse on the southern side of the grounds of Latchford Hall.

In my dream, or in reality, I stood breathing deeply, my lungs craving cool fresh air. A pinpoint of fire glowed steadily against the darkness of a tree that rose above a spreading shrub, a strangely misshapen growth which at one point took on the silhouette form of a horse's head. The glow came from a little higher, and a little beyond. With barely a flicker of interest I wondered what it might be. Much too big and too red for a glowworm . . . but if I were dreaming there need be no logical explanation.

The point of fire moved slowly down for a little distance, then suddenly spun through the air and dropped to the ground with a burst of tiny sparks. I closed my eyes and opened them again. Part of the shrubbery moved, the part that had looked so strangely like the head of a horse. From the darkness they moved out amid twisting feathers of mist, the horse and rider who had been so still against the dark background of trees and shrubs.

If I felt anything at all it was a shadow of surprise that I felt no astonishment, no fear, no alarm. The dream horse and rider, or the real horse and rider, moved at a steady walk across the grass. I could not tell the animal's color, but it was a beautiful creature, deep-chested, with a proud head and high-stepping gait. I was a poor rider, but a fair judge of a horse, and the one I now saw, or imagined, in the garden below me had the build of a mount that would carry a rider far and fast on a long day's ride.

I peered at the man in the saddle. They were moving across my field of vision, and for a moment moonlight shone full upon him as the dark shadows of the trees fell back where the broad walk ran through them. He sat tall, with head a little bowed, the reins loose in hands that were surely gloved, for I could see no gleam of flesh. There was a harmony between him and his mount which told of the true horseman, yet he sat strangely, with long legs reaching down so far that I wondered if he had stirrups. Those legs were encased in dark narrow trousers, not riding breeches, and he wore a long jacket. I saw nothing of his face, for it was in the shadow of a round hat with a wide brim, the crown low and flat like a shallow pillbox. I fancied that I glimpsed a chin-strap, but could not be sure. I had never seen anyone wearing such a hat before, and yet it was not completely unfamiliar. A fragment of memory flickered to life, and I recalled seeing in a children's encyclopedia long ago a drawing of a gaucho, one of the horsemen who herd cattle on the great pampas of Argentina. He had been shown wearing just such a wide-brimmed, low-crowned hat as the rider below me wore.

The gleam of moonlight upon him vanished, for he had crossed the broad walk and was no more than a silhouette again, a black shape becoming ever more shapeless as horse and rider were foreshortened to my view. Then they were gone. Still I felt no surprise, no fear, no curiosity. If I dreamed, then my lack of feeling was part of the dream. If I was awake, then the turmoil and tragedies of the day had drained me to the point where I was beyond feeling. It seemed to me that I let the curtain fall into place, but I have no memory of returning to my bed and to sleep, and if I dreamed other dreams that night, I was never to remember them.

three

Somebody was shaking me by the shoulder, calling anx-
iously. As I started to rouse from sleep all the horrors of
the day before came rushing in upon me, chilling my blood
and making me shrink from the misery of facing a new day.

"Bridie, wake up! *Please*, Bridie! It's Mama—I don't
know what to do."

Kate's voice. Kate's hand on my shoulder. I opened my
eyes and saw that the curtains had been drawn back and
sunlight was slanting into the room. Kate was bending over
me, her face pale and troubled. She wore a gray dress, and
had tied her hair back at the nape of her neck with a dark
ribbon. My head felt heavy and there was a sour taste in
my mouth. I was thankful to have slept, but wished now
that Dr. Carey's sleeping draught had not been quite so
potent.

"Just a minute, Kate," I said thickly. "Give me a moment . . . I feel rather sick."

"But you must *hurry*, Bridie!" she cried tearfully. "Mama
has taken the governess cart and gone out, and Henson
doesn't know what to do, and Nannie's fallen asleep in the
armchair in Mama's room, and even when I woke her she
didn't understand—"

I was out of bed, my heart pounding. The small clock
on the table beside me showed that it was only twenty
minutes past seven. Kate was weeping now, and I put my
arms round her. "Don't cry, dear. Please don't cry. What
do you mean, Mama has gone out?"

She pulled herself together and said tremulously, "I
washed and dressed, and when I went to her room there

was only Nannie there, asleep in the armchair. So I—I went downstairs, and Henson was very upset, telling Robert off. It seems Mama had got up and gone out to the stables without anyone seeing her. And she . . . she was just dressed anyhow, Bridie, with her hair loose, and wearing her big cloak. She told Robert to harness Daisy to the governess cart, and drove off."

I had looked to see that the door was shut, then thrown off my nightie and begun to put on the underclothes nearest to hand—those I had taken off last night. There was nausea in my stomach from the effects of the drug, and sickness in my heart from fear.

". . . Henson was cross with Robert for not stopping her," Kate was saying, "but Robert said it wasn't his place to tell the mistress what she could do, and . . . and so I ran to fetch you." She pressed her lovely long-fingered hands to her white cheeks. "Oh, it's so awful. Whatever's happening, Bridie?"

I said, "Come behind me and tie my hair up. It doesn't matter how." I was sitting down, pulling on my stockings. "Did Robert say which way Mama went?"

"She . . . she took the Selby road," Kate said in a frightened whisper. This was a small road which forked only half a mile from Latchford Hall. One fork led to the nearby hamlet of Selby, the other was barely used, for it led by covert and marshland to nowhere but a bay with only the ruins of a few cottages, long deserted, to show that a small fishing community had once dwelt there.

"Bridie . . . do you think Mama has gone to the sea to . . . ?" Kate left the last words unsaid, but they were in my own mind. Without quite knowing why, I did not believe that Mama intended to do away with herself by drowning, yet I could think of no other reason for what she had done.

As Kate finished tying up my hair with shaking hands I said, "I'm sure it's not what you fear. But I must catch up with her as soon as possible. Run and tell Robert to saddle Punch. I'll be down in just two or three minutes. Make him *hurry*, Kate."

She ran to the door, then paused to look back, round-eyed. "The sidesaddle, Bridie?"

"Dear heaven, no! I'd fall off a dozen times. Tell him I'll use Papa's saddle, and I'll just have to do the best I can."

Less than five minutes later, with my face unwashed and my hair in a tangled pile, I rode out on the Selby road in the morning sunshine. Robert could have ridden faster, so could Kate, but the groom was a shy and awkward village boy who would have no idea how to deal with a woman who was not only mistress of the household but also half out of her mind with grief. Kate could not have managed, either. She was too young for a task which might well be very frightening and could even call for physical strength if Mama was hysterical. At least I was quite strong, and for once I was thankful to possess this unladylike quality.

Punch was moving at an easy canter. I dared not urge him to a faster pace, for even now I was bouncing about in the saddle, gasping in time with the jolts as I tried to match the movements of my body to those of the horse. I had had the sense to put on a very full skirt, but even so it was rucked up above my knees, and with my hair falling loose and my ungainly seat I presented a ludicrous sight to anybody who might have been on the Selby road that morning.

I did not see a soul before reaching the fork, and after that I did not expect to see anybody. The narrow road had fallen into disrepair, and my heart was in my mouth with fear of Punch putting his foot in a hole and coming down. It did not occur to me to take the fork to Selby village. I knew, somehow, that my mother was on the bay road. After ten minutes I began to find the rhythm of the canter, so that I was not going down as the horse came up, and after that the ride became a little easier.

With the rising sun full in my eyes I could see almost nothing of the road winding across the flat ground stretching before me to the sea, and it was not until we turned a little north for the last half mile that I was able to make out the

governess cart in the distance, halted where the road joined
the line of crumbling cottages. I dug my heels into Punch,
and three or four minutes later I slid to the ground beside
the little trap, lost my balance, and fell over. Panting with
effort and anxiety I picked myself up and looked about me.

My mother had moved down past the cottages and was
walking out along the old stone jetty, her hair flying in the
breeze from the sea, her cloak flapping about her. I tried
to call out, but could find no breath to overcome the sudden
closing of my throat with fear. Stumbling on the green algae-
covered cobbles I began to run, but I had covered no more
than twenty paces when my feet slipped from beneath me
and I fell again, coming down hard this time, with an impact
that jarred my bones and left me sick and dizzy.

I could have screamed aloud with frustration, and I hated
myself in that moment for my clumsiness, which had en-
sured that I would now never catch up with my mother
before she reached the end of the long jetty. I scrambled to
my knees and called to her as loudly as I could, but my
voice was still feeble from lack of breath, and the wind
snatched the sound away. I remember plodding across more
cobbles, then over sand mixed with shingle, weed, and
crumbled rock. At last I reached the jetty. On each side of
it the sea came swirling over a bed of rock fragments, large
and small, where the land had been eroded, but at the far
end the jetty was almost awash in deep water. I looked up
and saw that my mother had stopped. She had half turned,
and was looking down at something she held in her hands,
a small square object . . . red. A box. A casket.

Even as I recognized it, she leaned back a little, then
suddenly swung her arm high over her head, hurling the
casket far out over the sea. At the zenith of its flight the
lid flew open. Tiny glittering things scattered and fell. There
was a cluster of small white splashes, then a larger one as
the casket struck the water.

My mother stood staring at the sea, then slowly turned.
I was twenty paces away, and limping a little as I moved
toward her. She blinked, then stood waiting listlessly for
me to come up to her, and though I knew how deep her

grief must be I was still shocked by the way her eyes had sunk back in that bone-white face, framed by a tangle of wind-blown golden hair.

"Oh . . . there you are, Bridie," she said vaguely. "Whatever are you doing out here at such an hour?"

I reached her at last and took ice-cold hands in mine. "I've come to take you home, Mama."

"That was a kind thought, dear. Yes, I really don't feel very well, but at least it's done now, so I can rest."

She had regularly worn three rings apart from her wedding ring, beautiful rings my father had given her. One was a half-hoop of diamonds, another was set with three superb emeralds, and the third was a ruby and diamond cluster. All three were gone, and on her fingers there was now only the plain gold band.

I turned, slipped my arm through hers, and began to walk slowly back along the jetty with her. Inwardly I was trembling with new shock and fear, though without quite knowing what the nature of it was. After a few moments I said in as normal a voice as I could manage, "That was your jewel box you threw into the sea, wasn't it, Mama?"

"Yes, dear." Her voice was low and confiding. "All my jewelry, everything your poor dear papa ever gave me. Those policemen can nose about as much as they like now."

I turned to stare at her ravaged face. "But Mama, that was *your* jewelry! It wasn't stolen!"

A furtive look showed for a moment in the deep-sunk eyes. "We can't be too careful, Bridie."

"But you mustn't believe what the inspector told you!" I cried, aghast as much at what she had said as what she had done. "Papa wasn't a robber who went about stealing jewelry! It's ridiculous, Mama. And we—we have to be brave and keep denying it until the truth comes out." I felt tears running down my cheeks. "Oh, Mama, how could you throw your jewelry in the sea like that? You can't believe that Papa would ever have given you *stolen* jewelry?"

"No, dear, I'm sure he would never do that. It would be so foolish, and he always used to say, 'You can't be too careful, Mary darling.'"

"Yes, but he was speaking about other things then, about his business, I expect. He didn't mean..." I shook my head, "Oh, Mama, you make me so confused."

"I'm sorry, dear."

We came from the jetty on to the beach, then crossed to the cobbled road where the remains of the cottages stood. My head ached dully, and it was hard to gather my thoughts. After a few moments my mother said in a faraway voice, "Your father was a very unusual man, Bridie. So different. He was... superior, you know. Superior to other men."

I did not know what to say, and left her while I brought Punch across and tethered him on a long rein behind the governess cart. As I helped my mother to mount the step she continued in the same remote voice, "I always worried about him, but he would laugh and lift me up in the air... he was very strong, you know. Then perhaps we would walk arm in arm, and he'd tell me such stories, Bridie, such stories... and in the end I'd find myself laughing with him, and promising I wouldn't worry any more. But I always did, the next time he went away..." She leaned forward, put her hands to her face and began to weep.

There was nothing I could do. From her strange ramblings I feared that her mind had slipped, and I prayed that it would be only temporary. Mounting the step at the back of the little trap, I moved forward, sat down, gathered the reins, and clicked my tongue to set Daisy moving round in a circle and back on to the road.

It was after half past eight o'clock when we reached Latchford Hall. Kate was waiting in the porch, full of questions, but I hushed her and told Ellen to take Mama to her room and put her to bed. Only a few minutes before, I had remembered that the two men from Scotland Yard would be arriving at half past nine o'clock to continue their search of the house, and as yet I had made no toilet and eaten no breakfast, though truth to tell I had no appetite.

Henson was in the hall, holding a copy of *The Times*. I knew from the stunned look on his face that it was today's copy, and that he had read something about my father in it. He waited till Ellen had taken my mother upstairs, then came forward and said in a hushed voice, "Miss Bridie . . . oh, Miss Bridie."

I thought with longing of the moment when Bernard would arrive in response to the note I had sent him last night. Once he was beside me I would have a loyal companion with broad shoulders to help me bear my burdens, and I would not feel so desperately alone. But Bernard was not here yet, and the moment had come when I could no longer hold back the awful shock from my poor Kate.

I held out my hand to Henson, and he gave me the paper. "In the drawing room please, Henson," I said. Then, to Kate, "Is Nannie awake now?"

She nodded wanly. "Yes, she went to get dressed a little while ago."

"As soon as she's ready, take her to your room and wait for me. I'll come and see you in five minutes, but I must speak to Henson first."

Her eyes grew large and her lip trembled. "What is it, Bridie? I have such a dreadful feeling that there's more bad news, but I can't think what it could possibly be."

"Dearest Kate, please bear with me," I said, my voice wavering. "Just five minutes. Please." My heart was breaking for her, but there was nothing I could do now to delay or even to soften the blow. She stared at me, at first hurt, then with tearful defiance, and for a moment I feared she would refuse, but suddenly she gathered her skirts and went running across the hall and up the stairs.

I went into the drawing room and stood by the fireplace. When Henson had closed the door I said, "Give me a moment to read this, please."

With grimy hands, scratched on the palms from my fall on the cobbles, I unfolded the newspaper. The report was contained in two columns at the foot of the page, under a title that sent a shiver through me.

A GENTLEMAN JEWEL THIEF

A report which can only be described as remarkable was published by all major French newspapers yesterday. It concerns a Suffolk gentleman, originally from Ireland, who came to a violent end beneath the walls of a French castle whilst engaging in his secret profession of jewel thief.

Our enquiries reveal that Roger Chance, aged 52, of Latchford Hall, Wynford, in the county of Suffolk, was an art expert and dealt in pictures. He pursued his profession almost exclusively on the Continent, where he resided in Paris, returning to his home in England three or four times a year to spend a few weeks with his family at Latchford Hall. It was here that he had resided since shortly after his marriage, more than twenty years ago, with his wife (Mrs. Mary Chance) and his two daughters (Miss Bridget Chance and Miss Kate Chance).

The report of the French police states that unknown to anyone, except perhaps to a fellow criminal who received stolen property, Roger Chance led a second life as a highly accomplished burglar. This report has now been confirmed by our own authorities, the Criminal Investigation Department at Scotland Yard. Senior Officers have studied a number of statements from witnesses to the events at Château Montpalion on the night of 3rd July, including statements from two French police officials of high rank.

The C.I.D. have informed us that for many years the police forces of several continental countries have been baffled by a thief who specialized in stealing expensive jewelry from the houses of the rich. These exploits were not frequent, but always yielded a haul of considerable value, and the methods of the thief were so skillful and baffling that in the course of time he acquired the nickname of Le Sorcier. *(Translation: The Magician.)*

I looked up from the newspaper, for the words had begun to dance before my eyes. Henson stood with head bowed, staring down at the floor. The report was longer than I had at first thought, and horrifying in the way it bluntly declared my father's guilt. I rubbed at my eyes with finger and thumb, then looked down again and made myself continue reading.

According to Scotland Yard it is now over a year since their French colleagues made a new study of all the seemingly unimportant facts, accumulated over a very long period, regarding these baffling thefts. From this study there emerged certain common factors which gave rise to the scarcely believable theory that the mysterious felon might be none other than a well-known art dealer named Roger Chance, a foreign gentleman living mainly in Paris but who traveled the Continent widely and was a popular guest at many of the best houses.

After much discussion, a trap was laid by the police in collaboration with Baron Montpalion and one of his guests, the Contessa Vizzini, at a week-end house party given by the baron at his beautiful château north of Angoulême. In the weeks preceding the house party, to which Mr. Roger Chance had been invited, small reports appeared in a number of French and Italian newspapers concerning a magnificent diamond pendant made for the contessa by Rome's famous jewelers, Mirel & Capelli.

It was hoped that this would prove a tempting bait for Le Sorcier, and these hopes were realized. Mr. Roger Chance had accepted the invitation to attend the house party and was among the guests. In the early hours of Saturday last, his face masked by a close-fitting hood, he effected entry into the boudoir of the contessa by way of the balcony, using certain burglarious instruments, and began a silent search for the diamond pendant.

He was not to know that by prearranged plan the contessa had been moved to another suite, and that French police officials were awaiting him. They allowed him to find a cheap duplication of the pendant in a jewel box on the dressing table, then burst from their hiding places as the miscreant made to depart in the same way that he had come.

The masked man evaded their grasp, darted out on to the balcony, and leaped from the balustrade to grasp the cornice by which he had presumably traversed the last part of the perilous journey from his own room. In the haste of his desperate attempt to escape, he lost his grip and fell sixty feet to the cruel stone flags below. Other police, who had been lying hidden in the courtyard, closed in at once, but Le Sorcier was never to move again, for he had been killed instantly on striking the ground.

When the black hood was drawn from his head, the truth of Le Sorcier's identity was revealed at last, and an astonishing theory was confirmed, for the face of the dead man was the face of Roger Chance, a member of cosmopolitan society, art dealer of Paris, and gentleman of Suffolk.

In a statement issued last night, Scotland Yard confirmed that detectives began yesterday to carry out a search of Latchford Hall in the hope of recovering some at least of the ill-gotten gains of this criminal who for so long had led such an amazing double life. Success in their search would appear highly unlikely, since it is apparent that Chance confined his felonious activities strictly to the Continent, doubtless to protect his family. Further developments in this remarkable case will be closely followed by your correspondent, but it is to be doubted that any future revelations will be as dramatic as those now reported.

I folded the newspaper and rubbed my eyes again. Henson said in a shaken voice, "I just don't understand, Miss Bridie. I . . . I never heard the like of it before. How can they say those things about Mr. Chance? It's a wicked slander, miss. Isn't it?"

"I don't suppose it's a legal slander," I said heavily, "or they would never have printed it. But there must have been some truly dreadful mistake somewhere."

"I know, Miss Bridie. But, begging your pardon, what sort of mistake do you think it was? I mean, that's what they'll all be asking me below stairs, so I want to be able to tell them."

I shook my head. "I don't know. I can't begin to think, Henson. But Mr. Whitely, the solicitor, is going down to London today, and I hope he will clear things up. In the meantime you must go and tell the servants about this newspaper report. Explain to them that those two detectives who were here yesterday will shortly arrive to continue searching the house. You must also warn them that things are going to be very difficult for a while. Very difficult indeed."

"Yes, Miss Bridie. The gossip's going to be something awful. I'm afraid there's going to be lots of people coming just to stare at the house, and at anyone coming or going."

"Oh, dear Lord," I said, cringing inwardly at the thought. "And we shall have reporters here soon."

"I'll put Robert on the gate, Miss Bridie, and I'll send for that brother of his."

"The big farm hand?"

"That's right, miss. Strong as a bull, Jack is, and looks it. If I give him a shilling he'll make sure nobody troubles you today."

"All right, Henson, thank you, and you had better arrange it without delay, even before you talk to the staff. I must leave all that to you, for I have to break the news to Miss Kate now."

As I crossed the hall I caught sight of myself in the big looking glass. Much of my hair had escaped from the ribbon and now straggled loosely about my head. The dress I wore was smeared with dirt, the skirt torn where I had twice fallen. When rubbing my eyes I had transferred grime from my fingers to my eyelids and eyebrows, giving me a grotesque appearance. I was stiff and sore from the ride, and despite the warmth of the day I was inwardly cold with dread of what I must now do.

Kate was in her bedroom with Nannie Foster. I made her sit down, told her that a hideously false report about Papa had appeared in *The Times*, then read it out to her, my voice failing me several times before I finished. Nannie sat blank-faced, shaking her head slowly from side to side. Kate had begun to cry quietly halfway through, and now sat with her face in her hands, her shoulders shaking. I knew that when she recovered from the first shock she would have a dozen questions to ask that I could not answer, and there was so much to be done that I could spare no time even to comfort her.

I put the newspaper on the bed, patted her shoulder and

bent to kiss her head. "I'm sorry, darling," I said wearily. "Stay here with Nannie and try to be very brave. We'll talk later, but I must bathe and change now, before the detectives arrive. Oh, and Dr. Carey, too."

Ellen, bless her, had set out my hip bath on the bath sheet in front of the fireplace and brought up hot-water cans to fill it. She had also laid out fresh clothes for me, with a navy blue dress from which she had somehow found time to remove white trimmings at collar and cuffs, so that it would serve temporarily for mourning until black dresses were ready.

Twenty minutes later, feeling almost calm for the first time that morning, I emerged from my room to find Ellen coming to the top of the stairs with Dr. Carey beside her. He gave me a strange, embarrassed look and said, "Good morning, Bridie."

"Good morning, Doctor." I knew that he had seen the newspaper report, and I had a strong feeling that he did not wish to be in Latchford Hall at this moment, but felt duty bound to call. I wondered how often in the coming days I would see that look in people's eyes, a look of shocked distaste overlaid with avid curiosity. I said, "Excuse me, just for one moment please, Dr. Carey." Then, to Ellen, "Thank you for all you have done, Ellen. I'll go with the doctor to see Mama, and I want you to run down to the kitchen and hear what Mr. Henson has to tell you."

"To tell me, Miss Bridie?"

"Yes. Go along now. I'll ring from the bedroom if I need you."

Ellen had washed my mother's face and hands, brushed her hair, and put a fresh nightdress on her. She was asleep when I entered the room with Dr. Carey, and I was glad to see that the terrible stress had vanished from her face. Her eyes were still sunken and bruised, but there was a kind of calm about her, and she looked almost beautiful again. She stirred when Dr. Carey felt her pulse, but did not wake. He felt her brow, wagged his head as if in surprise, then turned to look at me. "I take it she slept well?"

"I believe so, Dr. Carey." I had decided to say nothing

to him about my mother's wild trip to the coast unless it seemed necessary.

He nodded. "She seems to have sustained the shock very well. No more sleeping draughts, I think. She's still almost comatose. See that she eats something later, something light for preference, and she should be able to get up tomorrow, if she wishes." He picked up his bag. "I don't think there's any need for me to call again."

We went down to the hall together in silence, and I felt sure that Dr. Carey would not be calling again in any event. Perhaps for the first time I realized that all our acquaintances in the district, from village people to gentry, would now see us, my mother and Kate and me, as the family of a notorious criminal. We would be stared at, we would be the subject of endless gossip, and we would be avoided as if we carried some plague. Nobody would wish to have dealings with the wife and daughters of a felon. Once again I felt a surge of thankfulness that I could at least count on Bernard for support.

Henson was at the door, and as he opened it I saw the figures of Inspector Browning and Sergeant Dean approaching.

"Well . . . ah, good morning, Bridie," said Dr. Carey.

"Good-bye, Dr. Carey." I could not keep the bitterness from my voice. He went out, clapping his hat on his head, and I stood back as the two detectives entered. They greeted me politely, the inspector giving me a rather keen look as he said, "You're very pale, miss. Are you all right?"

"I'm a little tired, Inspector."

"I don't suppose you've eaten any breakfast, miss. You really ought to eat something."

"Yes, I will do so as soon as I'm free. Did Mr. Whitely speak with you yesterday evening?"

"He did, miss, and I understand he's gone to talk to my superiors at the Yard today. A very sound gentleman, Mr. Whitely is, if you ask me. Now, once again I'm sorry we have to intrude, miss, but I'd like to carry on, please."

"Of course. Mr. Henson here will give you every facility."

Inspector Browning looked at the sergeant. "Make sure the seals are intact, then start with the dining room and work your way through on this floor."

"Right, sir." Sergeant Dean marched briskly away.

The inspector hesitated, then said, "I would like to see your mother's jewelry now, miss, and also any jewelry belonging to you or your sister. Then I regret to say I must search the—um—sleeping accommodation."

I think my face must have taken on an even deeper pallor then, for my head began to swim. I felt the inspector's hand on my arm and heard him say, "Steady, miss."

After a moment or two I could see again, and said, "A word with you in the drawing room please, Inspector." It was useless to withhold the truth from him. He would soon find out that my mother had possessed jewelry but now had none, and he would quickly wring from one of the servants the story of her ride out that morning.

When the door had closed behind us I turned to him and said, "The shock of my father's death, and in particular of the terrible accusation you made yesterday, have combined to cause my mother great disturbance of mind, and she acted in a completely irrational manner this morning. No doubt obsessed by what you had told her, she gathered her jewelry together, drove out to the bay, and threw it all into the sea. I regret that I was too late to stop her."

Inspector Browning whistled faintly on an indrawn breath, then stared at me in silence for a while. At last he said mildly, "Well, thank you for telling me, miss."

I felt a pang of guilt. He had been very kind to me last night by leaving his search unfinished, and this was the result. I said, "I'm sorry, Inspector. I suppose your superiors won't be very pleased with you over this?"

"Oh, don't worry about that, miss. I'm sure you can give me a description of all the pieces, and that it can be vouched for by your mother's maid."

"Yes. That would not be difficult."

"Mind you, I'm quite sure we won't find that it matches anything on the list of stolen jewelry the French police gave us. I told my superiors so, right from the start. That Mr.

Chance was a very clever gentleman, I told them, much too clever to make a silly mistake like giving bits of the stuff to his family."

I glared at him now, and my voice cracked as I said, "My father did *not* steal any jewelry, Inspector!"

He sighed and fingered his chin. "Perhaps not, miss, perhaps not," he said quietly. "But your mother seems a lot less sure about that, doesn't she?"

At ten o'clock Bernard still had not come, and the next train would not bring him to Wynford for another hour. Ellen brought me a boiled egg, some bread and butter, and a pot of tea in the breakfast room, and stood there to make sure I ate it, her face pinched with distress. All the servants knew the worst now, and the house was full of whispering and tiptoeing, as if we were all in attendance at a funeral.

At eleven o'clock Bernard did not arrive. I went to Kate's room and sat with her for a while. We did not talk very much, for now it seemed that there was nothing to say. Twice Kate asked me what we should do without Papa, and I could only tell her that I did not know yet, and that I would discuss everything with Mama, when she was well enough.

Kate's room was on the front of the house, and from the window I could see beyond the tall shrubbery to the main gate. A dozen or more village folk stood on the other side of the lane, simply gawking at the house. Robert, our groom, was at the gate, and pacing slowly back and forth across the drive was the huge figure of Robert's farmhand brother, Jack, idly twirling a yard-long blackthorn cudgel. Twice Robert had brought me a message from a reporter on the *East Anglian Daily Times* requesting a short interview with a member of the family. Twice I had replied that no interviews whatever would be given to the Press, and that we should be grateful to be left untroubled by further requests.

At twelve o'clock, from the library window, I saw the station carriage trundling up the drive. I flew out to the hall and was running down the steps even as Bernard climbed from the carriage.

"Oh Bernard, thank heaven you've come. I've been so dreadfully alone—" I was clinging to his hands, and so overwhelmed with relief that my voice failed me completely, and I stood gulping to hold back tears. His eyes were steady, his jaw set, and as I looked up at him I felt an aching solace begin to expand within me, an emotion so strong that my head spun, and Bernard caught me quickly by the shoulders. He threw a word to the cabbie, then tucked my arm tightly through his and spoke again as we moved away together.

I said shakily, "I'm sorry . . . what did you say, Bernard dear?"

"I asked where we could talk, Bridie." His manner was crisp and determined, kindling new hope in me.

With an effort I gained control of my voice. "Oh, please . . . not in the house. It's so dreadfully sad and miserable, and there are two detectives there, searching."

"Yes. That was mentioned in the newspaper. Lord, you look ill, Bridie. Have you called a doctor?"

I made a little sound that was between a laugh and a sob. "Dr. Carey has been twice, to see Mama. And you need not worry about me. I shall be quite all right now, my dearest." We were moving along the front of the house to the point where the drive led off to the stables and coach house at the back. The noon sun was warm on my face, and I felt stronger with each passing moment. We did not speak as we walked slowly across the main lawn behind the house to the shade thrown by trees on the edge of the small copse beyond the shrubbery, and I was grateful to Bernard for understanding that I needed time in which to catch my breath and gather my thoughts.

When we halted by the trees I turned to him, putting my hands on his arms and looking up at him so that he would see how much I loved him for coming to my side at this dreadful time. My heart lifted a little as I saw the hard determination in his wide-set blue eyes.

"Are you feeling steadier now, Bridie?" he said quietly.

"Yes, much better, Bernard dear. Thank you with all my heart for being here now."

"I had to come, Bridie. I couldn't just write you a letter."

"A letter?" I echoed.

"That's what my father wanted me to do. I mean, after he had read the report in *The Times*. We had rather a row, as a matter of fact, but I couldn't do it, Bridie. I felt the only decent thing was to speak to you face to face."

I took my hands from his arms and put them behind me, clasping them tightly as sickness swept through me, and trying to prevent myself trembling. "What is it you have to say to me face to face, Bernard?" I asked at last in a high, wavering voice.

He ran a hand through his hair. "Surely you must know that, Bridie? Surely you realize that everything has changed now? Your father was a criminal, and however unjust it may be, you and your family are going to suffer from that for the rest of your lives. You are the family of Roger Chance, the notorious jewel thief."

I nodded slowly, and managed to say in a flat voice, "I see."

"I hope you do, Bridie. The best thing for you is to go abroad, change your name, start afresh somewhere, somehow. Wherever you go in England, there's going to be a finger pointing at you." He drew in a long breath, then went on firmly, "I came to say that I cannot possibly be your husband in such circumstances. It would put an end to my career, it would reflect on my own family; and it would make me a social outcast. That's what I've come to tell you, Bridie, and I'm sure you understand."

I nodded again, unable to speak. My hopes of comfort and support had been shattered as if by a thunderbolt, and I was alone again to face all that would have to be faced, to do all that would have to be done. Yet I did understand what Bernard had said, and though I was terrified and desperate, I could not find it in me to blame him. It had been foolish of me not to realize just how great was the stigma that would cling to the family of Roger Chance, a stigma I could not expect any man to share.

I found I was making one of my grimaces. My lips were folded in and pressed tightly together, at the same time stretching in an absurd attempt to smile. My eyebrows were raised high to indicate regret and acceptance. With my deep pallor I must have looked like one of those cloth-faced rag dolls with features drawn on them in simple lines.

Bernard stood looking down at me with an uneasy frown. I could have laughed, if I had dared, to think that the determination in him which had so gladdened me was not what I had imagined, but was a determination to end our engagement honorably by speaking rather than writing.

I brought my hands from behind me, and carefully took from my finger the sapphire engagement ring Bernard had put there only a few months ago. When I held it out to him he hesitated, then put up his hand for me to drop it into the palm. "Thank you, Bridie," he said doggedly. "It's all a beastly business, and I'm very sorry. I hope that in the end you and your family will find your way to ... well, to a satisfactory outcome. I'm sorry, but there's really nothing else I can say."

I wagged my head in agreement, feeling like a self-animated puppet. When Bernard continued to stand there, fidgeting uncertainly, I closed my eyes. I must then have looked even more like a cloth-faced doll, but it did not matter. My hands were pressed against my chest, and I could feel my heartbeats. Without volition I began to count them. When I had reached a hundred I opened my eyes, blinking in the bright sunlight, and found that I was alone in the garden.

In those moments when I stood in darkness something had happened to me. I was no longer close to tears, and my panic at the thought of bearing my burden alone had faded. Somehow I would have to comfort and care for my mother and Kate and Nannie. I would have no time for tears, no time to feel sorry for myself. I was not a very competent person to take charge of the family and to fight all the battles that would have to be fought, but there was nobody else now.

With a sudden surge of affection I remembered Mr. Whitely. Regardless of what he might believe about my father, he had received me kindly and continued to treat me with kindness after he had heard my story. Now he had gone bustling off to London in my service, putting all other matters aside. At least I could be thankful to have one such ally.

I had been standing with head bowed, staring down at the grass, and now found that my eyes had been focusing on a small object that lay at my feet. It was a thin brown cylinder, perhaps half the length of my forefinger, blackened at one end. Brown leaves, tightly rolled. Tobacco. I bent to look more closely. It was a very thin straight cigar, of a kind I had never seen before, with black ash solidified at one end where dew had extinguished it. But except when Papa was at home, nobody in Latchford Hall smoked at all, and the two gardeners smoked only clay pipes.

I gave an angry shake of my head as if to clear it, turning away from the dark brown stub and wondering what possessed me to speculate even for a few seconds on a matter so trivial at a time when my whole world was crumbling. For a little while I stood thinking, trying to plan what I must do in the days ahead. Certainly I would not be returning to Girton, that was out of the question. Tomorrow morning I would drive to Mr. Whitely's office in Southwold again, to hear what he had to tell me about his inquiries at Scotland Yard and to ask him how I might arrange for my father's body to be brought home from France. There would then be the funeral to arrange, and many matters to be discussed with my mother once she was well enough.

Beyond the immediate future it seemed to me that we would be well advised to sell Latchford Hall and move to a more modest house in another part of the country, a house just large enough to be comfortable for ourselves and Nannie Foster, with a cook-housekeeper, a kitchen maid, and parlor maid. I felt miserably certain that wherever we went the story would follow us, and I wondered if it might be better for us to settle in London, where we would be more anonymous.

There seemed to be many different strands of thought struggling for my attention as I walked slowly back to the house and crossed the terrace. The windows stood open, and as I entered the dining room I heard Kate playing. Papa had bought the Broadwood piano for her three years before, when it became clear that she had great talent. It stood in the drawing room, and as I crossed the hall I saw Inspector Browning standing quite still with head bent a little, eyes half closed as he listened. She was playing "Les Préludes" of Liszt, and I had never heard her play better, for it seemed that her heart's sorrow was flowing from her fingers to the keyboard. I wished I could have given release to my own sorrow in such a way.

The inspector gave a little start as he saw me, then collected himself and sighed, shaking his head and making a small open-handed gesture which seemed to express both sympathy and regret. He did not speak, but moved quietly away toward the stairs. I went on into the drawing room and stood behind Kate, resting a hand gently on her shoulder. Still playing, she ducked her head to brush my hand with her cheek, then said, "I'm all right now, Bridie. I won't cry any more."

I squeezed her shoulder, then stood simply listening for a while, letting the music wash through me. At last I said, "Have you been to see Mama?"

"About half an hour ago, but she frightened me, Bridie. She didn't say anything, she just seemed to be asleep with her eyes open."

"It's shock, darling. You mustn't be frightened."

"Bridie . . ."

"Yes?"

"Do you think it's true? I mean, what the newspaper said about Papa?"

"Kate, how could you!" I moved so that I could see her face. "Of course it's not true. Can you really imagine Papa doing anything like that?"

She played with frowning concentration for perhaps half a minute before saying softly, "Yes, I can imagine it, Bridie."

"Kate!"

She stopped playing and looked at me. "He was a laughing, reckless man." Her hands lifted, then pounced down, fingers flashing as she played a fragment in a minor key, as insolent, dancing, devil-may-care little melody from a new work by Dukas, *L'Apprenti Sorcier*. "He was like that, Bridie," she said. "Did you never feel it? Did you never feel that he saw the whole world as a joke to be laughed at?" She played some linking chords to bring back "Les Préludes" again, and gazed absently into the distance, dark smudges beneath her eyes showing plainly against the pallor of her face.

It was hard for me to find words, but at last I said, "That's silly wild talk, Kate, and I hope you'll never speak in such a way again." I would have said much more, once started, but I did not want to upset her at a time when she was so vulnerable, so I put my hand to her cheek to show I was not angry with her, then moved away and sat down to listen, hoping that the music would help to calm me, for I found my heart was pounding with a mixture of shock and indignation. It had never occurred to me for a single moment that the newspaper report could be true, no matter what the French police or Scotland Yard or anybody at all might say, yet my sister Kate was in doubt within an hour of hearing the dreadful story.

I had been sitting for no more than a minute when Henson came to say that the policemen were leaving. I went out into the hall to find the inspector and his sergeant waiting, hats in hand.

"Sorry to disturb you, miss," said the inspector, "but I thought you'd like to know we've finished here now."

"I'm sure you found nothing of what you expected to find, Inspector."

"Quite so, miss. I'd like to thank you for not making a fuss. You've been very good, if I may say so. It's a cruel blow for you and your family." He hesitated, then went on, "Might I make so bold as to offer two words of advice, miss?"

I tried to smile as I said, "I welcome advice at this moment."

"Well, don't hide yourself away. Just come and go freely, and those people hanging about outside will clear off all the sooner. As for the reporters, would you like me to tell them that you have nothing to say? I think you'll find they'll take my word for it."

"I should be most grateful, Inspector."

"Just one more thing, miss. If anything sort of . . . well, sort of strange happens, anything puzzling or maybe a bit alarming, I'd be glad if you'd send me a wire at the Yard. I've left my card on the hall table."

I stared at him. "Strange or alarming in what way, Inspector?"

"I can't really say, miss. It's just a notion at the back of my head." Holding his brown bowler hat to his chest, he gave me a courteous bow. "We'll bid you good day now, and if I may make so bold, miss, I'd like to say it's been a rare treat, listening to your sister play. I heard Paderewski himself at St. James's Hall a few years ago, and I reckon the way she played that Liszt piece is something he wouldn't be ashamed of himself. All right, sergeant, come along, we don't want to hang around all day."

As Henson closed the door after them I reflected vaguely that this surprising detective with a taste for classical music had shown more genuine sympathy than my erstwhile fiancé.

"May I ask about luncheon, Miss Bridie?" said Henson.

"Oh . . ." I collected my thoughts. "Tell Mrs. Ryland I leave it to her. Something very light and simple. I shall go and sit with my mother for a little while now."

"Very good, Miss Bridie."

My mother was awake when I tapped and entered her room. Ellen had brushed her hair and made it into two plaits to keep it tidy. Strangely, Mama looked younger than I had seen her look for many a day, her eyes quiet and serene, her face without strain. She gave me a little smile, and beckoned me to sit beside her. "I've been waiting for you, Bridie," she said in a gentle whisper.

"There were one or two things to see to, Mama." I took her hand and held it. "Are you feeling a little better?"

"Yes, dear. I shall be quite all right now." She made a sound that was almost a giggle. "The inspector isn't going to search this room after all. He sent Ellen to say it would be pointless, under the circumstances. What do you think he meant?"

"He knows you threw all your jewelry into the sea, Mama. I told him."

She looked reproachful. "Oh, Bridie, that wasn't very sensible. I'm sure your papa would have thought you a silly goose."

I did not want to argue with her, so I just nodded and continued to hold her hand. There were many things to be discussed, but I knew this was not the moment. My mother's gaze was wandering vaguely, and I was sure that she could not give her attention to any matter requiring a decision.

After a few minutes she closed her eyes. I thought she had fallen asleep, but then I saw her lips curve in the faintest of smiles and she whispered, "He was so clever... and I loved to hear him laugh with the stories he told me. Such stories, Bridie. I was never frightened while he was here, telling me all about it, and laughing... but I would think of the stories when he was away, and then I would be frightened. I suppose I never quite understood how he saw things... because he was a gentleman, you see. A gentleman born. And they laugh at different things, you know."

I found it hard to follow her rambling words, but there was something in them that evoked a shadowy unease within me. I said nothing, hoping that she would drift into sleep. For a minute or so she was silent, then spoke again in the same whispering voice. "Such stories, Bridie. There was that time in Austria long ago, in a place called Witt... Witt something. I could never remember all those foreign places. There was a safe in the big house belonging to a titled gentleman, and it had a special kind of lock, you see. But he made two little holes with a drill, and then sucked the air out with... with an air pump, I think, and he said it drew the powder in through the other hole. Gunpowder, I suppose it was. Then he... oh, there was a thing called a fuse, and the whole door came loose with the explosion. Can you imagine? Such beautiful emeralds, and the velvet they were wrapped in was barely scorched. Wasn't it clever of him? That must have been before we were married, I think, because I saw them that day when he took me to the Capricorn Stone. Oh, how he laughed about leaving the special lock of the safe quite untouched. That was the part he liked best, you see...the joke of it. Like the time in Rome...at the fancy dress ball, when he told a baroness that she was wearing imitation pearls. She was so indignant at first, but it was true, you see, because he had made the substitution himself..."

The voice rambled on. I sat looking at the hand with which I held my mother's hand, trying to think a coherent thought, trying to feel any kind of emotion, but I might have been a block of wood. Nothing moved in me.

Some time later, I could not tell how long, I realized that Mama had stopped talking and was asleep. She looked small, beautiful, and at peace. My numbed brain was beginning to come slowly to life again, and I was thinking to myself that what I had now learned made no difference to the situation. Except perhaps for Nannie Foster, I was the only one in the world who would have utterly refused to believe what the police and the newspapers said.

Very well. I would have been wrong, but this did not matter, for nothing else had changed. My father, Roger Chance, that laughing reckless man as Kate called him, had indeed been the notorious thief known as Le Sorcier. But the world believed this anyway, and it seemed to me now that the fact of it being true made no difference to what lay ahead for my family and for me.

Perhaps I was stupid not to realize it made a frightening difference. If I had done so, I might have been better prepared for the web of mystery, terror, and danger that was to entrap me in time to come.

I woke that night to find myself standing by the window and looking out on to the garden. Nothing stirred, and no horseman moved out of the shadows as in my dream of the night before.

A spark of memory flared within me. I rubbed my eyes, patted my cheeks sharply enough to sting, and rested my forehead against the cool pane. Now I could be sure I was awake, not dreaming, and I remembered the strange thin cigar, half smoked, which I had seen near the shrubbery this morning. I remembered, too, that in my dreaming or waking of the night before I had seen a fiery glow curve from on high to the ground, leaving a trail of sparks, just before the rider with the gaucho hat emerged from the blackness.

A cigar, tossed to the ground by a man on a horse, would have appeared to me in just that way. Suppose, then, that it was not a dream? In that event there had indeed been a horseman, riding strangely with a long stirrup, wearing a gaucho hat, and smoking a cigar, who had prowled the grounds of Latchford Hall in the early hours of the morning.

I gave a shrug of contempt and turned back to my bed, annoyed with myself for even considering that such nonsense could have been real. I told myself that I had been overwrought last night, and had dreamed a strange dream; tonight I had partly followed the pattern, even to climbing out of bed and going to the window, but then I had woken up. As for the half-smoked cigar I had found by the trees, that was no more than a coincidence.

I did not know, as I got wearily back into bed, that I had just come to a wrong conclusion for the second time in twenty-four hours.

four

In the next few weeks I discovered that there is a point beyond which another blow is almost meaningless because it cannot be felt. Two days after I had learned that my father was dead and had been a professional thief, and the day after my fiancé had broken our engagement, I drove out from Latchford Hall at nine o'clock in the morning, my cheeks flaming as I approached the dozen or more men, women, and children loitering in the lane near the entrance to the drive.

There were two dogcarts and a tradesman's cart. The men and women had formed two small groups, gossiping. A man was sharpening a sickle, a woman was knitting a stocking, a small child was licking a toffee apple. The other children were playing a game, chasing one another, and there was a little air of holiday about the whole scene. As I turned the gig out into the lane, everybody became quite still, as if in a tableau, staring, staring...

All through the journey, and especially during the drive through the busy streets of Southwold, my imagination made me feel a thousand curious eyes on me, and I seemed to hear the wordless whispering of a thousand gossiping tongues.

Mr. Whitely, as dry and polite as ever, received me in his office and came straight to the point. "I am bound to tell you, Miss Chance, distressing though it is for me, and indeed I am aware that it must be even more distressing for you, that after long discussion with the Assistant Commissioner, and after studying translations of a substantial number of documents from the French police, I can see no way

69

whatsoever in which we may hope to assert your father's innocence, for we should be attempting to do so in the face of what I have been compelled to concede is incontrovertible evidence from persons of unquestionable probity."

I sat looking down at my hands in my lap and said, "I'm sure you won't expect me to believe the evidence, Mr. Whitely, however strong it may be."

"Certainly not. I wish only to convey to you that you should have no hope of ever overturning such evidence."

"Very well, Mr. Whitely, and thank you for all your efforts on my behalf. Under the circumstances, do you now wish no longer to have me as a client?"

"I am perfectly willing to act for you, Miss Chance, along the lines that I mentioned when we last met. Indeed, the application for Letters of Administration is being attended to now, and I shall be in touch with your father's bank later this morning. Do you have any further instructions for me at present?"

"I should like my father's body to be brought home for burial here, if that is possible."

He nodded absently, stroking his nose. "Quite so. I anticipated this request, and took the opportunity of making inquiries into the situation while I was in London. My understanding is that there will be no difficulty about this, but there may be some delay. Certain French laws require that— pray forgive me—where mortal remains are to be transported by rail they must first undergo certain preservative procedures."

"I beg your—? Oh. Yes. I see." I put a hand to my throat and went on quickly. "Could I ask you to do whatever is necessary, Mr. Whitely? I don't suppose it falls within your responsibility, but I should be deeply grateful. My mother is not well enough to deal with anything, and I really seem to have nobody to turn to."

"Leave the matter with me." A gleam touched his eye for a moment. "I shall instruct my brother to discharge this particular responsibility. As to other matters, I hope that within a few days I shall be able to make a reasonable assessment of the financial situation with regard to indigenous assets. As to the question of foreign assets, I am informed that inquiries by the French police have so far revealed that your father kept a modest balance in a Paris bank for normal living expenses, but as yet they have not been able to trace any other assets or cash deposits of any kind. It would appear, Miss Chance, that whatever substance your father may have possessed, he kept it well hidden." Mr. Whitely tilted his head regretfully, and sighed. "Perhaps too well hidden, I fear. However, we shall pursue our inquiries and keep you fully informed at all times. I am greatly obliged to you for calling, Miss Chance..."

In the days that followed I took the advice of Inspector Browning and went out and about on household matters openly. During that time I learned to armor myself with dogged resignation against stares and whispers, sidelong glances, and mutterings wherever I went. Kate came with me once into Wynford, but could not bear it and scarcely managed to hold back her tears until we reached home again.

Nannie Foster had pulled herself together and was of great help in looking after Mama and in keeping Kate from brooding, but Latchford Hall had become a sad and somber house. Within a few days Henson came to me and asked apologetically if I would write references for all the servants. It was not, he assured me, that any of them wished to leave because of what the newspapers had said, but with the master's sad passing they could see that it might be necessary for them to find new positions. Nannie was indignant, but I did not think them disloyal, or blame them.

My mother remained in bed, and did not ask me a single question. She seemed to have withdrawn into a long daydream where she found a kind of contentment. In a way I was glad for her, but at the same time I worried because she left her food untouched and was asleep through most hours of the day and night. At first I had feared to leave her with Ellen or Nannie or Kate, in case she rambled as she had with me, revealing the truth. Kate had her doubts about Papa's innocence, and perhaps the same might be said of Ellen for all I knew, but I could not bear the thought of those doubts being replaced by certainty. In the event, I am sure Mama did not speak revealingly of the past with any of the others, for I would have known, and after a few days I felt the danger was past.

A letter sent by hand from Mr. Whitely told me that arrangements to bring my father home had been satisfactorily made, and that the coffin would be delivered to the Chapel of Rest of Messrs. Harris and Cole, Funeral Directors of Southwold, via Harwich, in approximately two weeks' time, the precise date to be confirmed within ten days. He suggested I might make provisional arrangements for the funeral, and asked if I would be kind enough to call at his office on Friday morning next, at eleven o'clock, when he expected to have all necessary information to enable him to advise me concerning the matter of my father's estate. He added that he hoped my mother had recovered from her grievous shock sufficiently to be present with me, since she was of course the natural inheritrix.

I wrote to thank him and to confirm the appointment, but said my mother was far from well and would be unable to attend. This was true, and by the Thursday I was so concerned for her that I sent for Dr. Carey. I half feared that he might make some excuse and ask me to seek medical advice elsewhere, but he came within forty minutes. It was clear, however, that we no longer held any position in his eyes, for his manner was short and unsympathetic.

When he had made a brief examination of my mother, he spoke to me as I walked along the passage and downstairs to the hall with him. "She is physically sound but undernourished, so you must get her to eat. Broth. Bread and milk. Anything. If you don't, she'll go into a decline."

I said, "We keep trying, Doctor, but she just takes a spoonful or so, then falls asleep. I'm very worried."

"Nervous debility following shock. It's hardly to be wondered at. I'll make up a tonic and send a boy round with it later today. Ought to stimulate her appetite. That will be two shillings, please, plus sixpence for the tonic."

"Oh." I managed to control a silly grimace of surprise. "Oh, I'm sorry. I... please wait while I fetch my purse."

When he had gone I shut myself in my bedroom and

wept a little with humiliation. I could have said coldly, "Kindly submit your bill in the usual way, Doctor." Or I could have said, "If you insist on cash, I will send it by the boy who brings the medicine." There were many cool, dignified phrases I could have used. But I was Bridie Chance, so I had pulled a face, apologized, groped for words, and thought of all the things I could have said far too late.

On the Friday morning I drove out of Latchford Hall at a quarter to ten, allowing myself ample time to drive into Southwold for my appointment with Mr. Whitely. Robert's brother, on guard there, saluted me, and I drew up for a word with him.

"On'y two women and a brace o' kids waiting about today, miss." He nodded at the little group by the low wall across the lane. "Don't nobody try coming in like before. Nine-day-wonder for 'em, I rackon."

The Roger Chance scandal was very much more than a nine-day-wonder, but I was thankful that at least the house was no longer besieged by inquisitive gossips and journalists as it had been during the first few days. I said, "Thank you for your help, Jack. I should be glad if you would keep taking turns here with Robert until after the weekend, just to make sure we're not pestered."

"Pleasure, Miss Bridie. It's them newspaper fellers was the worst, but they lost 'eart a bit now."

"So I understand. Here's an extra shilling for you, and very well earned."

I knew, from Henson, that earlier in the week Jack had thrown a particularly persistent journalist into a hawthorn hedge. Since then they had, as Jack now put it, "lost 'eart a bit."

Ten minutes later, as the gig swung round a bend in the winding lane which skirted the wood beyond Liddington, I pulled hard on the reins to stop short of a horse and rider standing quite still in the middle of the road, the horse's right flank toward me. At Daisy's modest pace there was no danger of collision, but the sudden encounter startled me, and perhaps because my nerves had worn thin over the past days I felt a surge of anger.

Before I could speak the man turned his head, took off the gray top hat he wore, and gave me a smile of greeting so warm and direct that I caught my breath in unexpected pleasure, then flushed at having done so. He was a man of above average height, with very dark hair making a cap of short curls above a square face with hazel eyes that were warm with gentle amusement.

He did not wear riding breeches or jacket, but a most elegant suit of fine gray check and a silk cravat fastened with a gold pin. There was something odd about the cut of his suit and about the way he sat his horse, but before I could wonder about it he spoke, and I realized that he was not English.

"Forgive me, mam'selle." Even if he had not used the foreign word, I would have guessed that he was European and probably French. His voice was rather deep, and his slight accent was similar to that of a professor from Grenoble who had visited Girton to lecture on French literature of the eighteenth century.

I had noticed that the man was riding with long stirrups, and I thought at once of the only other occasion when I had seen this style in the saddle. Confused by a mixture of half-formed thoughts, I blurted out, "Do you ever wear a different kind of hat?" With the words I felt color flooding my cheeks. Surely nobody but Bridie Chance would ever have chosen such words in response to a polite apology from a stranger. I was thinking of the way he sat his horse, and of the flat, wide-brimmed gaucho hat worn by the night rider I had seen or dreamed of on the night when disaster had first struck our family, but my question must have seemed idiotic.

The man showed no surprise, but pursed his lips thoughtfully and regarded the hat he held, as if giving the matter due consideration. At last he said, "I occasionally wear a cap, mam'selle. Is it a matter of importance?"

"No...no, not at all. Please excuse me." I drew in a frantic breath, stretching my mouth in a grimace of embarrassment, then remembering not to, but too late.

The stranger watched with interest. "It is for me to offer

excuses, mam'selle," he said. "I offer my most humble apologies for having intruded upon you, but allow me to introduce myself. My name is Chatillon. Philippe Chatillon, at your service."

It was hard for me to think clearly with those wide hazel eyes seeming to encompass me, but I forced myself to be wary. "Do you mean that you stopped me on purpose, M'sieu Chatillon?"

"From me, mam'selle, you will always receive an honest answer, and so I must tell you that I did indeed position myself here so that I might speak with you."

Anger flared within me as I said, "Are you a journalist?"

His smile was totally disarming. "Ah, please do not hurl insults at me, mam'selle. No, I am not a journalist. I am, in a sense, a policeman. A French policeman, naturally. And I was, in a sense, a friend of your father, the delightful Mr. Roger Chance."

"A friend?" My voice was husky with shock.

"In a sense." He gave a shrug which spoke expressively of regret. "It is possible to admire an opponent. Do you know that a few months ago, when your father was about to return from France to England, I urged him to remain here with his family? We shared a bottle of wine in the Champs Élysées, and I pressed him to retire from his profession, whatever that might be. He understood me well enough, but chose to pretend that I referred to his dealing in paintings. Ah, well...I am glad that I was engaged on other matters, and so was not involved in the final scene."

It was a long time before I spoke, but he waited without impatience. At last I said, "You...you mean when my father died at Château Montpalion?"

"Yes, mam'selle. I lost a most entertaining friend the night that you lost a father." His eyes were warm and comforting. "The grief is not to be compared, of course. I offer you my deepest sympathy."

"Thank you." I was so confused that I found myself wondering what to say next, then realized with a little shock that I had not yet asked the most obvious question. Now I said, "I am waiting to discover why you stopped me here on the road, m'sieu. I imagine you have something to ask me."

"No, mam'selle. Something to tell you."

"What is it?"

"I knew Roger Chance well, in some ways better even than his own family, perhaps. We called him Le Sorcier, and he well deserved such a name, but he was a man of strange prejudices, strange fancies. He was both brilliant and naïve. Clever without being wise. I believe you will find that he has left a riddle to be answered. When the time comes that you find my belief to be correct, I urge you to seek my help, mam'selle."

"A riddle? Your help? I don't understand."

"I have posted a letter to you today, containing my card with my address in Paris. A telegram will bring me to you in less than a day. Please keep the card for the time when you need it. Please do not throw it away."

I felt a stupid urge to giggle, though there was no laughter in me. "Is this why you came here to Wynford, and stopped me on the road today?" I asked. "Simply to tell me this?"

"If I had written to you, mam'selle, you would not have believed me to be serious. I think you cannot doubt it now."

The desire to giggle was gone, and I nodded slowly. "You would scarcely have gone to such trouble for amusement. I think you are a most unusual policeman, sir."

He gazed thoughtfully up at the sky, then looked at me again. "Yes, I am a most unusual policeman. I do not speak like one or dress like one or behave like one. I might almost, perhaps, be mistaken for a gentleman. But there are exceptions to be found everywhere, are there not? My friend, Roger Chance, for example, was a most unusual gentleman."

Strangely, I was not distressed by his words. I sat looking at him with a feeling of increasing ease, glad simply to be for a few moments with somebody who seemed to have a complete understanding of the man who had been my father. He moved his horse to one side, and leaned forward, resting an arm on the pommel. "I will detain you no longer, mam'selle," he said. "It has been an honor to meet you, and a true pleasure. I have known your name for a long time now," his eyes danced with sudden humor, "but I had no idea that you were so beautiful."

The feeling of comfort splintered under his mockery, and again I felt the blood rush to my face. Tears were trying to flood my eyes, and my hands were shaking as I gathered up the reins. With an effort I made myself turn my head to look up at him, and with an even greater effort I made myself speak. "You need not fear being mistaken for a gentleman, sir."

I shook the reins to rouse Daisy from her doze, but the Frenchman leaned quickly down and caught my wrist, his grip gentle but firm. "Forgive me, mam'selle, but I cannot let you depart with a wrong impression." His face was very serious now. "It is clear that you believe I spoke in jest, but I did not."

I stared at him without understanding, and said, "I beg your pardon?"

He released my wrist at once, and smiled again. "Dear young lady, you do not have the prettiness of the English rose, with the china-doll face, and I doubt that many Englishmen would ever see that you are beautiful. At this moment your eyes are sad and your cheeks are drawn with grief, but nothing destroys true beauty, for it is from within, and will be with you if you should live to be eighty." He reached down again, picked up my limp hand, and bent to touch my fingers to his lips. "*Au revoir*, mam'selle."

Still smiling, he settled his gray top hat on his head, gathered the reins, touched heels to his horse, and went cantering off down the lane. After a few moments I gave a brief laugh, and was startled that I could do so. "That was a Frenchman," I said thoughtfully to Daisy as I coaxed her to a trot. "I've sometimes heard that they pay flowery compliments, but I didn't know they could be so convincing."

I drove on in a strange and dreamy state, reliving the encounter and trying to make sense of it. Somewhere within me it had given birth to a small feeling of excitement, even of pleasure. I was not sure why. Certainly I had not taken M. Philippe Chatillon's flattery seriously, though I was glad it had been well meant. I was also glad that he had been a friend of my father's, even if the nature of their acquaintance was somewhat obscure. When I reflected on it, everything about the strange policeman was somewhat obscure, but I was still glad that we had met. It was the first time I had been at least momentarily taken out of myself since that black day when I had returned to find the detectives at Latchford Hall.

By the time I reached Southwold my spirits had lifted quite a little and I was optimistically beginning to think that perhaps the very worst of our ordeal would soon be behind us. It was in this mood that I was conducted by the clerk to Mr. Whitely's office, there to receive a blow so savage as to leave me feeling that I had been beaten by cudgels.

Even when Mr. Whitely greeted me I sensed unease behind his usual dispassionate manner as he made sure I was comfortably seated before taking his place in the big swivel chair behind his desk. "I regret adding to your burdens at this time," he said in his thin, rather high voice, "but I am bound to tell you that I am disturbed about your family's financial situation, Miss Chance. As I intimated at our last meeting, no substantial assets have been discovered, and the only funds available are those kept in the current account your father maintained at Messrs. Goslings and Sharpe's Bank, which amount to only a few hundred pounds."

This was no more than I had expected. It meant that our whole fortune was vested in Latchford Hall, but that would be quite a large fortune, which would permit us to live very comfortably in a more modest residence. Mr. Whitely cleared his throat and continued, "We have been in touch with the Crédit Lyonnais, your father's French bank, but their lawyers inform us that they expect the modest balance there to be completely disbursed in settling various liabilities such as the rental due on his apartment and gallery, and the normal outstanding bills of tailors, wine merchants, etcetera."

Mr. Whitely paused. His hands were resting on the large white blotter which lay on his desk, and he was gently tapping the tips of his fingers together. After a moment or two I said, "You were good enough to warn me that this would probably be the case, Mr. Whitely. It just means we shall have to sell Latchford Hall, but I'm sure my mother would wish to do so in any event. I have been looking at property advertisements in appropriate newspapers and magazines, and it seems to me that with its extensive grounds Latchford Hall should realize a sum not less than twenty thousand pounds."

Mr. Whitely continued to look at his hands as he said slowly, "Your father did not own the freehold of Latchford Hall, I regret to say. Twenty-one years ago he bought the remainder of a ninety-nine year lease, which expires at the end of October next. On that date the property reverts to the freeholder, which is the Latchford Trust, set up some fifty years ago by Lord Royston for the benefit of his family."

There was a very long silence in the big, musty office. I sat looking at a large sepia picture on the wall behind Mr. Whitely, showing two cats looking at a ball. As a wound hurts only after the first numbness has passed, so I did not at this moment feel panic and fear and wild desperation. All that was to come later.

Mr. Whitely broke the silence. "You will wonder why I did not tell you this before, Miss Chance, but the truth is that I did not know. I only suspected it from my limited knowledge of your father, and I could not speak without being sure. The fact is that when he signed the lease, in the year before you were born, he employed a London solicitor, since it was from London that he came to live in Suffolk. It was later more convenient for him to employ a local firm, but I fear he did not arrange for any transfer of documents. We became apprised of the true situation when I made inquiries concerning the ownership of Latchford Hall and found myself in touch with solicitors representing the Latchford Trust, who have kindly given me sight of their copy of the lease. It appears that they were on the point of writing to us, since your father had been in communication with them during his last visit. He wished to renew the lease, and asked for the draft of the new lease to be sent to us as his legal representatives—a matter on which, I fear, he had neglected to inform us."

I did not take in much of what Mr. Whitely was saying. He was not a man to make mistakes, and I now knew that Latchford Hall did not belong to us. How it had all come about was unimportant. The chilling fact was that our family faced a future in which we had no breadwinner and no more than a few hundred pounds to our name, some of which would surely be absorbed in funeral and legal expenses.

I kept looking at the picture of the two cats and trying to think what I could do. We would have to find somewhere to live, though I could not imagine where, and we would have to find money to live on. Somehow I would have to work out how to take care of my mother and Kate and Nannie Foster.

My mother was ill, and I did not know how long her illness would last, but it was certain that I would have no support from her for a long time to come. Nannie Foster might have a few pounds saved, but she had expected to see out her days with us and had no home to go to. Then there was Kate, who must be decently lodged and kept in London so that she might take up the scholarship she had won.

I began trying to work out sums in my head, but my mind kept going blank. Stupidly I remembered the eighteen pence that Inspector Browning had placed on the mantelpiece after I had paid his cabbie. I vaguely recalled that I had put it in the top of the bureau, meaning to transfer it to my purse later. Eighteen pence. I wondered how long it would take me to earn eighteen pence.

Mr. Whitely was speaking, and I dragged my mind from a dreamlike emptiness to say, "Please excuse me, I'm afraid my attention wandered."

"That is scarcely to be wondered at, Miss Chance. I fear I have given you most disturbing news. I was simply saying that I shall be pleased to continue to act for you in any way you may wish, and that you may rest assured that my firm's charges will be—ah—quite nominal."

"You are more than kind, Mr. Whitely. Please believe me to be grateful."

"You have my respect and, if I may say so, my admiration, to the extent that you are by far my favorite client, Miss Chance," he said in the same tone as he might have used for commenting on the weather. "It is my pleasure to be of assistance, and my regret that I am able to do so little. May I speak plainly?"

"Please do."

"Without income, you and your family will shortly be close to penury. Latchford Hall was leased fully furnished, so only such items as have since been purchased, and are therefore not on the inventory I shall obtain from the lessor, will be available for sale, together with two or three horses and small carriages. Furthermore, there will, I fear, be a substantial sum required to meet the charges for repairs, renewals, and the restoration of the property to the condition required to meet the terms of the lease. Your mother's jewelry is—ah—no longer available, and I would doubt that you and your sister have possessions of substantial value. It will therefore be important for you, Miss Chance, to find some source of income as soon as possible. Would you agree with my analysis of the position?"

I nodded. "Yes. There is nobody else to support the family."

"Fortunately you are a very well educated young lady of academic bent, and I think it should not be difficult for you to secure a position as governess in a good family, despite the disadvantage of your family association with—ah—pray forgive me—with the recent scandal. There are good Christian folk who do not approve of visiting the sins of the fathers upon the children, and I should be happy to use my good offices for you with one or two such families of my acquaintance, if you so wished."

I was suddenly so weary that I found it hard to think, and several seconds passed before I was able to formulate the question that hung in my mind. At last I said, "Could you give me some idea of the sum a governess might expect to earn, Mr. Whitely?"

He stroked his nose with a finger. "It would vary with circumstances, of course, but she would, as you know from your own experience, be fully kept in a manner appropriate to her position as regards bed and board, and would also be paid a sum in the region of, let us say, sixty pounds a year."

I sat looking at the cats again for a little while, then got slowly to my feet. "I have responsibilities that call for a great deal more than that, Mr. Whitely. Thank you very much for your suggestion, but I feel I must now go away and give myself time to digest all the implications of what you have told me before I shall be able to think clearly about the future."

He had risen with me and now moved round the desk. "Should you feel the need to talk over matters which are not in any way legal, please feel free to call upon me, Miss Chance."

"I'm sure I shall avail myself of your kindness, Mr. Whitely. Thank you once more." He had moved to open the door when a thought from nowhere struck me, and I said, "When you had discussions at Scotland Yard, was any mention made of a French police officer by the name of Philippe Chatillon?"

For once Mr. Whitely showed surprise, his eyebrows lifting by perhaps a quarter of an inch. "May I ask where you heard that name, Miss Chance?"

"I met the gentleman less than an hour ago."

"Here? In Southwold?"

"On the road near Wynford. He introduced himself to me."

"Extraordinary."

"So I thought."

"May I ask what he said to you?"

I gave a brief account of our conversation, leaving out the concluding flattery. When I had finished, Mr. Whitely pinched his lower lip and said thoughtfully, "What a remarkable fellow. Yes, I came to know his name during my discussions with the Assistant Commissioner, but he is not precisely a police officer, Miss Chance. He is in fact a rather well-to-do gentleman with a profound interest in criminal investigation. A detective. A private detective I suppose one would call him. The Assistant Commissioner said he is very highly thought of in France, and has helped to solve some notable cases."

"I wonder if I shall receive his card."

"I think it most probable." Mr. Whitely opened the door, gave a little bow, and put out his small bony hand for me to shake. "If so, I would advise you to keep that card, Miss Chance. The gentleman is said to be very efficient at solving riddles."

I was halfway home when panic struck at me. I felt it surging in my breast and sweeping through my limbs so that I shook as if with ague, and had to pull Daisy to a halt off the road. For ten minutes I sat shivering in the sunshine, racked by fear, wondering what in heaven's name I could do to save us all from penury.

One thing was certain. As soon as I reached home I would have to give all the servants a month's notice. Every pound, every shilling I could save had suddenly become of real importance now. Then, when I received the inventory from Mr. Whitely, I would make a list of all we possessed, to see what might be sold. After that . . .

My mind was empty. I picked up the reins and put Daisy to a trot, but took the fork leading away from the Wynford road. I was ashamed of my cowardice, but I could not yet summon the courage to go home, and so I had taken the lane that would bring me to old Tom Kettle's cottage.

Fifteen minutes later I brought the gig round the small copse that screened the cottage. Tom had a pump set on trestles before him and was working on the spout. He looked up as Daisy came to a halt, then laid down his mallet and chisel and plodded toward me, lifting the old brown felt hat he wore.

"Miss Bridie."

"Hallo, Mr. Kettle."

"You'll stay for sharin' a pot o' tea wi' me?"

"Yes, please. You know about . . . my father?"

He nodded, grim-faced, made a hawking sound deep in his throat, and said with huge contempt, "Them Frenchies."

"Well . . . let's not talk about it, Mr. Kettle."

"Best not."

He took my hand as I stepped down, then led the way toward the open cottage door. "Do yew mind to come inside, Miss Bridie? Tes cooler, an' there's words to be said."

"All right, Mr. Kettle, but please don't worry about the words. I know you liked Papa, and I'm sure we have your sympathy. It's very difficult to find the right things to say, so please don't try."

"More to it than that, miss." In the cool, rather dark cottage he pulled forward a beautifully made wooden arm-chair for me, and gestured with a calloused hand for me to be seated. "You set quiet now while I make tea. I niver could think o' more than one thing at a time."

I had no energy left to wonder what Tom Kettle might have to say to me. It was not likely to be of importance, and I had often known him to speak rather portentously about some triviality. For the moment I was glad to feel that I was away from the world for a little while, in a place where I could rest and try to recover what little courage I had to face the future.

The kettle was simmering on the small range, and he opened the damper for a minute or two to bring the water to the boil, then made tea in a large brown china pot. Five minutes later he set down the teapot, a jug of milk, and an earthenware bowl of sugar on the round table at my elbow, and drew up another of his chairs to sit opposite me.

"P'raps you'll kindly pour, Miss Bridie."

"Thank you, Mr. Kettle."

For a while we sipped our tea in silence. I did not want to talk or to listen, and I was sorry when at last he spoke. "I'd ha' come to the house to see your mam, but I hear tell she's faring right sick, Miss Bridie."

I was puzzled. "To see my mother?"

"I got something to give her from your dad, see."

I sat up straighter in my chair and put down my cup and

saucer, quite astonished now. "Whatever can you mean, Mr. Kettle?"

"No more'n I sez, miss." He drank some tea, frowning. "Your dad, he come to see me every time he was home from foreign parts."

"I know. He used to bring me with him when I was a little girl."

"Ah. But I reckon you never knew how he stopped old Briggs turning me out from this cottage where we're sitting now. Seventy pounds he give old Briggs, ten year ago, so's I could see me time out here."

"I'm very glad, Mr. Kettle. I know it's the sort of thing he would do. Papa was a generous man."

"A good 'un, he were. Trusted me, he did, Miss Bridie. Trusted old Tom Kettle better'n them lawyers an' banks an' suchlike, so he give me this letter I was to take to your mam if I iver heard he was dead, beggin' your pardon, Miss Bridie."

My nerves crawled. "A letter? When did he give it to you?"

"Ooh, nine or ten year back now. I got it wrapped in oilskin and hid safe away. I told him, mind. I'm nigh seventy, Mr. Chance, I sez, so I reckon it's me as'll be dead fust. But he just laughs, like he always did, an' gives me a sovereign. You're good fer twenty years yet, Tom, he sez, and as fer meself, he sez, why, I'm the sort o' gentleman that might vanish in a puff of smoke one fine day. Then he laughs again, big an' hearty an' throwing his head back in the way he had, just like as if he'd made a sort o' joke." Tom Kettle shook his head somberly and set down his teacup.

Not many days ago I would have found it difficult to believe that Papa would entrust an important letter to an uneducated old man such as Tom. Now, nothing I learned about him could surprise me, and it even crossed my mind that the fact of Tom being unable to read might have been a factor in my father's mind.

I said, "Do you wish me to take the letter to my mother for you?"

"Well, first of all, Miss Bridie, can you tell me certain sure as how your dad's dead an' gone, if you'll excuse me. On'y I don't trust them Frenchies, nor them newspapers, neither."

"Yes, it's quite certain, Mr. Kettle." I managed to keep my voice steady. "He was identified by several people who knew him well in France."

"Ah. Well now, you tell me what's proper, because I got to deliver that letter to your mam, but I can't do that while she's sick abed, along of what young Fred tells me, him what read the newspaper to me. So is it proper if I send it by safe hand, meaning your hand, Miss Bridie?"

Now that the first surprise had passed I felt oddly incurious, perhaps because I was still numbed by the shock of what Mr. Whitely had told me. I poured more tea for us both, and said, "I think that would be the best thing to do, Mr. Kettle. I don't feel my mother is well enough at the moment even to be given such a letter, but if you're willing to trust me with it, I'll take it home with me now and try to choose the right moment to give it to her."

He sat back with a gusty sigh of relief. "Ahh. I were wishly you'd say that, Miss Bridie. I on'y hope as your mam'll soon hold right well again." He got to his feet and went to the corner of the room where two steps led up to the door of his bedroom, which must have been very small. Lowering himself to his knees, he struck with the side of his fist against the riser of the lower step, and at once it swiveled back a few inches. Reaching into the cavity, he brought out a thin, dusty packet tied with string.

"Do you be wanting that unwrapped, Miss Bridie?"

"No, I'll take it as it is, thank you."

He moved to the open door, blew the dust off carefully, then came to the table again and set the oilskin packet in front of me. "There's none too sorry I am to be free of that," he said.

"Yes, it was a great responsibility, Mr. Kettle. Thank you very much."

I sat looking at the packet for a while, then picked it up and put it in my handbag, wondering what new trouble it would bring in due time. I had loved my father dearly, but there were times now when I felt almost angry resentment at the tribulations he had left me to struggle against by his reckless improvidence in so many matters.

Ten minutes later I said good-bye to Tom Kettle, thanked him, and drove on again to Latchford Hall. Kate met me in the hall with a letter which had come by the mid-morning post from Signor Peroni. It was addressed to my mother, but she had shown no interest and had only roused from her half-sleeping state long enough to tell Kate that I would deal with it.

Reading the letter as I stood with Kate in the drawing room, I felt a tiny spark of comfort being kindled within me. Signor Peroni wrote that he had heard of our sad bereavement and of "other afflictions" which had descended upon us, and expressed his deepest sympathy. He went on to say that he had refrained from making his regular visit, since he did not wish to intrude upon us at a time of such grievous trouble, but that he hoped my mother would write to him when she felt it appropriate for him to resume Miss Kate's lessons, as he considered it a privilege to have such a rewarding pupil.

Kate gave a little sigh of relief as I finished reading the letter aloud. "Well, that's something to be thankful for," she said. "At least he isn't turning his back on us, like everybody else."

I nodded, and summoned up my courage. "Yes, it's heartwarming. But I—I don't quite know how we shall be placed for a while, Kate dear."

"Placed?" She gave me a puzzled, rather frightened look, and at that moment Nannie Foster came into the room. We all three wore black dresses now, and I felt a stab of new panic at the thought that the dressmaker's bill was to be met.

"Ah, you're back then, Bridie. Would you like some tea, dear, or perhaps some nice lemonade to refresh you? It's such a hot day."

"Not now thank you, Nannie, but I'm glad you're here. There's something I have to tell you both. I'm afraid it's very bad news, but it's quite impossible for me to shelter you from it in any way, and the sooner you know, the better. The truth is that I've just come from Mr. Whitely, and it seems that all we have in the world, apart from any personal possessions, is a few hundred pounds."

I went on hastily to explain that Latchford Hall did not belong to us, and that it appeared my father had left no money or investments apart from a small sum in the bank. I think I repeated myself, for I was afraid to stop talking because I knew there would be questions to which I had no answers. Nannie Foster stood with hands clasped rigidly in front of her, blinking as if troubled by the light, though in fact the room was gloomy with the blinds drawn. Kate put a hand to her mouth and stared at me in disbelief. When I stumbled to a halt at last she said, "But Papa always had plenty of money. His wallet used to bulge with it, Bridie, don't you remember?"

"He always carried a lot of money, dear, yes. But that's not the same thing. It's still possible that something will be found, I mean that some funds will be discovered, but Mr. Whitely isn't optimistic because he says it's not in character. Papa wasn't the sort of man to hold investments or buy property."

Nannie's round old face was like a mask. I had known her, over the years, both stern and loving, happy and sad, brisk and weary, but I had always regarded her above all as a placid woman, and certainly I had never seen the gray fear that gripped her now. "Is there nothing, Miss Bridie? Nothing?" she said in a shaking voice.

Her fear made me afraid myself, and again the horror of our situation swept over me. "There's just enough to manage on for a little while, Nannie," I said. "But we have a lot of expenses to meet."

"Is it the workhouse for me, Miss Bridie?"

I went to her quickly, suddenly understanding, and put my arms round her. Now I remembered that both her parents had died in a workhouse in Bradford while she was a young girl in service. I bent a little to touch her cheek with mine, and said, "Don't be silly now. I'll look after you, Nannie, I promise."

I looked over my shoulder at Kate. She was very pale, her eyes like holes burned in paper. "You must neither of you tell Mama about this," I said. "She's not well enough to know yet."

"What about the servants, Bridie?" Kate whispered.

"I'm going to give them notice. I'll have Henson get them all together in the kitchen and do it now."

"Oh, Bridie. You're so brave."

I could have laughed. I could have shrieked with laughter until I collapsed. Patting Nannie's shoulder I said, "There's so much to be done that we shall have no time to fret. Mr. Whitely is sending me an inventory of all the fittings and furniture that belong to Latchford Hall, so you two must start making an inventory of everything else here, everything that belongs to us."

Kate said in a voice she struggled to keep from shaking, "Do you think I shall have to give up my music scholarship, Bridie? I mean, I was to live as a paying guest with the Branscombe family in London. Papa arranged it all at Easter, but if we haven't any money . . ."

She trailed into silence. I was thinking that in any event the Branscombe family would be unlikely to want the daughter of Roger Chance, notorious criminal, in their house, even if we could have afforded it, but I managed a small smile and said, "Of course you'll be able to take up your music scholarship. I'll think of some way to manage."

She looked at me uncertainly. "You look so strange, Bridie. Your eyes are funny, and your mouth, and your face is white with red patches. Are you all right?"

"Yes, quite all right." I went to the door and managed another smile as I looked back. "It's always been a bit of a funny face, anyway."

In the hall I stopped and pressed my hands to my eyes, wondering what madness possessed me. In the last few minutes I had made two promises without having the haziest idea of how I could possibly keep them.

Later, when I said what had to be said down in the

servants' hall, there were murmurs of sympathy which I knew were genuine, but I also sensed an element of relief. After the first excitement of being in the public eye, the servants were beginning to feel uneasy, perhaps fearing that something of their late master's reputation would rub off on them if they did not soon find new positions.

When this task was done I spent ten minutes sitting with my mother, who smiled but said nothing, then went to my room, locked the door, lay on my bed, and allowed all the devils of pain, sorrow, and fear to have their way with me as I let go the tight hold I had kept on myself, crying soundlessly with my face buried in the pillow.

When the long spasm was past, I poured cold water into the bowl on my washstand and sponged my face. I tidied my hair, straightened the bedclothes, opened my handbag, and stood weighing in my hand the oilskin package Tom Kettle had given me. I knew that if I went to my mother with this letter from her adored husband, the quietness that now possessed her would be broken, and she would again be racked by all the grief and horror she had known in the first two days of our ordeal. I knew, also, that she would want me to open the letter and read it to her, and I had yet to find the courage to do this, for some instinct within me kept warning me that to open the letter would bring fresh and unimaginable disaster upon us.

I realized this was foolish, as foolish as all the presentiments my mother had experienced for as long as I could remember, which had invariably proved false. Yet still I could not overcome my dread, and at last I slipped the packet into the bottom of my chest of drawers, empty now that I had turned out the little collection of gifts received from my friends at Girton when I became engaged.

The sight of that empty drawer did not bring to my mind the man I was once to have married, Bernard Page. For what seemed a long while now it was as if we had known each other in another world and another time, so that he was scarcely real to me anymore. Strangely, the man I thought of at that moment was one I scarcely knew and had forgotten in the turmoil of the last hour or so. As I closed the drawer and stood up, the one who came to my mind was the man I had met on the road only a few hours ago.

At six o'clock that day the card Philippe Chatillon had sent me arrived by the evening post, an embossed card, very elegantly printed. I did not believe I should ever have need of it, but remembering Mr. Whitely's advice I put it away carefully in my writing case. As I did so, the Frenchman with laughing hazel eyes and friendly smile leaped suddenly into my mind's eye again, so suddenly and powerfully that for a moment I caught my breath.

five

My mother died two days before the coffin with my father's
body reached Southwold station. It was unexpected, for
though she had declined a little each day Dr. Carey had not
felt that she was in danger when I called him to see her the
day before her death. I had the money ready for him this
time.

She died quietly during the night, and it was I who
discovered it when I went to her room soon after seven next
morning to see if she needed anything. To Kate and to
Nannie Foster it was a most dreadful surprise and shock. I
was beyond both, and at first could only register in a dull
sort of way that my mother had gone and that she had surely
wished to. Then, to my utter shame and horror, I began to
find that there were moments when I would catch myself
in a feeling of furtive relief that the burdens which were
overwhelming me had been reduced in some measure by
her passing.

I told myself that although I had never really understood
my mother I had loved her as fully as I was able, and that
death had released her from a future not only of endless
grief but also of penury. Yet I knew in my heart that a part
of my feeling was totally selfish, and I hated myself.

Ironically, my mother's death eased the problem of my
father's burial. I had spoken twice with the vicar about
arrangements for Papa's funeral once his body was brought
to Southwold, and the response had been somewhat evasive.
On the second occasion I realized that he did not want the
burial to take place in the churchyard at St. Mary's Church.
He was a timid man and new to the living, so I guessed

that his church wardens and more important members of the congregation were protesting at the idea of Roger Chance, criminal, being buried in hallowed ground where their forebears lay and where they expected to lie themselves one day.

When my mother died it offered the vicar a way to follow his conscience without too greatly offending his flock, for they could not object to my mother being buried at the church where she had worshipped for twenty years, and they would have found it hard to argue against her husband being buried with her, whatever his sins.

I arranged for the double funeral to take place in four days' time at ten in the morning, and paid another visit to Mr. Whitely to discuss the legal situation. He was very kind, and told me that my mother would be deemed to have inherited my father's estate, and that this would now pass to her two daughters. As to the substance of the estate, he had nothing to offer for my comfort. No further assets or funds of any kind had come to light, and the amount we would in due time receive was likely to be less than four hundred pounds.

Even before Mama died, my difficulties had been made more trying by Kate becoming hostile. I could not blame her. In a matter of days we had suffered hammer-blows of shock and grief, and now we were on our own, all that was left of our family, with a future too dark to bear contemplation. The servants were on edge, Kate had too little to occupy her, and I was too wrapped up in practical problems to give her the time and sympathy she needed. I am sure she did not really blame me for all the small tribulations that arose from our larger ones, and which seemed to beset us daily, but by her attitude she seemed to do so. I realized that she was frightened, her nerves were raw, and she needed a whipping boy to blame for all that had come upon us, but though I tried not to feel hurt by her sulks, silences, and occasional cutting remarks, there was more than one occasion when I had to go away to my bedroom so that she should not see me weep.

To help her, I had written to Signor Peroni, thanking

him for his letter and saying that I would like him to continue Kate's lessons. It was an extravagance we could ill afford now, but to me it seemed worth the small sum for his fare and fee if only Kate could be lifted out of her sour and bitter mood. With the shock of Mama dying, I completely forgot that I had written to Signor Peroni in these terms, with the consequence that he arrived at Latchford Hall in the early afternoon of the day after her death.

When Henson told him what had happened he was full of apologies and made to withdraw in great distress, but I happened to be coming downstairs at that moment, and was equally distressed to realize that I had forgotten about his visit. I invited him into the drawing room, and thought it only fair to tell him that we would soon be leaving Latchford Hall, and that our circumstances would then be so straitened that we had as yet been able to make no plans for the future.

Signor Peroni was a small dark man in his middle forties, with an English wife and three children—a boy and two girls. The boy was four, and the oldest girl ten, so it was a young family. His wife had been an English lady's maid, and Signor Peroni had met her in Rome during the time when the lady's husband had been an official at the British Embassy there. They had married a year later, and for a time had lived in Rome, but his wife had pined for England, and in the end Signor Peroni had brought her to London with their year-old daughter. He had inherited a little money from his father only a few months before, and this had been sufficient to enable him to take a modest but pleasant house in Kensington. There he had gradually established himself as a teacher of the pianoforte, the profession he had pursued in Rome.

All this I had learned from him during the times I had taken tea with him, after Kate's lessons and before he left to make the journey back to London. He was paid a special fee, since Kate was his only pupil for that day, but I had always felt that he must be out of pocket. He had been teaching Kate for four years now, ever since Papa decided that no local teacher was of high enough caliber for Kate's talent. After making inquiries during one of his spells at home, Papa had taken her down to London with him to play for Signor Peroni. My father had a great gift for persuasion, but I think it was Kate herself who had made Signor Peroni feel that here was a pupil he could not bear to lose.

When I told him, on the day after Mama's death, that Kate and I were now alone and in a very difficult situation, his dark eyes widened in alarm. "But the music scholarship, signorina!" he exclaimed. "Surely she must go there to the Prince Consort College of Music. It will be a great sorrow if she misses such opportunity." He gestured with long fingers. "She has the possibility to be a great artiste, and she is of good heart to work long and hard, as is necessary. Please, she must not be permitted to lose this chance."

I said, "With all my heart I agree with you, signore. There is nothing I want more than that Kate should continue her studies, but the difficulties are much greater than I expected."

"Ah," he said eagerly, "but please, you will make it possible, signorina?"

I sighed, and found I had started to twist my face into an exaggerated look of helpless resignation. Hastily I started to control the expression, then suddenly decided it did not really matter to anybody now if I pulled faces to my heart's content. "Signor Peroni, I will be very frank with you," I said. "In a few months we shall have no money except what I am able to earn, and there will be three of us to keep, including Nannie Foster. I understand that the incidental school expenses, together with the expense of Kate being a paying guest with the Branscombe family, would amount to almost one hundred pounds a year. At the moment I have no idea how I shall manage to feed, house, and clothe the three of us, so you can see how little hope there is for Kate to go on with her studies."

He shook his head, looking very upset, and lifted a deprecating hand. "Please, I did not mean to inquire into your family affairs, Signorina Bridie."

"That's quite all right, signore. I'm really not concerned to hide anything from anybody."

He studied me for a moment, then lowered his eyes

quickly to hide the pity in them. "I am very sorry that you have such great troubles, signorina," he said quietly. "Please permit me to say that I liked very much your dear father. He was a..." he groped for words, then gave a small shrug. "...a happy man, a man with much laughter in him. I do not regard what has been said, or what has been done. I remember him with much liking."

I was deeply touched, and it was a moment or two before I was able to reply, then I said, "Thank you for those words, signore, and also for coming here today. I'm afraid Kate is too distraught to have a lesson this afternoon, but I hope very much that you will come next week, and perhaps for a few weeks after that, until we leave Latchford Hall. I'm sure it will help to take Kate out of herself a little, and ease her grief."

"Then I shall come," he said, and stood up. "Please convey my most kind regards to Miss Kate. As you know, she has been my pupil since four years now, and I hold her in much affection."

Later that afternoon Kate was cross with me for not having called her down to see Signor Peroni. Her eyes were red-rimmed, her face pale and blotchy, and I knew she would have been equally cross if I had called her. I felt very low, and would have given anything to have Kate put her arms round me and say something warm and comforting, but she went into the drawing room and began to play a Chopin scherzo, a piece quite unsuitable for a house in mourning. I knew she expected me to reproach her, so that she could have another reason to be angry with me, but I said nothing and went out into the garden. I missed Kate's affection badly, but at the moment she was quite unlike her real self, and I could only wait for her to pass through the bad time.

The garden was at its best just now, with honeysuckle and clematis frothing from the old wall beside the orchard, and the beds full of color with lupins and sweet Williams, delphiniums, and border carnations. I had seen the seasons change year after year in these comely grounds, and had loved each season in turn. It made my heart ache to think that after a very little while I would never walk here again.

As I moved round the main rosebed my foot touched something that lay on the grass. It rolled away, and when I looked down I saw that it was the stub of a thin dark cigar, but it was not the one I had found on the night of that first dreadful day when our world began to crumble, for this was fresher, a little longer, and in a place a stone's throw from where I had found the first stub.

I stared down at it, thinking of the gaucho horseman I had seen or imagined, then thinking of the horseman in the gray top hat I had met on the road to Southwold. He at least had not been a creature of my imagination. Philippe Chatillon had been very much a living breathing human—

My thoughts made a sudden jump, and I caught my breath. Philippe Chatillon, then Mr. Whitely, and then Tom Kettle. I had seen all three that same morning, and Tom Kettle had given me the packet that contained a letter from my father to my mother. It still lay in my bottom drawer, and had gone completely out of my mind. Now I felt hot with guilt because I had not given it to my mother, even though I had known at the time it would be wrong to do so.

I had no curiosity about the contents of the letter, in fact I shrank from the thought of reading it, for I knew I would feel as if I were eavesdropping, yet it seemed to me that I had no choice but to open it now, for it must surely contain something of importance. My father had adored my mother, and I could well imagine that he might have written her a kind of love letter to be given her in the event of his death, but he would not have been so secretive about it unless it contained more than words of love and solace. The thought occurred to me now that it might even tell of some source of money that he had kept so secret that Mr. Whitely had been unable to trace it.

Five minutes later I sat in my bedroom, taking off the outer wrapping of oilskin. The envelope within was of fine quality and sealed. I slit it open with my nail file and took out the sheets of plain writing paper it contained. The letter was in my father's surprisingly neat hand, and he had written just as he spoke, so that I could almost hear his voice.

Mary darling,

I'm sure you'll never read this, for it's just in case I'm unlucky, which I've no intention of being. I'm sorry to spend so much time away from my beautiful girl, but I am what I am, Mary dear, as you well know, a fool who can't live without excitement bubbling in his veins like champagne, and that's the truth of it.

A fellow like me should be a soldier, maybe, but that means taking orders from idiots much of the time, which I couldn't abide, and anyway I'd be gone from you for years at a time, and not have the lovely home-comings I can always look forward to in a few weeks or a few days.

Now here I am writing this letter to you, sitting at my desk and looking out over Paris on a fine day, and laughing at myself a little, for I'm sure it's all a great waste of time to be writing words that I'll be the only one ever to read. So why am I writing them, I wonder? I'm not a pessimistic fellow, or a cautious one either, but I have in my head the thought that Bridie and Kate have far to go before they're grown up, and I have to think about how you'll be taken care of if I found myself in professional difficulties. Or worse, if the good Lord is absent-minded one day, forgetting that I'm to live to be a hundred, and sends that creature of Nannie's to carry me off— Black Shuck, is it?

Now then, you're not to be sad and full of tears, my lovely girl, for if you read this, and I'm gone for good, then I'll be waiting for my sweetheart in an even better world than this, where the grass is gold and the wind never blows cold.

Meanwhile I'm writing this for remembrance, Mary dear, to remind you of all things said between us when we drove out from the little smithy and up into the high valleys that fine summer day, when I told my secrets and you loved me still. Will you make a pilgrimage there, and will you remember the poor poetry I spoke? Do that for me, my darling. Walk again where the stream runs golden from the hills, and on to the valley of the Capricorn Stone. Remember me then, and have no fear of the shadow, Mary dear, for the darkness at eventide leads only to the dayspring of rainbow's end. Remember me then, and have no fear of the waiting crow, for it serves only to reveal the emptiness that is filled with brightness. Remember.

                              Ever with my love,
                              Roger

I sat gazing down at the last page of the letter written ten years before by my bewildering and enigmatic father. Kate had said that Papa was a laughing reckless man, and how truly she had spoken, for it came through even in the way he had put together the words in his letter. He was also a romantic, which I knew, but I had never imagined him attempting to be poetic. I read the final paragraph again. The first few lines seemed to refer to a particular place and a particular day when Roger Chance had told his wife the truth about his secret life of crime, and had found that it left her love for him unaltered. This did not surprise me. I had always known that in my mother's eyes my father could do no wrong. Then there was mention of the Capricorn Stone. I had no idea what this might be, and had never heard of it until my mother spoke the words during her ramblings shortly before she died. The rest of the paragraph seemed to be an attempt at what my English teacher used to call poetic prose, but it was a very poor attempt. The imagery was weak, the word "crow" struck an extraordinarily discordant note, and the concept behind the words was too obscure for me even to guess at.

On the third reading I wondered if it might be a secret message which only my mother could understand. According to folklore, a crock of gold was to be found at rainbow's end, but I felt sure Papa was using analogy. There could be no actual crock of gold. So what followed must be a cryptic direction indicating . . . what? A person? A bank? A safe deposit of some kind?

I read the paragraph a fourth time, and the notion that it was a secret message became more doubtful. Without warning I was swept by sudden irritation, for it was as if my father was reaching out from beyond the grave to tease and harass me. I stared into the looking glass above my dressing table and pulled a deliberately angry face, then folded the letter, put it back in the envelope, wrapped it in oilskin once again, and dropped it back in my bottom drawer.

It was meaningless, except as a kind of posthumous love letter from a man of warm heart and wild ways who gave no thought to the future. Or if it did contain a message, then it was one that had meaning only for my mother, and that meaning would never now be unraveled.

Three of us followed the funeral, my sister Kate, Nannie Foster, and I. At the church there was no organist to ease the silence and the muted sounds of movement. Mr. Garth, the organist, was a man whose fiery puritan outlook was daunting even to the most virtuous, and he had declined to give his services. The coffins were borne one at a time by Robert and his brother Jack assisted by two men from the village they had either bribed or coerced.

The Reverend John Irving was kindly in his manner and performed his office with a steady dignity that was unusual in him. Since there was no eulogy and no music or hymns, the service was short, for which I was glad. Nannie Foster was bearing herself very well, but my poor Kate looked waxen, and I was afraid she might faint at any moment.

As we rose to follow the first coffin out, I took her arm and held it tightly against me for comfort and support. She responded, and I heard her whisper faintly, "I'm sorry I've been horrid to you, Bridie."

"It was nothing, silly. Don't worry."

To my surprise I saw now that one or two other people had entered the church after us, and were now standing waiting to follow us out. There was Mr. Whitely, old Tom

Kettle in a black suit that looked faintly green with age, the Misses Cole, who were two spinster sisters from the village, Mrs. Burns, who was our dressmaker, and a stranger I had never seen before. He was a man in his middle fifties, short and very broad but not fat, with a rubbery face and brown hair plastered to his head with oil. The white center parting of his hair might have been made with a ruler it was so straight. He wore a dark suit and a black tie with a pearl tiepin, but though the suit was well made it sat uneasily on him, and I felt he was a man who would have looked more at home in rather loud tweeds.

As we passed, I looked at each person in turn and tried hard to show that I was grateful. At the graveside the first coffin was lowered and then there was a painful wait while the bearers returned for the second. At last the coffins lay side by side, and the vicar completed the ceremony. When the handfuls of earth had been thrown, I drew Kate quickly away and moved to where those not of the family had hung back a little. I shook hands with them all, thanked them for attending, and apologized for being unable to receive them at Latchford Hall now that the service was over, since we had made no preparations.

My apologies were hastily brushed aside, and it was all rather awkward and embarrassing. I came at last to the stranger, who looked as if he would have liked to slip away but felt it would be impolite to do so. Offering my hand I said, "Good morning, I don't think we have met."

He looked at me very hard from pale brown eyes. "Alfred Perkin at your service, miss. I trust I 'aven't displeased you, coming to pay my respects." He had a throaty voice that sounded as if it could be very powerful when he chose to exert it, a voice made husky by use, I fancied, and for some reason I thought of a sailor on a clipper, shouting orders above the noise of wind and sea.

"My sister and I are grateful for the attendance of any friends at such a time, Mr. Perkin," I said. "I take it you knew my father?"

"Slightly, miss, slightly." He hesitated. "But I knew your

mum better, really. We were colleagues, like, before she got married."

I was taken by surprise and did not know what to say. Mama's past was something I knew nothing about, and at any other time I might have been greatly intrigued to meet somebody who had known her long ago. As it was, I felt too close to tears to be able to do any more than was called for by good manners. Beside me, Kate was squeezing my arm and whispering in a shaky voice, "Please, Bridie..." Behind us I could hear the thud of earth being shoveled into the grave, and my skin seemed to contract with sudden cold.

"If you will excuse us, Mr. Perkin...?"

"Of course, miss. Very honored to 'ave met you." He held his black silk hat over his breast and bowed, not stiffly but in a very easy and unaffected manner, his eyes on Kate. I wished him good day and moved away toward our carriage, Kate holding my arm, Nannie Foster following.

Much later that sad and exhausting day I thought about Mr. Alfred Perkin again, and spoke of him to Kate, wondering who he might be. She was reading one of her books on music theory, and shrugged as if she had no interest in the question, so I did not pursue it. As I settled down to write some letters of thanks to those who had attended the funeral I thought it unlikely that I would ever see Alfred Perkin again, or learn in what way he and my mother had been colleagues. I did not dream that within a matter of weeks this roughly spoken man from the past would change my life in a way that would have defied my wildest imaginings.

I went to the churchyard alone next morning. With the grave now filled and the headstone set, I wanted to arrange the several wreaths and sprays of flowers sent by those who had defied the general ostracism to attend. There was one small wreath which I was sure had not been there the day before, and also a beautiful little bouquet of flowers. The wreath was for my father, and the words on the card it bore had been written in a neat, angular hand: *Dormez bien, mon vieil adversaire—Philippe Chatillon.*

Sleep well, my old adversary...

So the Frenchman I had met, the private detective who had dueled with Le Sorcier, had arranged for a wreath to be laid on the grave of his old opponent before returning to France. My eyes prickled, and I felt a little touch of gladness at the thought.

The card attached to the bouquet had been written in a very different hand, careful and laborious. It said: *Dear Mary, Yrs. faithfully, A. Perkin.*

I looked at the card in puzzlement for a few moments, then laid the bouquet carefully down. As I straightened I glimpsed a movement from the corner of my eye, and turned to see Mr. Perkin himself moving quietly away along the southern wall of the churchyard. His head was turned toward me, and he knew that I had seen him. He stopped, uncertain what to do, and I called, "Good morning, Mr. Perkin."

Hat in hand, he came toward me. "Good morning, miss," he said, his voice hushed, like a muted foghorn. "I saw you coming and didn't want to intrude, so I was just slipping away, as you might say."

I found myself liking this man, for he struck me as having the heart of a gentleman and a natural kindness. I said, "Please don't feel that you're intruding. I'm glad we have met again."

"That's very 'andsome of you, miss. You'll be Miss Bridget, unless I'm much mistaken?"

"Yes, but how did you know, Mr. Perkin?"

"Read the announcement in *The Times* when you were born, miss. Same with your sister, a few years later. My word, but I 'ad a shock when I saw Miss Kate yesterday. Image of your mum when she was young. Talk about beautiful."

I said rather wonderingly, "Why, yes. And since I think you must have been fond of my mother, you'll be pleased to know that she remained very beautiful all her life."

Mr. Perkin nodded. I saw him bite his lower lip, head bowed, struggling to control sudden emotion. After a moment or two I said, "Do you mind if I ask where you have come from?"

"London, miss. That's where I spend more than 'alf my

time, but I travel about a lot, too. Birmingham, Sheffield, Manchester—the whole circuit. Only I'm resting now for a few weeks."

"Oh, have you been ill?"

He started to smile, then remembered where he was and fidgeted with his hat. "No, miss. It's a professional term. In the theater, if you're not working, you're resting. It usually means you 'aven't got a job, but that's not so with me." He produced a card from his waistcoat pocket and handed it to me. "We've got all the bookings we want, but I always make sure we take a few weeks off in the summer. It keeps you fresh, so to speak."

The card said:

Mr. Alfie Perkin and Company
Comedy Sketches
10 Grant Chambers, Holborn, London

I found I was staring at him with one of my open-mouthed exaggerated expressions, and hastily modified it. "Good gracious, you're on the stage, Mr. Perkin!"

"On the music halls, miss, yes. Thirty years now. Made my first appearance at the Canterbury back in sixty-seven, when George Leybourne 'imself was topping the bill."

I looked down at the card again to hide the shock I knew would show in my face. Almost everything I had heard or read about the acting profession argued that the theater and immorality went hand in hand. Only three years ago there had been much condemnation in the newspapers of the notorious "promenade" behind the dress circle at the Empire Theatre in Leicester Square, where better-class women of easy virtue strolled among young bloods and Bohemians, inviting their attentions.

It was generally accepted that stage people could not possibly be respectable, and on this question I had heard only one dissenting voice, which was my father's. During his summer weeks at home the previous year there had been a scathing letter in *The Times* concerning the decline of morals brought about by the salacious nature of the entertainment provided by variety turns. He had read the letter out, laughing, and said, "Now isn't that fellow a fine ripe prig, Mary? I'll wager he's never sat in the Oxford or the Alhambra and laughed his head off at the comics, or joined in a chorus of 'Ta-ra-ra-boom-de-ay' with Lottie Collins. How I detest these Misery Dicks with not a spark of fun in them."

At the time I had wondered vaguely why he should comment on the subject, but now I realized that it was in some way relevant to my mother's past. I looked up at Alfred Perkin and said, "Thirty years? Then you were a . . . a music hall comedian when you met my mother?"

"Not exactly, miss. I hadn't got going with the comedy act then, and I was still doing the conjuring when your mum came in as my assistant."

I put fingers to my mouth, and felt my eyes opening wider than ever. "Your *assistant*? On the stage?"

"Why yes, miss. I—um—I suppose you didn't know." He twisted his hat round in his hands, looking embarrassed. "I do 'ope I've not given offense, saying all this after your mum married well and you were brought up gentry. But she was a real lady in 'erself, if you know what I mean. In service in Belgrave Square as a lady's maid she was, when we met." He glanced at the headstone, and lowered his voice even more. "Don't think bad of me, Miss Bridget, but I really fell in love with your mum and I asked 'er to marry me."

For the second time in a few minutes I felt tears pricking at my eyes. Nannie Foster would have been horrified to be told that my mother had once been on the stage and that a music hall comedian had asked for her hand, but I was deeply moved by the simple way in which Alfred Perkin had opened his heart to me. "Why should I think badly of you, Mr. Perkin?" I asked. "There's surely nothing to be ashamed of about falling in love."

He nodded slowly, his eyes distant now. "She wasn't sure," he said softly. "Then she met Mr. Chance, your dad, and she was really sure about him. But I never forgot her, miss. And I never wanted to marry anyone else." He drew in a breath and straightened his back. "I read about your dad passing away, and all the trouble in France," he went on, "and I was coming up to see Mary, in case she needed a friend to give a helping hand. But I saw in the paper the other day that she'd passed away, too, so I just came to pay my respects, as you might say."

I stood deep in thought for a little while, then said, "How long will you be staying, Mr. Perkin?"

"I've got a room at The Woodman, and I reckoned on going 'ome tomorrow, but I can stay on for a bit if there's anything I can do to 'elp, Miss Bridget."

"No. No, I wouldn't ask you to stay on, but I have some problems and I would very much like to have your advice about the possibility of finding some kind of work for myself in London."

"Work?" His eyebrows jerked up and his eyes widened in just the sort of expression I might have used myself. "But surely—?"

"I don't want to explain now," I broke in quickly, "but would you be so very kind as to come and have tea with me at Latchford Hall this afternoon, say at half past three o'clock?"

"I . . . I'd be delighted, miss. Delighted."

It was not an empty word, for he looked quite overcome with pleasure as he bowed again and said, "Well, I'll take my leave of you now, Miss Bridget, and I'll look forward to your kind invitation for this afternoon."

He moved away, treading with measured step until he was out of the churchyard, then walking more briskly as he turned down the road that led to the village. I stood holding his card, filled with astonishment at what I had just learned and at my own temerity. Yet what I had done by instinct, almost without thought, made good sense on reflection. I had to find work, and London would be the best place to begin. I would be more anonymous there than in a country town, and there would surely be more opportunities of work for a young woman. Above all, if some miracle permitted Kate to take up her music scholarship, it was important that we should live within easy distance of the Prince Consort College of Music.

Mr. Alfred Perkin was a Londoner. He would know what sort of work I might try to find, and how much I could earn. He was also a friend, I could feel it in my bones, and I had powerful evidence that he was faithful in his friendship, for today he had come to the funeral of the girl he had fallen in love with more than twenty years ago and had not seen since.

Later, when I told Kate of the encounter, she showed little surprise. We were in the drawing room, and she was playing the first movement of Beethoven's "Moonlight Sonata," which had been Mama's favorite piece. Nannie Foster was not there. She did not think it proper for the piano to be played at all during a time of mourning, but I had encouraged Kate. Without taking her eyes from the keyboard she said, "Are you really surprised that Mama had been on the stage, Bridie? We always knew she wasn't born a lady."

"Oh, don't speak so unkindly, Kate!"

"I wasn't. At least, I didn't mean it unkindly. I loved Mama, and thought she was a wonderful person to manage so well, especially as she was worried and anxious for so much of the time. What you've told me doesn't surprise me though, I think it's rather exciting in a way. Quite a lot of stage ladies have married into the gentry, and some of them even have titles, so it's not really strange that Mama married Papa, or that Papa married her, for he was a quite extraordinary man. What do you want to talk to this Mr. Perkin about, Bridie?"

"Kate dear, I've *explained*," I said, trying hard not to be irritable. "Soon there will be no money for us to live on, so I shall have to find a way to earn some."

"Is it true that you're arranging to sell this piano, Bridie?" She stopped playing abruptly and swiveled round to look at me.

"Well, yes," I said defensively, "I have to, surely you can see that. Wherever we find to live, it won't be a house that can take a grand piano, I'm sorry darling, but—"

"Oh, that's all right." She gave me one of her beautiful

smiles, then swung round and began to play again. "Don't worry, Bridie. I'm sure that when we go to London you'll meet a man who'll fall desperately in love with you. He'll be very rich, and you'll marry him, and then everything will be perfect. After all, that's what happened with Mama and Papa, wasn't it?"

I did not answer. Kate was sometimes hopelessly romantic, sometimes severely practical. At the moment she was in one of her romantic moods, and I was content for her to be so if it helped ward off the chill misery of anxiety. We would soon have more than enough practical problems to face.

six

Alfred Perkin presented himself promptly at half past three o'clock. He wore morning dress, carried stick and gloves, and brought these with his hat into the drawing room in the correct manner. I had already summed him up as possessing natural good manners, but was surprised at the extent to which he seemed to know the niceties of etiquette.

I introduced Kate, and could see after the first few minutes of small talk that she was greatly taken with him, perhaps because he was completely unlike anybody we had ever met before. I had wanted Kate to be present because I felt she must now be brought face to face with the realities of our situation, and as soon as I had poured tea for us all I said, "Mr. Perkin, can you tell me what sort of work is available in London for an educated young lady? For myself, in fact."

He frowned down at his cup of tea. "Well, I've been thinking about that after what you said this morning, Miss Bridget—"

"Forgive me," I broke in, "but I should be pleased if you would call me Bridie. Since you are a very old friend of my mother's, it seems more appropriate."

He flushed a little with pleasure. "Most kind of you—um—Bridie. Well, there's work in service, there's factory work, there's work in shops, there's teaching work, and there's quite a few young ladies doing office work now. That puts it in a nutshell, as you might say, though educated ladies only do teaching or office work, but p'raps I can tell you a bit more if I know what you 'ave in mind, see?"

"That's very simple, Mr. Perkin. This house is rented

and the lease expires shortly. My father's estate amounts to only a few hundred pounds. Apart from that, and some few chattels worth as much again, we have nothing. The woman who used to be our nannie and was later a companion to my mother is quite old now, and has virtually no money of her own. I have to take care of her. My sister Kate is a very fine pianist, and I want her to take up a scholarship she has won to the Prince Consort College of Music. I also have to provide for myself, of course."

Mr. Perkin drew in a whistling breath through pursed lips and looked unhappy. "I 'ate to be a Dismal Jimmy, but I can't see where a young lady can earn that sort of money, miss. I mean, Bridie. Tell you the truth, I don't see 'ow you can keep the three of you in plain bed an' board. With rent, food, and clothes, you're going to need . . . what? Let's say best part of a hundred and twenty pounds to live anything like decent." He looked about him. "And it wouldn't be like this, neither."

Kate said, "That doesn't seem a great deal of money, Mr. Perkin."

He looked at her, and I saw his face soften. I knew he was seeing my mother in her, and his throatily strident voice was very gentle as he said, "I don't suppose you've 'ad to think much about money, Miss—er—Kate. But you take a girl in service, a housemaid. She'll get all found and p'raps twelve pounds a year. A housekeeper, maybe a pony. Beg pardon, that's twenty-five pounds."

He looked at me. "I can't say what a governess might get, but it wouldn't be 'alf enough. If you taught in a school you'd earn more, naturally, but then you wouldn't 'ave bed and board thrown in. Same thing applies with office work, and anyway I expect you'd need to do typewriting on one of those new machines."

I said, "I'm quite a good needlewoman, Mr. Perkin. Would there be any opportunity in that line?"

He threw back his head, eyes closed, wincing as if in pain. "Lord, no. You 'ave a think about what you pay your dressmaker, begging your pardon. And it's worse in London. Look, you walk around Hackney, Bow, Bethnal Green,

where all the workshops are. Thirty bob a week for a skilled
bootmaker. Maybe two pound for a first-class cabinetmaker
with seven years apprenticeship and another ten of experience behind 'im. A pound a week for a docker. And
women? Twelve bob a week sewing furs. Ten in the book-
binding. Sweated labor, that's all you'll find in the workshops.''

I nodded, trying to look unruffled though my heart was
sinking with despair. Kate was gazing at Mr. Perkin as if
fascinated, but I was sure it was only the man himself and
his manner of speech that intrigued her; she still did not
apply what he was telling us to our own condition.

"Twelve shillings a *week*?" she said wonderingly. "However do they manage?"

He gave a shrug of his broad shoulders. "They live like
pigs, my dear," he said simply. "That's the top and bottom
of it."

Kate blinked, then put down her cup and stood up. "Excuse me," she said in a subdued voice, and went from the
room.

Mr. Perkin had half risen with her, and now he looked
at me in distress. "Did I offend 'er? I'm very sorry, I didn't
realize."

"It's all right, Mr. Perkin, please sit down. Kate can be
very realistic, but there are times when she doesn't wish to
be."

"Ah. Facing facts can 'urt, Bridie."

"Yes. And she's very sensitive, but if ever you hear her
play the piano you'll forgive her anything. Thank you for
all the information, Mr. Perkin, and now let us talk about
something else. I'd be most interested to know how you
came to meet my mother, if it won't distress you to tell
me."

"Why, no," he said slowly, "I don't mind a bit, but
there's not much to be told, really. Like I said, she was a
lady's maid, and one of the footmen was trying to court
'er, so he brought her along to the Oxford one evening. I
was doing an act called 'Marvo the Mystic' then, and well
down the bill, but I was working three halls a night, so I

wasn't doing so bad. Anyway, there was one trick where I got a young man to come up from the audience to 'elp. Well, this pertickler night I spotted your mum, and I got a bit of the devil in me, so I pointed 'er out and tried to coax her up on the stage."

I said wonderingly, "But Mama was such a shy person. I'm sure you didn't succeed."

"It was only because of all the people around 'er," said Mr. Perkin. "They were jollying 'er along and made a great bit of fun of it, and in the end she reckoned it was best to come up and get it over with. That's what she told me later."

"How did you meet her later?"

He smiled and scratched his cheek, eyes looking back into the past. "I was smitten," he said softly. "I was smitten so 'ard I followed 'er back that night to where she worked, her and the footman. The Oxford was my last turn, so it was easy enough. Then I waited my chance to see her when she came out next morning, and I introduced myself, and we talked, and I think she was a bit impressed, what with me being on the stage and all that."

I took his cup and refilled it. "And she became your assistant? Actually on the stage with you?"

He smiled suddenly. "Only three weeks later that was, because her mistress was going abroad and Mary was under notice anyway. I offered her a job at good money, and she never had to say anything on the stage. She was just dressed in a very pretty frock, bright with spangles but cut very modest, and she used to hold things and pass me bits of apparatus, and keep smiling. She was a girl who was beautiful but with a kind of dignity, if you know what I mean, and she brought a bit of quality to the act. The blokes in the pit never whistled or called out when she was on. I think they liked 'er being shy, because most of the girls in variety acts or in the chorus are a bit forward, a bit bold. They 'ave to be, really."

He sipped his tea. "Taught me proper manners, too, Mary did," he said with a touch of pride. "She knew about 'ow to behave, from being in service and taking note of the gentry."

"My sister and I have never known about her early days," I said. "Did you meet any of her family, Mr. Perkin?"

He shook his head. "No. There were no real ties there, Bridie. All I knew was that she was the last of ten children and was put out to service as a tweeny in Cambridgeshire somewhere, when she was twelve. Her mum had died and her dad just wanted to be rid of her. Then the son of the 'ouse where she was in service got married, and Mary became parlor maid to him and his wife down in London. Mary was sixteen then, and about two years later she got to be lady's maid."

For a brief while I had forgotten the chilling fear of the future which beset me, for I was fascinated to hear about this other world in which my mother had lived. I said, "Was she on the stage with you for very long?"

"Just over a year."

"It must have meant a tremendous change in her life."

"Yes, it did that. We worked three months in London, then went on tour for six months, then back to London again." He looked at me with sudden anxiety. "It was all very respectable, though, with your mum and me. My young sister, Ethel, lived with me in London and went with me when I toured. She wasn't much to look at, so she'd never been part of the act, but she used to look after me and take care of everything backstage and so on. It was only when I went in for comedy that I brought Ethel in. But what I'm saying is, your mum shared a room with Ethel, and it was all respectable."

"I'm sure it was, Mr. Perkin. But if you were so smitten and were courting her, I'm surprised she didn't marry you."

He smiled. "That was a nice kind thing to say, Bridie, but I wasn't surprised myself, not really. Oh, she liked me well enough, and she was always ever so grateful I'd taken 'er on, but that was all. I asked her to marry me several times, but she always said she didn't feel sure of herself. Not sure whether she loved me, she meant. And then Mr. Chance came along, your dad."

"How did that happen?"

"Oh, he saw the act at Gatti's, and he sent her flowers and waited at the stage door for her. Wasn't the first gent to do that, mind you. There's always a few of what we call Stage Door Johnnies, and your mum 'ad been asked out to dinner a few times, but she always said no. It was easy enough, because she always came out with Ethel and me, and that put the Johnnies off a bit, but your dad was different. He walked up to the three of us, smiling like he'd never been so delighted in 'is life, and says he'd be honored if we'd all come to dinner with 'im at the Café Royal."

"I can imagine him doing it. Oh, I'm sorry, more tea, Mr. Perkin?"

"No thank you, my dear."

"Please go on."

"Well, I thought it'd be a bit of fun, letting this gent take us all out to a posh dinner, so I winked at Ethel and your mum, and said we'd be 'appy to oblige." He shook his head, gave a little chuckle, and rolled his eyes in a comically rueful way. "My word, it was a bit of fun all right, because your dad was a real marvel, telling stories and making jokes, and saying nice things to poor Ethel just as much as to your mum. But that was when it 'appened, Bridie, because your mum was fair spellbound by Mr. Chance. I knew I'd lost her, even before we got 'ome that night."

"That was very sad for you."

"Well...I think I'd known for quite a while that your mum wasn't meant for me. The thing was, though, I didn't know if Mr. Chance's intentions were honorable, did I?"

"Oh. No, I suppose gentlemen's intentions toward ladies on the stage are often not very honorable."

"I'm afraid that's so, Bridie. Anyway, Mr. Chance asked Mary out twice more, and then I buttonholed 'im and asked 'im straight. And you know what he said? He said in that voice with a bit of the Irish, he said, 'It's high time you asked me that, Alfie, for I could be the worst sort of rake, and Mary's the least suspicious girl in the world, bless her. So now let me tell you. She's the one I'll love till the day

I die, and I want to marry her as soon as she pleases, and I'm hoping you'll be the one to give her away.'"

Mr. Perkin had closed his eyes, as if trying to recall the exact words spoken. Now he opened them, and I saw a hint of moisture in the corners. "Well, that's how it fell out," he said. "They were married three months later, and I gave your mum away, and they went off to live here in Suffolk. I told Mary I wouldn't write to her and she mustn't write to us, because she was going to be gentry and she must forget all about being in service and on the stage. She was a gentleman's wife now, so she'd got to live up to it, and she couldn't 'ave common friends."

I nodded, remembering her through all the years, and said, "She did wonderfully well, Mr. Perkin. You would have been proud of her. And my father spoke the truth, for he really did love her until the day he died."

"I never doubted it. Oh, I could see he was a real lively devil-may-care sort of gent, and I—um..." Alfred Perkin scratched his head and gave me an embarrassed half-smile. "Well, I won't say it didn't *surprise* me to read about all that French business in the paper, but it didn't knock me flat, as you might say. I knew your dad was exceptional, what stage folk sometimes call a nonpareil, but I never doubted he meant what he said about Mary."

There was a silence, and I felt suddenly very tired. Mr. Perkin took a slim watch from his waistcoat pocket and said, "My word, I'm sure I've stayed too long. I 'ope you'll excuse me."

"I've enjoyed every moment of your visit, Mr. Perkin. It was very kind of you to come and give me the benefit of your advice, quite apart from the pleasure of learning how you came to know my mother and father."

He stood up, frowning a little, hesitated for a moment or two, then said, "I'm sorry my advice wasn't much 'elp, Bridie, but it's no use me painting a rosy picture when it's not rosy. The thing is, I've been thinking at the back of my mind while we've been talking, and I'm very worried. You're Mary's daughter, and here you are in deep trouble from being short of money, to speak bluntly. Well, I've done not too bad over the years, and I don't throw money away like a lot of theatricals do, so I reckon I could 'elp you out a bit—"

"Oh, no!" I came to my feet, my face crimson. "Oh, no, no, no, Mr. Perkin! That isn't why I told you of our difficulties. Oh, whatever can you think of me?"

"I think very well of you, young lady," he said, lifting a hand in a calming gesture. "And if you won't let me 'elp in one way, then p'raps I can 'elp in another, so I'll just say this. It's quite a big flat we've got in Holborn, me and Ethel and young Charlie—that's her son, who's part of the act. Now, when the time comes that you've got to leave 'ere, and if you've got nowhere to go, then you come down to London with your sister and there's a spare room you can share. Nothing wonderful, but you could make a bed-sitting room of it until you've got your bearings and found work, and young Kate could go to her music college, couldn't she?"

I stood very still, my mind whirling. To know that we could go to London, have a roof over our heads, and not be on our own was a huge blessing. I could pay Mr. Perkin a small rent, and perhaps would have a little time to spare before our money was exhausted so that I could learn to do typewriting and obtain a better paid position than would otherwise be possible. There was still Nannie Foster to be thought of, but just before Mama died I had begun to have a glimmer of a notion as to how I might secure Nannie's future.

"We'll be in London right through till the spring now," Mr. Perkin was saying, "because we've just done a tour. Course, we're out working every night 'cept Sunday, me and Ethel and Charlie, so you'd 'ave the place to yourselves quite a bit. Mostly we get up late and go out to eat at restaurants or p'raps send out for stuff, because Ethel's no great shakes in the kitchen, and anyway it saves work, but you could look after yourselves, I expect . . ."

Quite suddenly I found that tears were running down my cheeks, and they were not tears of grief. I did not try to hide them, but impulsively reached out to Mr. Perkin and put my hand on his. "Thank you with all my heart," I said. "I hope we shan't need to trouble you, Mr. Perkin, but it's truly a wonderful relief to know that we have somewhere to go, a little friendly haven where we can have time to collect ourselves and prepare to face a new kind of life."

Alfred Perkin looked about the drawing room. "Yes," he said quietly, "it's going to be ever so different, Bridie. You can't 'ave any idea, really."

I dabbed my cheeks with a handkerchief, and smiled without having to make myself do so. "Never mind. I've been so frightened, but you've put new heart into me now."

His mobile face creased in a great beam of pleasure. "Well, I'm very 'appy about that, and no mistake. I'll trot along now, but you just write me a letter when you want to come down, and I'll see you're met at the station and everything."

When he had gone I went to find Kate. She was in the library, studying the score of a sonata, and looked up with a small apologetic smile as I entered. "I'm sorry if I was rude, Bridie," she said as I sat down beside her. "Somehow that man made me suddenly realize how awful it will be for us to be poor."

"He didn't think you were rude, darling, and I know how you feel. I've been quite frantic, trying to work out ways and means."

"Have you, Bridie? I didn't know."

Much as I loved Kate, I could have shaken her at that moment, for it was infuriating to think that she had been quite unaware of the panic that had possessed me for many days past. Our situation was so desperate that once, in the night, I had found myself wondering if the only way I could provide for us all was to become the mistress of some well-to-do gentleman. Even as I shocked myself by the thought, a practical part of my mind was acknowledging that I really had no idea how to go about becoming a loose woman, and that in any event my looks were not likely to attract success in that field. Our situation was still desperate, but it had at least been a little alleviated by Mr. Perkin's offer. I sat down with Kate and explained this to her now.

"That's very kind of him," she said thoughtfully, when I had finished. "Do you think there will be a piano there, Bridie?"

I managed to suppress a sigh. "I don't suppose so, dear."

"Well . . . never mind."

"I do mind. I want you to be able to practice as much as you need, and do everything that was planned, but it's all going to depend on what work I can find."

"I wish you could say something to Nannie to comfort her. She's so worried."

"Oh, I've decided about Nannie. I made up my mind just a few minutes ago. There's that tiny cottage at the end of the shops in Wynford, beside the haberdashers. It's been empty for quite some time, and when I inquired I found it was for sale with a twenty-year lease for ninety-five pounds. I'm going to buy it for Nannie to live in. She'll be happier here than in London because she has friends here. Then if I can send her fifteen shillings a week, she'll be able to live fairly comfortably."

Kate leaned her head against my shoulder for a moment. "Don't forget that rich, handsome young man who's going to fall in love with you," she said dreamily. "Or perhaps it will be me . . . oh, I do hope he's a lovely laughing man, full of dash and devilment, like Papa."

I said nothing. Dash and devilment were all very well, and I too had loved Papa and his ways, but the price to be paid for those ways had proved a heavy one for his family, and one that it seemed I would be paying for as far into the future as I could see.

Mr. Alfred Perkin's visit had refreshed my spirits, and the following week came another piece of good fortune. Signor Peroni arrived, as promised, for Kate's lesson on the appointed day. He said that he first had something to tell us, and while we sat in the drawing room he explained that he and his wife had carefully discussed a notion he had suggested to her. They would be happy to have Kate come to live with them in their Kensington home, where she could have a small bedroom of her own and would live as one of the family. She would have Signor Peroni's piano on which to practice, and would be able to attend daily at the Prince Consort College of Music. Signor Peroni and his wife had worked the whole matter out very carefully, and had decided that they could provide all Kate's needs, including her board and lodging, for fifty pounds a year.

"I must tell you," said Signor Peroni with a little gesture of apology, "that for my family are not bought clothes and footwear of high quality, as those to which Miss Kate is accustomed, neither is our house large with a big number of servants. But my wife is an excellent cook, and we eat most well. We have one maid, and a woman who comes each day for doing rough work. So I can say to you that Miss Kate will be cared for with much attention, as if to be a relative of our own."

Kate was sitting up straight, her eyes sparkling, and I felt a great wave of relief sweep over me. It was a few seconds before I could control my voice sufficiently to say, "Oh, Signor Peroni, I don't know how to find words for such kindness."

"Miss Kate has much talent. I cannot bear that it is lost. Also I have much affection for her, and I am sure that my wife and children will also have much affection. We shall be pleased to take her into our family. I hope she will not find it difficult to accept a home more modest."

I said, "I'm quite sure your home will be far better than anything I could hope to provide once we leave Latchford Hall. She is a very lucky young lady, signore."

I was longing for Kate to say a word of gratitude herself, but then saw that her pleasure had moved her to tears. As I looked, she jumped up, ran to the little sad-faced Italian, hugged him as she pressed her cheek to his, choked out a muffled "Thank you!" and hurried from the room.

Signor Peroni said in a low voice, "Poor child. It has been most hard for her. Hard for you both." He spread a long-fingered hand and looked apologetic again. "Forgive me that I have had to request payment, Miss Bridie, but of course I am not a rich man. I say only this, that it is not a matter of urgency. Please send what is possible when you have the convenience—"

I broke in quickly, "No, signore, I would like to pay you fifty pounds in advance. I have sufficient capital to do so, and then I can breathe easily, for I shall have only myself to worry about for a full year."

"Well . . . if that is your wish, Miss Bridie."

"It really is. How soon could Kate come to you? Now that I'm trying to tidy up our affairs, I have a great wish to finish here and be gone."

"I think my wife will desire a small time to prepare, and also you will wish to do similar, and decide what articles your sister will bring." He thought for a moment, then, "Suppose I would come by morning train on this day of the next week? I can give the final lesson here, and then escort Miss Kate back to London with me."

I had no doubt that Kate would be in very good hands with Signor Peroni and his family. We had led sheltered lives, never knowing real want or anxiety or discomfort, and I had been dreading that the huge change about to take place would prove a crushing affliction to Kate. Now at least she would be in the care of a decent family, and I knew that she had both affection and respect for Signor Peroni himself. I said, "That would be a splendid arrangement, signore, and I look forward to paying you a visit as soon as I come to London myself. One thing I must say. Kate is not at all a difficult young lady, but while she is under your roof she must be under the authority of you and your wife, and you must not hesitate to act as you would if she were your own daughter. I shall say this to Kate herself, of course."

Signor Peroni smiled. "I think we shall not have any troubles," he said.

One week later I stood on the platform waving my handkerchief as the train pulled slowly out on its journey to London. Nannie Foster stood beside me, a tear running down her cheek. Kate waved excitedly from the open window. She had good company, for Signor Peroni had shown extreme kindness by bringing his wife with him to Latchford Hall by the morning train, so that I could meet and talk with her. She had suggested this herself, I learned, because she felt that if Kate was to be put in her care then I had the right to meet her since I was now head of the family. Anne Peroni was a plump smiling woman, quietly spoken, and with a calm manner. I liked her at once, and felt that Kate could not have been more fortunate.

The next few days were very busy. As soon as Letters of Administration were granted for my father's estate, Mr. Whitely put in hand the purchase of the cottage I had found for Nannie Foster. He had saved time by doing all the preliminary work in advance, and the following week I saw Nannie comfortably installed there.

In the same week I suffered a hard blow. With the ending of the lease at Latchford Hall the liability for various repairs and renewals proved much greater than expected. This completely swallowed up all that I had been able to produce from the sale of the piano, ponies, carriages, and lesser items of furniture and ornament, and it also ate into the money in the bank. Mr. Whitely fought the assessment quite ferociously, and I think that but for him I would have left Wynford penniless. As it was, when all bills, servants' wages, legal expenses, and other liabilities had been settled, I had just over one hundred and twelve pounds left. This was after the payment of fifty pounds to Signor Peroni, and now I arranged with the bank for Nannie Foster to draw three pounds five shillings each month.

I spent several evenings working out sums on paper, but the answers I found were always very bleak. At the end of a year, if I allowed myself one pound a week for all purposes, I would have twenty-one pounds left in the bank. My liabilities would then continue at the rate of one pound a week for Kate, the same for myself, and fifteen shillings for Nannie. So I would have to earn at least two pounds fifteen shillings a week to keep our heads above water. I certainly could not earn as much as that by becoming a teacher or governess, even if I were able to find a position, and I had no other skill or qualification to offer. Alfred Perkin had opened my eyes regarding the kind of wage that might be earned in various forms of work, and I had lately been studying advertisements which confirmed what he had said. The brutal fact was that I could not earn enough money, or even half enough, to meet my obligations.

I told myself that I had a full year in which to solve my problems, and wrote to Alfred Perkin, saying that I should be grateful to take up his kind offer of temporary accommodation with his family if he had not changed his mind. By return of post came a letter in a round, careful hand, with several spelling mistakes. Mr. Perkin said he would be delighted to be of assistance, and would I please inform him as to when I expected to arrive in London, because he would be honored to meet my train at Liverpool Street.

I wrote again, thanking him and giving a date just over a week hence, saying that I would catch the morning train. I was careful to avoid a Saturday, as I had discovered by a thorough study of the newspapers that music halls often held matinee performances on Saturdays.

The servants completed their month's notice and departed from Latchford Hall. For three days I was alone there, with only family ghosts of my own imagining to keep me company. I slept poorly, and on the second of those three nights, in the early hours, I saw the gaucho horseman again, moving silently across one of the lawns. When the shadowy figures of horse and man passed from my sight I went back to my bed and slept soundly till morning. Strangely, I felt comforted rather than afraid. Alone in the great empty house, I had felt on edge once the sun went down, but after I imagined the horseman to be there it was as if I had a protector. I had seen no firefly glow on this occasion, and when I walked the lawn next morning I found no thin dark cigar stub. Afterward I felt foolish for having looked, and told myself that if I could not help dreaming a strange dream, at least I could have the sense not to mistake it for reality.

Next day I said good-bye to Nannie Foster and Tom Kettle, then drove into Southwold to say good-bye to Mr. Whitely, who had helped me so much in the long ordeal I was so ill-equipped to face. At eight o'clock the following morning, Mr. Whitely's servant, Frederick, came to Wynford on the early train and walked up to Latchford Hall. He carried my trunk and suitcase down to the gig, watched me lock up, then took the keys and drove me to the station. The gig and pony, all that remained now of our personal belongings, had been sold as from today, and Frederick was to deliver them to the purchaser in Southwold.

At nine o'clock on that warm September day I sat in the corner of a third-class compartment, wearing a summer gown of gray muslin and a black velvet hat with the brim turned up on one side. On my wrist was the small watch which had been a present from my father, but I wore no other jewelry, for I had none now, and in any event I was still in half mourning.

In my handbag, apart from the usual contents, I carried the card sent me by Philippe Chatillon and the letter that had been left by my father, still wrapped in oilskin. I would have found it hard to give a reason why I had kept the French detective's card and the bewildering letter from my father. Perhaps I was afraid to throw them away, though something within me urged me to do so, for now that one part of my life had come to an end I desperately wanted the break to be complete.

In that moment of departure I felt very lonely and plain and frightened. Angrily, I told myself that it was self-pitying to feel lonely, that I should be used to feeling plain, and that it was cowardly to feel frightened. No doubt all this was true, but where fear was concerned I had yet to learn that it was possible to be utterly terrified even when there was no genuine cause.

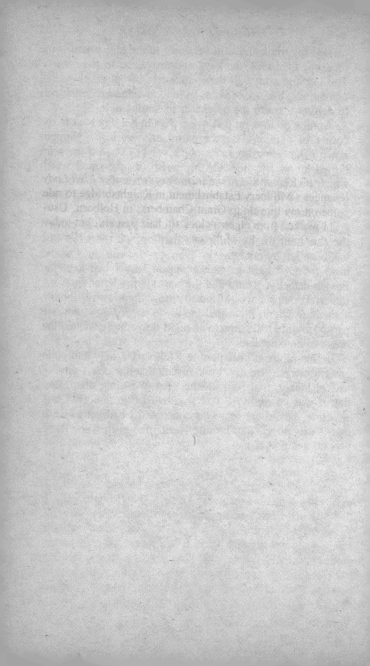

seven

At one o'clock on the first Saturday of November I left Lady Grainger's Millinery Establishment in Knightsbridge to ride home on my bicycle to Grant Chambers, in Holborn. Usually I worked from eight o'clock till half past six, but today was the first Saturday of the month, on which I was allowed a half day off.

Even after six weeks as a shop girl I still felt leg-weary at the end of the day, and it was a joy for me to be finishing with hats and gloves, difficult ladies and spoiled children, after only a morning's work. It was Ethel, the sister of Alfred Perkin (or Alfie as I now called him at his earnest request) who had secured this job for me after I had been unable to find a position during my first two weeks in London.

"There's this friend of mine who serves at The White Swan," she had said in the high, penetrating voice that was so unlike her brother's. "Well, she's got a cousin who's a maid to Lady Grainger what runs a hat shop up the West End, and this cousin says how her ladyship's looking for another girl to serve there, only she's got to be ever so refined, just like you, Bridie."

I had looked at her long angular face in surprise. "But I didn't know ladies kept shops, Ethel. Are you sure?"

Alfie had been studying a horse-racing paper, but now he put it aside and gave me a grin. "Ah, well, that's what's funny when you come to think of it. I mean, the gentry turn up their noses at anyone in trade, don't they? But somehow it's all right for a lady to run a shop selling clothes or flowers. Well, it is down 'ere in London, anyway. I don't know about anywhere else. You ought to try for that job, like Ethel says. Leastways you'll be dealing with a nice class of people."

"Will it be best if Bridie doesn't use her own name, Alfie?" Ethel asked. "I mean, people are going to remember about Mr. Chance and all that, and Lady Grainger might not like it."

"She's daft if she don't," said Alfie. "More likely to bring in customers than turn 'em away. I mean, you know what people are, Ethel. They'll come just to 'ave a gawp at Bridie." He wagged his head with a grimace of regret. "Sorry, Bridie dear, but that's the way it is."

I nodded. I had grown used to being gawped at in Wynford, and had learned to endure it. "I won't change my name or use a false one, Alfie," I said. "I made up my mind about that right from the beginning."

"Quite right, too."

"I'm not so sure," Ethel said doubtfully. "I mean, it's all right as far as the job goes, but what about when she gets married?"

I could not help laughing, but she went on, "No, honestly, Bridie, you just think about it. One day some young gentleman's going to fall in love with you, but what about his position in society? I mean, I liked your dad, rest his soul, but what young gentleman is going to take on his daughter after all those things in the papers?"

Alfie said in his distant foghorn voice, "Why don't you just shut up, Ethel?" But I was not upset. I had shed all my tears long ago.

Two days later I was interviewed by Lady Grainger and was accepted as a shop assistant at a wage of fourteen shillings a week. The first thing I did was to spend two pounds from my meager capital to buy a lady's bicycle, second hand, so that I could travel to and from the shop without further expense. I did not enjoy the work. On the few occasions when I saw Lady Grainger she behaved as if she regretted having taken me on, and eyed me with dark suspicion as if she felt I might have had my hand in the till. The two other girls, both senior to me, were great friends and made it very obvious that they did not want a third person in the shop. They had not been as fortunate as I had been in the matter of education, and perhaps this was why they spoke in very exaggerated accents and were such tremendous snobs. But all this was nothing. I was truly thankful to have a job that was not sweat labor in a factory.

Each week I gave Alfie three shillings as my contribution to the household expenses. This excluded food, which in general I bought for myself. Three shillings was still too little, but Alfie had only agreed to accept it when I almost cried and said I would have to leave if he refused, and then it was as much as he would take.

Ethel was a thin woman with a bony face and a great mass of splendid chestnut hair which she wore piled in a very tall chignon. Her features were vaguely horsey, and she seemed always to be balancing her chignon as she moved, as if it might fall off. Her voice was high-pitched and with almost no variation in it, so that she spoke on one long and monotonous note. This was of great effect in the variety act of "Mr. Alfie Perkin and Company," but it was not an assumed voice, for she spoke in just the same way offstage.

Ethel was known as "Mrs." Perkin, and her son, Charlie, was the third member of the act. He was twenty-two, and used his mother's surname. I did not at any time hear his father spoken of, but gathered from an idle word or so that Alfie let slip one day that Charlie Perkin was a result of the very brief and only romance Ethel had ever known. He was a tall, loose-limbed young man with red hair and a very pale face, who was rarely at home and who spent all his time on his own private pursuits except when he was onstage or rehearsing or in bed. What those pursuits were, neither Ethel nor Alfie seemed to know. Charlie spoke little, but was quite friendly. It seemed to me that he simply had nothing he wanted to say to any of us, and during the brief moments when he was at home his main method of communication was by a grin, a wink, a click of the tongue, or a wag of the head.

Home was at 10 Grant Chambers, Holborn. This was a large flat in a building comprising twelve flats varying in

sizes, on three floors, with a lift and a hall porter. Our flat
was on the top floor and we had a very pleasant view, with
St. Pauls to the east and Big Ben to the south. Charlie shared
a large bedroom with Alfie, while Ethel and I had a small
bedroom each. There was a spacious living room, a small
dining room, a kitchen, and a splendid modern bathroom
with hot-water taps.

Radiators attached to the walls kept all the rooms beautifully warm. They were connected to a boiler hidden away
in the basement, and this was tended by a very old man
who rarely emerged from his hot gloomy cavern except to
have bitter arguments with the hall porter, Henry, who was
given to complaining that the building was either too hot
or too cold. Henry was a staunch supporter of the Perkin
family, probably because he received many free tickets from
Alfie, and he made it his business to take charge of my
bicycle, which he kept in his small lobby for me.

Every morning at nine o'clock, except on Sundays, a
brawny woman named Minnie, wearing a flowered hat and
carrying an immense basket, arrived at the flat, bringing
with her bed-linen, clothes, towels, and other items she had
taken away for laundering the day before. She would then
make breakfast for Mr. Alfie Perkin and Company before
settling down to three hours of cleaning. In the two or three
weeks before I found work at Lady Grainger's shop I tried
to help Minnie with the cleaning, but she would have none
of it.

I made myself useful in a small way by doing whatever
mending I could find, and there was more than I at first
expected because of the constant wear and tear on the stage
costumes. For the rest of the time I wrote letters of application for work, and practiced typewriting on a machine
Alfie had produced, which he claimed to have borrowed
from a friend.

I was quite awed by the unexpected luxury in which we
lived, for I had expected nothing like it, and I sometimes
wondered how it was possible for a music hall performer
to live in such style. The occupants of the other flats were
gentlemen in various professions. One or two were bach-

elors, others had a wife and a small family, though no young children were allowed. For the most part they ignored us, except for an occasional stiff nod. This did not trouble any of us. Alfie always gave our neighbors a genial and courteous, "Good day," but amused himself by addressing every gentleman as "Sir George" and every lady as "My Lady." I followed Ethel's example and responded in exact measure to whatever greeting or lack of greeting I was offered. Charlie simply did some of his head wagging, or winking, or tongue clicking, sometimes adding a few paces of a very strange and comical walk which I later discovered he used on the stage.

It was only on Sundays that I was able to spend much time with my new friends. Every weekday I would arrive home at about seven o'clock, only half an hour before Alfie, Ethel, and Charlie left in a brougham for the first of their nightly appearances at two and occasionally three music halls in the same evening. By the time they returned at eleven o'clock or sometimes later, I was long asleep. When I left in the morning at ten minutes to eight o'clock, they had not woken.

During the days before I began to work in the shop I had spent several evenings at the theater with them. On the first occasion I watched their performance from the stalls, accompanied by the redoubtable Minnie as my protector. On the second occasion I watched from the side of the stage, which everybody called the wings.

Alfie had tried to prepare me for what I would see and hear, and had explained that there were different classes of music hall. "First there's the posh West End 'alls, Bridie, mostly around Leicester Square, like the Empire and the London Pavilion. Then there's the 'alls still in the West End but not quite so posh, like the Hungerford or Westons. Next you've got some big music 'alls outside the posh areas and down into the suburbs, like the Bedford in Camden Town, and last you've got the little old places that started as song-and-supper rooms for gents, or tavern music 'alls for the working class. I've played 'em all, Bridie, but we 'aven't played the bottom end for years now. We've built

up a good name, see? I mean, we never come out lower
than number four on the bill for the posh 'ouses, and we're
mostly at number two for the second-class London 'ouses
or in the provincial 'alls."

It was during the morning before my first visit to a music
hall that Alfie explained all this to me. I listened, I am sure,
with round eyes, for he was talking about affairs of which
I was almost completely ignorant.

"Mind you," he went on, "things 'ave changed since the
days when I was doing the conjuring act with your mum as
my assistant. You get quite a lot of gentry at all kinds of
'alls nowadays, mainly the young bloods and what they call
the Bohemians, and a few ladies on their own what aren't
really ladies, if you take my meaning. But the profession's
a bit more respectable than it used to be, really. I mean,
we get a lot of decent trades people now, people who keep
shops and suchlike. What 'appens is, they put up the posters
in their shops, and the management gives 'em free tickets,
so they come along regular with their families, and that
encourages more of their own sort."

Alfie produced a scrapbook full of photographs, pro-
grams, and yellowing slips cut from newspapers, ranging
back over twenty years and more. "You might like to look
through this some day, Bridie. It's a sort of 'istory, in a
way." He turned to a page near the front, and there in the
middle of it was a sepia photograph of Alfie as a much
younger man, in evening dress and wearing a short cloak.
He held a small box with zodiac signs on it in one hand,
and a short black stick with white tips in the other—a
conjurer's wand. From the box had come a string of flags,
and holding the other end of the string, smiling a shy smile,
wearing a pretty white dress with a tiny waist was Kate, a
little older perhaps . . . and not Kate, in fact, but my mother
as she had been twenty-odd years before.

"She should've been born a lady," Alfie said softly.
"Right, Ethel?"

Ethel nodded, her eyes misting. "Couldn't be brassy if
she tried, Mary couldn't. And we always dressed her like

that. Nothing vulgar. The men always behaved themselves when Mary was onstage."

Alfie closed the book and looked at me. "When she left, it was your dad who put me on the right road." He shook his head and scratched an ear, half laughing. "Alfie, he says to me, you're not a bad conjurer, but you'd make a much better comic. You've got the face for it, he says, but you haven't got the vanity a feller needs to make a go of it solo. Comic sketches for my money, he says, that's the thing for you. Think about it, Alfie. You'll need a company of three or four, but you might find Ethel a good bet for one of them, with that funny voice. So work out a comic sketch and try it."

"We thought it was a barmy idea," said Ethel. "Made me nervous just to *think* about going out there on the stage."

Alfie nodded. "But we couldn't get it out of our minds," he said, "and in the end we worked out a sketch with me and Ethel and a young chap called Nipper Jennings." He made one of his brow-wrinkling, eye-rolling grimaces. "Got the bird with it when we tried it out first time at the old Royal Standard in Pimlico."

I said, "The bird?"

"Got booed. Fell flat as a pancake, Bridie. Anyway, we worked away on it, changing a bit 'ere and polishing a bit there, and Ethel got over being nervous, and suddenly it seemed to take. So we worked out another sketch, and that's what we've been doing for the last twenty years, more or less, working the two sketches turn and turn about. Nipper Jennings got pneumonia and died five years ago, but we'd been training Charlie anyway, and he just stepped straight in."

I looked my astonishment. "Only two sketches, Alfie?"

He grinned. "The people out front like best what they know best, Bridie dear. I mean, Charlie Coborn can sing 'The Man Who Broke the Bank at Monte Carlo' every night of 'is life, and they'll love it. In fact, they'll call for it if he don't. They like to know what's coming next, and I reckon they laugh more at a joke the second or third time. I mean, you take young Fred Kitchen with that sketch, *The*

Bailiff. There's that line when he says, 'Meredith, we're in!' and the people laugh their 'eads off. It's not even a joke, really, but it just caught on. Now you get people saying, 'Meredith, we're in!' even if they've just walked into a pub or something."

I shook my head wonderingly. "It doesn't sound at all funny, Alfie."

He chuckled and picked up his racing paper. "You wait till you 'ear Fred Kitchen say it."

I had my first experience of music hall at the Canterbury, in Westminster Bridge Road, watching from the stalls with Minnie, and in spite of all I had been told I was quite dazed by the end of the evening, for it was as if I had suddenly been transported to another world—raucous and gaudy, but somehow honest; vulgar, but lusty and bursting with life; exhilarating, but a little frightening.

Minnie and I were seated among the young gentry, some of them with female companions who laughed uproariously at every word from their escorts. We drew a few curious glances before the performance began, but in general the atmosphere was friendly and genial. Behind us, the audience changed by degrees to a different class of person, and the hubbub grew louder with the chaff and chatter of young clerks and local bloods whose mark of distinction appeared to be the carrying of a small cigar behind the ear.

There were also a few families of tradesmen, as Alfie had explained to me, and a scattering of couples. By far the greatest noise came from above—not from the circle but from the gallery beyond it, which I could barely see even when I craned my neck. Here, according to Alfie, was where the fate of an artist was really decided, up in "the gods."

Every man in the audience seemed to be smoking, and the air was thick with it. There was much coming and going with refreshments, and I felt quite shaken by the thought that when the curtain rose a lady called Nellie Hastings, who was billed as "Serio-Comic and Dancer," would have the awesome task of securing the attention of this mass of humanity called the audience. Minnie had explained to me that this would be the first turn, because as the orchestra was finishing an overture two stage footmen in splendid livery had put a very large card with a number on it into a gilded frame on each side of the forestage. This was the number that appeared beside the name of Miss Nellie Hastings on the program.

In the event, this dark-haired and vivacious lady did not really capture the attention of the audience, for many of them continued chatting and laughing among themselves, but she persevered undaunted, and finally brought the house to a measure of silence when she sang a song about a soldier who died while trying to save his injured horse. I did not care much for the song, but I was glad to hear her receive a good round of applause at the end of her turn.

Mr. Alfie Perkin and Company came on for the last turn before the interval, and when the two footmen set up the big cards bearing Alfie's program number I found myself holding my breath with anticipation, yet at the same time I was apprehensive that I might not enjoy the performance my friends were about to give, for truth to tell I scarcely knew what I felt about the program so far.

Of the comedians I had seen, two had gone in for a great deal of shouting and capering as if trying to bully the audience into enjoying itself. Most of what they shouted was a kind of nonsense and almost meaningless to me, but there were phrases that the audience evidently recognized, and they always produced a roar of laughter. They were not funny phrases in themselves, but simple things like, "So I told her, I *told* her!" Or, "Don't talk to me about pease pudding!"

The third comedian was a lugubrious man who wore a hopelessly ancient and tattered tail suit and dress shirt. He simply stood there delivering a monologue—"The Problems of Being a Nob"—and I thought he was very funny. A black-faced comedian told poor jokes and sang beautifully. A comedienne with impossibly red hair delivered a stream of comic patter which was quite witty. And a baritone sang several overly sentimental songs which I did not enjoy but but which were warmly appreciated by the audience. Beside me, Minnie wept happily into a large handkerchief at a song about a little boy who was a powder monkey in the days of Nelson and kept carrying the powder up from a burning hold until his ship blew up.

A dark-haired young woman with tremendous vivacity, wearing a pink dress and carrying a parasol, sang a song with entirely innocent words which she managed to invest with far from innocent meaning. The audience was greatly taken with her. Beside me, Minnie guffawed till the tears ran down her cheeks, and I was laughing myself, even though I did not understand some of the innuendos, for with all her winks, eye-brow raisings, meaningful looks, and clever pauses, the young woman performed with a sense of fun which, for me, took away all offense. Even so, it was not the kind of entertainment that I was used to and very different from the musical concerts at Cambridge.

I reminded myself that variety artists had to appeal to a broad mass of people with tastes that had not been shaped by university education, and this made me a poor judge of performance, but still it was with mixed feelings that I watched the curtain rise on Mr. Alfie Perkin and Company, for I wanted so much to be able to say truthfully that I had enjoyed their performance.

The program announced that the sketch was entitled *The Water Board Man*, and there was a murmur of gleeful anticipation from the audience as the orchestra ended a short piece of introductory music. The center of the stage was occupied by a stretch of canvas with a brick wall painted on it, about as high as a man's shoulder. There were one or two pots with artificial flowers, representing a garden, and a post with a clothesline attached. The other end of the line ran off into the wings. A rainwater butt stood beside the wall, with a short pair of stepladders leaning against it. On the floor, a large iron plate, like a manhole cover, had been lifted at one end and propped open as if to reveal a hole in the ground.

Alfie Perkin, wearing a uniform slightly too small for him and a cap with a shiny peak, was moving toward the "hole," notebook and pencil poised. Behind him followed

Charlie, in a uniform too large and carrying a shapeless bag of tools. He walked with a curious chickenlike step, one of those steps I had sometimes seen him use briefly at home, his head moving forward and then back in the most peculiarly comic way.

The audience began to laugh. Alfie stopped by the hole. Charlie went walking on. Alfie watched him, pencil poised over notebook, with silent and dignified irritation. Charlie passed completely offstage. Ten seconds later he came back, using a different walk in which he seemed to exude witless embarrassment. When he halted by the hole, Alfie continued to eye him, and as he did so there passed over that rubbery face a whole range of emotions: indignation, outrage, resignation, menace, and finally a kind of hopeless acceptance. When the chuckling of the audience had died down, Alfie spoke, and for the first time I heard that powerful voice used to the full, yet without effort, reaching to the uppermost tiers of the gallery. Pointing down with his pencil he said slowly and deliberately, "Arnold, this is what we call *a hole*."

A roar of mirth went up, and my own laughter was a part of it. Anybody might have gone through the same movements and spoken the same words, but there were a dozen nuances in every move, gesture, and expression that gave a gloriously comic effect to the simple scene.

The idea of the sketch was that Alfie was *The Water Board Man*, and Charlie was his assistant. They had come to inspect a water main, and Ethel was the householder, Mrs. Fortescue, who was somewhat deaf. I learned later that the "hole" was really a solid wooden frame a few inches deep, with water pipes and turncocks set in it, these being fed through a slim hose from a hermetically sealed churn in the wings. Air had been pumped under compression into this churn, to provide a powerful jet of water.

With her shrill monotonous voice, Ethel was remarkably funny as the hard-of-hearing Mrs. Fortescue, who was trying to hang out her washing and who misunderstood all the explanations of the Water Board man. Alfie, long-suffering and growing steadily more exasperated, gave instructions

to Charlie, who did everything wrong, sending a jet of water
up Alfie's trouser leg, knocking his cap off with another
jet, and getting ridiculously tangled up in Ethel's washing.
Charlie uttered no word at all throughout the whole performance, but mimed and winked and twitched and gestured
through all his tribulations. When a jet hit him in the back
of the neck, or when the Water Board man accidentally
struck him with a water turnkey, or when Mrs. Fortescue
dropped an immense spanner on his toe, he would reel and
totter about the stage with brief and brilliant displays of
what I later learned was called eccentric dancing.

As I watched, my fears and troubles were completely
forgotten, for I was helpless with laughter and lost in admiration. All three were really quite splendid, but Charlie
was the greatest surprise to me, for I had not dreamed he
could be so funny. There were some ridiculous mishaps
with the clothesline full of washing, and disaster when Charlie mounted the steps to free the pulley of the clothesline,
and fell back into the rainwater butt with his legs, head and
shoulders sticking out.

The sketch ended in an absurd way when Charlie, soaked
from knees to armpits, was required by Alfie to hand him
a crowbar from the tool bag. The object produced and handed
over was a clarinet, which Alfie eyed with prolonged astonishment before resignedly starting to play it, whereupon
Charlie and Ethel began to dance a solemn minuet, bowing,
curtsying, and linking hand to hand as they stepped grace-
fully round the hole in time to the music. It was on this
scene that the curtain came down.

There was a wild inconsequence about the whole sketch
which I found quite hilarious, and certainly the audience
enjoyed Mr. Alfie Perkin and Company, applauding rap-
turously as they stood to take their bows.

Next day, after breakfast, and after I had lain awake for
a long time that night with the events of the evening running
through my mind, I made a special point of congratulating
Charlie as he emerged from his bedroom buttoning a smart
new blazer. I had already expressed my admiration to Ethel

and Alfie, but was a little shy with Charlie, for I felt I neither knew nor understood him at all.

I thanked him for the way he had made me laugh till my ribs ached, and added, "Oh, and I do admire your dancing, Charlie. You seem as light as a feather, and it's just as if you were made of rubber, the funny way you use your arms and legs."

He grinned, winked, gave a twitch of his head, and floated aside for a pace or two on effortless feet. "Ah, well, Uncle Alfie taught me, didn't he? Easy enough when you know how." He lifted his rather thin voice and called to his mother, "I'm off now, Ma. Ta-ta."

"Ta-ta, Charlie. See you tonight."

Then he was gone, to wherever it was that he followed his mysterious pursuits.

I first saw the other sketch in the repertoire of Mr. Alfie Perkin and Company from the wings of the Metropolitan, Edgware Road. It was called *The Paperhanger's Mate*, and the scenery consisted of a few pieces of furniture set in the angle of two high wooden walls. This represented a room that was to be papered. I learned that items used on the stage were called props, short for properties, and for this sketch there was a trestle table, some rolls of paper, a bucket of special paste, some stepladders, large brushes, and long paperhanger's shears.

Alfie had three sets of scenery, props, and costumes for each sketch, so that the company could appear at three different halls in the same evening, if need be. There were also important requisites in the little cramped dressing rooms, for washing off paperhanger's paste and changing out of wet clothing before hurrying to a waiting brougham and scuttling across London for another performance. To assist in this, and to take charge of scenery and props, Alfie employed a man called Harold, a thin, sad, stoop-shouldered man from Yorkshire, who lived in digs and had only two topics of conversation. One was the Yorkshire cricket team, and the other was the mean and grasping nature of his landlady. Harold's duties were by no means easy, for he had to make sure that everything was always in the right place at the right time and in perfect working order, but he had been employed by Alfie for eight years now, and performed his tasks unfailingly well.

In the second sketch of the company's repertoire Alfie was the paperhanger, Charlie was his mate, and Ethel was the lady of the house, who was greatly concerned for her furniture in general and for a very large picture in particular, a portrait of a man with a huge moustache and wearing a bowler hat, whom she referred to in an exaggeratedly refined voice as "mai departed 'usband."

Dreadful things happened to that picture, and Alfie's harassed attempts to conceal them or put them right were hilarious. Again, the humor of the sketch was based on a series of ingenious mishaps, with Charlie as the cause and with Alfie responding in a variety of ways, sometimes with an explosion of rage, sometimes with plaintive despair. Perhaps most comical of all was his flirtatious gallantry toward Mrs. Prendergast, played by Ethel.

It was not until later, when I had seen both sketches several times, that I realized how truly clever Alfie was, and Ethel too in her own way. Charlie played the fool and was regarded as the funny man, but everything depended upon the way Alfie and Ethel reacted. In time I found myself marveling at the way they timed their pauses and their interventions to a split second, even taking into account the slightly different response from different audiences.

When I began work at the shop I had no time for evening visits to the music hall, except on Saturdays, when I could sleep a little later on Sunday mornings. I missed seeing my friends perform, but I did not particularly miss going to the music hall, for I had discovered that I enjoyed less than a quarter of the entertainment from other artists. I was introduced to quite a number of Alfie's fellow performers backstage, and found them just as mixed as any other group of people. Some were warmhearted and outgoing, some reserved, a few almost hostile. Alfie and Ethel were friendly with the friendly ones, regardless of where they stood on the bill, and ignored those who were not. Charlie smiled or winked at anybody, but was as much a lone wolf in the profession as he was in the family.

After my second week in London I took to cooking a Sunday luncheon for the family. I was by no means a wonderful cook, but I had been sufficiently interested to learn the basic art from Mrs. Ryland, our cook at Latchford Hall, and I was certainly much better than Ethel.

"My word, that was good," Alfie said with a contented sigh after the second occasion. "A real treat, I reckon. I wonder how it is that you can cook the same food and make it so 'orrible, Ethel. Funny, isn't it?"

Ethel nodded agreement. "I never really got the hang of it, I suppose. Thanks ever so, Bridie. Best dinner we've 'ad for ages, that was."

I felt enormously pleased to have performed some small service for these kindest of friends.

Every Sunday after luncheon I took my bicycle and rode to Kensington, to Signor Peroni's house. There I would spend the afternoon with Kate and the family, take tea with them, and return to Holborn at about six o'clock. To my relief Kate seemed to have settled in very well. At first, like me, she had found it disconcerting to live in so small a dwelling, but she was used to it now and was also very happy in her studies at the Prince Consort College of Music, which she attended daily.

On the Sunday following my November half day off, Kate was in one of her practical moods. Signor Peroni and his wife always made sure that we were left together for half an hour so that we could discuss any private matters, and as soon as we were alone on this occasion Kate said briskly, "Bridie, are you sure you can manage this sixpence a week you give me for pocket money?"

"Yes, dear, of course. After all, you were entitled to half of what little was left to us."

She smiled. "At least I had enough sense to ask that you should have charge of everything. Poor Bridie, it must have been a terrible time for you."

"Well, it's over now, and don't worry about the sixpence. Now listen, I want to talk about Christmas."

She sobered, and I knew her thoughts. This Christmas would be quite unlike any other we had known. We would not have the joy of Papa being at home with us, of Mama being happy and at ease, and all the warmth of a family Christmas. I said, "Alfie hasn't made any bookings for the Christmas week, but he starts in pantomime at Drury Lane on Boxing Day. We thought it would be nice if you came to spend Christmas day with us, that's a Saturday, and then perhaps Signor Peroni would allow me to come here to spend Sunday with you. Alfie opens on the Monday, and says he'll arrange tickets for us all to go to the pantomime, if Signor Peroni would like that."

Kate sat up straight with excitement. "Oh, that sounds lovely, Bridie. Let's speak to Signor Peroni about it. I'm sure the children would enjoy a pantomime."

I smiled. "So will you. Alfie says they've worked his *Paperhanger's Mate* sketch into the book of the pantomime. It really is very funny, Kate."

"I'm sure it is." She thought for a moment. "Bridie, last Sunday you mentioned that the Perkins will be going on tour in the spring. What will you do then?"

"Just carry on, I suppose. They don't rent the flat out while they're away, so it won't matter if I stay there."

"But on your own?"

"Yes, I shall be quite all right. I'm sure I won't be carried off by that amazingly rich and handsome man you spoke of, who's going to come along and fall in love with me."

She gave an impatient shake of her head. "Oh, I was just being silly when I said that."

"You were in one of your romantic moods. Anyway, don't worry about me. I shall come and see you every week. Now let's talk about Christmas presents. You must try to buy or make some little token for each of the Peroni family, and I shall do the same for Alfie and Company."

We talked for a while about what we could afford to spend on each member of our adopted families, then came a tap on the door and the Peroni children came in, full of suppressed excitement, followed by their mother and father. They were most beautiful children, and now I learned that they had been practicing a little Italian song to sing to me. Kate made great pretense of having forgotten how to play, and there was much laughter and chatter in both English and Italian as the children took her hands and urged her to the piano.

They sang remarkably well, but I would have been just as happy and as near to tears if they had sung very badly, for I was so filled with a sense of thankfulness that Kate was part of a warm and loving family. I was no less fortunate myself, and when I thought how wretched the situation might have been for both of us, I felt an inward shiver.

In the few days before Christmas I saw more of my friends than usual, because they were resting. They still slept late, so I was away in the morning before they rose, but it was pleasant to spend a few evenings without them having to hurry off to work soon after I arrived home from the shop.

It was lovely to take a bath, change my clothes, and then go out to eat at a nice restaurant with Alfie and Ethel. The bill for the three of us would amount to almost as much as my whole week's wages, and this troubled me at first, but Alfie said very sternly, "All right, Bridie dear, we know you like to pay your way, but refusing to accept a bit of 'ospitality from an old friend of your mum's is something different. It's not nice, is it, Ethel?"

Ethel smiled the toothy smile that made people laugh when she did it onstage, and said, "We like to 'ave you with us, Bridie, honest. Just call it a little thank-you for them nice Sunday dinners you cook us."

It was hard to remember now, and I did not want to remember, that during my first few days in London I had felt awkward and embarrassed when going out anywhere in the company of Alfie and Ethel, because they were not of my kind. This snobbery was no credit to me, particularly under the circumstances, and I was bitterly ashamed of myself even at the time. I was still ashamed when I recalled my feelings, but they had long since passed. I had suffered enough humiliations in the shop to cure me of all condescension, and I was now quite indifferent to what any stranger might think of the obviously well brought-up young lady in the company of two common people. They were not common in my eyes, but truly uncommon, and I regarded them with great pride as my dearest friends.

When we had time to chat, there were no difficulties in finding subjects of conversation. Ethel belonged to two public libraries and was an avid reader of what she called "good stories by proper writers." It was disconcerting to discover that though I might know quite a little about French literature, Ethel's knowledge of Dickens, Hardy, Eliot, Thackeray, Emily Brontë, and other famous novelists, was far wider than my own. She was also well up in the tragedies of Shakespeare, which she had reread many times, but she did not like the comedies, and thought them silly. Alfie's reading was confined to *The Stage*, which was a magazine for theatrical people, and the racing papers, which he studied deeply without ever making a wager.

Two days before Christmas I arrived home to find only Charlie there. He was smartly dressed in a dark gray flannel suit with narrow stripes, and was about to go out, as usual, but he courteously helped me off with my coat, hung it up in the hall cupboard, and carried my shopping basket through to the kitchen for me. We then proceeded to have the longest conversation we had ever had together.

"Ma's out with Uncle Alfie," he announced in his rather creaky voice. "Bit o' Christmas shopping. Said you was to carry on 'aving your bath an' all that, and they'll be back by 'alf past seven. All go out to eat." His words were accompanied by the usual miming, winks, jerks of the head, and grimaces.

I said, "Thank you, Charlie. I expect you're off out yourself now. I hope you have a nice evening." I was not trying to end the conversation, it was simply that Charlie was always off out, and I did not want to detain him. To my surprise, he lingered on this occasion, squinted thoughtfully up at the ceiling, leaned in a rubber-limbed way against the wall, and said, "Chap was asking about you."

"A chap?"

"M'mm. About you."

I had started to take off my hat, but now stood holding the brim on either side, with the hat poised above my head, staring at Charlie. "Who was it?" I asked.

He gave a wriggling shrug, and wagged his head. "Dunno, Bridie. Some chap."

"When was this?"

"Last night."

"Where, Charlie?"

He gave a start, floated away from the wall, half closed his eyes in an agonized frown, and drew down his lower lip, sucking in air with an expression of much doubt. I watched, puzzled, my eyebrows lifting higher all the time, my lips turning in. I still held my hat above my head, and it suddenly struck me that in a way we were two of a kind, Charlie and I, though he had had no nannie to admonish him for making "exaggerated facial expressions."

I gave a half laugh, and put down my hat on the table. As I did so, Charlie opened his eyes wide and looked at me from the corners of them, with his head partly turned away. It was as if he was trying to make up his mind about something, then suddenly he dropped into a slight crouch, bent forward a little, rested his cane in the hollow between the finger and thumb of his left hand, and moved it backwards and forwards several times. I brought my eyebrows down, straightened all other parts of my face as much as possible, and said, "What do you mean, Charlie?"

He looked furtively over one shoulder, then the other, and said in a conspiratorial whisper, *"Billard 'all!"*

"The billiard hall? A place where men play billiards? Oh, is that where you go in your spare time, Charlie?"

He nodded vigorously, at the same time lifting a finger to his lips and saying, "Shhh! Don't tell Ma!"

I blinked in surprise. "No. Of course I won't, if you don't wish me to, but is that where you go *all* the time, to a billiard hall? Nowhere else?"

His head nodding changed to head shaking. "Just the billiards. Daft about it, I am. Cue in me hand, and I'm 'appy for ever." He rolled his eyes worshipfully.

I said, "But surely your mother wouldn't mind? I mean, it isn't like gambling at cards, or drinking heavily, or—"

"No, no," he broke in hastily, and drifted sideways without apparently moving his feet. "Two 'alf pints an evening, that's all. But Ma don't like billiards, see?" He twirled his cane and looked at the ceiling, lowering his voice to a whisper again as he said, "I think it's because of me dad. I think HE was a billiards player, see? And when he slung 'is 'ook, and left Ma, you know . . ." There followed a whole series of winks, eye movements, face twisting, and inhalations through pursed lips.

I said, "Yes, all right, Charlie, I understand. Does your Uncle Alfie know? I mean, that you go to billiard halls?"

"Might guess. Never says."

"I won't speak of it at all. Tell me more of this man who asked about me. What did he want to know?"

"If you were all right. If you were courting."

"Courting?"

"M'mm."

"But why?"

Another slow shrug, shoulders almost touching ears. "Dunno, Bridie. I just said yes an' no."

"What?"

"Yes you were all right, no you weren't courting. I was busy playing. On a break of thirty-eight, see?"

"Did you spare a moment just to look at him?"

"Er . . . 'ad a sort of brown face, 'air a bit longish. Spoke slow. Yankee all right."

"American? Are you sure? I've never even met an American—oh, except that I knew a girl at college who came from Pennsylvania, but I don't know any American men."

"Ah, well. That's about it, then." Charlie seemed relieved to have discharged what he evidently felt was his responsibility to tell me of the encounter. He tucked his cane under his arm, twirled his cap dexterously, looked at his watch, then jerked up his head in sudden surprise. "I just remembered, Bridie. This chap 'ad a horse. Some other chaps saw 'im go, and they were talking after I finished me break. Said it was a beauty, this 'orse."

I stood quite still, my memory reaching back to a night at Latchford Hall, and I said, "Was he wearing a low-crowned hat with a wide brim, a foreign sort of hat?"

Charlie rolled his head round on his shoulders, closed his eyes, held his cane horizontally just beneath his nose, like an enormous moustache, and caused his legs to undulate, all apparently in a supreme effort of memory. Then he said, "I never saw any 'at."

"Well...thank you for telling me about it, Charlie."

He opened his eyes fully, and lowered his cane. "Bit of a myst'ry?"

"Yes, but I don't think it can be of any importance."

"If I see 'im again, I'll take more notice."

I smiled. "Don't spoil a thirty-eight break, whatever that might be."

He grinned, put his cap on, raised it to me, and glided across to the door as if on wheels. "I'm off, then. Ta-ta, Bridie."

"Good-bye, Charlie. Enjoy your evening."

I slept uneasily that night. A man on a horse? I had dreamed of one such man and met another in Wynford, during the first dark days of calamity. But...an American? Charlie could surely never have mistaken the French detective, Philippe Chatillon, for an American. And if my dream had been reality, then who could the strange night rider be? Why was he now in London, asking about me, and asking in particular if I was being courted?

After a poor night's sleep I told myself firmly that I had sufficient to think of without fretting over matters that did not affect me and about which I could do nothing. Even so, I continued to wonder for many days, and the nagging puzzlement had still not faded completely when it was revived again by an encounter which left me dumfounded.

eight

Christmas came and went. For me, as for Kate, it was an occasion of very mixed emotions, and I am sure that it was also an occasion with anxious moments for the Peroni family and the Perkin family, since in their generosity they were concerned for us at what they knew must be a difficult time.

Kate was a little stiff and restrained with Alfie and Company when she was with us on Christmas day, and I wished so much that she could have been warmer and more at ease, especially with Alfie, for it was clear that he adored her as her mother's daughter and could scarcely take his eyes from her. By contrast, I felt very much at home with the Peroni family on the Sunday, and our Boxing Day visit to the pantomime was a huge success, with Mrs. Peroni stoutly declaring that the paperhanging scene by Alfie and Company was the best part of the whole performance.

I felt very proud and important when I was able to take them all backstage afterward, there to meet Alfie and Ethel, and to be shown the mechanical marvels behind the scenes. The children were entranced, and their parents were naturally delighted to see them so happy.

The new year was a few days old and I was busy in the store room at the back of the shop, arranging in size order some boxes of gloves that had been delivered that morning, when Helen, one of the two other shop assistants, appeared in the doorway, round-eyed, and said in a loud whisper, using her overrefined accent, "Ai say, there's a *gentleman* customer, asking for you by *neame*, Bridget, and quaite *insisting* that he wishes to be served bai *you*!"

A gentleman customer was a rare phenomenon in Lady

Grainger's Millinery Establishment, for though we stocked items other than hats, we carried nothing for men. Even more surprising was that the customer had asked to be served by me. I felt an inward giggle as I decided that it could only be Alfie, and I wondered what Helen and Maude would make of him, but then I realized that Helen would never have described Alfie as a gentleman.

There was a full-length mirror in the cubicle beside the store room. I slipped inside, made sure my hair was tidy, and adjusted my blouse where it had wriggled up a little at the waist from my exertions, then walked down behind the long shop counter. It was a constant admonition of Lady Grainger's that we girls should always move with dignity and decorum, and I was doing this quite well until a man with his back to me, in a fine gray topcoat, top hat in hand, gazing at a display of hats, suddenly turned toward me, and I found myself looking into the smiling face of Philippe Chatillon.

I stopped short, almost knocking a hat stand over, then stood gazing in astonishment, feeling my face do all sorts of things I could not help. He said, in the beautifully pitched voice I suddenly remembered so well, "Good morning, mam'selle. I apologize if I have startled you."

I drew in a deep breath, tried to urge my face into a dignified and decorous expression, rested my hands loosely on the counter, one upon the other, as I had been instructed, and said, "Good morning, M'sieu Chatillon, how may I be of service to you?"

His eyes, full of kindly amusement, held me without effort, and I could not have looked away if I had tried. "I hoped you would do me the honor of allowing me to take you to luncheon at Ferriers," he said. "The cuisine is French, and has been highly praised."

I felt heat rise from my neck into my cheeks with discomfiture that stemmed from a tangle of causes. I was taken aback by his presence here, and shocked by his invitation, for it was quite out of order for a virtual stranger to invite a young lady to take luncheon with him alone. I was also alarmed that Helen and Maude might report our encounter

to Lady Grainger in such a way that it would appear I had
been flirting with this unusual customer, which would bring
instant dismissal.

I said as calmly as I could, "I beg your pardon, m'sieu,
but I am here to serve you only in the capacity of shop
assistant."

He spread a hand in an elegant gesture of protest. "Ah,
but I imagine you are permitted time for luncheon, Mam'selle
Chance? And for that time, surely, you are not a shop
assistant?"

I managed to pull my eyes away, to glance at Helen and
Maude. They were listening breathlessly, eyes shining with
excitement. I looked at Philippe Chatillon again and said,
"I am allowed one half-hour for luncheon, m'sieu, and in
that time I eat one or two sandwiches brought from home.
In any event, it is not my habit to accept such invitations
from a gentleman of slight acquaintance." I felt quite glad
to sound so pompous, and heard little gasps from Helen and
Maude, but I did not look at them.

Philippe Chatillon said with a polite smile, "I was hoping
to make our acquaintance less slight, mam'selle. May I have
your permission to attend on you when you finish your work
for the day, so that I may escort you home?"

I began to feel rather desperate, and I think this must
have produced a grimace, for his smile broadened almost
into a grin for a moment as I said stupidly, "Thank you,
but I have my bicycle."

"I am really most anxious to talk with you," he said
gently. "May I call at your home in Holborn at a time
convenient to you and when we may be properly chaper-
oned?"

"I am surprised that you know where I live, m'sieu, and
also that you have found me here."

He shrugged a shoulder, tilting his head to one side as
he did so. "I am, as I have said, a kind of policeman by
profession, mam'selle. May I visit you?"

"I prefer that you do not, m'sieu." This was an answer
given from instinct rather than thought. It rather frightened
me that I felt weak when this man looked at me. I had once,

in my most desperate hours, shocked myself by wondering how one became a loose woman, and the thought came to me now that here was a man who would not find it hard to acquire a mistress whenever he so wished. But apart from this touch of fear—perhaps fear of myself rather than of him—I wanted above all to draw a line across the past. Our lives at Latchford Hall, Kate's and mine, had ended in nightmare, and I wished that nothing should reach out from the past to remind us of it. We might never completely shake off the taint of Papa's notoriety, but I was determined not to perpetuate needless links with our earlier lives.

My words of refusal had been spoken politely but were brusque in themselves. Philippe Chatillon stood eyeing me with a thoughtful expression, and I was glad to feel that I could now not only meet his gaze but also look away if I wished. After a long silence, broken only by faint whispering sounds from Helen and Maude, he said quietly, in French, "I believe you speak fluent French, mam'selle?"

I replied in the same language. "Reasonably fluent, m'sieu, though perhaps lacking in some of the more idiomatic expressions."

"I congratulate you on your accent. May I ask if you have discovered what I suggested you might discover when we last met?"

"I am not quite sure what you mean, m'sieu."

"I said you might find that my old friend and opponent, your father, had left you a riddle to solve, and I suggested that if this was the case I would be glad to assist you in the matter."

For the first time in weeks I thought of the letter that lay tucked away in my writing case, in my bedroom tallboy. I said nothing, but kept looking steadily at the French detective with what I hoped was an impassive stare. After a few seconds he said, still in French, "You have not answered my question, mam'selle."

"Please excuse me, but I have lost track of your question."

"I asked if you have found anything in the nature of a

riddle or cryptogram, anything which you feel may carry a hidden message."

I hesitated, and felt myself blink. Then I looked down at my hands and told a flat lie. "No, M'sieu Chatillon, I have found nothing such as you describe." I did not feel proud of myself at that moment, but at the same time I had no intention of amending what I had said.

As I looked up again he nodded slowly and said, "I see." I was very much afraid that he did see, and I was wondering apprehensively what he would say next when there came an interruption. I would have welcomed any other possible interruption, I think, but this one arose from the unexpected arrival of Lady Grainger herself, a handsome and formidable woman in her late thirties. She swept into the shop wearing a huge lilac-colored hat, staring with surprise at Philippe Chatillon and with suspicion at me. At the same time, and in her usual fashion, she was calling out a series of questions without waiting for any answers.

"Good morning. Did I hear you speaking *French*, Bridget? Why did you not tell me you spoke French? Are you being satisfactorily attended to, sir? Does he understand me, Bridget? What are you staring at, Helen? And you, Maude?"

Helen hurried forward. "Ooh, please Lady Grainger, this gentleman came in and asked for Bridget bai *neame*!" she said in a very audible whisper. "Then he asked her to teake *luncheon* with him! And when she said she hadn't taime, he wanted to escort her *home*, and then they started talking in *French*, ai think it was, and ai simply don't know *what* she was saying!"

Lady Grainger lifted her head so that she could glare down her nose at Philippe Chatillon, and drew in a long, menacing breath. But before she could speak he had turned the whole force of his easy magnetism upon her, bowing low with a gentle flourish, smiling as he straightened up, and saying, "I hope I have the honor to address Lady Grainger, for I am instructed to bring her greetings from La Comtesse de Toureilles."

Lady Grainger stopped as if her breath had suddenly been cut off. For a moment her mouth was open with no words coming from it. Then she blinked and said, "La Comtesse . . .?"

". . . de Toureilles," said Philippe Chatillon, and gestured toward me. "This young lady assisted her in the purchase of a hat and some gloves, here in your most excellent establishment, Lady Grainger, shortly before Christmas. My dear friend Marie—that is to say La Comtesse—was so delighted both with her purchases and with the attention given her, that she asked me to call while in London to purchase another pair of gloves for her." He gave a little bow in my direction. "And she insisted that I should ask by name for the same young lady who had served her."

Lady Grainger gazed at me in surprise. "You did not tell me of a visit by a *countess*!" she said indignantly.

I made a helpless gesture, no doubt accompanied by a suitable expression. I had no idea what to say, and could only reflect that when it came to telling a lie, this remarkable Frenchman showed far more imagination than I could ever hope for.

"Marie was traveling incognito," Philippe Chatillon said casually, "and Miss Chance therefore had no idea that she was serving a member of one of the highest families in France." He bowed again. "Pray forgive me for not yet introducing myself. Philippe Chatillon at your service."

Lady Grainger stared at him with interest. "How do you do?" she said, slowly recovering from her surprise. "You are actually a friend of La Comtesse, then?"

"Marie and I have moved in the same circles since we were children together." There was a hint of stiffness in the Frenchman's voice.

"Oh, quite so. Quite so," Lady Grainger said hastily. "But did she also suggest that you invite my shop assistant to luncheon?"

"Ah, no-o-o-o!" he said on a rising note, as if responding to a little joke she had made. He was smiling upon her with wickedly mischievous eyes now. "That was entirely my own idea, Lady Grainger."

I could almost see her suspicion and displeasure melting away under the warmth of his charm. She made a little pout that was very close to a simper, and said archly, "I think you are a rather dangerous man, m'sieu, and I shall certainly not allow you to take one of my shop girls out to luncheon, but I shall forgive you for such fast behavior because you are French."

He looked at her with laughing protest. "I am not so much a wicked Frenchman, my lady, as one who detests being at table alone. It is most kind of you to forgive me, but it is not enough. I beg that you will have the kindness to allow me the pleasure of *your* company for luncheon."

"Well, really, sir!" Lady Grainger's pretense of outrage did nothing to conceal her fluttery delight. "It is quite improper of you to invite a respectable married lady to take luncheon with you! What would people think?"

Philippe Chatillon looked at her with mock innocence. "I cannot imagine, madame. After all, I am a stranger here. What do *you* suggest people might think?"

Lady Grainger actually giggled. Then she looked thoughtful. "It would not be like *dining* with a man," she said, half to herself. "After all, Dolly St. Clair lunches with any man she can lay hands on, and it would be rather exciting, just for once, to mystify everybody. And Herbert won't be troublesome, he's much too busy with his wretched stamp collection." With a little toss of her head she looked boldly at Philippe Chatillon. "Where would you propose to take me for luncheon, m'sieu?"

He made an open-handed gesture, eyes sparkling. "But naturally, to a place where we shall be seen by as many people as possible, madame. The choice shall be yours."

It was then that I heard Lady Grainger laugh for the first time. "Very well," she said. "It is madness, of course, but I intend to enjoy a brief lapse from sanity. When friends or acquaintances greet me, I shall introduce you as an important customer from France."

He bowed, and crooked an elbow for her. "Delightful. Shall we go?"

"Certainly, M'sieu Chatillon." She took his arm. As they turned, he said politely, "Good day, young ladies," and all three of us responded, "Good day, sir." For a moment he was facing me, and only I could see his expression. In that moment he closed one eye in a solemn wink. Then Helen rushed to open the door for them.

When the carriage had gone clattering past the window, Helen and Maude looked at each other and at me, almost speechless with excitement. "Coo!" said Helen at last, momentarily forgetting her refined accent. "I never saw the like of that before. Never. Turned her ladyship's head proper, he did."

Lady Grainger did not return that day, and for the rest of the afternoon, whenever the shop was free of customers, Helen and Maude speculated endlessly together about the astonishing scene with the Frenchman. At first they plagued me with questions, but found me so noncommittal that they soon gave up and pursued the more exciting prospects offered by their vivid imaginations.

At ten minutes to seven o'clock that evening, as I reached Cambridge Circus, I saw Philippe Chatillon step out into the road ahead of me, take off his hat, and hold out his hand in a way which conveyed a polite request for me to stop. I did not want to, but I pulled on the brake and drew my bicycle to a halt beside him as he stepped back on to the pavement.

His face was rather serious as he said, "I must ask you to forgive me for any embarrassment I caused you this morning, mam'selle. I naturally did not expect your employer to enter just as I was talking with you."

I said, "She would have been fully informed by the other girls, m'sieu." Then I could not help smiling at the memory as I went on, "But I must thank you for the remarkable way in which you explained your presence and dispelled Lady Grainger's annoyance with me. I was somewhat in fear of losing my employment."

He nodded. "I could sense the danger of the situation, but I think you need not fear any adverse effects now."

"I am very glad."

He took something from the inside pocket of his jacket. "There were other matters on which I wished to speak with you, Miss Chance. As you know, I am a sort of policeman, and I would be obliged if you would tell me if you have been approached by this man."

I took the photograph from his hand and stared at the half-length portrait of a man in his middle thirties. He had a lean face, very wide-set eyes, and what appeared to be light brown hair, thick and short above a high forehead. I had no way of judging his stature, but gained the impression that he was of rather small build. After a few seconds I shook my head and held out the photograph to Philippe Chatillon. "No, I have never seen him. Why should he approach me?"

"Because he may think that you hold the key to great riches, mam'selle." He took a silver pencil from his pocket, wrote on the back of the photograph, and returned it to me. "Please keep this, and look at it from time to time to remind yourself of what I say now. This man is a fraud, liar, and cheat. He is also very clever and very dangerous."

Perhaps because I was so tired, the words made little impression on me. I realized that Inspector Browning and Mr. Whitely and Philippe Chatillon had all felt in varying degrees that my father must have had a hoard of valuable jewelry hidden away. For myself, I could see a measure of logic in this but felt that since nobody was ever likely to discover the truth of the supposed hoard there was small chance of it being actively sought by thieves and scoundrels of the underworld.

However, I did not want to treat Philippe Chatillon's concern brusquely, so I said, "What is the name of this man?"

He shrugged with a half smile. "Who knows? I could give you a dozen names he has used, but he can always find a new one."

Suddenly I remembered Charlie's encounter with a stranger who had asked about me, and said, "Is he an American?"

Philippe Chatillon looked puzzled. "No, but why do you ask?"

"Oh, it's quite unimportant. I was thinking of something else." Even as I spoke I recalled Charlie's description,

". . . brown face, 'air a big longish." The man in the photograph had short hair.

Philippe Chatillon said, "I regret to tell you that the man I am warning you against is a compatriot of mine. Please beware of him, and trust no word he may say to you."

I slipped the photograph into the handbag which hung from the handlebar of my bicycle and said politely, "You are most kind, m'sieu. I shall remember what you have said." My words sounded rather stilted to me, and in an attempt to be less formal I smiled and added, "I hope you enjoyed your luncheon with Lady Grainger."

"Well . . ." He considered for a moment or two. "I have no doubt she is a most formidable employer, but to tell the truth I found her quite pleasant company. However, it was not *her* company that I sought." He looked at me very directly and with no hint of smiling banter now. "It was your company I desired, mam'selle."

"Oh, dear. To ask more questions, m'sieu?" I said a little wearily, regretting that I had not ended the conversation a few moments ago. "I really do not know what you want of me, but I assure you it is not easy for me to cope with the problems arising from . . . well, from the events of last year. And I should be grateful to be left alone without distraction, to do the best I may."

For a moment he looked almost harassed as he said in a low voice, "I would be glad to help you in your difficulties, mam'selle, and I will tell you what I want of you. This is not at all the time or place, but you have left me no choice. Since I first met you near your home in Wynford I have been quite unable to forget you, and I speak now as a man of maturity, a man of thirty-two years, not a callow youth. In simple terms, I wish to call upon Miss Bridget Chance."

I stared at him in astonishment, unable to think of anything to say. After a moment or two he went on, "I have matters to keep me here in England for some time, but I would have come in any event, to say to you what I have just said, though I hoped it would be in a more appropriate place than on a corner of Shaftesbury Avenue." His smile flashed out ruefully with the last words.

I made a great effort to pull my scattered wits together and said at last, "I am . . . I am honored, M'sieu Chatillon, and taken very much by surprise."

"For that," he said quickly, "I must ask your pardon. It is a problem that you have no family for me to approach. I might have written, perhaps, but I prefer to speak with you face to face."

With his words I arrived at a decision that had nothing to do with logic or thought of any kind, and I said quickly, "I must tell you that I wish to sever all links with the past, m'sieu, and that I do not wish you to call upon me. You have been very kind, and I am sorry if I appear brusque, but I have had no time to phrase my words more appropriately, I simply wish to be left alone, and I beg you to respect that wish. Please, m'sieu."

He stood gazing down at me for long seconds with an expression I could not fathom, then nodded slowly. "I think you are a very resolute person, mam'selle, and I respect your answer. I ask only one small concession. It is that if you have need of my professional help, you will not hesitate to write to me." He slid a card from his wallet. "I have taken rooms for my stay in London, and this will be my address for the next few weeks."

I took the card and managed to smile as I said, "You are very kind, sir, and I will call upon you in case of need. I hope you will excuse me if I leave you now. I am rather tired."

"Of course."

I gave him my hand, and he raised it to brush the back with his lips. "Au revoir, Mam'selle Bridget."

"M'sieu."

I mounted my bicycle and pedaled away, thinking what an undignified way it was to end such a conversation. It was also typical of Bridie Chance.

An hour later, when Alfie and Company had left for the theater, I lay in the splendid bath, feeling the hot water ease the weariness from my limbs as I thought about the strange happenings of the day. It occurred to me that something at least of what Kate had predicted when in one of her romantic moods, and which I had treated as a joke, had actually come to pass.

Philippe Chatillon was certainly a very handsome man, and probably rich. He had not exactly asked me to marry him, but had asked if he might call upon me, which was the first step. And I had refused. I looked down the length of my too-long legs to my too-large feet, and sighed. If I had been asked why I refused I could not have given an answer, for my wish to break with the past was no more than a part of it. There was something else, and it was too deep within me to be discerned.

As I thought about what I had done, I gave a little laugh and shook my head. "What a fool you are, Bridie Chance," I murmured. It was true enough. Though my situation for the moment was far better than it might have been, this could not last indefinitely, and I was very much aware that what little money I possessed was going out at four times the rate of my meager earnings. Yet I had refused to allow Philippe Chatillon to call upon me, even though I was attracted to him and felt at ease with him.

It was very odd. A young lady was supposed to feel shy and maidenly when in the company of a man, but this was not so with me. I had known strong excitement under Philippe Chatillon's gaze, and it would have been very easy for me now to imagine him putting his arms about me and bending his head to kiss me. I knew I would have enjoyed it very much. Yet I also knew that if he came to me again in six months time with the same question I would give the same answer. As I sat up in the bath and began to soap myself, I wondered if by that time I might have discovered why.

It was at the end of February that the double disaster struck. Alfie Perkin and Company were just finishing their season of pantomime and would then be free of bookings for three weeks while preparing for a tour of the Midlands and the North. I knew that I would miss them dreadfully while they were away, and I was also troubled by the realization that five months had passed since we left Latchford

Hall and I had managed to save only two or three pounds toward the ninety I would need in another six months to cover my liabilities to Signor Peroni and Nannie Foster. I tried to hide my anxiety from Alfie and Ethel, and especially from Kate, though with her it was not very difficult since she had left her practical mood behind and now seemed to be going through a long romantic phase.

The first blow fell a few days before the final night of the pantomime, when Lady Grainger swept into the shop one morning and told me that she would not require my services beyond the end of the week. I felt ill with shock, and kept making mistakes all day long. Strangely enough, Helen and Maude showed great sympathy and helped me as much as possible. At first I wondered if my dismissal had anything to do with the Philippe Chatillon incident, but that had been long ago, and later in the day I learned from Maude that Lady Grainger wished to bring in a new girl she had rather taken under her wing, the daughter of her dressmaker. Helen and Maude had both been alarmed that one of them might be replaced, and I think their kindness to me sprang from relief that I was the victim.

When I arrived home that evening, Ethel took one look at me, then stood up and opened her arms. I ran to her, put my head on her bony shoulder, and sobbed. After two minutes I felt better, apologized haltingly, then sat down and told them what had happened.

"Miserable old cow," said Ethel indignantly. "Not fair, giving anyone the sack like that." She looked at Alfie. "How about me going along there and giving her a piece of my mind?"

"Oh, no!" I exclaimed hastily. "Please don't annoy her, Ethel. I have to work there for the rest of the week."

"No you 'aven't," Alfie said cheerfully. "You'll only be miserable as sin, and it's not worth it. Not worth Ethel wasting time on 'er ladyship either."

I was thoroughly ashamed of my outburst, and had myself under control now, so my voice was reasonably steady as I said, "But I won't get my money at the end of the week if I don't go back, Alfie. I can't afford to lose that."

"You won't, Bridie dear." Alfie leaned back in his arm-chair and spoke firmly. "You 'elp us with all that's got to be done in the next three weeks getting ready for the tour, and I'll pay you the same as what you've been paid at the shop." He lifted a hand as I started to protest. "Now 'old on, 'old on. You'll be earning your corn all right, even if you just do the cooking and look after Ethel and Charlie and me while we're seeing to the scenery an' props an' costumes an' orchestra parts an' servicing the mechanical stuff. You can 'elp with that typewriter you've been prac-ticing on, too. There's letters to be done, and lists to be made, and all sorts of things. My word, you'll be busy all right. I don't know why we never thought of this before. Eh, Ethel?"

I said, "Oh, Alfie. Are you really sure?"

"Dead sure, Bridie." He looked at his watch and stood up. "Come on, Ethel. Time we were off."

I ran to kiss him on the cheek, and said, "I do so hope that one day I can help you in some way, Alfie, in return for all you've done. I'd be so happy."

He patted me on the shoulder, then stepped back, eyes moist, smiling and embarrassed at the same time. "Well, you never know, do you? Now then, you come along with me to Drury Lane tomorrow morning, with a pencil and a notebook, and I'll 'and you over to Harold."

For a moment I could not think who he meant, but then remembered the lugubrious man from Yorkshire who looked after all scenery and props for the act. It was several weeks since I had last seen him, and then it had been for only a brief minute or two backstage.

"Don't take any notice of 'im groaning and sighing," Alfie was saying. "Harold can't stand the paperwork, he's very slow at it, and he'll be over the moon to 'ave someone like you doing everything nice and neat for 'im. Course, he'll never admit it, mind."

I said, "God bless you, Alfie. If I don't feel I'm giving you a fair return, I'll say so, and we'll have to think again, but I'd love to work for you."

All next day I spent with Harold, moving between the

Drury Lane Theatre, where Alfie and Company were appearing, and the big warehouse near Blackfriars where Alfie rented storage space for all the scenery and props used in the two sketches. These had to be dispatched by train when the tour began. One set of scenery for each sketch went direct to the theater in the first town of the tour, another set went into storage in the second town and yet another went to the third town. As soon as the booking in the first town had been completed, the scenery there would be sent on to the fourth town of the tour and this leap-frog system would be continued to the end. It called for considerable organization, but was well worth while.

"Right canny is Mr. Perkin," Harold confided to me gloomily as I sat on a crate in the wings of the Drury Lane, writing out address labels to be fixed to the scenery there. "Other folk just send their stuff on to t'next town on the Sunday, after last performance Sat'day night, like. Talk about fret an' flummox when there's anything goes amiss. But wi' Mr. Perkin, he's always got t'other sketch if there's owt goes wrong wi' first, like say the water pump, and he's never got to worry wi' the trains, because the stuff's there in store wi' weeks to spare, an' time to put things right if there's owt wrong." Harold shook his head in glum admiration. "Only one as does it like that, Mr. Perkin is. Right canny."

As Alfie had warned me, Harold showed no pleasure at having my assistance, but I noticed that as the day went on he thawed toward me quite a lot, in fact to such an extent that he shared his lunch-time pork pie with me, and even showed me his most precious possession. This was a card, kept for safety between two pieces of thick cardboard held by rubber bands. On the card was the autograph of Lord Hawke, captain of the Yorkshire cricket team.

By the end of the second day I was joyfully certain that I was being of genuine use to Alfie and earning my wages. By the fifth day all our plans were in ruins, for it was then that the second disaster struck. It happened on the Monday following the final Saturday performance at Drury Lane, which marked the beginning of our preparation time for the tour which was to start three weeks later.

At nine o'clock in the morning Charlie was walking along Holborn to buy himself some cigarettes. As he passed a brewer's dray which was being unloaded outside a public house, one of the great casks of ale slipped free from the rope holding it. The falling cask struck some thick coconut matting placed on the pavement to cushion it as it touched the ground, then bounced up and struck Charlie with great force, hurling him against the wall and breaking his right leg between knee and thigh.

Charlie did not lose consciousness, and five minutes later a bystander was at our door, panting out his tale of what had occurred. By great good fortune two nurses were making their way to St. Bartholomew's Hospital, by West Smith-field, less than a mile away. They arrived upon the scene only two or three minutes after the accident, and had taken charge by the time we came running along the road. Within an hour Charlie was in one of the operating theaters in St. Bartholomew's, having his broken leg set by one of the best surgeons in the country. Again it was a stroke of good fortune that the surgeon chanced to have a list of operations at Barts, as it was called, on that particular morning, but we were in dire need of any shred of good fortune now.

This was a day in which we scarcely knew what to say to one another or what to do with ourselves, for we were so dazed by the shock. Alfie and Ethel were allowed to see Charlie for a few minutes in the evening, and returned to say that he seemed quite comfortable but rather sleepy from medicine given him to dull the pain.

I, had busied myself making a nice dinner while Alfie and Ethel were away, and they made a good pretense of enjoying it, though none of us had any appetite and we only picked at the food. I was almost afraid to ask the question uppermost in my mind, but at last I said hesitantly, "Did anyone say how long it would be before Charlie is well again?"

They looked at each other. Ethel, gray-faced, lifted a hand to steady the wobbling chignon of her piled chestnut hair. "The sister reckoned p'raps three months if all goes well," she said, her penetrating voice strangely subdued.

"It was a clean break," said Alfie, "and she said Dr. Dawson, the surgeon, got it set very nice, so the leg shouldn't mend shorter than it was. But she says even when Charlie's up and about, say in ten or twelve weeks, he'll still be on crutches for a while, and it'll take the muscles a long time to get back to what they were. Anyway, they'll keep 'im in Barts for two or three weeks, then he can come 'ome or go to a convalescent place somewhere in the country or at the seaside. A place where they do proper nursing."

I said, "Won't that be . . . oh, please don't think I'm being inquisitive, Alfie, but won't that be very expensive?"

His rubbery face twisted into an expression of wry relief. "Well, it would be, 'cept I took out insurance for all of us about five years ago now, just after Charlie came in for Nipper Jennings. Got cover for 'ospital expenses and doctors and convalescence and suchlike for a whole year at up to five quid a week, and it wouldn't cost that much. Took out insurance for our old age, too. You should've heard the way some people laughed. They don't think much about tomorrow, not in our business they don't."

I thought how truly Harold had spoken when he described Alfie as being "Right canny." Wisdom and forethought were certainly proving their worth, but this answered only a small part of the problem. "How difficult will it be for you," I asked, looking from one to the other, "if you can't work for the next six months?"

Alfie sucked in air through his teeth and screwed up one eye thoughtfully. "Well, the trouble is, it might finish the act, Bridie. We're booked for the Moss and Thornton circuit till autumn, and their management won't be best pleased about 'aving to cancel. Besides, it's a funny thing, but if you drop out of circulation for a bit, you get forgotten. Well, it's worse really, you get looked on as a sort of has-been, if you know what I mean."

After a little silence I said, "Perhaps this is a silly question, but could you get somebody to replace Charlie for a while?"

"It's not silly, dear," said Ethel, "it's just going to be very 'ard to do. Oh, we know a few eccentric dancers who could do the funny steps and all that, but if they're good enough, they wouldn't come in for one tour an' then bow out again for Charlie to come back. Besides, there's a lot more to it than the dancing, and I can't think of anyone we know that would fit in with us nice and natural, can you, Alfie?"

He shook his head. "It's a lot deeper than it looks, making people laugh. You 'ave to what they call 'play off' each other just right. You do that, and they'll laugh their 'eads off. But if you get it just a little bit wrong, they'll sit on their 'ands."

I went to the kitchen, returned with a tray, and began to clear the table. In that time I decided this would be a bad moment for me to say I must fend for myself and cease to be a burden on them, but I would certainly have to speak soon. I had no work, and time was running out for me, but my friends had done enough and more than enough. Whatever the cost, I could impose on them no longer.

As I stacked plates and dishes on the tray I said, "What will you do, Alfie?"

He looked up, shrugged, and tried to smile. "I dunno yet, Bridie. I'm all at sixes and sevens just now, and I don't know which way to turn. It's either find a replacement, or cancel. And if we cancel, there's a good chance the act might die. I'll 'ave to make up me mind in the next couple of days, but I can't seem to think very clear at the moment."

Next morning I bought a small basket of fruit for Charlie and wrote a note to go with it, sending him my best regards and saying that I would come to see him as soon as the hospital allowed an extra visitor. Alfie and Ethel took the little gift when they went off to the hospital that evening. They returned in a mood I found hard to fathom, for they spoke little and seemed distracted. They said that the surgeon was pleased with Charlie, that Charlie himself had spent a fairly comfortable night, and that he had asked them to thank me for the fruit, but all the time it was as if their thoughts were really elsewhere.

When dinner was over, and Ethel and I had washed the dishes, I took off my pinafore and said I thought I would fetch my sewing box and do some mending. Alfie and Ethel looked at each other, then at me. Alfie rose from his chair and said, "Hang on a second, Bridie." He went out leaving the door open, and I saw him cross the hall, go into the bedroom he shared with Charlie, and emerge a minute later with some clothes over his arm. When he came back into the room I saw he was carrying the jacket and trousers of one of the several identical costumes Charlie used for *The Water Board Man* sketch. They had been brought home for mending some weeks ago, and evidently Charlie had not troubled to return them to Harold yet, since it was the other sketch that had been performed throughout the run of the pantomime.

Alfie said, "Will you do something for me, Bridie? Will you go an' put this costume on?"

I felt my eyebrows climbing up my forehead. "Put it *on*? But . . . but why?"

Ethel said, "It was Charlie's idea. It came to 'im in the night, while he was worrying about the act, and he fair burst out with it, soon as we got there. 'Bridie can do it, Ma,' he said. 'She moves right an' she's got the face, an' she'll work till she drops for you an' Uncle Alfie. She'll be top-'ole once she's got over 'er nerves,' he said. That's what he said, didn't he, Alfie?"

✦ nine ✦

I stared numbly from one to the other. At last I managed to say, "Me? Acting Charlie's part? But it's impossible! I can't act, and it's a man's part, anyway, and I could *never* do the eccentric dancing. I'd die of fright if I had to go out on the stage, and I'm sure Charlie must have been delirious even to *think* of it—!"

I went on talking agitatedly in this vein until I was out of breath, while Ethel and Alfie watched me with anxious eyes. When at last I trailed into silence Alfie said doggedly, "It's the best idea Charlie ever 'ad. We both wondered why we didn't think of it ourselves."

"But I'd be *hopeless*, Alfie!"

"No. It'll be very 'ard, but it's not 'opeless, Bridie. You've got the knack of using your face in a way that's naturally comic, like me, so that's one thing you don't need to learn."

"Oh yes, my face!" I gave a nervous laugh, and felt my eyes rolling in what must have looked like comic despair. "But there's the dancing, and that's absolutely vital to the act. The people *expect* it! If you perform those sketches with someone who can't do the Chicken Walk and the Crab Glide and all the other things, you . . . you'll get the bird! You can't possibly teach me to do eccentric dancing in three weeks!"

"I can teach you enough, if you're ready to work eight hours a day on it, Bridie. You move very nice, like Charlie said."

"I don't! I'm clumsy!" I cried indignantly.

"No you're not, dear," said Ethel. "I mean, you needn't

be. The trouble is, I expect you did a lot of what they call deportment when you were a girl, what with going to posh schools and all that, but it doesn't suit you, and you're much better moving in your own natural way, instead of sort of struggling with yourself to pretend you've got no legs."

There was a silence. I said, "But..." and stopped.

"After all," said Alfie, "you don't 'ave to speak a word in the act, do you? Now that would really be an 'ard nut to crack because you've got a soft voice, and I'd need months to teach you 'ow to reach the gods with it, even if you ever could."

Another silence. I muttered, "But..." and stopped again.

Ethel said diffidently, "It could save the act for us."

"Will you try it for us, Bridie?" said Alfie. "Please?"

I knew I could not do it. I would never have the ability or the courage to walk out into the glare of lights knowing that every move of the comic performance had to be timed to perfection or the sketch would fail. I tried hard not to remember how good Alfie and Ethel had been to me, a stranger from another world; how loyal, and generous, and affectionate. I did not dare think of the debt I owed them, for I was about to refuse them the only help they had ever asked of me.

I drew breath to speak, and my mouth said, "All right, Alfie. I'll try."

I heard the words with shock and astonishment, but there was no going back. After a long time, and with what felt like a terrible smile, I took the clothes from Alfie and walked to my bedroom.

As I went I heard him say, "Bless you, Bridie."

Ten minutes later, feeling very foolish, I returned wearing the costume: dark blue trousers, a jacket that buttoned to the neck, and a cap with a shiny peak. I had turned the trousers up a few inches, and was in stockinged feet because I knew that any shoes of Charlie's would be too big for me. My hair was pinned up with the cap perched on top.

Alfie and Ethel studied me carefully. Then without warning he glared at me, pointed down, and said in a very loud voice, "Arnold, this is what we call *a hole*."

I was startled, and must have looked it. Alfie and Ethel exchanged a pleased glance. "That's nice," he said. "Can you do that expression again, Bridie?"

"What expression?"

"The one you did just then."

"Oh. Um... like this?" My panic had faded and I felt calmer now, for I was comforted by the certainty that I would prove such a miserable failure in every respect that within a few days Alfie would abandon his plan.

"No, not quite like that," he said. "You'll 'ave to spend time practicing in a looking glass, but we won't worry about that now. You'll 'ave no trouble reaching the gods with your face, once I've taught you to keep your 'ead up, and I don't reckon it'll be too 'ard getting you to use your whole body and arms and legs for the miming, neither. It's the dancing that's the most difficult until you get the 'ang of it, so we'll start on that tonight. Let's 'ave a look at you first."

"Nice long legs," Ethel murmured as they eyed me appraisingly. "We'd 'ave to alter the costumes a bit, but that's nothing. I don't know what's best to do about the hair, though."

I said at once, "I'll have it cut short if you wish." I would gladly have had my head shaved to show my willingness, for with every passing moment I was more convinced that my own deficiencies would save me, and then at least I would not have to reproach myself.

Alfie shook his head. "No," he said firmly. "Leave it like that with the cap stuck on top, Ethel. I mean, it's no use trying to pass 'er off as Charlie. The customers wouldn't like that. We want to make a big show of 'er being a girl. Put it in *The Stage*. In a newspaper if we can get it in. I mean, it's like a special feature of the act, isn't it? She'll be a male impersonator, like Vesta Tilley, only in a Company."

Alfie's broad face was beginning to show increasing enthusiasm as he talked. "We'll get some proper boots tomorrow, and spend the day down at Mac's rehearsal 'all in Charing Cross Road. I can get Vera to play the piano for

us for a few bob." He patted my arm. "But we can make
a start tonight. Keep the trousers and stockings on, Bridie
dear, but go and take the jacket off and put on a blouse or
something light. No, better still, one of Charlie's shirts.
You find one for her, Ethel, she can't work in that jacket,
she'll be too 'ot."

It was nine o'clock when Alfie began to count slowly,
"One, two, three, four . . ." as he showed me how to perform
a step called the Crab Glide. With his bulk, he was not as
graceful as Charlie, but I was surprised to see how skillfully
he gave the appearance of floating sideways with his feet
barely touching the ground.

"It's a heel an' toe move, Bridie, see? Like this. But the
way you do it, you're really taking your weight on one leg
while you 'old your body like this, so it looks as if you're
moving on the other leg, except the foot's not touching,
see? Then you switch over, vice versa, as you might say.
Now you try it with me, ever so slow . . . one, two, three,
four . . ."

I stared down at my feet in dismay, for they had done
nothing right. Then I looked up. Alfie said, "That's a good
expression. Get the big looking glass off the 'ook in the
bathroom, Ethel, so she can 'ave a look whenever we see
a good expression. Right you are, Bridie. Again."

Again, and again, and again, into all eternity it seemed,
I tried to imitate that elusively simple movement of Alfie's
feet. After half an hour I broke into tears. Ethel said, "There,
there, dear, now don't be upset. Just keep trying. You can't
expect to learn it in five minutes, can you? Oh, just a minute,
keep your eyes screwed up like that and look in the glass
while I hold it for you. See? That's a lovely expression for
when Alfie gets cross after you pinch 'is fingers in the
stepladders, and you sort of cry. Remember?"

Alfie wiped his brow and said, "Once more, Bridie.
Now . . ."

By ten o'clock I hated both Alfie and Ethel. I had acquired what Alfie called four bars of the Crab Glide, but
the way I executed the steps was ridiculous. I knew what
to do with my feet, arms, and body, but I did it with leaden

slowness, plodding and hopping where Alfie swayed and floated.

By eleven o'clock I had discovered that what I had thought to be a whole series of steps was, in fact, a basic step repeated several times in rapid succession and with slight variations. I could now go through the movements of eight bars, enough to take me right across the average stage and back, and we were using the living room, the passage, and one bedroom—with doors open between—to get the distance we needed.

My shirt was wet with perspiration. My hair had long since come unpinned and hung limply down my back, tied with a piece of ribbon to keep it out of the way. I no longer hated my friends, I was too tired to nourish any particular emotion, and I had drifted into a strange kind of limbo, in which I simply went on doing the same thing over and over and over again without thought, for I no longer had to think what I was doing.

At half-past eleven o'clock Alfie's voice said, "Right. Again, Bridie." We moved back across the hall to the far wall of the living room and I took up the preliminary position, head back, knees slightly bent, hands in pockets (though they would come out during the third bar of Alfie's count) and my "tail" stuck out slightly. He said, "One, two, three, four . . ." and I began to move through the same steps I had now performed several hundred times.

There was something different. My mind woke abruptly to the realization that a change had occurred, though I could not have said how it had happened or what exactly it was. But I was gliding smoothly . . . almost smoothly . . . floating . . . almost floating . . . and despite all weariness my body felt lighter, more fluent, more harmonious within itself than ever I had known before. A sense of astonishment and delight touched me as I came to a halt.

Alfie said, "Not bad. Try it again, Bridie."

I tried, and the touch of magic was gone. Alfie said, "Stop thinking about what you're doing. Your feet and your body know what to do, so let 'em get on with it."

After another five attempts the magic came back, and it

remained through the next three attempts. Alfie said, "Right, you've made a good start, and it's nearly midnight. You 'op off now and have a good 'ot bath, Bridie. You'll be stiff in the morning, but Ethel can show you exercises to 'elp loosen you up, and in two or three days you'll be fine."

I slept very soundly that night, and was less stiff than I had expected when I rose next morning, perhaps because I had done quite a lot of bicycling. Minnie had prepared breakfast, as usual, and when she went off to clean the bedrooms Alfie looked up from his plate of kidney and bacon and said, "We didn't talk about money last night, Bridie. If you're going to be in the act, you've got to 'ave a proper wage. I've talked it over with Ethel, and we reckon four pounds a week an' all found."

I let my face run riot with the dazed astonishment it wanted to express, and at last I said, "But that's ridiculous!"

Ethel giggled at my expression, her great chignon swaying. "Charlie gets five pounds ten shillings," she said. "We'd make it the same for you, 'cept we know you'd make a fuss about it."

"But four *pounds*?"

"Rising to five after the first month on stage," said Alfie. He chuckled. "Don't look so flabbergasted, Bridie dear. There's plenty of professional gents like solicitors and doctors who'd be glad to pick up what a good music hall turn can get. A good 'un, mind. And that's nothing new. Blimey, I remember thirty years ago, when old Morton was really bringing the new music 'alls on strong, there was comic singers who'd been earning a guinea a week at Evans' Song and Supper Room in Covent Garden, and suddenly they were picking up thirty, forty quid a week at the Canterbury." He stirred his tea, gazing reminiscently toward the window which looked out upon Holborn. "Alfie Perkin and Company never take less than thirty-five quid a week," he said, "so when we're working two 'alls a night, or maybe three, we're doing all right, aren't we? I reckon we can afford your four quid easy enough, Bridie, and you'll be earning it all right, don't you worry."

I sat staring down the table at him, my head buzzing.

Four pounds a week was riches. Nobody in an ordinary occupation could possibly earn such a wage. Certainly it would solve all my money problems, at least for as long as it lasted. I felt torn between dread and delight, for quite suddenly the possibility of doing something I had thought I would never dare to do, of appearing on the music hall stage, had become real to me.

That day was spent with Alfie in one of several large rooms over a tavern in Charing Cross Road. These were hired out by the day or half day as rehearsal rooms. On the way we had stopped at a theatrical costumers in Drury Lane, and there Alfie had bought me three pairs of black boots. They were men's boots, but no ordinary footwear, for they were so soft and supple it was like wearing gloves on my feet as I tried them on. The lady shop assistant who served us showed no surprise at all at fitting me with men's boots. We also bought some thin woollen vests and drawers, socks, two pairs of light cotton trousers, and two loose-fitting tunics.

In our rehearsal room was a very ancient piano at which sat a plump, gray-haired lady called Vera. A glass stood on top of the piano, and on the floor beside her were three bottles of stout. Across this end of the room was an enormous looking glass. In a tiny, dingy dressing room I changed into a set of the rehearsal clothes Alfie had bought for me— vest and drawers, cotton trousers and tunic, socks and boots. My own clothes I folded into a suitcase we had brought with us, then carried this back into the rehearsal room and stood it beside the piano. "You get a light-fingered lot around 'ere," Alfie said cheerfully. "Anything that's not nailed down, they'll 'ave it."

He had traveled from home in his own rehearsal clothes, and as soon as I returned from the dressing room we began to work. To my infinite relief, I was able to perform the Crab Glide straight away, and with the almost magical effect of floating. I could see myself in the great looking glass now, and Alfie spent the first hour making me use my arms, head, and even fingers in a particular way to enhance the quaint effect of the step.

After an hour, I was suddenly able to combine all the elements of the little dance, though in a somewhat rough-and-ready way. It was then that Vera, at a word from Alfie, put down the magazine she was reading and began to play some of the familiar music that was used as a background in parts of Alfie's sketches. This seemed to help me far more than I would have expected, and I became inwardly quite excited as I watched the betrousered figure in the looking glass go skittering across the floor in a very poor imitation of Charlie.

"Right," said Alfie at last. "We'll spend 'alf an hour every day polishing that up. Now let's start the Chicken Walk, and you keep your back to the glass till you've got 'old of the steps, Bridie. Like this, watch me now . . . you do a sort of contrary movement with your 'ead and tail, see? The opposite of normal. And you straighten each leg 'ere, at this part of the stride, not 'ere, like you usually would. All right, try it with me."

After another hour's work we took a light lunch in a small pie shop not far from the rehearsal rooms, for I could not go into the tavern below. I wore my top coat over my rehearsal clothes, and drew one or two mildly curious glances, but Charing Cross Road seemed to be an area much given over to theatrical and musical people, and unusual garb or eccentric behavior attracted little attention. I saw several people costumed or partly costumed, and discovered from Alfie that they were the cast engaged in a dress rehearsal for a play called *The Lady Lawyer* which was to open at the Garrick next day.

Vera had guarded our belongings, and we brought her back two more bottles of stout to sustain her through the afternoon. After half an hour Alfie allowed me to watch myself do the Chicken Walk in the great looking glass, so that we could work on refinements of it, and then I began to practice the step to music.

By the end of the day I was tired, but strangely enough I was not nearly so leg-weary as I had been when serving in Lady Grainger's Millinery Establishment. By the end of three days I had gone on to learn the Skip Shuffle, the

Willow Strut, the Stork Step, and the Hesitation Walk, and I was able to combine them in all ways necessary to execute the various dances that Charlie performed in each of the sketches. At present I performed them badly, but it appeared I had developed something of a personal style that was funny in itself. This was quite involuntary, it simply happened. On the fourth day Ethel came to the rehearsal rooms. Alfie had asked her to stay away before, so that she could view my progress with a fresh eye, and in any event she was very busy with Harold, making all preparations for the tour.

I felt nervous, but I went through all my steps to music, and at the end of it there was no doubting the genuineness of Ethel's delight. "Oh, my word, you've done wonders, Bridie dear, you really have. My Charlie said you would, he was quite sure about it. She's going to be fine, isn't she, Alfie?"

He nodded, closing one eye in a wink. "We're going to be all right. Now let's work it out, Bridie. We'll take four more days to polish up the dancing—no, three and a half. Tomorrow's Sunday, and you mustn't miss seeing your sister Kate, so we'll make that a half day. Then Wednesday we'll 'ave to start doing 'alf a day on dancing and the rest on a sketch. We'll make it the paper-'anging one, because the water board one needs more rehearsal, getting them jets to go just right. You'll have to be 'ere every afternoon for the sketch, Ethel, because we've got to keep rehearsing it all in one go at least four hours a day, otherwise we'll never get our timing right."

That evening I went with Ethel to the hospital to visit Charlie for the first time. His conversation was as jerky as ever, but he seemed very pleased to see me, and kept assuring me that I was going to be "top 'ole" in the act.

"You make sure you 'ave plenty of practice with the props, Bridie. 'Specially the paper-'anger's paste. Mustn't get it on your boots, or it mucks up your dancing. Sticky, see? Ooh, and I thought of something else last night. Your cap. Make sure it's got a really stiff peak. I got a very thin bit of wood in mine. It's when Uncle Alfie stands you against the wall an' runs the big paste brush right down you from top to toe. If the peak's a bit floppy, you get your eyes pasted, see?"

I said, "Thank you, Charlie. I'll come again in a day or two, and I'll be glad of all the hints you can think of. I'm really very frightened."

He grinned, winked, and slid his head from side to side on a seemingly elastic neck, a movement Alfie had painstakingly taught me as part of the Willow Strut. "Course you're frightened," he said. "It's enough to frighten anyone. Tell you what I did first few times I was on. Kept thinking, 'Oh, thank Gawd I 'aven't got to open me mouth!' You remember that, Bridie. It'll 'elp ever so."

"I'm sure it will, and thank you, Charlie."

Next day, a Sunday, I went to Signor Peroni's house as usual to have tea there and spend some time with Kate. After careful thought I had decided to make this my last visit and to say my goodbyes now, so that I could spend the whole of next Sunday working with Alfie and Ethel. Every hour of practice was precious to me, and also I wanted to have my mind completely clear of everything else. Kate was still in a rather strange, absent-minded mood, but when I told her what was happening she collapsed in her chair with a fit of the giggles, hands clapped over her mouth.

"Oh Bridie, no! You mean you'll be on the stage in that sketch we saw at the pantomime?"

"Yes."

"Doing funny dances, and getting paste all over you, and—"

"Yes, dear. And getting shut in the grandfather clock, and doing silly things with the plank, and dancing with Ethel at the end. I'm playing the whole of Charlie's part."

"But Bridie, you *can't*! I mean you don't know how!"

"Well, I've been working like a mule at it, and Alfie's sure I can manage. I have another two weeks to practice."

"But won't you die of fright?"

"Quite possibly, but I shall try not to."

"May I tell Signor Peroni and the family?"

"Oh yes, of course. I was going to tell them myself, while we're having tea, because I shall be away on tour for several months, and this is the last time I shall see you for a while. We'll be traveling to Nottingham on Saturday week."

Kate looked a little taken aback. "Oh dear, I shall miss you so much, Bridie."

"I'll write to you every week, and I'll give you a list of dates and theaters so you'll know where to write to me."

"Yes, please do, I shall be so anxious to hear from you, but you won't be cross if my letters aren't very frequent, will you? I seem to be so busy all the time."

I laughed. Kate had always been a reluctant writer of letters. "No dear, I won't be cross," I said.

She looked down at her hands, gently massaging the long beautiful fingers, and said slowly, "Bridie, did Mama or Papa leave any message for us? A letter, perhaps?"

For many weeks now I had not thought of the letter left with Tom Kettle, and was not sure I wanted to speak of it. To give myself time to think I said, "A message? What makes you ask?"

"Oh . . . I was just thinking about it one day. I felt sure Papa would have left some sort of word for Mama. You know how he adored her."

In those few seconds I made up my mind that Kate was entitled to know the truth, and I said, "Yes. He left a letter for Mama with Tom Kettle, who gave it to me, but Mama was too ill to be shown it, and then she died."

"Tom Kettle?" Kate stared, then gave a funny little laugh. "Yes, I suppose it's just the kind of thing Papa would have done. Did you read it, Bridie?"

"Yes, after Mama died. It was a kind of . . . well, a love letter."

"Without any message?"

"Oh, I did wonder briefly if part of it was a cryptic message, but I'm sure it wasn't."

"Have you kept it?"

"I've got it tucked away somewhere. But why?"

"Oh, I was just thinking I'd like to see it. You can't be *completely* sure there's no cryptic message."

"Well, if there is, Mama was the only one who could possibly have understood it." I felt suddenly uneasy. "I'll look it out and show it to you when I have time, but I'm sure it's just a private letter. Now, tell me how you're getting along at the college."

Her lovely face lit up, eyes aglow, and she said, "I'm so happy there, Bridie, I really am. As for my music, well, you must ask Signor Peroni."

I felt immensely thankful that all had gone so well for her. When I told Signor Peroni and his wife what had happened to Charlie, and that I was to take his part in the music hall act, they tried politely to hide their astonishment, but with small success.

"Do you think you'll be happy, dear?" Mrs. Peroni asked. "It must be a funny sort of life for a young lady like you."

I managed to smile, and said, "Well, I'm very happy with my friends, but at the moment I'm frightened out of my wits about performing on the stage. I expect that will get better in time, though." I looked at Signor Peroni. "It's very well paid work, amazingly so, and I shall certainly be able to provide for Kate's keep for another full year by the time I return. Do you think I could hear her play before I leave this afternoon?"

"But of course." He spread his arms a little, and smiled at me. "You are not simply her sister, Miss Bridie. You are also her fairy godmother, as in the pantomime, yes?"

She played my favorite Chopin nocturne, and there was an exciting new quality in her rendering of it, even to my rather undiscriminating ear. I listened that day with every fiber of my being, and watched her as she played, for I knew it would be many months before I saw her again. I could not know that when this came to pass it would be in another country, and in circumstances so cruel for my beloved Kate that my heart would break for her.

Holborn was almost deserted and dusk had fallen as I neared home that evening. I had lit the acetylene lamp on my bicycle, and the lamplighter had just made his rounds as I passed the top of Kingsway. A man was hailing a cab a little way ahead of me, standing under the light of a street lamp and lifting a walking stick on which I caught a glint of silver. I had no more than a glimpse of his face as I passed, and I knew at once that I had seen the man before, but could not think where. He was not one of the residents in Grant Chambers, and I could not place him among Alfie's friends and acquaintances. I had certainly never seen him at the shop, and was quite sure his face was not one I remembered from Suffolk or Cambridge.

It was an irritating puzzle, and kept nagging me at intervals throughout the evening, despite the fact that we spent two hours going through various parts of the sketch to give me the rudiments of timing. At three in the morning I came suddenly wide awake with the shock of recollection. Climbing out of bed, I lit a candle and went to my dressing table. From beneath some papers in one of the drawers I took out the photograph Philippe Chatillon had given me, and stared at it. A lean face, wide-set eyes... short thick hair. This was the face of the man I had seen hailing a cab in Holborn, the man Philippe Chatillon had called a fraud, liar, and cheat. I turned the photograph over and looked at the words penciled there by the French detective in a round, untidy hand. *This man is dangerous.*

For a little while I sat wondering what to do, and then realized how foolish I was being, for there was nothing to be done. I had seen the man near my home, but doubted that he had seen me at the same moment. Certainly he had made no attempt to speak to me, either then or before. If he did approach me, I would be very wary, I would not trust him, and I would tell Alfie and Ethel all about it. Until that happened I had more than enough problems and anxieties to occupy my mind, and the best thing I could do at this moment was to go back to sleep. Yet for some while longer I sat gazing down in the flickering candlelight, studying the face, then turning the photograph over to read the words on the back.

Something was wrong. Something was amiss. It was like hearing a single wrong note in a series of chords, and not quite knowing where it had occurred. After a while I shook myself irritably, put the photograph away, and climbed back into bed, telling myself that I was letting my imagination run away with me.

By the end of the second week of my training I could have performed what Alfie called my "routine" in *The Paperhanger's Mate* in my sleep, in fact I frequently did so, but with nightmarish disasters constantly occurring. By day I was either physically going through the routine in a rehearsal room, or mentally going through it at any other time, from the moment of my entrance carrying a bucket and doing the Hesitation Walk, to the final moment of stepping out in a slow, exaggeratedly elegant minuet with Ethel, for this was the finale Alfie used for both sketches.

I no longer worried about the eccentric dancing, for I now had far greater worries arising from the hundred and one tiny details I must not forget. We were rehearsing with props now, and I had once spent two hours with a plank on my shoulder practicing to turn round at exactly the right speed to match the timing with which Ethel, her back to me, kept bending down slightly to speak to Alfie, who sat trying to get his foot out of a bucket in which it was stuck.

Each time Ethel bent, the swinging plank had to miss her piled chignon by inches. Ethel's role was always to be immensely dignified, so the plank must never touch her chignon, neither must any disaster ever befall her, yet the near escape from such business as the swinging plank always brought great roars of excitement from the audience—at least, this had been so whenever I had seen Charlie performing. I had yet to discover what would happen when it was I who was playing the part.

During the third week of my training we rehearsed the sketch in short sections all morning, going over each section time and time again. Every afternoon was devoted to going through the full sketch as much as a dozen times, but never automatically, always struggling to polish and improve.

On the Saturday we went to see Charlie for the last time before the tour, visiting him by special arrangement for a short spell in the morning, since we would travel up to Nottingham in the afternoon. Harold had already gone on ahead to do all that was necessary regarding our scenery and props, and to arrange lodgings for us, or "digs" as everybody called them.

To our great relief Charlie had suffered no complications from his broken leg. In another week, if all went well, he would be taken down to a hospital in Margate, on the east coast, where there were also facilities for convalescence. Alfie had made arrangements for him to be accompanied by a nurse and a hospital porter, and to travel on a special trolley in the luggage van.

We lunched early that day and left Grant Chambers at two o'clock. As our train pulled out of St. Pancras station I was suddenly swept with horror. What on earth was I doing? How could I ever have imagined that I might become a variety artist and replace Charlie Perkin? It was wild lunacy. Bridie Chance was a plain, clumsy girl who was prone to accidents. I had been chuckled at almost all my life, not because I was witty or clever at making people laugh, but because I was the kind of person people laughed at.

We were traveling first class, and a good tea was served in the restaurant car, but I felt too sick to eat. I was sure Alfie and Ethel knew what I was suffering, and glad that they had the good sense not to try to reassure me and allay my fears. Perhaps they knew that these were fears that simply had to be faced and endured. When we reached Nottingham we found Harold waiting with two carriages to take us with our luggage to the digs he had secured for us. He reported morosely that everything was in order and that he had made special arrangements with the manager of the Royal for Alfie Perkin and Company to have the use of the stage for two hours on Sunday morning. There would be the usual Monday morning band call for everybody on the program, but Alfie wanted us to run through the sketch two or three times the day before, so that I could get the feel of the stage where I would actually be appearing for the first time.

"You'll get no band for Sunday," Harold said flatly as we stood on the platform waiting for a porter to unload our trunks, "but I got a piano player to come from Dooley's Tavern for 'alf a crown, Mr. Perkin."

"You'll ruin me one of these days, 'arold," said Alfie. "Never mind. Did you get us decent rooms at Mrs. Pratt's?"

"Not bad. Yours isn't that big, but I got the nice double for Mrs. P. an' Miss Bridie. The one you usually share wi' Charlie."

"That's all right then, all I use me room for is going to sleep. Ah, 'allo Maggie, how are you, duckie?" The last words were addressed to a dark-haired and very nicely dressed young woman who had alighted from another part of the train and was passing along the platform, followed by a porter trundling a trolley with a large trunk on it.

She stopped and said, "I'm all right, Alfie. Sorry about Charlie, though. I hear you're using a girl to replace him?"

Alfie nodded toward me and said, "That's right. Friend of ours, Bridie Chance."

As he spoke I remembered the young woman. She was a serio-comic called Margaret Dane, and I had seen her perform from the wings of the Metropolitan, the first time I had watched Alfie's paperhanging sketch. Now, as he gave my name, she looked at me curiously and said, "Chance? Wasn't that the man who—?"

She broke off. Alfie said, "That's right, Maggie."

The young woman gave me an apologetic smile and said, "I'm sorry. Good luck with Alfie and Company."

I said, "Thank you," and with a friendly little nod she moved on.

Alfie murmured, "That bother you, Bridie?"

I shook my head. "No. It doesn't seem very important now."

"Good. You won't find it's important to music 'all people, mostly. They've got better things to worry about."

"I saw her at the Metropolitan, didn't I?"

Ethel said, "That's right, dear. She was on just after the intermission."

Alfie grimaced. "She usually is. Not much of an artist, poor old Maggie, but she's a nice girl." He looked up and down the platform. "Looks as if she's the only one except us who's traveled up today. Most of 'em will come up tomorrow, after they finish the week in London tonight. Maggie must've been resting. And what's 'olding up our luggage, I wonder?"

"Three of 'em gawping into that van," Harold said irritably. "Just look at 'em. I'll go and wake them up, Mr. Perkin."

"No, 'ang on, they're getting a horse out. Look."

We were all staring down the platform now, and I saw the most splendid mount step quietly from the open doors of a van which evidently contained a stall or horse box. It was a red roan, and it moved with the unruffled arrogance of a creature aware that it was a king among its kind. At first I could not see the man who moved on the far side of the horse, holding its bridle, but he must have saddled the animal before leading it out, for now he swung up on to its back, paused to speak to the porters, then began to move at a walk along the platform toward us.

He rode with long legs in long stirrups, wearing narrow trousers, a colored shirt, and a jacket of fine leather. On his head was a black hat, broad-brimmed, low-crowned, the kind worn by the gauchos of South America, a kind I had never in my life seen before, except in the dream which had come to me on two occasions in the dark of night at Latchford Hall . . . if indeed it had been a dream.

ten

Ethel said, "Ooh, my word! I never saw anyone like that before."

"Nor me," said Alfie. He looked toward the stranger. "He's what they call a cowboy, Ethel. You ought to know about cowboys, with all them books you read."

"I don't read books like that," Ethel said with indignation. "Ooh, I did once though, come to think of it, when I'd got nothing else and Charlie said he'd got a book I could have. By a man called Buntline, it was, and more like a magazine, really, with pictures in it. Ooh, my word, it was all about shooting outlaws and Indians and suchlike."

I was only vaguely aware of what was being said, for I was gazing at the approaching rider and trying desperately to make sure that my telltale face was not showing the astonishment, tinged with alarm, that consumed me at this moment. I could make him out more clearly now. He was tall and loose-limbed, with a very brown and weathered face. Beneath the brim of the hat I could see a thatch of straw-colored hair, rather long. He wore a moustache a little darker than his hair, trimmed short and extending fully across his upper lip before turning down slightly, in a fashion strange to me.

"I wonder what a cowboy's doing in Nottingham?" Ethel mused. "Seems funny, doesn't it, Alfie?"

"Well, it would," agreed Alfie, "if it wasn't this bloke Nathan McFee."

"Who?"

"Yankee bloke. Jimmy Samuels, the agent, was telling me about 'im. Says he does a novelty act with a horse and a lasso. You know, a rope. Jimmy says it's a real eye-opener. He's well down the bill for this tour, because he's new, isn't he? But Jimmy says give him a year and he'll be up in the top five."

I could see now that the man's eyes were vivid blue. There were crow's-feet at the corners, as I had seen on fishermen in Southwold, men accustomed to staring out over the long emptiness of the sea. His manner as he rode was completely relaxed; I had never seen anyone appear more placid. He had a nose which looked as if it had been broken at some time, a thin white scar from just below one temple to halfway down his cheek, and a square chin, clean-shaven.

I might have said anything in my surprise, but being Bridie Chance I said something quite trivial and meaningless. "That's not an American cowboy hat. It's a gaucho hat."

Alfie said, "Eh?"

I did not answer, for the man had almost reached us, and now he inclined his head in our direction, lifted a lazy hand to the brim of his hat, and said, "How do, ladies." The blue eyes rested amiably on Alfie. "Sir."

Alfie said, "Hallo, friend. Nathan McFee?"

The man smiled, reined to a halt, then swung down from the saddle and took off his hat. "Recognized you, Mr. Perkin. I've seen your act more than once. Didn't figure you'd know me, though." His voice was deep and drawling, with a pleasant twang that reminded me of the voice of the American girl I had known at Girton.

Alfie said, "Jimmy Samuels mentioned your act. Where you staying, Mr. McFee?"

"Jimmy fixed for me to lodge with a lady name of Mrs. Pratt while we're in Nottingham." Nathan McFee pronounced it Nottingham.

"Ah, you'll be all right with Ma Pratt," said Alfie. "Very nice theatrical digs. Always stay there ourselves." He glanced at two porters who were now arriving with our trunks and cases. "We've got a couple of cabs waiting, so we'd be glad to take any luggage for you."

Nathan McFee studied Alfie quietly for a moment, then

gave a little nod of acknowledgment. "That's real neighborly of you, but I guess I have the habit of traveling light." He indicated his saddlebags with a movement of one big brown hand. "Got my main needs with me, and I figure to buy anything else I want as I go along. Be glad to follow your cab, though, if you'll allow. Save me hunting around for where Mrs. Pratt lives."

"You're welcome. And we all 'ope you 'ave a big success with your act, Mr. McFee."

"Why, thank you, sir." He considered for a moment, then went on, "I'm new to burlesque, or music hall as you folks call it, and I've no great ambitions in that direction, but I always hankered to see your country, and this is a way of earning a little money while I do it."

Alfie laughed. "You're lucky to 'ave an act at your fingertips, then."

The porters passed us with their trolleys. Nathan McFee hung back with Alfie, bowing slightly as Ethel and I inclined our heads and followed the porters. In a procession we made our way along the cobbled path of the station exit, and I heard Nathan McFee say, "I was sorry to hear about the accident to the young feller, sir. That was real bad luck."

"It was an all," Alfie agreed. "Still, we got a first-class replacement for Charlie."

"A girl, Mr. Samuels told me."

We halted by the two cabs. Alfie said, "That's right, and this is the young lady 'erself." He snapped his fingers in annoyance. "There. I'm forgetting me manners, not introducing you proper. This is my sister Ethel, Charlie's mum, and this is an old friend of the family, Bridie Chance, who's taking Charlie's place for the time being."

Again Nathan McFee gave a little bow. "Mrs. Perkin. Glad to know you, ma'am. I greatly admire your comedy work." The blue eyes rested on me, and I could read nothing in them. "Miss Bridie. Pleasure to make your acquaintance, and I wish you all the luck in the world, ma'am."

Ethel blushed and looked pleased. I dropped a small curtsy, caught a heel in the hem of my dress, and would have overbalanced if Nathan McFee had not shot out a long arm to catch me by the elbow. It was astonishingly quick for a man who moved in such a leisurely fashion. I should of course have tried to remain dignified, but before I realized it I had sighed, rolled up my eyes despairingly, and was saying, "Oh dear. Thank you, Mr. McFee."

He grinned slowly, but his eyes were friendly as he released me. "My pleasure, ma'am." He leaned down to pick up the hat he had let drop to save me from falling. As he slapped it against his thigh to dust it, I voiced yet another remark of complete irrelevance by saying, "Surely that's not a cowboy hat, Mr. McFee. Isn't it a gaucho hat?"

Alfie said with a touch of pride, "Bridie's very educated. She knows about things."

Nathan McFee looked at the hat thoughtfully. "That's correct, Miss Bridie," he said. "It's a gaucho hat, but I guess a gaucho is a cowboy anyway."

"Yes, I suppose so. Do you come from Argentina then, Mr. McFee?"

He shook his head. "No, ma'am," he said amiably. "I was born in Wyoming, but I'm a wandering sort of man, and I once spent a few years down on the pampas south of Gran Chaco." He lifted the hat to put it on, and smiled. "Always liked myself better in this than a Stetson."

Harold had finished supervising the loading of the luggage. He looked at the stranger with some disfavor and said, "I wouldn't wear one of them if you paid me. You play cricket in America?"

"Cricket? Now that's a game I've heard of, but I don't know too much about it, friend. Can't say I ever came across folks playing it anywhere I've ever been back home."

Harold gave a faint snort. "Well, there you are, then. All right, Mr. Perkin, I'm ready, aren't I? We going to hang around all day?"

Mrs. Pratt's boarding establishment was a tall, four-story house no more than half a mile from the Theatre Royal, where we would open on Monday. The room Ethel and I were to share was large and pleasant. It had no running hot water, but a maid brought a large copper container of piping-hot water within five minutes of our arrival. There was an ample washstand with a screen for privacy, and a bathroom at the end of the passage.

Ethel chattered away happily in her rather shrill monotone, needing no comment from me. I remained quiet, and thought about Nathan McFee. Or rather I wondered what to think about him. It was extraordinary that I should have dreamed of a night rider in a gaucho hat at Latchford Hall, and now I had met a horseman who wore just such a hat and must surely be the only man in England to do so. It was even more extraordinary if what I had seen earlier had not been a dream.

Ethel's voice penetrated my consciousness. "I don't know about you, Bridie, but I'm not going to stay up late tonight. We've all been working ever so hard, and I reckon we could do with an early night, what with all that's to be done tomorrow."

Tomorrow. Sunday. The day of special rehearsals for Alfie Perkin and Company, the last day before I would have to face my dreaded ordeal. At once everything else was swept from my mind, and I could almost feel the blood chill within my veins. Nathan McFee and his hat ceased to exist for me, and I was in the grip of raw fear once again.

At ten o'clock on the Sunday morning I was on the stage at the Theatre Royal, looking out over the tiers of empty seats in stalls and pit, looking up to circle and gallery, trying to coax my perverse face into one of the often rehearsed expressions, only to find that it seemed to have frozen and become completely expressionless for the first time in my life.

Again and again we went through the sketch, with Alfie and Ethel using soft voices rather than the penetrating pitch required for a real performance. A half-drunk pianist called Reg pounded on the piano at appropriate moments, while I mimed, danced, grimaced, and tried not to wish that it was I who had broken a leg rather than Charlie.

Toward the end of the morning I passed through the barrier of despair to a gray limbo where I no longer cared about anything, and then things began to go better. For the last two rehearsals we put on costume and went through the sketch completely, using props, and with no breaks.

Alfie seemed not to be too displeased. "It's much 'arder when you've got no people out front," he said. "I mean, they're part of it, really. You get a sort of response going between them an' you, and then you can time everything better. It'll be different with an audience, Bridie, you'll see." I was quite certain it would be different with an audience, and it was this difference that terrified me, but Ethel chatted away quite cheerfully and seemed not to be worried as we left the stage and made our way to the dressing room allotted to us.

The size and position of a dressing room depended on the reputation of the performer, and ours was considered to be quite large, though it seemed tiny to me. We could not have two dressing rooms for the Company, and though Ethel and I could have used a communal ladies' room, or Alfie a communal men's room, we had decided to share. Each night, Alfie would put on his costume and make-up well before we were called, then would leave the dressing room so that Ethel and I could get ready.

After the performance the order would be reversed, for I would be liberally coated with paste, as I was now. Ethel and I would go straight to the dressing room, where there would be a screen across one corner with a small hip bath behind it, filled with warm water as part of Harold's duties. There I could strip off my costume, which Harold would take away later for cleaning and pressing. In the hip bath I could sponge myself thoroughly clean, then put on my own clothes, transforming the paperhanger's mate into Bridie Chance again.

All was ready for me as we finished the rehearsal, and while I sat in the bath Ethel called, "Did you get any on your hair, dear?"

"No, it's all right, thank you. Alfie's very good, he jerks my cap down hard just before he runs the brushful of paste down me, and that keeps if off my hair. Oh Ethel, I'm so frightened about tomorrow."

"I know 'ow you feel, dear. But you just 'ave to go

through it, Bridie, then you get used to it, and sometimes it's really lovely when you've done a nice performance an' you're taking a curtain call. You feel all the applause and 'appiness coming at you because you've made 'em laugh, and it's ever so nice. What would you like to do for the rest of today, dear?"

"I don't know . . . yes, I do, I'd like to go into the country for an hour or so. Except from the train, I haven't seen any countryside for so long, and I do miss it."

"All right, dear, we'll see what Alfie says, but I'm afraid he might be too busy to take us."

We found Alfie still onstage with Harold, discussing details of lighting, scenery, musical cues, and prompting. He was uneasy about our scenery, feeling that the size of the stage called for "the room" to be opened up a little by having the side walls more widely angled.

"You say that every time we play Nottingham," Harold sighed dolefully.

"Well this time we'll *do* it instead of just talking."

"But it's going to muck up Miss Bridie's distances," protested Harold.

"She can manage," said Alfie. "Matter o' fact, Miss Bridie can use a bit more distance, with them long legs of 'ers. She's a bit cramped, I reckon."

"Well, it'll take all day," declared Harold gloomily.

"Then let's get on with it. Yes, Ethel? You wanted me?"

When Ethel said we would like an afternoon in the country Alfie shook his head with the first sign of impatience I had ever seen him show. "Blimey, 'ave a heart, Ethel, I got too much to do. Can't you two go on your own?"

Ethel said, "Well, we don't want to be shut in a cab, Alfie. I thought you could hire a phaeton and take us somewhere."

I began to say, "No, please don't bother, Alfie—" when a voice spoke from the back of the theater, a drawling American voice. "Hope you'll pardon me for butting in, Mr. Perkin, but I'd be happy to escort your two ladies. I had a fancy to look at some country myself today."

We peered across the tiers of seats, and saw the tall figure of Nathan McFee rise to his feet. He was hatless now, wearing a white shirt with a dark green neckerchief.

Alfie called, "Hallo, young feller. Didn't know you were 'ere today."

The tall man strolled down the center aisle, hat in hand. "Came along to get the feel of the house, Mr. Perkin. Didn't want to intrude, so I just sat there and watched that last rehearsal of yours." He reached the orchestra pit and stood looking up at us, smiling placidly. "Wasn't easy to keep from laughing out loud all through it." He looked directly at me. "You're going to be fine, Miss Bridie. Just fine."

I felt a small thread of hope, a spark of prayerful relief, come to life within me, and I returned his smile with a glow of pleasure. "I hope you mean that, Mr. McFee."

"I do, ma'am."

Alfie scratched his head and said, "What about it, Ethel? Do you and Bridie want a run out with Mr. McFee here?"

Ethel had blushed slightly and was almost simpering. "Ooh, well, yes, that would be ever so nice, wouldn't it?"

"I'd count it a pleasure," said Nathan McFee. He looked at Alfie. "They have open carriages for hire at the livery stable where I keep Lucifer. I could be ready for the ladies as soon as they finish lunch, and I'll take good care of them, Mr. Perkin. I'm a fair driver."

Alfie grinned. "I bet you are, son."

At two o'clock he was waiting for us outside Mrs. Pratt's boarding establishment, and he had evidently inquired about a route, for within thirty minutes we were moving slowly along a grassy broad walk in woods where early buds of spring were beginning to speckle the dark branches. Ethel had chattered almost without pause for the first twenty minutes, and then had relapsed into a sleepy silence. Nathan McFee drove with a sure hand and spoke little except to murmur occasionally to the horses, seeming well content to look about him in that easy way of his, taking in all that the countryside had to say to him.

Gradually I began to feel more at ease myself, with the peace and beauty of the early spring day helping to slacken the tautness within me. I was glad we had come into the country, and I drew in long breaths of good air such as I had not tasted since leaving Suffolk. After half an hour the sun broke through some thin white cloud, bringing a pleasant warmth to the afternoon and dappling the greensward with shadow from the branches of the trees.

Nathan McFee half turned and said politely, "Will it trouble you ladies if I smoke?"

Ethel roused and said, "Not at all. I like a nice tobacco smell, really."

"Miss Bridie?"

"Please do."

From under his jacket he produced a cigar which he clipped between his lips, then with the same hand he produced a match which he struck on his boot. His head was turned almost in profile to me, and as he lit the cigar I saw that it was thin and dark, like the stubs I had twice found in the grounds at Latchford Hall.

A kind of untroubled wonderment possessed me as I sat looking at those broad shoulders, remembering the two occasions when I had seen or dreamed of the night rider, being startled the first time and strangely comforted the second time. But I asked no questions now, for I could not think how to begin.

Ten minutes later he drew the horses to a halt where the broad walk ended in a cluster of small paths. Climbing down from the driving seat he began to stroll slowly back and forth, drawing on the cigar every now and then, and looking about him with quiet appreciation. As his gaze touched mine, I started to speak, but he lifted a finger and nodded toward Ethel, beside me. When I turned my head I saw that her eyes were closed and she was dozing, even though sitting upright. I had often seen her do this at odd times of day. She could simply close her eyes, drop her chin on her chest, and fall asleep for ten minutes or so. Alfie had once said rather proudly, "I reckon she could sleep standing up, like a bloomin' 'orse."

I reached out a hand toward Nathan McFee, and he helped me to step down from the phaeton. As we moved away a little I said quietly, "I think you would like to stretch your legs, Mr. McFee, and so should I. Perhaps we could walk awhile."

"A pleasure, ma'am."

Keeping within sight of Ethel in case she woke, we strolled for perhaps a hundred yards along the grassy path in silence, yet it was not an awkward silence. As we turned I said with a smile, "We're both very quiet today, Mr. McFee."

"I hope you don't think me impolite, Miss Bridie. I figured you were busy with your own thoughts, and I didn't want to intrude."

I heaved a sigh and made a wry grimace which brought a sudden twinkle to his eyes as I said, "I'm busy worrying about going onstage for the first time tomorrow, and I should be only too glad if anyone would intrude, but I thought perhaps you were a man of few words."

"Well, sometimes, I guess. Other times I can be real talkative." We were strolling back along the path now, and he was looking all about him with the same air of quiet pleasure I had noticed before. "Maybe another reason I didn't say much was because I was busy taking everything in. First few weeks I was in England I fell in love with your countryside." He drew in a slow breath as if savoring the air. "I know deserts and mountains and plains, and they're all good places to be, each in its own way, but your woods and lanes, your little fields and small hills and green grass, they've bewitched me, Miss Bridie. I just want to go on looking and looking."

His blue eyes were warm as he gazed about him, and I knew he had been speaking from the heart as I said, "Do you not have this kind of countryside in any parts of America?"

"Oh sure, ma'am. They tell me New England's much the same as here in many ways. It's a part I've never seen, for I've lived and worked mostly in the West, apart from a spell down in Argentina." He smiled suddenly. "But I'll surely go take a look when I get back to the States, and if it's all they say, then that's where I'll hope to buy a nice farm one fine day when I settle down, where the land's green and gentle, and nothing's too big, and the flowers smell good."

I said in surprise, "Why, Mr. McFee, you're quite a romantic."

He laughed. "Most cowboys are, ma'am. They all dream dreams."

We stopped a little way short of the phaeton where Ethel was still sleeping bolt upright, and turned to retrace our steps again. I said, "Well, I hope your particular dream about a farm in New England comes true, Mr. McFee."

"Thank you, Miss Bridie."

"You don't seem to be worried about your performance when we open tomorrow, but of course you're not a beginner, like me. Were you apprehensive the first time?"

"If I wasn't, I guess it was because I don't have the job of making folks laugh, thank the Lord. I'd sooner get kicked by a mule." He chuckled and shook his head, the thick fair hair glinting. "No, I just go on and do what I can do easy enough. Spin the rope, do a few tricks with Lucifer, and that's all. But this job you've taken on for Mr. Perkin would scare the living daylights out of most folk, if you'll excuse the expression."

"Oh, it scares whatever you said out of me, that's true enough. I'm only doing it because I owe it to Mr. Perkin."

"That's courage, ma'am. And you've shown it in other ways, too."

"Other ways? I don't understand."

He hesitated. "Well...I hope I won't offend you by speaking of it, Miss Bridie, but I know your story."

We strolled in silence for perhaps fifty paces before I said, "You mean you have read what was published in the newspapers?"

He nodded. "I was in England at the time. It must have been very tough for you." He looked at the stub of the cigar and tossed it away. Watching it arc through the air and fall to the greensward, I remembered seeing the small fiery glow in the darkness from my bedroom window, and then the trail of sparks curving down to the ground.

I said, "Mr. McFee, have you ever been in the village

of Wynford, in the county of Suffolk?" As I spoke I halted and turned to face him, so that he could do no other but follow suit.

Looking up into his face I saw a flash of wariness, then it was as if a veil had come down behind his eyes as he said consideringly, "Wynford? Yes, I reckon I could well have passed through thereabouts while I was up in Suffolk last year."

"May I ask where you were staying, Mr. McFee?"

"Little place called Thetcham, as I recall, ma'am. It was just at the time when the trouble hit you, and that's when I read about it."

"Did you have Lucifer with you?"

He smiled placidly. "Sure. We'd been appearing at a music hall in Norwich, and after that we were resting for a while, so we stayed to have a slow look at Suffolk."

"For no other reason?"

His eyebrows lifted a little. "What other reason were you thinking of, ma'am? Like I said before, I fell in love with your English countryside."

"Yes. Please forgive me for being so curious, but do you make a habit of riding at night?"

"Oh, sure. It's a different world at night, and a new experience. When I was on a cattle drive I always liked watching over the cows at night. Excuse me, but you're looking mighty fierce, Miss Bridie."

"Oh, I'm sorry. No, I'm not sorry. I really must ask you—did you ever ride through the grounds of my home, Latchford Hall, by night?"

He appeared to think hard for a few seconds, then nodded slowly. "That's possible, ma'am. I might easily let Lucifer just wander where he fancies for a while." He looked at me anxiously, but the veil was still there. "Hope I didn't upset you by trespassing?"

I had asked a whole string of questions, and now I suddenly found myself with nothing more to say. Nathan McFee, an American who had once been a cowboy, and who had a liking for wearing a gaucho hat, had been staying at Thetcham, five miles to the west of my home, when disaster had come upon us. He liked the English countryside, and occasionally rode out at night. I had twice seen him in the grounds of Latchford Hall, seemingly because his horse, Lucifer, had simply wandered in.

It was all quite possible, but I was strongly convinced that there was more to it than Nathan McFee had told me. I studied his brown face for a few seconds longer, trying to read it, but his look of polite patience revealed nothing to me. At last I said, "Is there anything more you can tell me, Mr. McFee?"

He shook his head. "Why, no ma'am. There's nothing more to tell. Since we're going to be neighbors for a while, I felt it right to tell you what I knew, and that's all. Don't think me a pushing kind of man, but I hope maybe you'll look on me as a friend."

A chord of wariness sounded deep within me. From nowhere came the thought that Nathan McFee could make a very good friend, but he could also make a very frightening enemy. I put the thought aside, smiled, and said, "Thank you, Mr. McFee. Are you sure it doesn't trouble you to offer your friendship to somebody whose father was the notorious Roger Chance?"

To my astonishment he threw back his head and burst into quiet laughter that could only be genuine. "Why no, ma'am, it doesn't trouble me at all," he said after a moment or two. "You see, my pa was the notorious Hank McFee."

I blinked, rummaging through my memory, but the name meant nothing to me. "I'm sorry. Should I have heard of him?" I asked.

"I doubt it, ma'am. He was only wanted in two states, and I don't figure he'd get into your newspapers over here. As bank robbers go, he wasn't very successful."

I think my mouth fell open then. When I could speak I said, *"Bank robber?"*

Nathan McFee nodded, amusement still dancing in his eyes. "That's right. He robbed three banks, all told. Just used to tie a neckerchief over his face, walk in with a forty-five in his hand, and tell them to hand over the money."

"Oh, dear." I felt utterly confused. "Er . . . where did all this happen?"

"Well, first one was in Elson, Wyoming, and he picked a time when they'd just locked up the day's money and gold dust in their safe, so he got away with about twenty dollars. Second bank he tried to rob was in Santa Marta, and one of the tellers pulled a gun and let fly, so Pa just ran for his horse and got out of that town quick as a whip."

"Oh, Mr. McFee, I'm sure you're joking with me."

"No, ma'am. That's how it happened, according to what he told my ma and she told me later. I was just four at the time, and I don't really remember him. We had a patch of ground outside Blackwood, but he got tired of hard work and left my mother to do all that while he went off robbing banks. Third time was in Loganbridge, and he got away with a real big bag of gold dust, but then his old horse went lame and he had to leave it and hide in a dry gulch, because there was a posse after him."

I did not know some of Nathan McFee's words, like "forty-five" and "posse," but could guess their meaning from the context of his story. I said, "Did he give up after the third time?"

"Yes, ma'am, he gave up sure enough, because that posse found him in the dry gulch, and they strung him up from the first tree they came to on their way back home."

I put a hand to my lips. "They . . . hanged him?"

"That's correct, Miss Bridie."

"Oh, how . . . how dreadful for your poor mother."

"She was a mite upset at the time, she told me, but she'd been pretty sure that's how he was going to finish up, and she kept telling him so all along. Anyway, she was too busy trying to scratch a living out of our patch to have time for fretting."

I shook my head slowly. "It all seems so strange, so different . . ."

He inclined his head. "We're a new country, and a big one. There hasn't been time yet for us to have settled ways of doing things, like you have here. Besides, this was thirty years back, when everything was a lot more primitive than it is now. But I can tell you this, Miss Bridie. Outside of a few snob families who reckon they came over with the *Mayflower*, nobody gives a cuss that my father was a bank robber. Over there, you start fresh when you're born, so I'm judged as Nathan McFee. Myself. Good or bad."

I think I would have gone on to ask about his mother and his years of childhood, but at that moment Ethel's high-pitched monotone pierced the quiet woods. "Bridie! Mr. McFee!"

As we walked toward her she waved an arm but made no attempt to alight from the phaeton. "Time to go, dear," she said as we drew near. "It's getting a trifle chilly, I think." She looked at the tall man beside me. "Thank you for taking Bridie for a little walk, Mr. McFee. I'd have come myself, but I just felt like closing my eyes for a few minutes. I wasn't asleep, you know." Ethel always claimed not to have been asleep whenever she woke from one of her upright naps.

As we drove back to our lodgings, my thoughts and feelings were in great disorder. Against a background of fears and imaginings to do with my performance next day, I was digesting what I had learned of the man who sat in front of us now, holding the reins. Nathan McFee had shown me every courtesy and had offered his friendship, but shadowy doubts hung in my mind. I was quite sure that almost all he had told me was true, but I was equally sure that he had been less than truthful about the reason for his presence so near to Latchford Hall at the time of disaster. And I did not want a friend I could not fully trust.

I dreamed wild dreams that night, and spent the next day feeling physically sick with nervousness. In the morning there was a band call for all the artists appearing in the program. We did not go through the whole of our various acts for this, only those parts where orchestra cues or musical tempo were important. Ethel was not needed for the band call, but Alfie persuaded the conductor to run through my eccentric dancing routines twice, which was a notable achievement.

I could eat no lunch that day, and felt quite unable to sit still. My stomach was tight with apprehension, and every nerve in my body seemed to be twitching and jumping. At the same time I was furious with myself, for the worst that could happen was that I should utterly fail to play my part, yet my terror could scarcely have been greater if I had been awaiting a tumbril to take me to the guillotine.

Ethel was reading a book, and I was standing by the window, trying with trembling hands to work a piece of embroidery in the corner of a handkerchief, when there came a tap on the door. Ethel took off her spectacles and called, "Come in." The door opened and Nathan McFee stood there, holding a small box and a flat rectangle of board. He took half a step into the room and said, "Hope you'll forgive the intrusion, ladies, but I've been sitting wondering to myself if maybe Miss Bridie plays chess."

Ethel said, "Ooh, how nice. I'm sure you do, dear, don't you?"

I pricked my finger and said, "Well, I used to play a little, but I wasn't very good, and I couldn't play at the moment."

"Whyever not, dear? There's nothing special to do."

"But you like to have a sleep for an hour," I said desperately.

Nathan McFee lifted a hand in protest. "I wasn't figuring to trouble Mrs. Perkin. It's quiet down in the sitting room, and we could play there."

"No. Really. I mean, I was never very good at chess, and today I can scarcely think what I'm doing."

He smiled. "Then you're just the opponent for me, ma'am. I play a terrible game. I learned when I was a boy, and most of the folks I've met since then were more inclined to poker, so I've had only myself to play against. Could you spare half an hour, Miss Bridie? I'd sure appreciate that."

I was drawing breath to refuse with abject apology when Ethel said firmly, "Go along, Bridie. Off with you. I can't take my nap with you flitting about like a grasshopper every other second." I was completely taken aback, and before I knew what was happening Ethel had jumped up, taken the embroidery from me, and was ushering me to the door, assuring Nathan McFee in her birdlike trill that there was nothing I would like better than to play a game of chess with him.

I was still dazed when we settled in a corner of the big sitting room and Nathan McFee unfolded the worn board. He set out cheap wooden chessmen, polished by much handling, and gave me the white pieces to play. "Trouble is when you play against yourself," he said, "you always know what the other feller's planning. This is going to be different, and I'm really looking forward to it. Your move, Miss Bridie."

I had played occasionally at Girton with one of my friends who was a good player. She had told me that I had little idea of how to win at chess, but that I was rather difficult to beat. After a while I came to the conclusion that Nathan McFee was much the same sort of player. We gnawed away at each other, occasionally exchanging a piece, taking longer and longer between each move, muttering an apology from time to time for being so slow, until eventually we were both reduced to three pawns, a rook, and a bishop. I suppose one good player would have finished the game very quickly, or two good players might have agreed on a draw, but we plunged into a prolonged end-game in which I finally made a mistake which allowed Nathan McFee to queen one of his pawns, and soon it was all over.

We laughed together and sat back. I looked at my watch and saw to my astonishment that an hour and a half had passed in which I had ceased to feel that nerve-racking terror of what lay before me. But it was lurking, waiting to pounce, and I said quickly, "I hope you have time to give me my revenge, Mr. McFee."

"Surely, ma'am. And if I'm not making too bold, I'd be glad to have you call me Nathan. I think you'll find stage folk are not quite so formal as others."

I smiled. "Yes, I've noticed. I think Harold is the only person who addresses Alfie as Mr. Perkin. Please call me Bridie, if you wish."

"I'll feel honored, ma'am. Bridie it is."

As he set out the pieces for a new game I sought for a quick distraction to hold down the thrust of fear, and said, "Who taught you to play chess when you were a boy?"

"My mother." He smiled. "Ma was a woman with a good education, and she wasn't going to have me grow up without schooling, so she gave me lessons five hours every day till I was fifteen. Used to have to get up before dawn for two hours' studying. Then another hour after eating around noon, and another two before supper." He shook his head, still smiling. "I hated it till I was about twelve, then somehow I got to like it."

"She must have been a very brave and determined lady," I said. "Is she still alive?"

"No. She died when I was seventeen."

"Oh, I'm sorry."

"She was pretty much worn out, I guess. I greatly admired her as I grew older."

I said, unthinking, "It seems strange that she—" I stopped short, angry with myself for being so tactless, but he smiled as he set out the last of the pieces on the board.

"Strange for an educated woman to marry a no-good bank robber? I guess it was, Bridie. My mother came of a good family. Farming folk up in New Hampshire, and she was sent down to Boston for her schooling. But when she came back, she felt she was being ridden on a rein so tight she couldn't breathe. They were strict folk, very strict . . . and by all accounts Pa was a man who could charm a bird off a tree."

Nathan McFee shrugged his big shoulders. "Ma never said a lot about it, but I think somehow he got her to fall so hard in love with him she just hadn't got a mind of her own for a while. Anyway, he'd come from out West and was working on their farm. She met him, and then they went on meeting secretly I guess, and she believed all his great talk about how they'd go away together and start a new life." He centered a pawn on its square, and looked up at me with quiet eyes. "It happens, so they tell me.

Sometimes a young lady can get swept right off her feet by a man who's real bad underneath."

I said, "Did your mother run away with him?"

He nodded. "They ran away, got married, and the family disowned her. She soon found that Pa was a wastrel who used her like a drudge, and she spent the rest of her life bringing me up and scratching a living from the patch of ground they bought with her own money, all she had."

I felt suddenly quite near to tears, and said, "How terrible for her. Do you never feel bitter on her behalf, Nathan?"

He shook his head slowly. "The way she taught me was different. You do what you want, but you pay for it. I'll say one thing, though. I'm real proud of the way she stuck out her chin and paid." He leaned forward and moved the white king's bishop's pawn forward one square. "This is the McFee Special opening gambit. I worked it out one night when we were bringing a herd up to Santa Fe. Come on now, Bridie, do your worst."

Within three minutes I was absorbed in the new game. It followed much the same pattern as before, except that the end-game went on longer and we were both so reduced in strength, with no pawns left, that we decided it would take better players than we could ever hope to be if a win was to be achieved, and we agreed on a draw.

I looked at my watch again, found that it was five o'clock, and stood up. As he rose with me I said, "Thank you, Nathan. I think you're a very kind man."

To my surprise he looked suddenly uneasy, and dropped his eyes to stare down at the black queen he held in the palm of his open hand. "You have a generous heart, Bridie," he said quietly, almost as if speaking to himself, "but don't be too ready to trust folk." Before I could say anything he looked up and gave me a quick smile. "Thanks for the games, and good luck for tonight. I'll be wishing you well every moment."

eleven

I stood in the wings, my heart thundering so loudly in my ears that I could barely hear Ethel talking beside me, or even the orchestra playing furiously while two jugglers tossed glittering clubs at each other in front of a drop scene with a circus background painted on it. Behind this I could see Harold and two stage hands working quickly but without flurry to set up the scenery for Alfie Perkin and Company. They could complete the whole thing, with all props in place, in less than two minutes, and could strike everything in one minute as soon as our performance ended.

The orchestra struck a long loud chord, the jugglers took their bow, the audience applauded, the curtain came down, and on each side a bewigged footman moved out on the apron stage to change the number in the frame, so that everybody would know that Mr. Alfie Perkin and Company were about to appear.

Beside me, Alfie patted my shoulder, said something I did not take in, then moved onstage. Ethel, in a too-large dress with a monstrous floral pattern, touched her cheek to mine and followed him. When the curtain rose, Alfie the paperhanger and Mrs. Prendergast, the lady of the house, would be discovered in the "room" that was to be decorated, discussing how it could be done without disturbing the portrait of the late Mr. Prendergast, which she would not permit Alfie to move. There were thirty seconds of dialogue before the cue came for me to enter.

I stood alone, though there was all the usual bustle of offstage activity going on behind me. Harold stood ready with the props I would need. My hair was pinned up securely on the crown of my head, with my large cloth cap perched on top. I wore a shirt with the sleeves rolled up, a short gray woollen scarf knotted in front of my neck and tucked into the shirt, trousers with thin legs and a baggy seat, and a short decorator's apron splotched with paint. The trousers were inches short of a normal length, to show my ankles and boots. Beneath the shirt a band of linen was laced round my chest to flatten my bosoms, which were quite large. "You've ever such a nice shape there, dear," Ethel had said, "but you bounce about a bit when you dance. I know we want people to realize you're a girl, like Alfie said, but we don't want to overdo it."

My mind was blank, and I could remember nothing. No cues, no moves, no steps, no business. The orchestra played our introduction, the curtain rose, and there was a burst of applause. As it died away, Ethel's splendidly penetrating voice lifted indignantly in the over-refined tones which always reminded me of the girls in Lady Grainger's Millinery Establishment.

"You may say what you laike, Mr. Perkin, but ai will nevah allow mai late 'usband to be moved. Nevah."

Alfie turned from her, pushing back his bowler hat, and I knew he was using his rubbery face to show the audience eye-rolling despair. There was laughter, quickly hushed as they waited for the next words.

"All right, Mrs. Prendergast, we'll just cover 'im up, then."

"Cover 'im *up*?" Ethel's spirelike chignon seemed to wobble with indignation. She used almost no facial expressions at all, but seemed able to convey everything with her voice and her head movements. "Mai word, he would never forgive me, Mr. Perkin. Most laikely turn in 'is grave."

The words became a blur in my ears and I knew I was dreaming, for unreality possessed me. Frozen, unable to move, I watched the two strangers on the stage, and heard the man call, "Arnold! Fetch the bucket, lad!" Now he was climbing the stepladders, as I had seen him do so often in other dreams. Somebody was jabbering furiously in my ear.

On the stage, the man on the steps said, *"Now* what's become of him? Ar-*nold!"*

I shivered. This was different from my usual dream.

The strange woman with the piled hair lifted her voice. *"A-a-ar-nold!"*

The audience guffawed. A hand slapped my face and I jumped. Harold. Jabbering. Thrusting the bucket into my hand. "You're on, Miss Bridie, you're *on!"*

Oh, dear God.

Reality exploded about me. I seized the bucket and next moment was moving onstage, passing behind the open-ended wall of the scenery so that I would enter by the door, stepping out in the curious gait of the Hesitation Walk. I was entering from the prompt side of the stage, and from the vast black cave beyond the footlights on my left came a blare of sound, part of it from the orchestra picking up the accompaniment to my walk, and part of it laughter from the towering creature with a thousand eyes which crouched beyond, huge as a mountain, unpredictable as an avalanche. The audience.

Sweat was trickling down my neck as I strutted through the doorway, swiveled on one foot in a clownish way which brought another guffaw from the darkness, put the bucket down at the bottom of the steps, swiveled again, came face to face with Ethel for the first time, recoiled in startled alarm, and floated back across the room on rubbery legs in a reverse Skip Shuffle.

Alfie called, "We'll want the plank too, Arnold."

Circle the room and out through the door, using the Willow Strut. My mind almost closed, my face and body worked by instinct now, doing all those things which have become automatic by hundreds of repetitions. Take the plank from Harold. Alfie and Ethel continuing their dialogue. Onstage again with the Stork Step, plank on shoulder. More laughter. Not huge, but laughter. No boos or silence.

Remember Charlie's advice. Think: "Thank God I don't have to open my mouth!" A tiny slackening of the fierce tension that grips me. Into the room. Alfie has just descended the steps and got his foot stuck in the bucket I placed there. Begin the business of swinging the plank, missing Ethel's chignon by inches each time she bends to help Alfie. Count the tempo inwardly, hearing the clash of the cymbals. Turn-two-three, look surprised two-three, turn again two-three . . .

Alfie's foot is free. Dialogue. I keep quite still so that all attention is on Alfie and Ethel for this part of the sketch. Laughter. Mrs. Prendergast goes out to make tea. Business of starting to paste and hang paper. Accidental papering over the portrait, which is unglazed. (We have scores of them, crudely painted by a man in Battersea for two shillings each.) Peel the paper off, and half the paint comes away from the portrait. Frantic mixing of paint to restore the portrait ourselves, before Mrs. Prendergast returns. Ludicrous result, disaster follows disaster. Miming, dancing, dialogue. An absurd outcome, in which Alfie is left with no alternative but to propose to Mrs. Prendergast and thereby provide her with a new husband. The familiar ending, with Alfie playing his clarinet while I dance a slow, ridiculous minuet with Ethel.

I have been onstage for a hundred years in eight minutes. The curtain falls, and rises again when we have lined up to take our bow, with Alfie in the middle. Once more. Alfie says sharply from the corner of his mouth, "Cap off, Bridie. Pull the pins out and shake your 'air loose."

Startled, totally bemused, weak with relief, I obey as we move out between the two front curtains, or "tabs" as everybody calls them. Steady applause. The feel of the audience is good. I am pulling out the pins, and now shake my hair loose. A sudden extra surge of applause.

Alfie mutters, "Don't let's milk it." He takes my hand, passes me across in front of him and off between the curtains. The same for Ethel. One quick solo bow and he is off before the applause has died. We are in the wings at last. My legs are like jelly and I am sagging with exhaustion, sticky with paste. I am also crying now. Behind a pastoral drop scene, Harold and the stage hands are striking the scenery and clearing the big protective tarpaulin off the stage. In front of the drop scene two comedians are playing one-string fiddles. Alfie's big arm clamps about my shoulders. "Well, there you are then, Bridie!" I turn and cling to him. "Oh, Alfie, can you ever forgive me for missing my first cue? And then I didn't get the business with the fruit bowl right, and—"

"Bridie dear, you made four tiny mistakes, but we covered 'em. You'll never do the same again. There's a few places where we want to tighten things up a bit, but that's nothing." He held me gently away, his face split in a great grin of relief and delight. "You didn't bring the 'ouse down, and nobody's going to offer you a solo spot at the top of the bill, but I'll tell you something, Bridie girl. I reckon you were just a bit better than Charlie when he made his first appearance. Right, Ethel?"

Ethel beamed and flung her arms around me. "It's true, dear, honest it is. You've got that funny little style, all your own, and it's really ever so comic." She stepped back to look at me, and I saw that her eyes were moist with tears. "I know it wasn't our best performance, because we were all a bit nervous, weren't we, Alfie? But it'll get better and better now we've broken the ice, you'll see."

Ten minutes later I was sitting in the hip bath behind the screen in our dressing room, cleansed of paste and grime and perspiration, barely able to keep my eyes open with the huge sleepiness that had descended upon me. I felt limp as a rag doll, and was inclined to giggle now and again, as if my stupor had been caused by drink.

Ethel was highly amused, and also kept giggling as she helped me to dry myself and get dressed. Later, while we were waiting backstage for Alfie to take off his costume and make-up, Nathan McFee approached. He was dressed ready for his act in black trousers with silver buttons down the legs, a red shirt and a white neckerchief, carrying his gaucho hat in his hand.

"Been looking out for you to congratulate you, Bridie," he said, smiling.

I pulled myself together. "Thank you, Nathan. I very much want to see your act . . ." My voice trailed away as I set my teeth against a huge yawn.

He said, "Another time, Bridie. Good night now, and good night to you, Mrs. Perkin." He moved away toward the men's communal dressing room, and as he did so Alfie appeared, dressed ready to leave.

"What a nice young man that American is," said Ethel.

"M'mm..." I could hold the yawn back no longer. "I wonder why he said...what was it, now? Oh yes...said I mustn't be too ready to trust people. You know, Ethel, it was almost as if he was...talking about himself."

Then my mind stopped working, and I left it to Alfie and Ethel to take me home as if I were a sleepwalker.

I slept late next day, and ate heartily when I woke. Beneath my all-pervading sense of relief I was well aware that only the worst of my ordeal was over, for already I was beginning to worry about tonight's performance, and I wondered if music hall artists ever became so experienced that they felt no apprehension at all.

When I put the question to Alfie he grinned. "It'll get easier, Bridie, but I'll tell you one thing—the day you don't feel a few butterflies in your tummy just before you go onstage, that's the time to pack it in. If you don't feel a bit strung up, you 'aven't got the juice to make a real impression on the audience, if you see what I mean."

I nodded, for I could see very well what he meant. "Yes, Alfie. No wonder a real performance is more tiring than half a dozen rehearsals." I looked across at Ethel. We were the only three left at Mrs. Pratt's breakfast table now. "Shall we go shopping today, Ethel? I'd like to buy myself a new dress, to celebrate my debut." I giggled as I said the last words.

Alfie tapped a finger on the table. "You've 'ad nothing new since you came down to London, so you're going to buy yourself a whole new wardrobe, young Bridie, and at *my* expense. Blimey, I've got to say thank you some 'ow, haven't I? But you won't find time today, because I've booked a little 'all for us to rehearse in this afternoon, and every afternoon for the three weeks we're playing 'ere, plus a few mornings as well, p'raps."

I wanted to do three things at once. To protest about his paying for my new clothes, to thank him for the thought, and to ask why he had arranged three weeks of rehearsal. Perhaps my face conveyed a medley of these thoughts, but all that came out of my mouth was, "Rehearsals?"

"We'll be doing the Water Board sketch 'alf the time we're playing Sheffield, dear," Ethel trilled placidly.

I pressed my hands to my cheeks and stared frantically from Alfie to Ethel. "Oh, dear Lord," I whispered at last, "I'd completely forgotten the other sketch. Alfie, I'll never do it, I'll never be ready in time—!"

"Don't talk daft," Alfie broke in amiably. "It's just the same steps, and your dancing is first chop, Bridie, real gold. We've got to practice the business and the timing, so that means setting up the water tank and using the jets. It's tricky, but you're not starting from scratch, like before, and we've got a week *longer* for this than for the other."

In the event, I was glad that my days were busy during the first three weeks as a member of Alfie Perkin's company, for this allowed me little time to worry about the evening performances, and made the familiar paperhanging sketch seem relatively simple.

As I stood in the wings waiting for my cue on the second night I was full of trepidation, but in no danger of panic, and by the end of the first week my fears had dwindled to little more than a quickening pulse, a dryness in the mouth, and a tight feeling under the heart for perhaps half an hour before the callboy banged on our door and shouted our names.

On the third day Ethel and I went shopping in the morning; and that same evening, after I had bathed and changed following the sketch, we joined Alfie and slipped into some seats the house manager had arranged for us at the back of the stalls. We waited until after the intermission to do so, for though nobody would have recognized me as "Arnold," almost anybody would have known Alfie or Ethel at once, and we did not want to attract attention.

Nathan McFee was the second act after the intermission, and was billed in the program as "Nathan McFee—Wild

West Artiste." When the footmen displayed his number in the frame I felt almost as nervous as if I had been about to appear myself. The curtain rose, and he was already onstage in his splendid gaucho costume, black hat tilted back on his head, brown face impassive above the white neckerchief, great silver buttons that adorned the trouser legs glinting in the lights. The orchestra was playing a brisk, cheerful little melody I had not heard before.

He held a white lasso, some of it coiled in his left hand. His right hand held the rope near to a wide noose at the end, and he was using that part of the rope as if it were a spoke to turn the noose, which was spinning parallel to the floor. With a seemingly casual jump he was in the center of the rope circle, spinning it faster and at the same time feeding more rope into the noose so that it expanded, whirling round him at waist height, white against the black backcloth. The noose grew smaller again, then began to bounce, shooting up above his head and falling almost to the floor, yet still spinning smoothly all the time.

After several more tricks with the noose spinning parallel to the ground he flicked it into a vertical position and began to move it rapidly from side to side in front of his body, giving a kind of butterfly effect. Slowly the noose expanded again, spinning on his right now, until it reached from just clear of the floor to above shoulder height. Next moment he had made a sideways jump through the elongated noose, bringing it to the other side of his body and instantly jumping again and again, passing the noose back and forth each time.

I glanced at Alfie, saw him shaking his head, and found it easy to guess why. After each trick, the audience had started to applaud, but Nathan had not once stopped to take a bow before starting the next trick. This was a mistake, for it made everything he did look too easy, and it tended to stifle any response from the audience. I knew that his act was timed for six minutes, and judged that almost four had passed before the orchestra crashed out a final chord as Nathan let the flying lasso spin away from him and vanish into the wings. He stood to take a bow, not center stage but near the side I had learned to call o.p., meaning "opposite prompt."

The audience applauded. Lucifer appeared from the wings upstage, saddled and bridled, carrying a coiled rope in his mouth. He looked at the audience, moved forward, butted Nathan gently from behind with his nose to send him staggering aside, then went down on one knee as if taking the bow himself. The audience roared and clapped. Lucifer stood up and carried the coiled rope to Nathan, who shook out the noose and started to spin it round himself like a crinoline hoop. Then, quite suddenly and astonishingly, he sprang into the saddle without using a stirrup and without disturbing the spinning rope.

Quickly the noose expanded to encompass both horse and man, rising and falling as Lucifer moved in a small circle round the stage. The noose grew larger still, for this was a longer rope, and at last Lucifer could move no more for the great circle of rope occupied the whole stage from orchestra pit to backcloth. Then, to a splendid galloping tune, the curtain swept down on the scene.

Nathan came out and took a bow to satisfactory applause. When he did not appear again for a second bow the applause dwindled quickly. Alfie nudged me, and we slipped quietly out of our seats.

"It's clever all right," Alfie said as we rode home to Mrs. Pratt's in a growler. "It's clever, and novel, and a good spectacle, but I reckon it could be polished up to look twice as good. A lot of the timing's wrong, and he don't use that horse nearly enough. Still, if he's not in it for a career, there's no point in saying anything, I suppose. None of our business anyway."

On the following Wednesday I was free all day until the evening, for Alfie decided it would be good for us to have a break from rehearsal. Nathan hired a horse for himself, put me up on Lucifer in a pair of corduroy rehearsal trousers, and took me riding in the woods for most of the morning. Perhaps the countless hours of dancing had given me a better sense of balance and co-ordination, for I was surprised to

find that I was much more at home in the saddle than I had
ever been before, and I greatly enjoyed myself.

In the afternoon I wrote letters to Kate and Charlie. The
letter to Charlie was much the longer, for in it I spoke of
all kinds of details to do with the sketch and with rehearsals
for the new sketch. I also wrote to Mr. Whitely, thanking
him for his kindness at the time of my worst troubles, telling
him of my good fortune, explaining what I was doing now,
and asking him to treat this as confidential. I did not want
to revive the story of the Chance family by setting tongues
wagging about the astonishing phenomenon of Bridie Chance
becoming part of a music hall turn.

After three weeks at the Royal, we moved on to Sheffield,
traveling on the Sunday. I was in a state of some apprehension about my first performance in the Water Board
sketch, which we would start in the middle of our second
week there, but again Alfie had arranged a full rehearsal
on the stage for the whole of the preceding Sunday morning.
My fears were nothing like so great as they had been on
that terrifying first night at the Royal, and in the event, the
sketch went down very well.

By the time we came to appear at the Empire, in Hull,
I had six weeks of onstage experience, and I was cautiously
confident that I could play my part in either sketch without
letting Alfie and Ethel down. Every week I wrote to Charlie
and Kate. Every week I had a lovely letter from Charlie,
the grammar hopeless, the spelling atrocious, but letters that
delighted me and brought tears to my eyes with their un-
bounded friendliness, their invaluable advice, and their en-
thusiastic reassurance.

I had two rather hasty letters from Kate during those first
three bookings. They were very loving but did not tell me
much. In the second letter she again spoke of the letter Papa
had left for Mama, asking me to make a copy and send it
to her when I had time, as she would like to see if I was
right in thinking it contained no cryptic message.

I did not want to do this. In fact I had a strong aversion
even to reading the letter again myself, though I would have
found it difficult to say why. After thinking it over, I wrote

in my next letter that I felt unhappy about doing what she suggested, but that when I returned to London I would bring the letter with me to Signor Peroni's house so that she could read it.

In our second week at Newcastle, and ten weeks after my first heart-stopping appearance on the stage, I was suddenly aware of a subtle yet very positive change. It happened during my longest piece of dancing foolery in *The Paperhanger's Mate*. In those moments I knew that in some strange way I had moved into another class; that until now my work had been adequate but rather labored; that in fact Alfie and Ethel had been carrying me through by a score of tiny responses and reactions, pointing up my strengths and covering my weaknesses.

On that night in Newcastle it was as if all I had learned and practiced suddenly became a part of me. I had never floated so deftly, with my feet seeming not to touch the floor. I had never glided so smoothly, or run without moving forward so effectively, or undulated, swayed, tottered, or strutted so freely and effortlessly.

The applause was very big that night, and became even louder when I shook my hair out to show I was a girl. In the wings, as we came off, Alfie gave me a great hug, grinning from ear to ear, and said, "Now you know! Blimey, you got there quick, Bridie. Some people never do."

Nathan always watched us from the wings now. He came to me, smiling, took my hands and said, "That was a humdinger of a performance, Bridie. You really laid them out with laughing."

The magic stayed with me all through our booking in Newcastle and then in Edinburgh, but any pride or overconfidence I might have felt was soon to be dispelled. On our third night at the Gaiety, Glasgow, as we waited to go on I could see that Alfie was furious and Ethel upset. Harold, too, was glowering as he came off after setting up the scenery for our act. In front of a drop scene with a military background, a Scottish comedian called Jackie Blair was finishing his turn by playing the bagpipes as he marched up and down. The applause had begun already, and was deafening. This comedian had joined the tour for Edinburgh and Glasgow only, and for these bookings he had so far played the last turn before the intermission, which was a very good position on the program.

As we stood in the wings I did not ask why there had been a change of order, for I did not want to distract Alfie, or myself for that matter, just before going on. In fact, I was never to learn the cause of the change for that one night only, but I was soon to learn the disastrous effect of it.

I could not judge whether the Scottish comedian was good or not, for his accent was so broad I had been unable to understand more than one word in six of all he said, but the audience rose to him and he took six curtain calls before the applause finally ceased. When the curtain rose for Mr. Alfie Perkin and Company there was complete silence, and as the moments passed the silence continued except for an occasional mild ripple of laughter from a handful of people here and there.

After four minutes I was in a state of utter desperation, and I could see that Alfie and Ethel were in no better case. We were working as we had never worked before, fighting to reach the audience. I could see sweat trickling down Alfie's face, could feel it running down my body as I clowned and mimed, could see the straining tendons of Ethel's neck quivering as she struggled to keep her voice up.

We did not get the bird when our ordeal ended at last, but there was no more than a patter of applause as the curtain came down and then rose for us to take our bow. When it fell again, Alfie signaled for it to be lifted no more, and we took no call in front of it. As we came into the wings I burst into tears. Nathan was coming toward us, but Alfie waved him away. He hesitated, and then to my relief he turned and walked quietly off. Ethel leaned against the wall beyond the proscenium with her eyes closed, exhausted.

I stammered, "I'm sorry, Alfie, I'm so sorry, but I don't know what I did wrong—"

"You did nothing wrong, Bridie." He put his arm round my shoulders. "It was that blooming 'alf-wit of a house manager, Kincaid."

"Ought to be shot," said Ethel angrily, her eyes still closed. "Fancy doing that without telling us."

"Telling us what?" I asked, wiping a blob of paste from my lips.

"About changing the program," said Alfie grimly. "Blimey, he ought to know that when you play the Glasgow Gaiety there's no English act *anywhere* that can follow a top Scotch comic like Jackie Blair. It's plain murder, that's what it is. Only place for someone like Jackie when he's playing Glasgow is last before the intermission or last turn." He breathed in hard through his nose, then abruptly the anger vanished from his face and he grinned at me. "Never mind, Bridie, it's an experience, and you didn't break. You worked like a Trojan. Now off you go with Ethel and get changed. I'm going to find Mister blooming Kincaid and shake 'im till 'is 'orrible Scotch teeth rattle."

I never knew what passed between Alfie and the manager, but for the rest of the booking we played in our original position on the program, and all was well. Certainly I was very nervous for a few days, for it had been a chastening experience and had taught me how different one audience could be from another, and how a seemingly minor change could have a profound effect.

From the day we opened in Leeds, on our way south again, we were a great success. The magic of movement was always with me now, and not only in my miming and eccentric dancing onstage. For the first time in my life I seemed no longer to be clumsy. It was as if my mind and body had never fully understood each other before, but now were at one.

To my joy, Charlie was now on his feet again and was to join us in Manchester. His leg had mended well, and he had been following a careful course of exercise to strengthen the muscles. To add to my joy, Alfie had said that there was no question of my leaving the act as soon as Charlie returned. I was to continue for the rest of the tour, and meanwhile Alfie would rewrite the sketches to incorporate an extra character.

I was astonished when he first told me of this, and said,

"Oh, that's unfair to you, Alfie dear. It just means you'll have the extra expense without getting any extra fees."

"Don't you believe it, Bridie." He folded his face in a splendid wink. "Look, first of all I can't stand waste, so I'm not 'aving you go back to a shop. Second, you an' Charlie'll play off each other a real treat. Third, it's about time we put a bit of new life into the sketches, and this is a perfect chance. And fourthly, you needn't worry about the money, young Bridie, because there's been a lot of extra pull with the act because of you being a girl. I've never pushed 'ard for money, so if I go for an extra fiver or tenner they'll pay it all right, don't you fret."

When I reviewed my situation I felt quite overwhelmed by the good fortune that had come my way. I had acquired a new family of which I was immensely fond. I was earning six or seven times as much money as most girls of my age, or most people of any age for that matter, so I was able to take care of Kate and Nannie Foster. Our music hall act was a success, and I was becoming more experienced all the time. Charlie would soon be well again. My inward scars from the dreadful and wounding shocks of last summer were fading. And in Nathan McFee I had a friend and companion with whom I was never ill at ease, and whose soft drawling voice told tales of his life in the Americas which I found of endless fascination.

And yet... despite all this I found to my shame that I was often troubled by a profound melancholy stemming from some nameless cause. I made great efforts never to let it show, but during our time at Leeds and again during our first week at Manchester both Nathan and Ethel asked me on more than one occasion if there was anything wrong.

In Manchester I was able to offer an excuse with some truth in it, for the second day there I received a letter from Signor Peroni. Kate's letters had been few and erratic, but Signor Peroni had written to me regularly once a month and I had answered with equal regularity. In his latest letter he wrote that he was somewhat anxious about Kate. This was a time when she should be making a big step forward in the technical aspects of her playing, but instead of working harder than ever she had become, as he put it, ". . . at times contrary, and antagonistic to discipline."

He went on to say that this was not unusual in a young person struggling to reach a higher level and perhaps fearful of failing, but he was concerned that she seemed secretive about her companions and fellow students at the college, and wondered if I could write to her and try in a discreet way to find out if she was under some disruptive influence there. I spoke of this to Alfie and Ethel, also to Nathan, as an excuse for those moments when I might inadvertently let a gleam of my inner melancholy show through, but truth to tell I was not greatly surprised or disturbed by the letter. I knew how capricious Kate could be, and felt sure the mood would pass more quickly if nothing was said or done.

I wrote a reassuring letter to Signor Peroni, saying that he should not be distressed by the situation and that I did not feel it would be wise for me to question Kate by letter, however discreetly. I told him that in another six weeks our tour would end, and on my return to London I would have a serious talk with Kate.

During our first week in Manchester I had another letter, sent on from Grant Chambers by Henry the porter. It was from Nannie Foster, a rather rambling letter in which she said that she was nicely settled in her cottage and keeping well. There were new folk in Latchford Hall, and people had now stopped asking her about the Chance family, since she never answered such questions anyway. She ended by saying that she hoped she was not too great a burden on me, and that she prayed every day that either Kate or I would come to see her soon.

When I showed the letter to Alfie at breakfast that morning his mobile face creased itself into a thoughtful look and he cocked an eye at the ceiling. "That gives me an idea, Bridie. You'd like to see her, wouldn't you?"

"Well yes, but—"

"Right, then. Now look, Charlie comes up next weekend, and I want to get 'im back into good shape. I'll do a week of rehearsals with 'im, and then he can take over from you for the third week while you go off to Suffolk for two or three days to see your old nannie. You take over again for Birmingham, and when the tour's finished, we'll spend a month changing the sketches to get both of you in, like I said. What d'you think, Bridie?"

"Oh my word, it's a splendid idea, Alfie. I could go to see Nannie midweek, spend the night and a full day with her, and come back the day after."

"Good-oh. You don't mind Charlie taking over for a week?"

"Mind? Why, it's Charlie's part I've been playing, and I think it's very good of him to let me finish the tour. Besides, I want to see him play, to watch his performance. I shall be seeing it differently now, of course, and I'm sure I can still learn a lot from him."

"That's settled, then. Oh, and you get paid for the week just the same, Bridie."

"No, you mustn't, Alfie—"

"Don't argue, young lady. Alfie Perkin pays his company fifty-two weeks, working or resting."

It was two days later when I discovered the cause of my strange melancholy, and it began when I came off after a good performance to find Nathan, in the wings as usual, leaning against a tall crate and chuckling so much that he found it hard to speak.

I said, "What is it, Nathan?"

He shook his head. "Just . . . just you, Bridie." Another splutter of laughter, rare in a man of so quiet and steady a manner. "You were tremendous. So darned funny. Lord knows I've seen the act often enough now, but you really caught me under the ribs tonight."

I smiled, and thanked him, and went to take my bath, but melancholy was like a stone within me. As I sat in the hip bath, sponging myself free of paste and grime, I suddenly knew the cause. In a small way I had become a successful clown, and this was how everybody saw me. Even to my fellow artists I was a funny girl. I had often noticed that they would laugh at some comment I made which was not meant to be particularly amusing. I was Comical Bridie Chance . . . smothered with paste, falling into a barrel of water, strutting, gliding, miming with monstrously exaggerated facial expressions. This was how the people of my small world saw me, even Nathan.

But I was a girl. Not pretty or clever, but still a girl, not the ludicrous and capering "Arnold" of Alfie Perkin and Company. And here was the root of my melancholy. As a girl, I longed to feel that one day I would be loved and wanted by a man I loved and wanted in return; but in my heart I had felt, without realizing it, that this could not come to pass for a girl who was a clown.

☙ *twelve* ❧

Charlie came up on the Sunday, and we met him at the
station that afternoon. He looked very smart as he alighted
from the train in a cream suit and boater, and I think we
were all watching anxiously to see if he showed any hint
of a limp when he moved. As we hurried toward him, with
Nathan following, Charlie stopped, blinked, mimed surprise
and alarm, then went floating back on those long elastic
legs as lightly and easily as of old.

I almost wept with delight, and made myself hang back
so that Ethel and Alfie could greet him first. She reached
up to hug him, moist-eyed, and said reproachfully, "Fancy
you wearing your best cream suit on a train journey. You
got no sense at all, Charlie."

"Oh, sorry, Ma."

She stepped back. "You all right now, then?"

"M'mm. Fine, thanks. I did tons of exercise. You
know. 'Allo, Uncle Alfie."

"Glad to see you, Charlie. I booked a hall for rehearsals
next week."

"Ah, good." Charlie peered past his uncle, beaming at
me. "'Allo, Bridie."

I went forward, put my arms round his neck and kissed
him, making him blush to his ears. "Hallo, Charlie. You're
looking wonderfully well."

"Thanks ever so for all the letters, Bridie."

"Thank you for yours."

"Going all right, then? You know. The old . . ." He undulated to one side with the Crab Glide, doing it so perfectly
that I realized I was still a novice by comparison, but I did

225

not mind that. Laughing, I lifted my skirt a few inches
above my ankles, and glided across on a parallel course
with the same movement. I suppose that six months earlier
I would never have dreamed of doing such a thing, even if
I had been capable of it, because I would have been too
concerned about what anybody who saw me might think.
Now I did not mind what anybody thought, for I had accepted that I was a kind of female comic and there was
nothing I could do to change myself.

As I finished the glide facing Charlie again I answered
the question he had half spoken, half acted. "Well, I'm no
match for you, Charlie dear, but I'm always trying to improve."

His eyebrows shot up and his peaky face was alight with
pleasure. "No match? You're 'aving me on! Crikey, that
was top-'ole, Bridie. I'm dying to see you do the act."

"You will, tomorrow. And I shall be very nervous,
knowing that you're watching, but never mind, I'm getting
used to being nervous. Now come and meet a friend of
ours. Nathan, this is Charlie Perkin. Charlie, this is Nathan
McFee. He's on the program with us, and he does a
marvelous turn with a lasso."

Nathan extended a hand. "Glad to know you, Charlie."

"Oh—er—pleased to meet you." Charlie blinked, and
his eyes flickered toward me with an almost panic-stricken
expression.

Nathan said, "Surely we've run into each other before,
somewhere?"

"Eh? Did we? No, I don't think so. Don't remember,
anyway. Ah, 'ere's the porter with me luggage. You got a
cab, Uncle Alfie? We in digs with Mrs. Curtis as usual?
I'm dying for a cup of tea."

I could see that Charlie was greatly disconcerted by the
meeting with Nathan, and I wondered why. It was not until
after we had taken tea at Mrs. Curtis's boardinghouse that
I had the opportunity of a private word with him, when I
came out of the room I shared with Ethel and found him
lurking on the landing.

"Bridie!" He spoke in an urgent whisper, looking over his shoulder. "Is Ma in?"

"No, she's gone down to play cribbage with Mrs. Curtis' father."

"Can I come in for a sec? Something to tell you."

"Yes, of course."

It was a large room, with our two beds curtained off at the far end. Charlie would not sit down, but drifted across to stand by the window that looked out over a tangle of roofs and small gardens. I stood with my hands on the back of a rather well-worn easy chair, and said, "What is it, Charlie?"

He gave a jerk of his head, and muttered hoarsely, "I didn't dare say, but that's '*im*!"

"Who?"

"Bloke I told you about! Him at the station! Oh, blimey. I thought he was going to say about . . . you know." He half crouched, extending his left arm and looking along it while moving his right hand back and forth. For a moment or two I was baffled, and then I remembered.

"Oh, billiards? You mean the billiard hall?"

"Shhh!" he hissed frantically. "Don't want Ma to 'ear! That's what I was afraid of, wasn't I? Him remembering that's where he'd seen me."

"Who, Charlie?"

"Him! The Yankee! You know. Bloke with the horse, asking about you!"

"Oh!" The mists of bewilderment cleared suddenly, and I felt rather shaken as I said, "You mean to say that Nathan, Mr. McFee, is the man who spoke to you in the billiard hall in London, who asked if I was courting?"

"M'mm, that's '*im*. I keep telling you, Bridie."

"Oh . . . well, I expect there's a perfectly natural explanation, though it's surprising he hasn't said anything to me. I shall ask him about it."

"Oh, crikey, don't do that!"

"But why not?"

"Same reason I kept quiet at the station! He must've

forgot where we met, and I don't want 'im remembering the billiard 'all and spilling it to Ma!"

"I don't think he's the kind of man who would forget having spoken to you, and where," I said doubtfully.

Charlie ran a hand through his spiky red hair. "Well, I dunno. But please don't say anything, Bridie."

It was impossible to refuse. I smiled and said, "All right, Charlie, I won't say a word. And if Nathan ever speaks to me about it, I'll make sure he won't mention the billiard hall in front of your mother."

He exhaled a long sigh of relief. "Thanks ever so, Bridie. You're the best girl I ever knew."

"That's very nice of you, Charlie."

"I'd better 'op along now."

When he had gone I reflected somewhat ruefully that since he spent all his spare time in a billiard hall Charlie could have known very few girls with whom to compare me. Then I sat down and thought about Nathan McFee. Over the weeks and months of the tour we had become good friends, but I had to acknowledge that Nathan had certainly concealed from me the fact that he had asked questions about me in London long ago, and this brought a sadness upon me.

I did not go to the rehearsal hall to watch Charlie begin his practice next day. After being right away from music hall for almost six months he would have much hard work to do to achieve his best form, and I knew it would be distracting for him if he had to begin with me watching him. I was very nervous myself at the thought that he would be watching my performance that evening, but when we came off at the end of *The Paperhanger's Mate* I felt I had not disgraced myself or let him down.

Charlie had chosen to sit in the audience, but he was backstage before Ethel and I reached our dressing room. His rather pale face was one huge grin of delight, and he was almost speechless with enthusiasm. "Cor, Bridie, you were...it was...you know...I never thought...eh, Ma? Honest, though...you were topping. First class. A-one. Oh, crikey. Yes."

I glowed with pleasure, for this was praise from a past master in the art. Then I had to thrust back a familiar pang of melancholy at the thought that the art he was praising me for was the art of clowning.

It was on the Saturday evening, during the last performance I was to give before Charlie took my place for the next week, that calamity befell Mr. Alfie Perkin and Company, right in the middle of our turn. We were doing *The Water Board Man*, and were only three minutes into the sketch when a valve stuck in the water reservoir offstage, and the jets failed.

I froze with horror, for the business with the jets of water was the basis of the whole sketch, and I was bending over the supposed hole in the ground, waiting to be struck in the face by a jet of water which would not come. A quick glance into the wings on the prompt side showed Harold wrestling with the connections to the churn which held the water, and Nathan moving to help him.

Nothing happened. Next moment I heard Alfie's foghorn voice saying, "'Allo! Look at these ants crawling all round the 'ole. I'll go and fetch some paraffin. You watch out they don't bite you, Arnold."

I took my cue, and sprang back as if in alarm. As I did so, Alfie muttered from the corner of his mouth, "*Dance, Bridie!*" and strode off. The sweat of fear broke out all over my body, just as it had on the night we had died the death on the stage of the Gaiety, Glasgow. Then I slithered sideways and began to perform a dance with the theme of trying to avoid hordes of ants which were running about the garden, and which I feared might crawl up my trouser legs. I did not improvise any new steps, for that would have been beyond me, but I strung together all that I had learned, modifying the steps to fit the theme of the dance, and miming appropriately.

Ethel was simply splendid. As I glided, tottered, and fluttered around her like a great lunatic puppet, she turned her head slowly to watch, face frozen in a hilariously haughty expression, chignon quivering with astonishment. The orchestra had been unprepared, of course, but the conductor

was quick-witted, and after the first few seconds he must
have signaled the drummer to match my movements with
quick touches on the side drum, cymbals, and skulls.

My impromptu solo lasted for perhaps a minute, and
brought continual bursts of laughter, but my alarm as I
dodged the imaginary ants was very little assumed, for I
was wondering what on earth we should do if the men failed
to get the jets working. I could have cried with relief as a
thin stream of water suddenly shot up from the framework
of the manhole, and I immediately varied my steps so that
I backed into the jet and was soaked. Alfie came stalking
back onstage, and he had remembered his own cue, for he
was carrying an old paint tin he had picked up, and splashing
water from it as if dousing the ants with paraffin. We muddled through for the next ten seconds or so, and then were
able to pick up the sketch where we had broken off.

The applause was good, and I received a special burst
when Alfie held up my hand during our final bow. As we
came off into the wings he said, "Blimey, you'll never do
better than tonight, Bridie. I was too busy to look, but you
'eld 'em all right, I could 'ear 'em laughing."

Ethel said, "She was just lovely, Alfie. I was scared out
of my wits, but she came out with the impromptu just as if
it 'ad always been part of the act. You ask Charlie."

I was immensely thankful to have played my part in
coping with the near disaster, but knew where the true credit
lay. "God bless you for the ant cue, Alfie," I said. "I wouldn't
have known what to do but for that."

Then Nathan McFee was in front of me, and on his face
there was a look I had never seen before. I was in my too-
big and soaking-wet uniform with its too-short trousers braced
up to show my boots. As usual, I had shaken my hair loose
for the last curtain call, so I looked a strange mixture, half
girl, half clown. But Nathan McFee had taken me by the
shoulders and was looking down at me with a glow in his
eyes that set my heart leaping and my stomach tingling with
an overwhelming excitement completely new to me.

Alfie and Ethel had halted on either side of me, but he
seemed unaware of them. "Bridie Chance," he said, lifting

his quiet voice a little above the music being played for the next act. "Bridie Chance, I love you, and will you marry me, please?"

I stood dazed. The world stopped. Tears mingled with the water on my face. Then it was as if something within me opened like a flower, revealing to me that I had been falling in love with Nathan McFee for several weeks past, perhaps from the time when I had first been troubled by that nameless melancholy.

He said, "Bridie?"

Beside me, Ethel exclaimed, "Well I never!" and simultaneously Alfie said in astonishment, "Cor blimey!"

I laughed, put my arms up to link my hands behind Nathan's neck, and said, "Oh, dearest Nathan, yes. But what a time to ask!"

"I couldn't wait any longer," he said simply. Drawing me to him, he bent to kiss me gently on the lips, then put his arms round me and held me close, ignoring grinning stage hands and everybody else backstage.

Ethel said, "You're making his nice shirt all wet, Bridie."

"No, ma'am," said Nathan, "that's entirely my doing." He released me and stepped back, smiling, a huge wet patch on his red shirt. "You go and change, Bridie. Come to supper with me at the Royston after my turn?"

"Oh yes, I'd love to, Nathan."

"Off you go then."

I lay in the hip bath in a hazy golden dream, letting Ethel's chatter pass me by unheard for a time, until she stopped, and I realized she must have asked a question.

"I'm sorry, Ethel dear," I called through the screen. "What was that?"

"I said will you go back with him to America, do you think, or will he stay here?"

"Oh. I haven't thought. I haven't had time to think yet, or to talk with Nathan. What about Alfie and Company? He's been planning to change the sketches, and I wouldn't let him down."

"Bless the girl, I've just been telling you not to worry about us. Charlie's all right now, so we'll just carry on like before. I don't say we're not going to be sorry at losing you, because we'll all be ever so sad really, but I know Alfie's pleased as Punch about what's 'appened. I can always tell."

I felt my throat tighten as if I were about to cry, and said, "I hope you're right, Ethel. You've all been so good to me."

For the next three days it was as if I were floating on a summer cloud. I knew that in another world I had once been engaged to a man called Bernard Page, but I could barely remember what he looked like, and I knew that I had never been in love before. I no longer felt like a girl clown, fit for nothing but to be laughed at. I felt like a girl who was greatly loved by a wonderful man, and who, for very sufficient reasons, had acquired a comic skill in which she might well take pride.

When we took supper in the dining room of the Royston Hotel that evening Nathan wanted to talk seriously about our future. This proved difficult, for I had taken two glasses of wine, which I was quite unused to, and I kept laughing, partly no doubt from the effect of the wine but partly, I felt sure, because I was so happy. Whatever the cause, it amused Nathan and set him chuckling.

"Now be serious awhile, Bridie," he said. "Tomorrow we'll go and buy an engagement ring—"

"Not tomorrow," I broke in, and giggled. "It's Sunday."

"All right, on Monday then. But how soon do you want us to be married?"

"Oh. How soon? Oh, dear. I'm dreadfully forward, Nathan, and I'd really like to marry you tomorrow, but I don't suppose that's possible."

"Think about things, Bridie. About your commitment to Alfie, and to your sister."

"Yes." I sobered a little. "Well, it's all right about Alfie. I'd like to finish the tour, of course. As for Kate, I'd like to see her thoroughly settled and through her next set of examinations before—well, it depends how far away we would be, I suppose. Would we live in England or America?"

"That's for you to say, honey."

"Honey? Oh, I like that, Nathan. It's a lovely word. I don't know. I think if Kate were settled, I'd like to go to America with you. I've found that I'm quite good at getting used to a new kind of life, and if we were to marry and have a family here, we'd always be living under the shadow of the Roger Chance scandal. You said it wouldn't be like that in America."

He shrugged. "Might be a few folk who'd look down their noses, but the rest wouldn't care a button." He grinned. "Maybe we could hang a picture of your pa and my pa each side of the fireplace and tell stories about them when we have neighbors in."

I giggled again. "And make the children laugh. After all, *we* didn't rob banks and steal jewelry, did we? Nathan, there are two men and two ladies dining a little way away, I can see them in the looking glass, and they keep staring at you very fur . . . furtively."

"Sure. They've been to the Palace recently, so they recognize me. Folk are always fascinated by people who appear on the stage, you know that."

"It's not fair, though. They don't recognize me as Arnold. Shall I get up and give them the Crab Slide and the Stork Step?"

He reached out, took my wrist firmly in one hand, and with the other removed my half-full third glass of wine. "Another time, honey. Lord, but I do love you, my sweet maverick girl."

"Maverick?"

"Not one of the herd. Now listen, Bridie, we have to talk about money."

I nodded, and made an effort not to feel so carefree. I had learned that money was very important. People who had plenty often said it did not matter, but they were wrong. Being rich did not matter, but having enough money to live without fear was something that mattered very much.

It was then that Nathan told me about the farm. He had not known about it himself until shortly before he came to England, when he had heard through a firm of American lawyers that his mother's father, Jonathan Rigby, a widower, had died without leaving a will. This was a man Nathan had never seen, who had disowned Nathan's mother when she ran away to be married.

The lawyers had told Nathan that, as the only grandchild, and in the absence of any nearer kin, he appeared to be the sole heir. It would be necessary to make due enquiries before confirming this, but in the meantime the Rigby farm was being satisfactorily run by the manager who had effectively been in charge of it for the last three years, when Jonathan Rigby had been too ill to play any active part.

"Had a letter from these lawyers when we were in Glasgow," said Nathan. "Sent on by Jimmy Samuels. They say it's all clear, so that means we have a farm, Bridie. It's called Greenways. Eight hundred acres in New Hampshire, about a third of it planted as orchards, the rest mixed farming. Real pretty there, they say, and the old man looked after it well, so there's a good living in it and maybe a little more. They don't have final figures on what money was left, but they estimate something over eighty thousand dollars. Say twenty thousand pounds in your money. I guess if you wanted to live in England we could sell the farm for a good figure, then buy one here . . . or do whatever else we fancy."

I was gazing at him from eyes suddenly grown so heavy I could scarcely keep them open. I understood his words, but seemed to have lost all power of response, so that I could only sit as if stupefied.

Some time went by, and at last he spoke again, struggling with suppressed laughter. "Do you think you could say something, honey? Anything would do, just to show you're still there."

"Well . . ." I said dazedly. "Oh, my goodness. I didn't realize you were rich, Nathan."

"I don't know about rich. But whatever it is, don't say 'you,' say 'we,' Bridie."

"Wait, please. I don't quite follow that, Nathan. You seem to be getting rather muddled."

"I'm sorry, I expect it's the wine," he said solemnly. "I

meant you should say *we* are rich. Assuming we are. Not *you*."

"No . . . I'm definitely not rich, Nathan. Oh, I do wish I hadn't arranged to go to Suffolk and see Nannie Foster on Tuesday. I shall be away for three whole days, and I shall miss you so much."

He must have signaled a waiter, for I saw now that he was paying a bill. I was embarrassed at having spoken that way in front of the waiter, but Nathan simply smiled and said, "No more than I'll miss you, honey."

The waiter went away, and I was suddenly overwhelmed by the sadness of parting from Nathan only two days after we had found that we loved each other. I said, "Nathan, I know this sounds silly, because I'm really very happy, but I think I'm about to cry."

My memory is vague at this point. I recall being in a cab with Nathan, weeping on his shoulder while he spoke soothing words interrupted by spasms of laughter. I recall entering the boardinghouse and sailing up three flights of stairs, never once touching them with my feet. The last thing I remember is Ethel trying to undress me while I insisted on demonstrating the secret of the Chicken Walk.

I slept till past nine o'clock next morning, and woke with a dry mouth, a slight headache, and a sense of great embarrassment. Ethel had gone. I put on my long dressing gown, went through to the bathroom at the end of the passage, found only half a container of lukewarm water left, took a very small and tepid bath, then returned to our room.

Ten minutes later I had dressed, done my hair, and was walking downstairs to the breakfast room. When I put my head diffidently round the door I saw the Perkin family sitting at table with Nathan and Margaret Dane, the serio-comic. They had finished breakfast, but were lingering over cups of coffee, chatting idly. As I entered Ethel trilled, "Ah, here she is!" Every eye turned toward me, and I was conscious that everyone was smiling, but the only smile I saw clearly was Nathan's as he rose and held a chair for me.

I reached out a hand for him to take, made a huge "Arnold" grimace of despair, and said, "I was tipsy! Oh Nathan, I was actually tipsy last night! I'm so ashamed."

"Ashamed?" It was Alfie who spoke first. "I should 'ope so, young lady. I understand you knocked back two whole glasses of wine, all on your own!"

Charlie got up and began to reel and totter about the room as if his legs had turned to rubber, Margaret started to sing "The Demon Drink Was Her Undoing," and Alfie performed a drum roll on the table with two spoons. Nathan bent to touch his lips to my cheek, smiling and shaking his head reassuringly. As the hubbub ended in laughter he said, "All my fault, honey, I'm sorry."

"I should have told you I wasn't used to wine. I didn't think. I was so happy, and I was thirsty, and—oh dear, it's simply awful to think I was actually drunk!"

"You weren't, Bridie. You were just happy, and beautiful with it."

"But you were laughing. I remember."

"Sure I was laughing. You're a very entertaining lady, and a joy to be with. Come on, now. Try to eat a little breakfast."

"It's given me a really good idea," said Alfie. "I was just talking about it. Even with you leaving the company, Bridie, I reckon it's time I brought something new into the repertoire, so I'm going to work out another sketch. I mean, suppose you 'ad a night scene in Covent Garden. Well, early morning really, and Ethel's got a fruit barrow and I'm a policeman, and Charlie's a toff in a top 'at and monocle, but drunk as a lord. We could 'ave a bit of fun with that I reckon."

Nathan put a cup of black coffee down beside me, and I held his hand. Despite the headache, my mind had seized on Alfie's suggestion at once, for I could see that eccentric dancing as a tipsy toff could be very funny indeed.

"Need more props," said Charlie. "Got to 'ave things to work with."

"There's the fruit on the barrow," I said thoughtfully, "and you could include tomatoes. A basket full of them for the toff to fall into. Oh, they have those baskets the porters pile up high on their heads, don't they?"

"Right," said Alfie. "And suppose a sandwich-board man left 'is sandwich board lying around? I've always reckoned that would make a good prop. Charlie could put it on for a bit."

Charlie giggled. "Clonk you on the 'ead when I bend forward, eh?"

I drank some coffee and said, "I expect you'll need a theme for the sketch, Alfie, won't you? Perhaps you could make it quite simple, like a wheel having come off Ethel's barrow. You're the friendly policeman trying to get it on again for her, and Charlie insists on helping."

Alfie gave a loud sigh, and jerked his head toward Nathan. "It's a shame, you throwing yourself away on this bloomin' Yankee," he said. "You've got a good 'ead for ideas, Bridie. And when I think what we could do with you an' Charlie playing as *two* tipsy toffs . . . well, I don't know, I'm sure."

Nathan chuckled. I pressed his hand and said, "I'm not marrying this bloomin' Yankee today, Alfie, so if you feel I could be any use at all in working out a new sketch, I'd be so proud to help."

It rained all that day, and a strong wind howled round the chimney pots, but I could not have been happier if the sun had shone from a perfect blue sky. We did not do anything special, but I was with Nathan and could wish for nothing better. In the afternoon he and I went out for a walk in the park near our boardinghouse. Nathan wore a kind of South American cape, I wore a long mackintosh and took an umbrella which Nathan held over us, but the wind blew it inside out, and we came home with heads drenched, laughing.

Next day I chose a ring with two small diamonds for my engagement ring. It was not expensive, and Nathan protested on this count, but the stones were beautiful, the design unusual, and I fell in love with this particular ring as soon as I saw it.

That evening I sat in the circle and watched Mr. Alfie

Perkin and Company perform *The Paperhanger's Mate*. Not
long ago I would never have dared to do such a thing without
an escort, but my life had changed beyond measure since
those days. Six months on the stage had given me a special
kind of confidence, and I was quite untroubled by thoughts
of what should or should not be done.

I suppose I had come to have quite a good opinion of
the way I played the part of "Arnold," but this was now
rapidly dispelled. I could never have been jealous of Charlie,
but I did feel almost crestfallen when I saw how much better
he was than I in so many ways. I stayed in my aisle seat
until after the intermission, to watch Nathan, and again
found myself full of admiration for his skill. It seemed a
pity that he performed his rope-spinning tricks so casually,
without any attempt to impress the audience, but I realized
that to him this was of little importance. He had never set
out to make a name on the halls, and his time there would
soon be coming to an end.

We had made tentative plans to be married in the spring.
Until then, we would remain in London once the tour ended,
and during that time Nathan proposed to take some bookings
rather than find himself with too little to do. There was now
no point in Alfie rewriting the sketches to bring me in as
an extra character, as he had once intended, but he had
declared that he would pay me a stand-by fee each week of
half my present wages in return for my being ready to take
Charlie's place if required; and he would also pay me half
wages for what he called "advice and consultation" in helping him devise the new sketch to be called *The Tipsy Toff*.
All this was no more than a device for ensuring that I was
fully paid at my present rate until the marriage, but he would
brook no argument about it.

Nathan and I had yet to decide where we would live. I
had a great feeling that I would like to go to the farm in
New Hampshire. I knew now that it would be hard for me
to return to the rigidly conventional life in which I had
grown up, and felt that America offered freedoms I could
not find here. Much depended on Kate. Unless she agreed,
I felt I could not leave her alone here and go to a far country,

for the only family we had now was each other. I hoped she would come with us, and Nathan was very willing, but there was so much to be discussed that we could make no decision until we had seen her.

Early on the Tuesday morning Nathan saw me off on the train for my visit to Nannie Foster. The journey was a wretched cross-country affair with two changes, and I did not reach Wynford until almost teatime. It was strange to be driven from the station to the green by the same dour George Cooper who had brought the men from Scotland Yard to Latchford Hall in what now seemed another lifetime.

He recognized me, and his eyes widened, but he looked down and knuckled his forehead as I told him where to take me. I realized then that I must have given him a very hard and formidable look. No doubt he would gossip avidly about his fare as soon as I had dismissed the cab, but he was certainly not going to have the impertinence to say anything to my face. I smothered a laugh, wondering at the way in which Bridie Chance had changed since last Wynford had seen her.

Nannie Foster wept with delight when she opened the door, and began at once to fuss over me as if I were a twelve-year-old returning from boarding school. "I've put the kettle on, dear, so you just run upstairs and wash your hands, then we'll have a nice cup of tea and some of Nannie's special *scones*! Gracious me, how pretty you look, Bridie, and what a nice hat. Here, let Nannie do it for you. There we are. Oh my, you've quite changed in the way you walk about, haven't you? So very nice and elegant, dear. I expect you've been practicing with books balanced on your head, the way Nannie tried to teach you."

I did not tell her that my new-found grace came from being a comic dancer in a music hall turn. She would probably not have been able to grasp what I meant, but if she had it would have upset her deeply. After tea we sat talking, and to my relief she was well content to spend most of the time gossiping about all the small domestic details of her daily life in Wynford. She asked after Kate, and said anxiously that she hoped I was not working too hard, but in general she was satisfied with simple and uninformative answers.

Later, when she had lit the lamps and drawn the curtains, she produced a plain but excellent meal of mutton chops, cauliflower, and dumplings, followed by blackberry and apple pie. I insisted on helping her to wash the dishes, and as we worked together in the tiny kitchen I explained that I would be going to visit Mr. Whitely and old Tom Kettle next day, but planned to spend the rest of the day with her, and to stay overnight before catching a train early the following morning for the wearisome journey back to Manchester.

It was a rather sultry September night, and I felt sleepy from the day's travel. When we sat down again I glanced at my watch, found that it was nine o'clock, and decided that at half-past nine I would ask to go to bed. There was no spare room or spare bed in the small cottage, but Nannie had brought down fresh linen and a pillow to make up a bed for me on the settee.

As she settled in the armchair she had brought with her from her room at Latchford Hall I said, "I've been waiting all this time for you to ask about my ring, Nannie. Look."

She took my hand as I held it out, stared down at the ring on the third finger, then looked up with shining eyes. "Bridie! You're not . . . ?"

"Yes, I'm engaged to be married, Nannie. It happened only two days ago, and even Kate doesn't know yet. I must spend an hour writing to her tomorrow, to tell her all about it."

"Oh, that's lovely, dear! A London gentleman?"

"No, he's American, and his name is Nathan McFee."

"*American*? Goodness me! Wherever did you meet him?"

"Oh—we met in the course of business, Nannie. He really is a most wonderful man, and I'm so happy."

"Then I'm happy for you, dear. I've been meaning to ask, what sort of work is it that you do?"

"I'm very lucky. I was able to find employment as assistant to the head of a company." This was a prepared answer. The words were true but the impression given was quite false, for I could not bring myself to distress Nannie by telling her the exact truth.

"Oh, that's splendid, Bridie," she beamed. "And it all comes of being well educated, you know. Your dear papa always said you had a good head on your shoulders. Of course, I've *heard* about young ladies going into business these days, but I've never *known* one before. Bravo dear, bravo. I'm sure he would be so proud of you."

"Yes, Nannie. I think perhaps he would."

"Oh, my." She shook her head, misty-eyed. "Little Bridie getting married, just to think of it . . ."

"I'm not exactly little now, Nannie. My legs are still too long."

"Oh hush now, dear!" she said with surprised reproach. "We don't speak of limbs in conversation, do we?"

I managed not to laugh, and said, "No, I'm sorry, Nannie."

"Just fancy. Our Bridie to marry an American gentleman. Oh, that reminds me. I won't be a moment, dear." She went upstairs, moving rather slowly, and came down two or three minutes later with a yellowing envelope in her hand. "You remember asking me to tidy your poor dear mama's room? Well, there were a few very old magazines in one of the drawers, and I took them to look at later, to see if she'd kept them for any special pieces in them."

She paused, sitting down beside me, and I said, "She often put such things aside to read again later, but I think she rarely did so, Nannie. It might be a recipe she felt was interesting, or an article or story. Did you find anything?"

"Not really, dear. I'm afraid I put them with my own things and forgot all about them till long after I was settled here, but I was having a tidy-up a week or two ago, and I found these photographs tucked away in one of the magazines."

"Photographs?"

"Yes. I'd seen them before, you know, years ago. Your mama showed them to me once, when you were just a baby. They were taken when she and your papa were on their honeymoon. In France, it was."

"Yes, they stayed at a village in the Dordogne valley."

"I expect you're right, dear. I can't remember foreign names."

"I've seen the photographs, Nannie. There was an album I looked at several times when I was a little girl, but I thought that was in the trunkful of family items I wanted to keep, the trunk I asked Mr. Whitely to have stored for me till I was settled."

"Oh, I'm sure you have the album in your trunk, dear, but these photographs were always quite separate. I don't know why."

There were only two, and I had not seen either before. Considering that they were more than twenty years old, the prints remained remarkably sharp. The first showed my mother as a young woman, looking so much like Kate. She stood with her back against what appeared to be the face of a rocky cliff, and was smiling a shy smile. On her head was a hat with a wide brim and long feathers. She had one hand raised to hold the hat in place, as if there might be a stiff wind about.

The second picture had been taken from much farther away, so that she was quite a small figure without discernible features, but the pose was the same. Now it was clear that she was not standing against the foot of a cliff, but against a natural pillar of rock about twice her height, a rather freakish outcrop jutting vertically from ground that looked stony and barren. The background was blurred, but I had the impression that low cliffs were rising up on each side of a small dry valley.

I said, "Yes, I remember Mama's hat from several photographs in the album, but I wonder where this place is? Most of the pictures were taken near the village, but this is very rocky, without a tree or flower to be seen." I looked at the first photograph again. "Papa must have taken them, I suppose, but how do you think he managed it?"

"Oh, with a camera, dear."

I laughed. "Yes, Nannie. But when this was taken there were no folding cameras or collapsible cameras. This looks the sort of place that's high up and difficult to reach, so it would be quite difficult to take a camera and tripod up there."

"That wouldn't trouble your papa, you know. When he decided to do something, he always found a way, and he was very clever with mechanical things."

I remembered Mama's rambling, half-delirious tale of gunpowder and a safe, and said, "Yes, Nannie, very clever in that way, but I wonder why he would go to such lengths to take photographs here?"

"Oh, I couldn't say, Bridie, I really couldn't say."

"Did Mama never explain when she showed you the pictures?"

Nannie Foster blinked. I saw the interest fade from her face, and knew that she was suddenly tired. "It's a long time ago now," she said vaguely. "I think the photographs were just a souvenir, you know. To remind her of the Capricorn Stone."

thirteen

I sat up straight. "The Capricorn Stone? What did she mean, Nannie?"

"Oh, I don't think she said, dear. I didn't really pay much attention. You see, she liked to talk to me because there wasn't really anybody else, most of the time, but I never asked questions, dear. That wouldn't have been polite. I know she spoke of the Capricorn Stone, though. When I was a young girl a fortune teller told me I was born under the sign of Capricorn, so I expect that's why I remembered, Bridie."

The Capricorn Stone. Those words had been among almost the last my mother had spoken to me, and I had seen them written down in the letter my father had left for her. I tried to recall phrases from the letter. *Walk again . . .* something about a stream in the hills . . . *and on to the valley of the Capricorn Stone.* I looked down at the second photograph once more. Here, surely, was the valley of the Capricorn Stone, with my mother standing against the stone itself. But what then? . . . *Darkness at eventide . . . rainbow's end . . . waiting crow . . .*

I could remember nothing in clear detail, but of one thing I was now certain. The last part of my father's letter was indeed a message couched in cryptic form, and my mother would have understood it, perhaps because it was no more than a reminder of something she already knew, a kind of *aide-memoire.*

What was the burden of the message? I felt it could only be a guide to the place where he had kept safely hidden the great haul of jewelry stolen during half a lifetime as a thief.

It was typical of his feckless nature that he should think he
had made provision for his wife and family by telling Mama
where to look for his spoils—as if she could or would have
been able to make use of them. In that moment I might have
hated him if I had not known that he loved her so truly and
so dearly.

Idly I turned the photographs over. At first I thought
there was nothing on the back of either, but then saw faint
markings on the second, the one that showed Mama against
the Capricorn Stone at a distance. Somebody had written a
word or two with a soft pencil. The lead had rubbed away
over the years, but when I moved to hold the photograph
at an angle under the lamp I saw that it was my father's
hand, and that he had written *Tête de Chèvre*! The excla-
mation mark still stood out boldly from the rest.

Head of the goat. Goat's head. I looked at the picture
again, but the words seemed to have no connection with
anything shown there. Suddenly I wished Nannie Foster had
never discovered the photographs. I knew that what I held
in my hands, together with the letter Papa had left, might
be made to yield the answer to a mystery, but this was
ground I shrank from disturbing. I could tell Inspector
Browning what had come to light, or I could write to Philippe Chatillon, the French detective, at the address in Paris
he had given me, for he would now have returned there
from whatever his business had been in England during the
summer.

I felt confused and uncertain. In my heart I wanted to
tell nobody about the photographs and the letter. Kate and
I had endured a long and frightening ordeal, but each of us
had now settled to a new life. I hated the thought of the
whole dramatic story being reopened and discussed in detail
in the newspapers.

Nannie Foster smothered a yawn and said, "My, my,
I'm a sleepyhead tonight."

I emerged from my thoughts, and slipped the photographs
back into the envelope. "Yes, I'm tired myself, Nannie. It's
been a long day. Shall we make up the bed for me now?"

"You just sit still, dear, I'll see to it. I have everything ready."

Twenty minutes later, as I lay snugly in the made-up bed on the settee, she bent to kiss me good night as she had done throughout all the years of my childhood. "Sleep well, dear, and call Nannie if there's anything you need."

Though I was tired, I lay awake for an hour or more after she had gone. At the end of that time I determined that I would talk everything over with Nathan, so that we could decide together what I should do. I also made up my mind that I ought to tell Kate, for it was as much her right to know as mine, and I already felt a little guilty for not yet having shown her the letter from Papa, even though she had asked to see it.

Next morning after breakfast I settled down to write a long letter to Kate, telling her the wonderful news of my engagement to Nathan, and explaining that we had yet to decide just what we would do and where we would live when we were married. I also told her something of the photographs Nannie Foster had found, and said they seemed to be linked with Papa's letter in a way which made me certain she had been right in thinking it held a hidden message. We would have a long talk about it, I said, on my return to London.

At ten o'clock I walked along the High Street to the little post office. I had no presentiment, as I slipped the letter into the box, that I had just set in motion a train of events that would lead to undreamed of danger, fear, and death.

When arranging to visit Nannie Foster I had also written to Mr. Whitely and received a reply to say that he would be most pleased to see me at his office in Southwold at half past eleven o'clock on the Wednesday morning. I felt that Nannie would enjoy an outing to Southwold, where she could look at the shops while I kept my appointment, and so I had arranged for George Cooper to call for us at half past ten with his growler.

Mr. Whitely received me with the same outward dispassion and the same underlying kindness he had shown me

in the dark days. I told him all my news, and said that I
hoped he would continue to act for me in any legal matters
that might arise concerning my marriage, and in any dis-
positions I might make to provide for Kate.

"I shall be most happy, I assure you, to do as you ask,
Miss Chance. May I say that I am delighted to see how
ably you have coped with the formidable problems you faced
last year? I was quite fascinated to hear of your exploits as
a ...um... music hall artist. The letter is in my private
file, I hasten to inform you, so no cognizance of it has been
taken by my staff." A touch of malicious satisfaction gleamed
in his eye. "Or by my brother, who was most curious to
know how you had fared. Pray tell me, if I am not being
overinquisitive, what is it precisely that you do? Recitations,
perhaps? Or singing?"

I hesitated, then spent five minutes describing just what
I did onstage as a character called "Arnold." His expression
did not change, but when I had finished he continued to sit
without saying a word or moving a muscle for almost a full
minute, as if turned to wax. Then at last his shoulders shook
as a thin dry chuckle escaped him.

"My dear Miss Chance, oh my dear Miss Chance, I do
beg you to accept my most sincere admiration."

I spent an hour in Southwold going round the shops with
Nannie, who was greatly concerned at the cost of keeping
the carriage waiting for us, then returned to Wynford for a
simple lunch before setting off on my own in a hired gig
to see old Tom Kettle. He was busy making a chair, and
greeted me without fuss, as if I had last called only the
other day.

I was glad he showed no curiosity about what I had been
doing, and during the half hour I stayed with him the only
time he referred to the past was when he asked me if I was
still "doing them drawings." At first I could not think what
he meant, then remembered that I had sometimes sat in the
garden of his little cottage with my pad and pencil, making
poor sketches. It all seemed very long ago now.

Later I drove to the church, where I put a posy on my
parents' grave before continuing to the vicarage. On leaving

Wynford a year ago I had paid one pound for the sexton to keep the grave properly tended for twelve months, and now I arranged for this sum to be paid regularly from my bank in future, so that the grave would never be neglected.

By teatime I was back at Nannie Foster's house once more, conscious as I drove into the village that more than one or two pairs of eyes were upon me now. The fact that Bridie Chance, daughter of the notorious Roger Chance of Latchford Hall, had returned to Wynford for a brief visit was becoming more widely known every hour. I did not much care, for I had been stared at by a thousand eyes, six nights a week for the past six months, but I was glad that I would be leaving next morning to be with my friends again, and especially to be with Nathan.

It was raining in Manchester, but still a joy to come home. Nathan was there at the station, and I knew that wherever in the world I might be, for me "home" was in his arms.

Later, when I could think clearly again, I told him what I had discovered, showing him the photographs I had brought with me and the letter from Papa which I kept with my few personal papers in my trunk. He studied them quietly, a little uneasily I thought, and said at last, "Yes, Bridie, I guess the last piece of this letter was some sort of reminder to your mother, telling her where to look for what your father had hidden."

"Do you think it really was a lot of jewelry?"

"Seems likely. I read the list of big items they reckoned he'd got away with over the years, and that was only part of it."

"Oh. Where did you see that?"

"In one of the newspapers, around that time."

"Yes. I didn't read them after the first story."

"Don't be upset, honey."

"I'm not, Nathan, truly I'm not. It's just that I don't want to do anything about this, but feel I ought."

"Why do you feel that, Bridie?"

"Well, I suppose that if the jewelry my father stole can

be recovered, I owe it to the people it was stolen from to do all I can to help."

"You don't owe them a red cent, honey. You're not responsible for your father."

"Well...no, but...oh, wait a minute. I'm not sure you're right, Nathan dear. I'm part of his family."

"It rests on the police, Bridie, not on you."

"But should I tell the police that I've found these...these clues? Should I tell Inspector Browning? Or that French detective I told you about? I don't want to, but I keep feeling it's the right thing to do."

He smiled, and bent to kiss me on the cheek. "Ma always used to teach me that the tough thing to do was usually the right thing to do. She figured it was a pretty sneaky way to arrange things, but there was no use complaining, you just had to go along with it. There's one thing, though. You don't have to make up your mind this minute, Bridie. Take a while to think it over. Whatever your father hid, it's not going to run away by next week or next year."

I felt a sense of relief. "Yes, that's true. A few days can't make any difference, and anyway I ought to wait until I've heard from Kate before I decide. After all, she's not a child. She's nineteen now, and entitled to have her say."

On the Monday I took over from Charlie and played the final week of our Manchester booking. I had felt diffident about this, but Charlie was very reassuring. "Eh? Course I don't mind, Bridie. For one thing, I found it a bit tiring last week, so Uncle Alfie wants me to sort of ease meself back into it gradually, with rehearsals, see? I mean, you know 'ow much more it takes out of you when you're onstage."

"Oh yes, Charlie. There's no comparison."

"Another thing. I want to watch you, Bridie. You got some tricks of your own I wouldn't 'alf like to learn."

"Learn from *me*? Oh Charlie, I shall never have a nicer compliment than that."

"No, honest, Bridie. You know that bit...'ere, wait a jiffy." We were on our own in Mrs. Ransom's big sitting room, waiting for the gong to sound for luncheon, and he pushed back one or two chairs to make more room. "Look, in the Willow Strut, it goes *one* and-a *two* and-a *three* and-a *four*, right? But you get an extra sort of twitch with your . . . well, you know."

"With my tail. Yes, but I don't quite know how, Charlie. See if you can tell." I pulled my skirt up a few inches and skittered across the room. Charlie followed me. Then we moved back, performing the step in unison, his head turned to watch me with great concentration.

"Ah," he said thoughtfully, "it's partly the 'ips and partly the way you 'ollow your back. I'll see better when you're in trousers. P'raps we could try it down at the rehearsal hall tomorrow, when we're working on the new sketch?"

"Yes, of course."

"Thanks, Bridie. And don't you feel bad about playing the last week 'ere and the next three in Birmingham. Suits me fine, what with the new sketch to think about. Anyway, it'll be your last run, I s'pose. Me, I'll 'ave donkey's years of it."

I was especially happy to have Charlie's reassurance that he did not feel put out by my return to the act, for I found to my surprise that I was looking forward quite eagerly to the excitement of going onstage again after a week away from it. "You're just a clown, Bridie Chance," I told myself, "that's the trouble with you. But Nathan loves you exactly the way you are, thank goodness."

The sketch went well that Monday evening. Nathan was in his usual place as we came off, and kissed me despite the paste all over my face. "You get better all the time with that crazy dancing, Bridie," he said in the quiet drawl I had come to love. "Seems a real waste of talent for me to take you away from all those folk busy laughing out there." He smiled. "Not that anything's going to stop me."

"I'll do my comic dancing sometimes especially for you, to make you laugh, shall I? Oh, and I'll do it to make our children laugh, too."

Ethel said, "Really, Bridie! You do come out with some shocking things, dear. Whatever's Nathan going to think of you, talking about children when you've hardly been engaged for five minutes?"

Nathan said, "I think she's just fine, Ethel ma'am."

I laughed with sheer happiness and excitement, thinking how wonderful it was that Nathan and I understood each other so well that we did not have to watch our words, but could say whatever was in our hearts.

The following Sunday we moved to Birmingham, where we were to end the tour. I still had not decided what to do about the discoveries I had made when visiting Nannie Foster, and in fact had mentally put the matter aside for the time being. Nathan had said nothing more, but I felt it was on his mind, for there were times when his thoughts seemed faraway.

At the end of the first week, after the matinee performance on the Saturday, Ethel and I went out to a tea shop to while away an hour or so. There was not time to do much between the matinee and evening performances, but we preferred to change and go out rather than remain in the dressing room, as some of the artists did. Alfie and Charlie had dashed off to spend an hour at a cricket match, and Nathan had said he might join us at the tea shop after his turn, but he did not arrive. I was not particularly worried by this, but thought that perhaps he had decided to spend some time grooming Lucifer or polishing his harness, for though Nathan made little effort to present his act as dramatically as he might have done, he always made sure that Lucifer appeared as a prince among horses.

When Ethel and I returned to the Empire I asked the stage doorman, Fred, if he had seen anything of Mr. McFee. "Funny you asking that, miss," he said in the strong Birmingham accent I sometimes found difficult to follow. "There was this feller waiting when Mr. McFee coom out, an hour back. Give him this note, he did, and you should ha' seen Mr. McFee's face when he luked at it. Then he steadies himself, like, an' reads it again, an' gives it back to the feller. I mean, that's funny, eh? Giving it back?"

I hid my anxiety and shrugged, not wanting to encourage Fred to gossip. "I don't suppose it's a matter of any importance, Fred. Is Mr. McFee in the theater?"

"No, miss. Went off, he did, walking. Then the other

feller called a cab and told the cabbie to take him to the station. Red-faced bloke. Shifty, I reckon."

I went in, found a callboy, and told him to look out for Mr. McFee and ask him to come and have a word with me as soon as possible. Ethel trilled some phrases meant to be reassuring, but looked worried herself. We had scarcely been two minutes in our dressing room when there was a tap on the door. It was Mr. Chapman, the manager, a middle-aged man with heavy jowls and a permanently worried air.

"Sorry to trouble you, Miss Chance, but can you spare ten minutes to come to my office?"

I was taken aback. "Why yes, but...oh, is it anything to do with Mr. McFee?"

He looked puzzled and shook his head, jowls wobbling. "No, dear, no. It's just I've got a friend of mine here, man I used to know when I was under-manager in London, and he's what you might call an old acquaintance of yours, too. Up here on business, saw the show last night, and couldn't get over what a clever young lady you are. Couldn't believe his eyes. I said would he like to meet you again—I mean, you know how people enjoy meeting you if you're on the stage, eh? So he said yes, but I was to tell you it wasn't official. Definitely not official."

I stared. "Whatever can he mean? What is your friend's name, Mr. Chapman?"

"Browning, miss. Inspector Browning from Scotland Yard. But it's just up to you. He was very particular about that. Tell Miss Chance it's just to congratulate her and wish her well, he said. Nothing official."

After a moment I said, "Yes. Very well, Mr. Chapman. I should be glad to meet the inspector again. Shall I come to your office in two or three minutes?"

"Thank you, miss. Much obliged. Always like to do a favor for the police, if I can."

When he had gone I explained briefly to Ethel as I tidied my hair in the looking glass.

"Are you sure you don't mind, dear? I'll come along

with you if you like. You looked very queer just for a moment, when Mr. Chapman said his name."

"Did I? Well, it was something of a shock, and brought back bad memories, but I don't mind seeing Inspector Browning. He was really very kind to me at the time, and if he says it's not official, then I believe him. If Nathan comes, please ask him to wait and say I won't be long. I'm rather worried about him, Ethel. I do hope he hasn't had any bad news."

"Well . . . try not to worry until you know, dear."

Three minutes later I tapped on the door of Mr. Chapman's office, and entered when he called, "Come in." He was not at his desk, but stood with his back to the window. Inspector Browning rose from one of two easy chairs, hat in hand. He looked exactly as I remembered him, and was wearing the same suit.

Mr. Chapman said brightly, "Well, here she is, Mr. Browning. No need for introductions, since you've met before. Now I hope you won't mind me leaving you for five minutes or so while you have a little chat, but I've got one or two things to attend to." He waved me toward a chair and hurried to the door. "Do excuse me. Busy time of day, Mr. Browning."

As the door closed after him Inspector Browning said, "It's very good of you to see me, Miss Chance. I fancy Chapman doesn't believe me when I say this isn't an official call, but it's perfectly true." As he spoke he came forward, putting out his hand, and looked relieved when I took it.

I smiled and said, "I believed you, Inspector, but I'm quite glad Mr. Chapman decided to go. Shall we sit down?"

"Thank you, miss." He waited for me, then seated himself. "You're looking very well, I'm happy to say."

"Yes, I've been most fortunate. I'm glad to see you looking well yourself. How did you know I was here?"

He looked a shade embarrassed. "Well, the file's never been closed, miss, so the Yard still keeps an eye on you, in a manner of speaking."

I stiffened. "You mean I am watched?"

"Oh Lord, no!" he said hastily. "Nothing like that. But

they took note of your sister being at the Prince Consort College of Music, and of that announcement in *The Stage* about Miss Bridie Chance replacing Charlie Perkin in the well-known music hall act of Mr. Alfie Perkin and Company."

"Oh, I see."

"Me being here in Birmingham is just a coincidence, miss. But when I saw the playbills I couldn't resist coming along last night to watch you do your turn." He shook his head, staring at me curiously. "You were absolutely splendid, miss. I couldn't believe it was really you, not until afterward, when you took off that cap and let your hair fall loose."

I was pleased to have impressed the inspector so greatly, and said, "I'm very glad you enjoyed the act."

"Oh, I did indeed." He smiled and made a baffled gesture. "I really can't get over it, the way you've managed to learn all that dancing and those comedy bits. It's flabbergasting to me, really it is, and I'm not one who's easily surprised."

"There are times when I'm still quite astonished myself, Inspector. If you would like to see the other sketch we shall be doing it tomorrow, and I could arrange a ticket for you."

"Ah, I'm afraid I have to be off back to London tomorrow morning, so I'll have to give it a miss this time." He took out his watch. "I'd better not keep you now. I expect you've got to start getting ready soon."

"Well, in a little while."

As we both stood up he said, "It was a bit of a liberty, coming along and asking to see you, but I think I really wanted to have a chance of saying how pleased I am that you've done so well, miss. It's a real credit to you."

"Thank you, Inspector." I hesitated. "I was surprised when you spoke just now of a file still being open at Scotland Yard. I suppose it must be the file on the Roger Chance case, and I was hoping that the whole affair was officially dead and forgotten now. Can you say how long it will be kept open?"

"Hard to tell, miss." He gave me a sympathetic look.

"It's the stolen property, you see. One day a piece of it might turn up somewhere, or we might hear a whisper from an informer. I'm sure the French police haven't closed the case, and you know yourself that Pinkertons are still on it."

"Pinkertons? I don't understand."

"The American people. Detective agency, working for that lady from Boston who lost a priceless bit of jewelry in Biarritz."

"Lady who...? You mean an American lady who was robbed by my—by Le Sorcier?"

"That's right, miss." He seemed puzzled by my lack of understanding. "Pinkertons have had one of their agents right alongside you for months now, though I can't think what good it's likely to do them. Still, I suppose they can afford to take a long chance."

I shook my head. "Inspector, I have no idea what you mean. Will you explain, please?"

His eyes narrowed in sudden surprise, and he slowly rubbed his chin. "I didn't realize you were unaware, miss. I'm afraid I've said too much."

"No. You speak of a detective agency, and you indicate that I have been watched for months, yet I know nothing about all this. I'm not a criminal, and I have a right to know. I beg you to tell me what it means, Inspector."

He looked troubled, rubbed the back of his neck vigorously, then seemed to make up his mind. "All right, miss," he said in a low voice. "I'm under no obligation to Pinkertons, and I took a liking to you right from the start, so here goes. It's a very big detective agency in America, been going for nearly fifty years now, dealing mostly with train robberies there, but they'll tackle any kind of robbery for the right price. The Boston lady engaged them, and they put three men into France to try and nail the guilty party. They knew who the French police thought it was, and they ferreted around for a few weeks without any results. Then, the day after your father was trapped and fell to his death, one of the men came over to Harwich and started keeping an eye on your family. The other two went home. Everyone thought that sooner or later a clue would turn up as to where the spoils were hidden." The inspector shrugged. "Everyone still does, including me, though that's not why I'm here. Anyway, you've been under close surveillance ever since. I thought you knew, miss. I thought something must have been said by now. I'm sorry if this comes as a shock."

I said slowly, "Surely you must be mistaken. It's more than a year now since my father died. No private detective agency would pursue a matter for so long."

Inspector Browning pursed his lips. "Pinkertons would. I was told they once kept two men on a case for three years. Besides, it's the Boston lady who's paying, and she's got three hundred thousand dollars' worth of jewelry at stake."

I turned away. I was lost somewhere in a dark place in my mind, and I did not want Inspector Browning to see my face. After a few moments I said, "Is the Pinkerton man who is watching me Mr. Nathan McFee?"

"That's right, miss. I fancy you must have had an inkling about him after all."

When I was sure that my face and voice were under control I turned to look at the man from Scotland Yard again. "No, Inspector," I said, and marveled that it was possible to feel such racking pain yet remain so calm. "No, I had no inkling about him at all. Thank you for explaining to me, and perhaps you will excuse me now. I must go and prepare to be funny."

He opened the door for me and said something, but I did not take it in, and I saw nothing as I made my way through the maze of passages and narrow stairs to our dressing room. Ethel looked up from the book she was reading, and for the second time in my life she simply stood up and opened her arms to me. I clung to her, shaking as if with ague, but I could not cry.

"What is it, Bridie dear, what is it? You tell Ethel. Come along, lovey, try an' tell me. There's plenty of time. Alfie won't be coming because he'll be late from the cricket, so he's going to change in the communal this evening. Was it that detective? What's he been saying, dear?"

I whispered against her shoulder. "If Nathan comes, I can't see him, I can't. Not yet."

"Whatever you say, Bridie dear. Don't you worry now. Look, sit down here and let me rub your hands. Ooh, my word, they're cold as ice. I'll send a callboy for some brandy, shall I?"

"No, Ethel. No, I daren't. It might make me stupid, so I couldn't go on."

"Charlie can do the act if you're not feeling up to it—"

"No!" I heard my voice crack. "Of course I shall go on tonight. I must. I'm a clown, Ethel. I'm a girl clown, for everyone to laugh at, only fit to dance about in comic trousers and big boots and get smothered in paste and water, not fit for anybody to love."

"Bridie, Bridie, you know we all love you."

"I'm sorry." I clutched her hands feverishly. "I didn't mean that. I meant not fit for a man to fall in love with. Oh, I've been such a fool, Ethel, such a stupid fool."

The tears came suddenly, and I clung to her again. She said nothing, but simply held me for long minutes until the spasm passed and I was quiet. Then she said sadly, "Is it Nathan?"

I nodded, found a handkerchief and blew my nose. "Yes. I've just discovered that he's really a sort of detective who works for an American firm. They think I know, or might come to know, where my father hid a whole mass of jewelry. Nathan was already watching our house in Wynford when the news came about my father, and he lied to me about that. He was watching me in London, he even asked Charlie about me, and during all this time that he's pretended to be my friend he's simply been spying on me. He even asked me once whether Papa had left any message, but I didn't suspect anything. Oh Ethel, I truly thought he loved me. It hurts so much, deep inside me, I can't tell you..."

She chafed my hands gently. "I know how it hurts, dear. I know."

I remembered then that she had been abandoned by the man who fathered Charlie, a man she must have loved dearly, and I felt suddenly ashamed of the exhibition I was making of myself. "I'm sorry, Ethel," I whispered. "It's just . . . such a shock at first. I'll be all right again in a few minutes."

She sighed and looked troubled. "Are you sure about Nathan, dear? I mean, quite sure? I don't understand about him being a detective and all that, but p'raps he loves you just the same. He seems such a nice honest young man to me."

I went to the washstand, poured water from the jug into the bowl, sponged my face, then dried it. When I had finished I said, "Yes, I'm sure, Ethel. I think his conscience troubled him once, and he almost gave himself away by telling me not to be so trusting. But to make doubly sure, I shall ask him tonight, after the performance, and he can speak for himself."

"It's better to have things out in the open," Ethel said hopefully. "Perhaps it will all come right, dear."

I went to her and kissed her cheek. "No. It won't, I'm afraid. Once I'd given him my friendship, he could have told me the truth if he really liked me. Why conceal it?" I was still holding the towel, and as I looked down my eye caught the sparkle of the engagement ring on my finger. It was like a knife-thrust piercing my heart. I gave a shaky laugh and said, "This will be the second ring I've returned. I've learned that you can get used to most things, so I suppose I shall soon get used to being humiliated."

We said nothing to Alfie in the few minutes that we were together before our number was shown in the frames. Later I noted with dull surprise, as if I had been an onlooker, that I performed well that evening. There had been no sign of Nathan in the wings as we went on, and he was still missing when we took our final bow.

"No Nathan?" Alfie said in surprise as we came off. "He's always 'ere to watch you, Bridie. What's up?"

Ethel said, "How should we know? All we know is that he's let our Bridie down, and don't you start asking questions now, Alfie, I'll tell you later." She took my arm and began to move briskly off. "Come on, dear, let's get you into the bath."

In the remote mood that lay upon me now I wondered vaguely as I bathed and dressed why Nathan should be absent from the wings on this particular night, since he could not know that I had learned the truth about him from Inspector Browning. Ethel was buttoning my dress for me when there came a tap on the door. She answered it to find Margaret Dane there, dressed ready for her usual place as first turn after the intermission. Looking both troubled and apologetic, Margaret said, "Hallo, Ethel, I just had to come and ask. Is it true about Nathan McFee?"

Ethel turned to look at me, not knowing what to reply. I came forward and said, "What have you heard about him, Maggie?"

"Well, Mr. Chapman said he's gone. Just walked out. Broken his contract."

Ethel gasped. "But that's awful!"

"Mr. Chapman's furious. I just couldn't believe it, but I thought Bridie would know." She hesitated. "Well, being engaged to him."

I said, "We didn't know, and I think the engagement is ended, Maggie. Do you know where Nathan is now?"

"Oh Bridie, I'm so sorry. I expect he's still at the digs. Molly said he was talking to Mrs. Bailey when she left half an hour ago, settling up with her because he was leaving. Oh dear, I'm sorry to be the one to bring such wretched news."

I said, "I'm glad to know. Thank you, Maggie."

She hesitated, then shook her head, made a little gesture of regret, and hurried off. Ethel closed the door and turned to me. "Will you try to see 'im before he goes, Bridie?"

I nodded, my face feeling stiff and pale.

"Want me to come with you, dear?"

"No. No thank you, Ethel. I'd better hurry now. Please excuse me."

I was lucky to find a cab which had just delivered a fare near the stage door, and ten minutes later I was outside Mrs. Bailey's theatrical digs in Manston Street. The dining room was in darkness, and the gas mantles in the sitting room had been turned low. I met nobody as I climbed three flights of stairs, passing my own room and continuing on up another flight to the next landing. There were five doors, and I was uncertain which was Nathan's room, but a light came from under only one of the doors, and I tapped on it.

Nathan's voice called, "Come in." When I opened the door he was on the far side of the room, his back toward me, fastening the straps of one of the big saddlebags he used for suitcases. Without turning he said, "Will you take these bags down, please? I want to go to the livery stables in Albert Street."

I said, "I'm not the cabbie, Nathan."

He straightened slowly, and remained facing away from me for several seconds. When at last he turned, his face was impassive. "Hello, Bridie," he said quietly.

"May I come in?"

He half lifted a hand. "As long as you don't mind."

"I'm not worried about my reputation, Nathan." I closed the door behind me and stood looking across the room at him, wishing I could stop myself aching with love for him. "May I ask you some questions, Nathan?"

He nodded, and I could read nothing in his eyes. I said, "This evening a man told me that you're an agent working for a detective organization called Pinkertons. He said that you were sent here to watch me. They believe that my father left a hoard of jewelry hidden somewhere, and that the best hope of discovering it is through me. Is it true, Nathan? Is it all true?"

His eyes narrowed a little. "Who told you this, Bridie?"

"A Scotland Yard detective."

Perhaps I imagined it, but I felt that he relaxed slightly at my words. After a moment he said, "Yes. It's true, Bridie. I'm sorry."

My heart felt like a great cold stone. I said, "So asking if you could be my friend, even asking me to marry you, was all just to win my confidence? You did it so that I would tell you anything I might know or discover about the jewelry?"

He looked away for a moment, and a muscle in his jaw twitched visibly, perhaps in anger. "It was business," he said in a flat voice. "My job was to recover a client's stolen property, and that calls for undercover work. We have to handle a case in whatever way seems most likely to get results."

"You could have told me the truth, Nathan."

He shook his head. "You'd have kept me at gun-shot distance."

I said tiredly, "Perhaps so." There was a little silence, and I held up my left hand, showing the ring. "Was this just business too, Nathan?"

He looked away. "Sorry, Bridie." His voice still held no expression.

I began to ease the ring from my finger. "Well, I've shown you the letter and the photographs, so you know as much as I'll ever know about the jewelry. I suppose you're going to France now, to the Dordogne valley?"

He looked at me again. "No. I've been called home, urgently."

"To America?"

"New York. I hope to be in Southampton by tomorrow night."

I moved a pace forward and put the ring down carefully on the corner of a small table. My face felt shriveled and ugly. "You must take the ring," I said. "I do wish you hadn't given it to me. It wasn't . . . necessary."

He folded his arms. "Depends how you look at it, Bridie."

My voice had faltered for a moment, but now I had it under control again. I said, "Yes, I suppose it's all in the way you look at it, and I've been very stupid." I turned, found the handle of the door, opened it, then paused to look back at him. Tall figure . . . blue eyes in a brown face beneath a straw-colored thatch of hair. The cold stone in my chest seemed to have grown so large that I found it difficult to breathe. I said, "I ought to hate you, but I can't. I wish you well, Nathan. I hope you're never hurt as badly as you've hurt me. Good-bye."

He was still gazing at me from brooding eyes when I turned again, went out, and closed the door quietly behind me. I stayed in my own room only long enough to sponge my face, then hurried out and took a cab back to the theater. If I had stayed, I would have found myself listening to the sounds of Nathan McFee departing, and that was more than I could bear.

When I entered our dressing room I found Ethel and Alfie sitting on the two bentwood chairs, and Charlie leaning against the wall, hands in his pockets. I had heard no sound of voices as I opened the door, and had the impression that they had been sitting in glum silence for some time now. Alfie had changed out of costume and was in his brown check suit. He rose as I came in, and took my hands in his own.

"Ethel told us. Did you see 'im, Bridie?"

"Yes." I tried to smile. "He admitted that it was all true."

Charlie said angrily, "Rotten swine. He's got no right to treat our Bridie like that, Uncle Alfie."

"I know, son. But I don't suppose Bridie wants us to make any trouble."

"Oh no, please." I held up my left hand to show the bare third finger. "I'm not engaged any more. I suppose I never was, really. He's been called back to America, and he's leaving this evening, so it's all over and done with now."

Ethel closed her eyes, the tall chignon quivering, and I saw a tear run down her cheek. "I don't know," she said plaintively. "I never dreamed he'd turn out like that."

"No, well, you're not the best of judges, Ethel," said Alfie briskly, "and what's done is done, so stop piping your eye or you'll 'ave us all at it." He looked at me, still holding my hands. "The thing is, what do you want to do now, Bridie?"

I did not need time to think, but said, "Will you have me back, Alfie? I mean, could we do what you were thinking of before . . . before Nathan McFee made a fool of me? Rewrite the sketches, and . . . and make the new one *Two Tipsy Toffs*?"

"Have you back? Blimey, girl, you never went, did you?" A smile added to the creases on his face. "Right, that's it, then. We'll get down to work on it tomorrow."

I looked across and said, "Charlie?"

"Course, soppy. Nothing I'd like better."

Somewhere deep within me I set a heel on all the joyous hopes I had known during the past days. They were dead for ever, and best forgotten quickly. I said, "Thank you, Alfie. From now on I just want to be part of Alfie Perkin and Company. I'll never think of leaving you again."

I meant those words with all my heart as I spoke them. It was not given to me to know that within three days they would prove false.

$\rbrace$ *fourteen* $\lbrace$

For much of Sunday we worked on ideas for the new sketch.
I was thankful to be kept busy. On the Monday I played
my part in *The Water Board Man.* I felt hollow and lifeless,
but strangely this seemed not to show through, and I think
we had the best Monday night reception I could remember.

At nine o'clock on the Tuesday morning, as we sat at
breakfast, Mrs. Bailey's son brought me a telegram. I opened
it apprehensively. The only person I could think of who
might send me a telegram was Kate, and then it would be
because something untoward had happened. Telegrams
rarely brought good news, I felt.

It was not from Kate, but it was about her. The words
danced before my eyes.

REGRET MISS KATE HAS RUN AWAY AND WE BELIEVE IT
IS ELOPEMENT PLEASE COME AT ONCE—PERONI.

Alfie's voice said from a distance, "Bridie? You all right?
You've gone white as a sheet."

I looked up, shaken to the roots of my being, keeping
my lips pressed together for fear that a dreadful and primitive
wail of despair would escape me. With shaking hand I
passed the telegram across to Alfie. He read it through
slowly, and I saw his face change. There were seven or
eight at the table besides ourselves, and all eyes were on
Alfie now. He glanced round, stood up, and said, "We'll
'ave a talk upstairs. Ethel. Charlie. Come on."

Alfie's room was on the second floor. We went upstairs
in a silent and somehow foolish-seeming procession. All

the way up my mind was saying numbly, "No. No, Kate. Oh, no. No. No, Kate..."

None of us sat down when we reached the room. Alfie closed the door and read out the telegram. His eyes were suddenly haggard, and I remembered that to him Kate had seemed a replica of my mother, the girl he had loved more than twenty years ago. Ethel said, "Oh, dear God, who do you think it is, Bridie?"

I shook my head. "I've no idea. She can sometimes be very romantic, very impulsive, but she hasn't spoken of anybody in her letters." I pressed the heels of my hands to my eyes, trying to clear the fog from my head. "There haven't been many letters, anyway."

Alfie looked at me. "You'll 'ave to get down there on the first train, Bridie."

"Yes. I'm sorry."

"Don't worry about that. Charlie's 'ere, and it's no trouble for 'im to step in. I'm just sorry I can't come down with you, but we've got to play out the rest of the booking."

"Yes, of course you have, and anyway I've no idea what can be done until I've spoken with Signor Peroni." My voice shook. "Perhaps nothing can be done. There may be no way of finding where she's gone, no way of knowing what's happened, until she writes."

Alfie said, "I'll nip down and borrow Mrs. Bailey's time-table, so we can see 'ow the trains run. You go and change to whatever you'll wear for the journey, Bridie. No, wait. Get packed, but don't put your traveling togs on just yet. Tell you why later. You go and 'elp 'er pack, Ethel. Just a suitcase. We'll bring 'er trunk with us when we all go 'ome, Sunday week."

Ten minutes later, as I tried to concentrate on packing while my mind churned in wild speculation, there came a tap on the door. Ethel straightened up from folding a dress, looked at me and said, "You all right, dear?" I drew my dressing gown about me, tied the belt, and nodded. She moved to the door and opened it to admit Alfie. He carried pieces of paper in one hand, and in the other something that looked like a thin white stocking which bulged in the middle.

"Train leaves at twenty-five past eleven, Bridie," he said. "It's an express, and you'll get to Euston in a couple of hours. I'll come and see you off, and I've ordered a cab for 'alf an hour before, to take us to the station. Right? Now before you get dressed, you put this on."

He handed me the strange white object, and I saw that it was of very fine suede, like a belt in the form of a tube, with something inside it, and a small leather-covered buckle at one end. Alfie said, "There's a row of little buttons along the top there, Bridie, to keep the money nice and snug inside."

I looked at him blankly. "Money?"

"It's a money belt, my dear. You wear it under your clothes. Look, you might 'ave to go chasing off anywhere over the next few days, and you'll need ready cash. I've put eighty quid in there in fivers, and twenty in ones—"

"Alfie, no!"

"Be quiet and listen, there's a good girl. If you don't need it, all well and good, but if you do, you'll be glad of it. Tell you the truth, I've got a funny feeling that young Kate's gone off abroad. Don't ask me why, because I don't know. P'raps I just always think of abroad when I think of 'er, because of that Mr. Peroni being foreign and your dad always being away in France. Anyway, you don't know what you might need, so apart from the ready cash I've written down the name and address of my bank in London. Tuck that away in your purse, Bridie. Now, you sign this other bit of paper, and I'll send it off to the bank manager today as a specimen signature, with a letter saying you can draw whatever you need from my account, see?"

I did not protest. I signed the slip of paper, then put my arms round Alfie's neck and wept against his shoulder. No words could have told what I felt.

The train brought me to Euston exactly on time. Ten minutes later I was in a cab and on the way to Kensington. I had sent a telegram from Birmingham to say that I would be arriving soon after two o'clock, and Mrs. Peroni had the front door open even before I had paid off the cab. Signor

Peroni hurried to take my suitcase, but said nothing until we were in the hall with the door closed behind us, then words burst from him.

"Oh, Miss Bridie, thank heaven you have come. We are desolate to face you." He pressed fingertips to his temples, and closed his eyes. "It is so bad, so bad that you entrust your sister to me and then that this happening takes place."

His wife stood with hands clutched together and said tearfully, "We didn't know. Really, we had no idea, Miss Bridie. It was such a shock, a terrible shock."

They both looked drawn with worry, and as I took off my gloves I said, "I'm sure you have nothing to blame yourselves for. You wrote and told me that Kate was being difficult, and I replied that it was best simply to do nothing for the time being." I managed a poor sort of smile. "So if anybody is at fault, I'm the one. Can we sit down now while you tell me all that you know about it?"

"*Si, si.* Of course. Come please, this way, Miss Bridie."

I was shown into the small but pleasant drawing room, and there Signor Peroni paced and paused, paced and paused with much gesticulation, while he told his tale with occasional interjections from his wife.

At the beginning of the previous week Kate had announced that she would like to spend the next weekend with a girl she had made friends with at the college, Sarah Patton. Sarah lived with her parents in Sussex Square, on the north side of Hyde Park. Her father was a barrister of some reputation, and Kate had stayed for a weekend once before at their house. As her unofficial guardian, Signor Peroni had first paid a call there to confirm the invitation and to assure himself that Kate would be staying in a respectable home.

On that earlier occasion, Kate and Sarah had gone straight from the college on a Friday afternoon, being driven to Sussex Square in the family carriage. The two girls had attended college together the following Monday morning, and Kate had finally returned to the Peroni household in Kensington at the end of the day's classes, so in fact she had been away from Friday morning till Monday evening.

On this second occasion, Signor Peroni had not felt it

necessary to confirm the invitation, but had naturally been quite content for Kate to spend a long weekend, as before, with a college friend of her own age in a household of unquestioned propriety. It was not until Kate failed to return on the Monday evening that he and his wife began to worry. When she was more than an hour late, he had taken a cab to the college, and there was fortunate to find a professor known to him, who said that to the best of his knowledge Kate had not attended her classes since the previous Thursday.

Shocked and bewildered, Signor Peroni had driven on to the house in Sussex Square, there to speak to Mr. Patton, and to learn that there was no truth in the story of the invitation. Sarah was summoned and questioned by her father. She was clearly startled to hear of the pretense, and of Kate's disappearance, but under stern questioning from Mr. Patton she admitted, with much reluctance, that she might be able to guess the reason.

Kate was in love, and had been in love for many weeks now. There was a man she often met secretly on days when she left college early. Sometimes she would miss a morning lesson, or return late after the luncheon break. Sarah had never seen the man, but had no doubt that Kate was completely enchanted by him, for of late she had seemed to live in a dream world, distrait, absent-minded, smiling at her own thoughts. The last thing Kate had confided to Sarah, some days ago now, was that this wonderful man had asked her to marry him.

I listened in alarm to Signor Peroni's story, yet in some ways I felt little surprise. There was great passion in Kate, indeed it played an important part in her musical ability, and if a man was clever enough to strike the right chord of response in her...

Signor Peroni said despairingly, "It was for me to know, but I did not see. Ah yes, I have known that she was at the most difficult stage in her work, you understand. It is similar to when a horse must jump a very high fence, I think. She was nervous. Afraid to fail. Perhaps, without knowing, she had looked for a way to escape, yes? All this I know, I understand. Why have I not seen also that she is a young girl in love?"

I said, "Did she leave no message for you? Nothing at all?"

Mrs. Peroni shook her head. "We've looked in her room and found nothing."

I rubbed my eyes with finger and thumb. "That's very strange. Kate could be wise or foolish, romantic or practical, but I've never known her deliberately unkind. To leave you without a word, after all you've done for her . . . that's cruel, and unlike her."

Signor Peroni waved a hand. "For a young girl in love there are no rules," he said. "To have a little madness is part of youth. My wife and I we do not mind for ourselves that Miss Kate left no word, but we have much fear that a man who would take her away in such manner is not a good man."

"Yes." I was fidgeting with my gloves, unable to keep still. "I have the same fear. This girl Sarah Patton seems to have been Kate's confidante. You have said she never saw the man, but did you ask if she learned anything about him?"

"Yes, Miss Bridie. This I asked. Oh, of course Miss Kate had told her that the man was handsome, wonderful, brilliant—er—kind, loving, intelligent, and etcetera. All the things that any young lady will see in the man she loves." He shrugged. "But apart from this, Sarah could say only one thing of importance she had learned from Miss Kate. The man is French."

I drew in a quick breath, startled as there came to my mind's eye the image of the man in the photograph Philippe Chatillon had given me, the man I had later seen near our home in Holborn. That photograph was in my writing case still, together with the photographs Nannie Foster had found and the letter from my father. I had packed them in my suitcase, scarcely knowing why. On the back of the photograph Philippe Chatillon had written: *This man is dangerous.*

"I don't know who the man is," I said slowly, "but I

believe I know what he looks like, and I have been warned against him myself." I suddenly found it hard to go on, for my throat seemed to be swelling with fear. "I think ... I think he is a scoundrel, a criminal perhaps, who set out to make Kate fall in love with him ... because he thinks she may be the means of finding some very important valuables that he and ... and other people believe were hidden by my father."

Signor Peroni and his wife exchanged a troubled look, then he went to sit beside her on the sofa, and held her hand. My mind had suddenly begun to work very quickly, and I now saw much that I had been unaware of until this moment. Kate's romance with the dangerous Frenchman had been going on much longer than I had at first thought. It had begun even before I left to go on tour. I remembered that she had asked about Papa's letter, speculating as to whether it held a hidden message. That question, I was now sure, had come from the Frenchman, and it had been echoed in one of the few letters she had written to me later.

I could not imagine what story he had told her to trick her into trying to worm such a secret out of me without telling me why, but a clever and unscrupulous man could have done it easily enough with an impressionable girl. It would be especially easy with a girl who had suffered a series of tremendous shocks, a complete change in her way of life, and who, as a student, was facing particular difficulties at this stage of her progress.

Remembering how easily Nathan McFee had deceived me, I could not feel that Kate had been any more gullible than I had been myself. The man had courted Kate, dazzled her, and bided his time. Then had come the moment when she received the letter I had written to her from Nannie Foster's cottage, telling her of the photographs and the cryptic part of Papa's letter. It must have been then, from the moment she told him of this, that the man decided to take Kate away with him ... to France, of course, to the Dordogne valley to seek that which had been hidden—

But no. My flow of reasoning faltered. Kate did not possess the photographs or a copy of the letter, and knew only as much as I had described or quoted. Why had the Frenchman not waited till he had access to every detail? And if what Kate had told him was sufficient, why continue his deception? What was his reason for persuading her to go with him? She would certainly believe that it was an elopement, and that they were to be married, of that I was sure. However romantic Kate might be, she had too much pride to accept the role of mistress.

I shook myself mentally, trying to free my thoughts from confusion. Speculation was fruitless, and the important thing now was for me to find Kate, wherever she might be, and tell her she had been duped... if she had not already discovered as much. And then? I could not plan beyond that point, for I was so much in the dark, but I knew that the man to help me now was Philippe Chatillon, the French private detective. Unless he had changed his plans, he would have finished his business in England long since. It might well be that the personal interest he had once shown in me had passed, but I knew from our first encounter, in Wynford, that he would be very much interested in what I had to tell him now.

"Miss Bridie?"

Signor Peroni's voice penetrated my deliberations. I came to myself and said, "I'm sorry, you asked me something, but I was busy with my thoughts."

"Of course. I was asking if it will be possible to find Miss Kate."

"Well... yes, I think there is somebody who is very much in a position to help me, but it means I must go to Paris as soon as possible."

"Paris?"

"I'm sure Kate is in France. Do you have a Bradshaw, Signor Peroni? I would like to look up the times of the boat trains."

It was now three o'clock, and from Bradshaw's Railway Guide I discovered that I could either catch the nine o'clock mail train from Charing Cross, and go by way of Dover and Calais to arrive at Gare du Nord shortly before six tomorrow morning, or I could take the night express from

Victoria, a quarter of an hour earlier, which would take me by way of Newhaven and Dieppe to Gare St. Lazare by half past six. After very little thought I decided on the latter, for by taking the longer sea crossing I could reserve a cabin on the steamer for only a few shillings more than the first-class fare, which was less than two pounds. In a cabin I could at least lie down and rest, even if sleep escaped me.

During the next few hours I wrote a brief letter to Alfie, rested for a while in Kate's bedroom, and forced down some of the very excellent meal Mrs. Peroni decided I must have before beginning my ten-hour journey. Signor Peroni came to Victoria with me in a hansom cab, greatly troubled at the idea of my traveling alone. I assured him that I would manage very well, and persuaded him not to wait for the half hour before the train was due to depart. The thought of trying to maintain some kind of conversation at such a time was too much for me.

Before leaving he saw me comfortably settled in a first-class carriage, then bowed over my hand and said, "Please to give to Miss Kate our affection. Tomorrow I will go with all my family to the church, to pray she has not come to harm."

"Thank you, Signor Peroni. I'm sorry she has caused you so much anxiety."

"That does not matter, Miss Bridie." He hesitated. "I hope she will not have a too unhappy experience. But whatever has passed, please say to her to come back to her music. It can heal all bad memories."

"I will tell her, signore."

"And please say also that she has the blessing of a good gift. She must not let it die."

"Yes."

When he had gone I sank back and closed my eyes, thankful to be alone. My head throbbed, and although I was desperately weary I felt I would never be able to sleep until I held Kate's hand in mine and could carry her away to safety.

For one long aching moment I wished I might look round and see Nathan beside me, quiet and strong, a man I could turn to, could lean on, could trust to stand with me through whatever might lie ahead. But the moment faded and died. Nathan McFee was no such man. He had played the false friend and humiliated me. Better to be alone than to have such a friend; and unless I could win help from Philippe Chatillon I would indeed be alone in my task, as I had been in those days which seemed a hundred years ago now, the days of grief and fear at Latchford Hall.

When the train clanked to a halt in Gare St. Lazare I was in much better case than I had expected. To my surprise and relief I had slept soundly for four hours in my cabin on the steamer, and dozed for another two during the train journey from Dieppe. From the moment of leaving Victoria I had somehow managed to keep a tight hold on my imagination, not allowing myself to speculate on what Kate's situation might be, and perhaps this had enabled me to seize the chance of sleep.

It was not yet seven o'clock. I could scarcely present myself at Philippe Chatillon's house before eight. To do so even at that hour would be quite outrageous, for in all likelihood he would still be abed, but I was determined not to be any later. I had been able to make a reasonable toilet before leaving my cabin at Dieppe, but that was two hours ago, and since I now had a little time to spare I engaged a porter to carry my case across to the hotel adjoining the station. I had money to pay him, for I had changed some on the steamer, and soon I was at the hotel reception desk, explaining to the clerk that I wished to take breakfast and to use the toilet facilities. I felt very thankful that my French was good, for I had never set foot out of England before, and would have felt a little nervous to be on my own here without the language, especially under the heavy anxiety that pressed down upon me.

There were only four other people in the hotel restaurant for breakfast at this hour, but the service was excellent and the coffee the best I had ever tasted. At twenty minutes to eight o'clock, a hotel porter carried my case out for me and whistled to bring a cab across from the rank outside the station. When it arrived, I read out to the driver the address on the card Philippe Chatillon had sent me long ago in Wynford, made sure I had been understood correctly, then settled back in my seat as the cab began to rattle along at a good pace down Rue Lafayette. Twenty minutes later I was speaking to a doleful man who was concierge of an apartment building so peeling and run down that I had at first thought the cabbie must have brought me to the wrong address. I could not believe that Philippe Chatillon lived in so poor a place.

Since I had not yet paid the fare, my cabbie was now in the hall with me, requiring the concierge to confirm for the third time that this was indeed number sixteen Rue Flavin. I said in French, "Yes, I agree that you have brought me to the correct address. Now please be quiet and wait while I ask some questions." Turning to the concierge I held out the card and went on, "You have no gentleman here by this name?"

"No, mam'selle."

"And he was not living here last year?"

A patient sigh. "No, mam'selle."

I felt utterly at a loss, and had a sense of growing unease. The concierge tapped the side of his nose with a finger and leaned forward to speak in a throaty whisper. "Sometimes a gentleman will use this address for correspondence, you understand. A gentleman who does not wish his true where-abouts to be known to another person, to a *petite amie*, perhaps, with whom he has little assignations."

The cabbie chuckled, and both men stared at me with interest. Once I would have flushed and been overcome by embarrassment, but I was no longer the Bridie Chance of old; I had been annealed in the fires of clowning before a hundred music hall audiences, and I could never again be disconcerted by laughter.

I said, "Any such gentleman would have to give you his correct address, so that correspondence could be sent on. Do you have such an address for M'sieu Chatillon?"

The concierge spread his hands and shook his head. "I regret, mam'selle. Gentlemen using this address must call for their letters, and I have a poor memory for names and faces."

The cabbie said, "Chatillon?"

I looked at him hopefully. "Yes."

"Not M'sieu Philippe Chatillon, surely?"

"But yes. He is a detective, I understand."

"Oh-ho. Oh-ho. Yes, yes. You understand very well, mam'selle. Naturally he is a detective, and of much fame except to such imbeciles as this." He surveyed the concierge with huge scorn. "But I, Charles Bouvet, I have driven him in my cab on *two* occasions, no less."

I said quickly, "Can you take me to his address?"

"Certainly, mam'selle, certainly, but it is far from this flea pit, I assure you. Come, we will go at once, and even though you are a foreigner I shall take you by the most direct route, for I am a man of honor, you understand."

For the next ten minutes, as we drove, he regaled me with a shouted account of how he frequently plied for hire near the Sûreté, which I gathered was the equivalent of Scotland Yard, and on *two* occasions he had been privileged to drive M'sieu Chatillon home from meetings with his important friends in the police. Because he, Charles Bouvet, was a man of honor, he continued, it was only proper to inform me that nine out of ten cabbies would have been able to take me to the house of M'sieu Chatillon. This gentleman had become well-known among them two or three years ago when he had proved the innocence of a cab driver accused of murder, who would otherwise have gone to the guillotine. It had been a most dramatic affair, I was assured, and since then M'sieu Chatillon had been a great hero among the cabbies of Paris.

We passed through the center of Paris and continued west for a full two miles before drawing up at last by the gates of a small but gracious house standing in its own grounds in a tree-lined road. Again I asked the cabbie to wait, left my suitcase in the cab, and thanked him as he opened one of the iron gates for me. Standing before the heavy door, I tugged the bellpull and waited nervously. A minute passed, and then the door was opened by a short, square, gray-haired woman in maid's uniform. She gave me a suspicious look and said in a far from encouraging tone, "Mam'selle?"

"Is this the residence of M'sieu Philippe Chatillon, if you please?"

"That is so," she acknowledged coldly.

"Is he in residence at this moment?"

"Who wishes to see him?"

I gave her look for look, and said, "I have traveled overnight from London on a very urgent matter in which I know M'sieu Chatillon to be deeply interested. Please give him my apologies for calling unannounced at this hour, and say that Mam'selle Bridget Chance wishes to see him." Since I had no visiting card, I had taken the precaution of writing my name in block letters on a slip of paper so that there would be no problem of pronunciation.

The maid stared, took the slip of paper, glanced at it quickly, then stepped back and said, "Please enter, mam'selle." She led me across a paneled hall to a beautifully furnished drawing room. "Please be seated. I will inform M'sieu Chatillon at once." She gave a slight shrug. "He gave instructions that he was not to be disturbed. For once he will be glad that I take little notice of his instructions." She turned, raising her eyes briefly to the ceiling. "Men are truly stupid, are they not?"

She went out without waiting for a reply, and I guessed that her position was that of an old retainer with a master who indulged her crotchety manner. Less than a minute later I heard quick footsteps in the hall, and the maid's voice again. "Certainly I have not kept her waiting. I am not a fool, M'sieu Philippe, and I know what you would wish."

A man's voice, drawing nearer, "Naturally you know, since you pry into my business and read my letters, Hortense. Now be so good as to fetch coffee—no, no, let it be tea. And a little something to eat, some biscuits, small cakes, perhaps—"

"Do you have to tell me? Am I an imbecile?"

"Then go and see to it, wretched woman! Off with you."

The door opened and he stepped quickly into the room, still buttoning a jacket which he must have been putting on as he hurried through the hall. But the man was not Philippe Chatillon, with those curiously magnetic hazel eyes set in the square face beneath the cap of black curls. This was another man. He wore a white shirt and a tie of dull gold material. No more than an inch taller than I, he was very well proportioned and moved lightly on his feet. The eyes were dark and wide-set, the hair light brown, and the face was one I knew. I had seen it, very briefly, under a lamp in Holborn one evening. I had also seen it in a photograph, and on the back of that photograph Philippe Chatillon had written, *This man is dangerous.*

I was on my feet, staring in shock and bewilderment as the man came forward extending his hand, a smile of inquiry on his lips. In excellent English, with an accent that was pleasant to the ear, he said, "I am delighted to see you, Miss Chance. I hope you are in good health, and your charming sister also."

I half put out my hand automatically, then drew it back and blurted out, "Where is M'sieu Chatillon?"

He looked puzzled. "I am here, mam'selle."

"But you are not Philippe Chatillon!"

He spread his hands, palms up, and there was amusement in his eyes as he said, "I am sorry you should think that, but I assure you I can bring many witnesses to confirm that my claim is true."

My mind was in complete chaos, and I pressed hands to my cheeks as I tried to think. I had been warned against this man by the French detective, Philippe Chatillon, yet this same man claimed to *be* Philippe Chatillon. The maid-servant might be part of some devious plot, but I did not see how the cabbie who had brought me here could also be an accomplice in it.

The man said, "You are clearly startled, mam'selle. May I ask why you think I am not Philippe Chatillon?"

With an effort I pulled myself together and said confusedly, "But I have met M'sieu Chatillon. I met him near the house where I used to live in Suffolk. He...he sent a wreath for my father's funeral. And I met him again in London." The man's eyebrows lifted in surprise and he seemed about to speak, but I hurried on. "He said that I should write to him if I discovered any sort of message left by my father, a message containing a riddle to be solved. He said he would come to help me. Here is his card." I had been fumbling in my bag, and now held out the printed card sent to me in Wynford.

The man took it, but kept his eyes on me and said, "Please continue, mam'selle."

"I . . . I did not write to him, but he came to see me again several months later, when I was working in a shop in London. It was then that he . . . he warned me against you, and gave me this." I put the photograph into the man's hand. He looked at it, smiled, turned it over, read the words on the back, gave a wry shrug, then studied the visiting card.

After a few moments he looked up and said, "I did indeed send a wreath on the sad occasion of your father's funeral. It was arranged by your local undertaker to whom I sent a card on which I had written, '*Dormez bien, mon vieil adversaire.*'"

I caught my breath, and there was an abrupt swirling in the turmoil of my thoughts. Suddenly I saw, in my mind's eye but with startling clarity, the neat angular handwriting on the card attached to the wreath from Philippe Chatillon. It was quite different from the round, untidy scrawl, *This man is dangerous*, on the back of the photograph. I had seen that scrawl penciled there myself by the man with hazel eyes, and when I studied the photograph later I had felt that something was amiss. I could not put my finger on it then, and had dismissed the feeling as false, but now I knew. The writing had not matched.

The man in front of me reached into his inside pocket and said, "Perhaps you would care to compare the calligraphy with the writing in my diary? I think you will agree that I can hardly have made preparations for your visit."

I looked at him, and knew the truth. "No," I said slowly. "It is not necessary for me to see your handwriting. I realize I have been greatly deceived." I put out my hand. "How do you do, M'sieu Chatillon. Please forgive my discourteous greeting."

He took my hand and bowed over it. "There is nothing to forgive, and I am truly delighted to make your acquaintance, mam'selle. Please sit down, and then we will talk. I think we may have much to say to each other."

"Thank you. Oh, I have a cab waiting, and have left my suitcase in it."

"Hortense will attend to all that in a moment."

"But I must give her the fare."

"Please be seated and do not trouble yourself further. I insist. Are you comfortable? Good." He stood with hands clasped behind his back, eyes thoughtful. "Well now, it is perhaps a little difficult to know where we should begin."

"Yes. I feel so confused, M'sieu Chatillon. Who can he be, this man who claimed to be you? And why did he do such a thing? I can describe him to you very easily. He is—"

"Forgive me, but there is no need," said Philippe Chatillon, lifting an apologetic hand as he interrupted. "He is French, of good height and build, short curly hair almost black, light brown eyes...and a power to charm which ladies are said to find quite irresistible. His name is Victor Antoine Jean-Pierre Sarrazin, and he is a criminal. The words he wrote on the back of my photograph may be truly applied to him. This man is dangerous."

The door opened and the gray-haired maid entered, pushing an elaborate trolley bearing a silver tea service with cups and saucers of beautiful blue and white porcelain, and a salver of very small honey-colored cakes. Philippe Chatillon said, "Thank you, Hortense, that will be all. Please go and pay the cabbie who brought mam'selle. Thank him, and give him a good tip."

"Rogues and scoundrels, the lot of them," sniffed Hortense. "Will mam'selle be staying for luncheon?"

"I hope and believe so. Please prepare accordingly."

"Very well." She glanced at me, then rolled her eyes toward him. "Are you going to languish over this one also?"

"Go and do as you are told, you stupid old woman, or I will have you sold for dog meat."

"Ha!" She shuffled away with a throaty chuckle, and when the door closed behind her Philippe Chatillon said, "Please excuse Hortense. She has been with my family for forty-five years now, and is somewhat privileged. Also, her husband is the best cook in Paris." He gave me a friendly smile, drew up a chair, and began to pour tea. "Now, concerning Victor Sarrazin, there is much I can explain to you, but that can wait. In a way I am glad that he used my name when he first met you, for by good fortune this has brought you here to me in Paris. You have come in haste, and you have said the matter is urgent, so I will delay no longer in asking you now I may serve you."

I hesitated to take the cup he was now offering to me, for my hands were suddenly shaking as I said, "I believe he has taken my sister, Kate. I think she has . . . eloped with him."

Very carefully Philippe Chatillon set down the cup and saucer, then stood up as if he could not bear to remain still. I saw to my surprise that his face had lost color, and he said in a low voice, "That dog Sarrazin has taken Kate? Oh dear God, no."

I said, bewildered, "You speak as if she was known to you, m'sieu."

He nodded, and paced away with his hands behind his back again, a small wiry figure. "Yes, I know her, though she does not know me. For much of the summer I was in London, watching her . . . because I was watching Sarrazin. Then, as I thought, he concluded that she could be of no use to him, and he returned to France. I realize now that it was a trick. He must have discovered my surveillance, and decided to throw me off the scent. Evidently he went back to England as soon as he had achieved his purpose."

When Philippe Chatillon turned to pace toward me I saw that his face was drawn and there was hot anger in his eyes. "Fool!" he muttered. "Fool that I am!"

I put a hand to my head. "There is much that I do not

understand, m'sieu, and I hope you will enlighten me, but above all I pray that you can help me to find my sister."

"I do not think it will be difficult to find her," he said quietly. "Sarrazin will have taken her to his home, which is a small and dilapidated château south of Brive. But I doubt that he can be accused of abducting her. It is even possible that he has married her. A special license would not be difficult to arrange."

I looked down at my hands in my lap. "Why has he done this, m'sieu? It is not for love of her, I am sure of that. When we met in London he... he was most flattering to me and said that he wished to court me."

"That does not surprise me. Did you find yourself attracted to Victor Sarrazin, mam'selle?"

I lifted my head and looked at him. "Yes, and in a way that I found frightening. Perhaps that was why I rejected him, because I felt that I would be... lost. He has more than charm, m'sieu, he has power, and if he exerted that power upon Kate, I cannot feel surprise that she yielded to it."

"Poor young girl," he said gently, and closed his eyes for a moment, then opened them and said in a businesslike manner, "You asked just now why Sarrazin has done this, but I think you know the answer."

"You mean... the spoils my father left?"

"Yes. That is the reason for everything our devious friend Sarrazin has done. The only two persons who might know your father's secret, or come to know it, are your sister and yourself. If you had found a message, a riddle, and written to Philippe Chatillon at the accommodation address Sarrazin gave you, then *he* would have received it, and his first move would have succeeded. But you did not write, and so he made a new move. Tell me, when he came to you in London did he ask then if you had found any letter or message?"

I cast back in my mind, and said, "Yes. Yes, he did. At that time I had come into possession of a letter my father had left for my mother. It was only later I found photographs that made me realize there was a message in the letter. But when Victor Sarrazin asked me, I felt I did not want anybody to know of the letter I had found, so I told him a lie."

Philippe Chatillon shook his head. "From you, that would never deceive Sarrazin. He would know at once that you were trying to hide something from him, and so he began an attempt to court you. When that failed, he turned his attention to your sister."

"But that was months ago, m'sieu. Would he pursue her for so long?"

"Once he knew that the secret existed, yes. For he believes, as I do, that the spoils will be enormous. The Pinkerton agency of America has had a man working on this case for over a year now, in the hope of recovering just two pieces of jewelry for a wealthy client."

I tried to keep the heaviness from my voice as I said, "Yes. Nathan McFee."

"Ah, he has made himself known to you then?"

"Not exactly. He was watching me, as this man Sarrazin was watching Kate, and for the same reason. I discovered by accident that he was working for an American detective agency. He has been called back to America now."

Philippe Chatillon gave a frown of surprise. "Strange to withdraw him when he is so familiar with the case. I met him when he first came to France, shortly before your father died. A very competent man, I would say."

"Yes. Very competent, I have no doubt." My mouth was dry. I managed to pick up my cup of tea and sip a little without my hands shaking too obviously. "I must accept that the spoils are worth all the time and effort that various parties are prepared to spend in the matter, m'sieu, but how can it help Victor Sarrazin to make Kate fall in love and run away with him? She knows something of the letter my father left, and of the photographs I discovered, because I wrote to tell her about them, but I cannot believe she knows enough for Sarrazin's purposes."

Philippe Chatillon looked at me somberly. "Mam'selle," he said, "Sarrazin will take the view that if he has your sister in his hands, then he has you also. I am surprised that you have not already received some sort of message from him."

I felt the blood drain from my cheeks as I set down my cup. "You mean he would . . . harm her? He would actually harm Kate?"

"If he thinks it necessary in order to achieve what he wants. He is capable of anything, I fear."

"Then I must go to the police, at once!" I stood up as I spoke, but he came toward me with hands lifted in a calming gesture.

"Please, mam'selle, do not think that the police can put this matter right for you. Sarrazin is very clever, and I am sure that a marriage has taken place. What passes between husband and wife is no concern of the police. The law is very wary of interference in that sphere. He may virtually do as he pleases with her."

It was pleasantly warm in the room, but I felt shivery with cold. After a moment or two I said, "Please advise me, m'sieu. Please help me. I ask your professional help now, and whatever your fee I will find a way to pay it."

He shook his head quickly. "Oh no, mam'selle. There will be no fee. I offer you not my professional help, but my personal help in this matter." He paused, biting his lower lip for a moment, then went on quietly, "Did you take note of a remark Hortense made as she was leaving us a few minutes ago?"

I thought back, and said uncertainly, "I remember her using a word which I think would translate into English as 'languish,' but I did not quite grasp the reference."

He gave a little sigh. "I am a bachelor of thirty-five, mam'selle. I am well-to-do, I follow a profession which interests me, and I have known more than a few young ladies since my youth. It therefore amuses Hortense that I should have found my emotions deeply engaged with a young lady I have never spoken to but have simply watched over for a number of weeks."

I said wonderingly, "You mean . . . Kate?"

"Yes. Your younger sister. I doubt that she would know my face, for I can claim to have some skill in the craft of surveillance, yet I spent many days within a stone's throw of her whenever she went out, watching her pass to and fro daily between home and college, observing her clandestine meetings with Victor Sarrazin, and feeling tormented by worry as I saw him bring her under his spell."

"Did you not warn her, m'sieu?"

"You ask an artless question, Mam'selle Bridget. Can you imagine how a young girl would respond to a stranger who tells her that the man she loves is a criminal?"

"But surely there was something you could do?"

He moved to a bellpull and tugged it. "You feel I might have informed you? That is true, though in the event it would only have brought confusion, for Sarrazin had already made sure that you believed me to be a very wicked man. A clever precaution on his part. In fact, I made no attempt to inform you because I felt better able to protect your sister by not allowing you, or her, or Sarrazin, to become aware of me, but by keeping watch and thwarting whatever move he might decide to make."

I said wearily, "But you have not done so, m'sieu. He has tricked you, and taken Kate."

"You cannot blame me more bitterly than I now blame myself," said Philippe Chatillon quietly. "I involved myself in this case because I wished to bring Victor Sarrazin to book, but that reason was replaced by one far stronger as time went by." He shook his head as if long baffled. "I cannot explain this, even to myself. I can only say that as I watched her walk, speak, or laugh, watched her look mischievous, severe, surprised, or troubled . . . I found she had captured a heart I had long thought immune."

He stopped abruptly as the door opened and the elderly maid entered again in answer to his summons. "And what is it now, m'sieu?" she demanded. "Oh, but you have a long face indeed."

He said sharply, "Hold your tongue, Hortense. Go and pack an overnight bag for me at once. I want it done in ten minutes. Tell Raoul to have the carriage ready. Off with you now."

She stared for a moment, then gave a brisk nod. "Leave it to me, m'sieu."

As the door closed I said, "What do you intend to do?"

He had moved to a bureau in one corner, opened it, and taken out a thick book with a gray paper cover. "I shall go at once to Château Valbrison," he said, flicking quickly through the pages, "for that is where Sarrazin will be with your sister. Let me see . . . ah yes, excellent, there is an express to Toulouse at shortly after nine o'clock. It stops only at Orléans and Limoges, but I will send a note to a friend of mine at the Sûreté, and he will arrange by telegraph for it to be stopped for a few moments at Brive, where there is a good connection for Valbrison, thirty kilometers beyond. I shall be there by soon after three o'clock if all goes well."

I stood up. "You must take me with you, m'sieu."

He looked at me, and gave a little nod. "I hoped you would wish to come. You realize that to travel with me unchaperoned is to endanger your reputation?"

"Please," I said impatiently, "we need not concern ourselves with matters of no importance. I am on the stage, and therefore have no reputation."

He gave a short laugh, made me a bow, and tossed the timetable aside. "I am informed of your achievements, Mam'selle Bridget, and I count it a privilege to meet you. I know that your father, my old adversary, Roger Chance, would regard his daughter with most joyous delight and pride."

I tried to keep all bitterness from my voice as I said, "That gives me small pleasure, m'sieu. I loved my father, but I cannot forget what he has brought upon my poor sister. I think he would take little delight in that."

"As you say." He stared bleakly into space for a moment or two, then came to himself and took out his watch. "We shall leave in five minutes, and I shall try to reserve a compartment on the train. It should not be difficult, I think. We can take luncheon on the journey, and, if you agree, discuss the letter and photographs you spoke of earlier."

"I have them with me, M'sieu Chatillon."

"Good. And since we are to be colleagues in this matter, may I ask you to do me the honor of calling me Philippe?"

"Thank you. And I am always called Bridie." I hesitated, then went on, "What will you do when we reach Château Valbrison?"

Philippe Chatillon gave a small shrug. "I shall confront Victor Sarrazin. I shall find out if he has married your sister. That being the case, I will offer to give all possible assistance in finding the spoils left by Roger Chance, with the categorical understanding that Sarrazin may take and keep them without hindrance from me, if he will release Kate into your care. Do you agree?"

"Yes, of course. But if he refuses?"

Cold menace flared suddenly in the dark eyes of the quiet man before me. He picked up the photograph of himself he had put down on the table, and turned it over to read what was scrawled on the back. "If Sarrazin refuses," he said in the same polite voice, "then he will learn that the words he wrote here are true." His head came up again. "I will do whatever may be necessary, Bridie. Whatever may be necessary."

❧ fifteen ❧

We caught the Limoges train with ten minutes to spare, and
Philippe Chatillon was able to reserve a compartment for
us without difficulty. As the train moved out along the left
bank of the Seine, heading south for Orléans, I began to
learn more of Victor Sarrazin, the strangely compelling man
I had first encountered in a country lane near Latchford
Hall; the first man ever to say I was beautiful, though he
lied; who later asked if he might court me, though he did
so entirely for his own dark purposes.

Victor Antoine Jean-Pierre Sarrazin, the youngest son of
an aristocratic family, was a gambler, a libertine, and a
receiver of stolen property, though this last was something
which had never yet been proved. His own family had long
since turned their backs on him, but he was still accepted
in most sections of cosmopolitan society throughout Europe,
for many ladies and gentlemen with too little to do were
greatly attracted not only by his considerable charm, but
also by the dark rumors that were whispered about him.

It did not matter that he was arrogant, heartless, unscrupulous, and often openly contemptuous of almost all those
with whom he associated. Such defects even added to his
attractions in some circles. There was one man only he
respected, and perhaps to a degree feared, for this man was
utterly unimpressed either by Victor Sarrazin's charm or by
his sinister reputation, and usually regarded him with the
kind of tolerant amusement that might be accorded to a
precocious youth. The man was Roger Chance, my father.
He used Sarrazin as a spy to keep watch on wealthy ladies
with valuable jewelry, and he used him as a receiver. Sar-

razin would willingly have become a lieutenant and disciple of Le Sorcier, but Roger Chance would have none of him in that respect. He was of use as a tool, and no more.

As I sat in the corner of our reserved compartment, Philippe Chatillon gazed distantly out of the window and told me of the extraordinary man who had been my father. "He could not help himself, Bridie. Of that I am sure. You must realize that when Sarrazin pretended to be me, as you have described, and said that I was both friend and adversary of your father, he spoke the truth for once. I knew Roger Chance long before he at last fell under suspicion of being Le Sorcier. Afterward, such was his confidence that it amused him to fence with me verbally when I made reference to these suspicions. You tell me also that Sarrazin, as Philippe Chatillon, claimed that he urged your father to retire to England. That also is true. I liked Roger Chance, you understand, and I knew that soon he must be brought down, if not by me, then by the police."

He sketched a shrug, and turned his head to glance at me with a wan smile. "There are people who must climb mountains though it will kill them. Roger Chance was a man with just such a compulsion, but one that was far darker. Because of it, your family suffered greatly, as the family of the man who falls from a mountain suffers greatly, though your case was much worse. But he was not a bad man, Bridie."

I said a little tiredly, "No. But I've learned that people don't have to be bad to cause a great deal of hurt."

He gave me a curious look. "You have suffered a painful hurt recently?"

I shrugged. "It's of no importance. I can think only of Kate now. Please tell me, is Sarrazin in any way like my father, or is he truly bad?"

"Oh, he is truly bad." Philippe Chatillon stared out of the window again with haunted eyes. After a moment or two he shook his head as if making an effort to clear it. "I must keep firm hold on my feelings," he said sharply. "Anger and worry are the enemies of clear thought, and we shall need all our wits about us in dealing with Victor Sarrazin. May we study your father's letter and the photographs now, please? If we can make some progress in deciphering his message, we shall have more to bargain with when we confront Sarrazin."

For two hours before we went to take luncheon, of which we both forced ourselves to eat at least a little, and for another hour afterward, we read and reread the letter, studied and scrutinized the photographs, seeking to draw coherence from the words my father had written.

At some time in the early afternoon, when we had still made no progress, Philippe said, "It is written in English, and I think it may be very hard for a Frenchman to perceive the nuances that may be here. Let us try again. He speaks of '*the little smithy.*' Is there any double meaning there, Bridie?"

I thought carefully, and shook my head at last. "No. I think it must really just be a smithy, a forge, a particular place from which you can go up into '*the high valleys.*'"

He said thoughtfully, "Yes . . . the high valleys. We shall be entering such an area toward the end of our journey, where there are many places not unlike this rocky valley where your mother stands in the photograph. Dear God, how like Kate she is. So beautiful—" He stopped abruptly. "Let us continue. Your father speaks of making a pilgrimage to this place, and asks your mother to remember the poor poetry he spoke. '*Pilgrimage? Poor poetry?*' Do the words have any special significance, Bridie?"

Again I shook my head. "No. Being Irish, he always tended to speak with a touch of poetry in his phrasing, but I think here it's simply to justify what follows, which is poor poetry and poor prose, all about '*darkness at eventide*' and '*dayspring of rainbow's end.*' I believe that's where the real message is hidden."

"Yes, I agree. But wait, Bridie, wait. Let us take the matter in sequence. '*Walk again where the stream runs golden from the hills . . .*' I would say that also is a simple instruction, except that a stream would be more likely to run golden toward sunset or shortly after sunrise. '*And on to the valley of the Capricorn Stone.*' This, surely, is where your mother stands against the stone pillar, but again it is not a unique landmark. So 'Capricorn' is written here to help identify it . . . but how? Why is this called the Capricorn Stone?"

"I can't think why, Philippe. Perhaps it was just a name my father gave it."

"But to know why he chose that name might help to guide us to it. Does the word Capricorn have any particular significance in your family?"

I thought carefully, then said, "Not that I know of."

"What does it mean to you in general?"

"Oh . . . well, it's the southern boundary of the earth's tropical zone, and it's also a constellation of stars. I can't think of anything else."

"Nor I." He sat gazing blankly out of the window for a while. "I am no astronomer, but I think the constellation comes into the zodiac. I have heard of people being born under Capricorn."

"Yes. I don't know which sign it is, though. Oh, yes I do. The constellation of Capricorn is The Goat, isn't it? So it must be the zodiac sign of The Goat—"

I broke off, and we stared at each other with wide eyes. After long seconds Philippe Chatillon said quietly, "Well done, Bridie. *Tête de Chèvre.* Goat's head. The words your father pencilled on the back of this photograph."

"Yes," I said doubtfully. "I suppose so. But it doesn't really tell us any more, does it?"

"We may find more meaning in it if we can solve other parts of the puzzle." He looked at the letter again. "It continues, '*Remember me then, and have no fear of the shadow, Mary dear, for the darkness at eventide leads only to the dayspring of rainbow's end.*' No fear of the shadow? What shadow? The Capricorn Stone would cast a shadow, of course, but why should she fear it?"

"I think," I said slowly, "that some of the phrases are put in simply to link up the important parts, and the important part here must surely be the shadow."

"Which he seems to equate with '*the darkness at eventide.*' And this leads to—ah, yes! It is a way of saying that the shadow points in a particular direction." He frowned, and looked up from the letter. "But shadows move with the sun."

"He says '*at eventide*,' so it must mean when the sun is going down." I sat up a little straighter in my seat. "Why, yes. That confirms what you said before, about '*where the stream runs golden*.' It would be more likely either at sunrise or sunset."

He gave a quick nod of agreement. "Exactly so. And now we can assume that the shadow of the Capricorn Stone at sunset points to . . . ." he looked down at the letter once more. "To the '*dayspring of rainbow's end*,' which by tradition is where a crock of gold is to be found. There will be a hiding place, of course, but of what nature we cannot tell until we find the Capricorn Stone and are able to study the surroundings."

I knew this part of the letter by heart now, and could recall the final words. *Have no fear of the waiting crow, for it serves only to reveal the emptiness that is filled with brightness.* The second half of the sentence, we had already agreed, must refer to the hiding place in which the spoils lay, but we had been unable to fathom the first half.

As if echoing my thoughts, Philippe Chatillon said slowly, "Again there are the words, '*have no fear*,' and I agree with your suggestion that they are make-weights without meaning. But what is '*the waiting crow*'? There surely cannot be a living bird in the hiding place, or a dead one either, for that matter."

"I believe that in England the word 'crow' can mean an inferior quality of coal," I said. "But that doesn't seem to make any better sense."

"No," Philippe Chatillon agreed after a little reflection, "but that is the way to think, Bridie. Let your mind be flexible."

My head had begun to ache, and I leaned back, closing my eyes. "Does it matter so much that we solve the riddle, Philippe?" I asked a little wearily. "My concern is for Kate."

"And mine," he said sharply. "That is why we are seeking

an answer. The more we have to offer Sarrazin, the greater our chance that he will yield Kate up in return."

"Yes. I'm sorry, I wasn't thinking very clearly. Let's go through it again from the beginning."

We had made no further progress when the train halted briefly for us at Brive, where we had fifteen minutes to wait for the train to Valbrison. It was warmer here than it had been in Paris. We sat on a bench together, saying little, for it was difficult to speak of ordinary matters, and we could not talk about our true concerns in public.

The sky was without a cloud. A short way from where we sat, three or four French workmen in blue overalls were renewing sleepers in a siding, levering the old ones out with thick steel bars. There were no more than six other passengers waiting for the Valbrison train. I watched the workmen, watched the passengers, but found it more difficult every moment to keep Kate out of my mind or to hold back the panic that threatened to possess me if I allowed myself to wonder about her plight. The workmen lifted another sleeper, then paused to lean on their picks and crowbars while they watched a train pull slowly out of the station on its way to Limoges. There was nothing to distract me from the thoughts I dreaded, and in desperation I closed my eyes and began to rehearse *The Water Board Man* in my head, going through Alfie's lines, Ethel's lines, then my own part, mentally playing and dancing my way through the moves which had now become so familiar to me.

I had almost reached the end of the sketch when the local train came in, and two minutes later we were on our way to Valbrison. I knew that Philippe Chatillon was as tense as I, for I could see his wiry hands working about the knob of the slender black cane he carried. We were traveling beside the river now, and as I gazed out I knew suddenly that I had failed to recognize some important thought that lay in the depths of my mind. What it was, I could not tell. Somewhere, sometime, I had heard or seen something that threw light on the riddle we had just spent hours trying to solve. No . . . not sometime. Recently. For whatever it was had not been in my mind for long; had not been there when we left Paris.

As the train rattled slowly along the valley, climbing gradually, I wrestled with the infuriating will-o'-the-wisp of memory. Sometimes the recollection seemed tantalizingly within my grasp, then it would fade so completely that I would wonder if I had imagined it. After twenty minutes I closed my eyes and tried to make my mind a blank.

Overalls. Blue overalls. I could see the old railway sleepers being pried up out of their flinty beds. Workmen, some smoking stubby pipes, one with a jug of wine...

The train was beginning to slow for a bend when I jumped as if stung, and clutched the arm of the man beside me, thankful that we were alone in the compartment. "The *crow*, Philippe!" I gasped. "The waiting crow! It isn't a bird, it's a common abbreviation of *crowbar*! Oh, what's the word in French? *Un levier? Une barre de fer?* A long iron lever for... for prying things up. There must be something in the hiding place that has to be pried up. The letter says that the waiting crow '*serves only to reveal the emptiness that is filled with brightness.*' It's a crowbar waiting there to be used for lifting something, Philippe! That makes sense, doesn't it?"

He nodded slowly, excitement lighting his eyes. "Excellent sense, Bridie! Crow... crowbar. It is a connection only to be seen by an English person." He leaned forward, took my hand, and touched it gently to his lips. "Only the precise location is lacking now, but we have everything else to offer Victor Sarrazin. I pray it will be sufficient." He sat back, closing his eyes. After a long silence he said in a low voice, "Dear Bridie. I have dreamed that one day I might call you sister."

I felt close to tears, and said, "That would make me very proud."

A spasm of grief plucked at his face. "But now..."

I said, "Perhaps it will all come right, Philippe. There must always be hope."

He nodded, his eyes still closed. There was another silence, and then he said quietly, "I wish Nathan McFee were with us. A good man, that one, with a good head."

I said nothing, but the aching emptiness that lay beneath my anxiety for Kate was like a great cold weight within my breast.

Château Valbrison stood at the head of a high valley, across the foot of which flowed a tributary of the Dordogne. In the heat of the afternoon an ancient cab brought us up the long winding road from the little station where we had left our cases, the two elderly horses straining against the gradient. For this journey Philippe Chatillon had paid handsomely, since it appeared that there were never any visitors to Château Valbrison except those who were expected, and then a carriage was sent down for them by M'sieu Sarrazin.

There were no doors at the entrance to the courtyard. The great hinges had rusted through a century ago, so our cabbie informed us, in his grandfather's time. He drove between the old pillars, then on through an arch into a smaller courtyard and up to broad steps that rose to a weather-bleached oak door with heavy iron fittings.

Philippe paid him off, and together we climbed the moss-grown steps. As the cab creaked away behind the plodding horses I felt my heart begin to race with mingled hope and dread. I longed to find Kate here, yet feared to do so. The thought that she was somewhere within this grim, dilapidated château with a man such as Victor Sarrazin appalled me, yet I knew that if we did not find her here I would be frantic.

Philippe had pulled on the thick chain bellpull which hung beside the door. His face was very composed, showing no sign of the anxiety which I knew to be burning within him. For a moment I felt a stab of envy to think that without effort, without even knowing him, Kate had somehow won the love of such a man. I winced with shame at the thought, and as I did so the door swung open. A burly man with cropped black hair and an untrimmed moustache stood looking at us, chewing something. He wore good clothes, but these were ill-matched by his coarse face and crude manners.

He swallowed, wiped his mouth with the back of his hand, and was about to speak when Philippe said in French, "Be so good as to tell Victor Sarrazin that Philippe Chatillon and Mam'selle Bridget Chance are here to see him on a matter greatly to his advantage."

As he spoke, Philippe stepped forward briskly. There was no obvious menace in the way he held his slim black cane, but as if by a careless flourish the tip pointed toward the man's face, causing him to step back, disconcerted. In another second I had followed Philippe across the threshold. He took my arm and we turned to face the man with cropped hair. "You have understood my message?" Philippe said.

The man eyed him narrowly and said in a gruff voice, "M'sieu Sarrazin is engaged at the moment."

Philippe leaned on his cane and said coolly, "Be assured that he will see us at once, however busy he may be."

The man hesitated, looking from one to the other of us. I was aware that the big hall in which we stood was a high-ceilinged, gloomy place which was much in need of thorough dusting and polishing. From what I had seen of Château Valbrison so far, the whole impression was one of reduced circumstances, and fitted the description Philippe had given me of Victor Sarrazin as a gambler, spendthrift, and prodigal.

A door opened on the far side of the hall, and as it did so there came a burst of laughter from the room beyond. A voice I knew said, "Who the devil is it, Felix? If it's that lively wench from the bakery, bring her in. We can always do with another girl—"

Victor Sarrazin stopped short at sight of us. He was clearly surprised, but in no way embarrassed. His shirt was unbuttoned at the neck, and he wore no jacket. From the clink of glass, the clatter of china, and the sound of voices, male and female, mingling in talk and shouts of laughter from the room behind him, I guessed that he had been drinking, but he showed no sign of it. There were two long scratches down his cheek, but the hazel eyes were clear, his face fresh and alert, and his whole manner one of leisurely assurance, just as I had seen him in Suffolk and London.

I had expected to look upon him in a completely new light, and was shaken to find myself unable to. For a dreadful moment I had the confused and shocking thought that the world had turned upside down for me once more, and that the man who had lied to me and deceived me was Philippe Chatillon. Then abruptly Sarrazin threw back his head and laughed. "The stars are with me," he said in English. "My stubborn wife refuses to do what I thought necessary to bring you here, yet now I find that you have brought yourself. Amazing." He looked back into the room, lifting his voice a little and speaking in French. "The devil looks after his own, my friends. Here is the stupid English girl"—his head turned again, and he looked at us with a smile of happy mockery—"and the great French detective."

Beside me, Philippe said, "Do you have Kate Chance here, Sarrazin?"

The hazel eyes gleamed with amusement. "I have Kate Sarrazin here, m'sieu."

"She has married you?"

"By special license, three days ago."

"Very well." Philippe's voice held no expression. "We are here to arrange that you release her to our care, with a view to annulment of the marriage as soon as possible. In return we offer to give you all the information you may need in order to lay your hands on the fortune in stolen jewelry which Le Sorcier accumulated over the years."

A dark flame gleamed in Sarrazin's eyes, and his head came up like the head of a listening dog. "So you have the answer, by God!" he said softly. Then, in sharper tones, and lifting a peremptory hand: "No! Say nothing more for the moment. This is a time for discretion, I fancy." He stepped back, opening the door wide and extending an arm. "Welcome to Château Valbrison, mam'selle, m'sieu."

Philippe touched my arm and I moved forward. From the moment of first hearing Sarrazin's voice I had felt that I might be living through an ugly dream, but as I passed in front of him I shuddered under the impact of some shapeless horror, as if his very aura had chilled my blood.

It was a large, ill-kept room. Three men and three women lounged round a long table on which lay platters of cold meats, long crusty loaves, cheeses, dishes of butter, baskets of fruit, and many bottles of wine. However rundown the castle might be, it was clear that those who lived here did not stint themselves for food and drink. The men were of the same type as Felix, who had opened the door to us. They were not of the class that Victor Antoine Jean-Pierre Sarrazin had been born into, but neither were they servants. My immediate thought was that they must be henchmen of his, and I had no doubt that they were criminals. The three women were dressed in tawdry finery and had the brazen air of strumpets. They did not strike me as being local country girls, and I thought they might have been brought in from Brive or Limoges.

At my elbow, Philippe said in French, "Ah . . . so here you are, Didi. Taking a rest from picking pockets in Place Vendôme, perhaps? And there is my old acquaintance André l'Apache, from Montmartre, for whom I once had the pleasure of securing three years in prison. The other scoundrel is unknown to me."

The men looked at us stonily. One of the women giggled, another lifted her glass unsteadily, winked at me, and slopped wine down herself as she drank. I looked round at Sarrazin and spoke for the first time, thankful to find my voice quiet and steady.

"Where is my sister?"

He smiled. "Madame Sarrazin is in her room at present, but you may see her very shortly." He looked toward Felix, who had followed us into the room, and said curtly, "I have business to attend to. Take the women down to the station, leave them to catch the train, and return immediately."

"Bien, Victor."

There were half-giggling half-indignant protests from the three women as they were quickly ushered out of the room, Felix holding the most reluctant one by the arm and hustling her along without ceremony. When the door closed after them Sarrazin flung himself down carelessly in a chair, refilled the glass in front of him, and looked at me with the same air of polite mockery he had adopted from the moment of our arrival. "You will no doubt wish to see Madame Sarrazin alone, in the first instance?" he said.

I glanced at Philippe, who gave a little nod of his head, then answered, "Yes, I wish to talk with her alone."

"Then you shall do so at once, while the famous M'sieu Chatillon explains to me what he has discovered and deduced from the letter left by your father." He glanced at the man Philippe had not known. "Take her up, Alex. Leave them together and come straight down."

Alex, a skeletal man with small black eyes, gave a nod, moved to the door, opened it and went out, leaving me to follow him. Sarrazin was saying, "And now, my dear Chatillon, pray be seated. I must confess that your presence here is quite unexpected . . . but not inconvenient, I fancy. Not inconvenient. What have you to offer?"

"Nothing until I am assured of Kate's well-being." Philippe's cold voice was cut off as I closed the door and hurried after the man called Alex as he mounted the wide and once elegant staircase with its worn and grubby carpet. On reaching the gallery he turned to the right and led the way past several doors to one near the end of a wide passage. When he bent to turn the key I felt sick at the realization that Kate was locked in, though it was foolish of me not to have anticipated this.

He gave a jerk of his head, telling me to enter, and when I passed in front of him he shut the door again and I heard the click of the lock behind me. The room was lofty, with threadbare carpets and a few pieces of good but neglected furniture, including a four-poster bed in one corner. Kate stood by the window, looking out, her back to me. She wore a plain gray dress with a high neck, a day dress she had used for half-mourning. Her hands, hanging by her sides, were tightly clenched, and her whole body seemed rigid.

My throat closed, and as I struggled to speak she said

in a flat, hard voice, "I will not do it. You may kill me, Victor, but I will not write that letter."

I moved across the room toward her, and managed a husky whisper. "Kate . . . oh, Kate."

She spun round. *"Bridie!"* A whole range of emotions flickered across her white, startled face. Gladness and alarm, shame and stubborn pride, relief and despair. There were dark smudges under her beautiful eyes, and a blue-yellow bruise was like a stain from her right cheekbone almost to the chin. She started toward me, then held herself back, standing very upright, her chin lifted. "You needn't scold me, Bridie," she said in a strained, unnatural voice. "I know I've been a fool. I've been as big a fool as any girl has ever been."

I went toward her with my arms outstretched, groping for words, choking on them. "Kate . . . scold you? No. Oh, Kate darling, no. I know how strong his fascination can be—"

She lunged forward into my arms and clung to me, her head pressed into my shoulder, and I stood gently patting her back and murmuring words of comfort. "There, darling, there. It's all right, I've got you. There, now. I understand. Please don't worry . . ."

I could feel her sobbing, though she made no sound. After a little while the spasms eased, but still she clung to me. I said gently, "Kate dear, I have to ask. He says you're married to him. Is it true?"

She nodded against my shoulder, and said in a muffled voice, "Yes. It was a . . . private wedding. Special license. In Paris."

My heart sank. I held her close and said, "Has he . . . used you?" Again she nodded against me, then lifted her head to look me in the eyes. "In Paris. Before we came here. Before I knew he was . . . a monster. A monster, Bridie." Tears suddenly came, and she buried her face against me once more. "Oh, Bridie, I loved him so. I thought he was . . . so wonderful, I would have died for him. And then, when we came here . . . suddenly it was as if he took off a mask."

Her sobs were heartbroken, and I held her quietly in my

arms till she could speak again. She lifted a tear-stained face to me, and stubborn anger glinted in her eyes as she said, "He hasn't touched me since, Bridie. He tried. He tried in front of those women, but I tore his face with my nails."

I stood there holding my sister and knowing with cold certainty that if I could find a way to kill Victor Sarrazin I would do it. I said, "Was that when he made this bruise on your face?"

She shook her head. "No, he did that before, when I wouldn't write the letter." Her face twisted with alarm. "Oh, dear God, Bridie, you shouldn't have come! That's what he wants. That's why he tried to make me write the letter."

"It's all right, darling, I didn't come alone." I took her hands and drew her toward a settee by the empty fireplace. "Let's sit down while you tell me what happened."

We sat side by side, turned toward each other, still holding hands. She spoke haltingly at first, but then the words came tumbling out. The elopement had been planned in the way I already knew, except that she had written a letter to me and another of thanks and apology to Signor Peroni. Sarrazin had pretended to post them in Dover on the Friday afternoon, to be delivered next morning, but she knew now that the letters had never been posted. Next day she and Victor Sarrazin had been married in Paris under special license by a priest from the Anglican church there. She did not know how this had been arranged, and now suspected that bribery might have been employed, but she had no doubt that the marriage itself was legal.

They had spent two nights at an excellent hotel in Paris, and traveled down to Valbrison on the following Monday. It was then that Victor Sarrazin let fall the mask he had worn. His cronies were already at the château, and the women from Brive had soon been brought in. For Kate, the unbelievable nightmare had begun. She was Victor Sarrazin's wife, completely in his power, yet knew that she was no more than the means to an end, for I was the one he wanted. I was the one who held the key to the fortune in jewelry stolen by Le Sorcier, and Sarrazin knew it, for I had lied to him about the letter left by my father, and he had seen through me with contemptuous ease. When his attempt to court me failed, he had turned his attention to Kate, for as Philippe had guessed, he knew that if he had her in his grasp then he had me also.

"He . . . he planned to have me write you a letter to bring you out here," Kate said, her hands shaking in mine. "He had it all composed, ready for me to copy out, saying that I was very happy but wanted urgently to see you. I wouldn't do it though, Bridie. He got so furious I thought he was going to kill me, but he only knocked me down." She bowed her head. "When I turned round and saw you just now, I was terrified for you at first, and then I thought perhaps you had come with your fiancé, Nathan McFee. He's from an American detective agency, I expect you know, and Victor is afraid of him. You said . . ." She lifted her head. "You did say he was with you, didn't you, Bridie?"

"I told you I wasn't alone, but it isn't Nathan with me. He . . . he had to go back to America. I'm with a man called Philippe Chatillon. He's a French private detective, and quite famous, I think. He was a friend of Papa's, in a way."

"Chatillon? Yes, I've heard Victor speak that name to his dreadful cronies. How is it that he came with you?"

I told her all that Philippe had recounted to me of his surveillance in England, how he had watched over Kate, and found himself falling in love with her. She shook her head in bewilderment at this, then sat looking down at our clasped hands, biting her lip and trying to speak without breaking down.

"I . . . I don't suppose Victor will allow me to see this gentleman," she said haltingly at last. "But please thank him for me, and say that I am . . . honored to learn of his feelings, and am deeply sorry that he should find me so foolish and . . . so wicked as to do what I have done." She pressed my fingers. "Thank God he is with you, Bridie dear. At least it means you will go safely away from this place."

"But we're not going without you, Kate!" I exclaimed. "All Sarrazin wants is the spoils Papa left hidden some-

where, and between us Philippe and I have found most of
the answers to that riddle. Philippe will offer him all we
know in return for . . . you."

She looked at me from eyes that were now far older than
they had been such a little time ago. "It isn't all he wants,"
she said quietly. "A small part of the reason he made me
his wife is because he relishes humiliating a daughter of
Roger Chance. He envied Papa so much that it became
hatred. Oh, they were colleagues up to a point, but for years
Victor tried to find where Papa stored the jewelry he stole.
Papa only ever produced a single piece of it at a time for
Victor to sell, when he wanted cash, and then it was always
something stolen years before. Victor was obsessed with
finding Papa's hoard, and Papa knew it. He was amused
by it, and took delight in laying false trails for Victor to
waste his time on."

I felt a chill of apprehension, but tried to sound confident
as I said, "If he was so obsessed, then I'm sure he'll give
you up in return for the spoils. Philippe will bargain with
him, and get a written undertaking to have the marriage
annulled . . ." I had no idea whether this could be done, and
was talking simply to put heart into Kate. How I might have
continued I have no idea, but at that moment the lock clicked,
the door opened, and the skeletal man, Alex, stepped into
the room.

Looking at me, he jerked his head and said in French,
"He wants to see you downstairs."

I stood up, drawing Kate to her feet. "Very well."

"Not her. She must stay."

I hesitated, then squeezed Kate's hand hard and said,
"I'll be back very soon. Try not to worry, dear. You're not
alone any more."

To my surprise Sarrazin was by himself in the dining
hall when I followed the man in. He was lounging in a
chair, a glass of wine in one hand, booted feet up on the
table, and gave me a smile of such warm affection that I
felt my stomach churn with nausea at his hypocrisy. "I trust
my wife enjoyed your visit," he said.

With a tremendous effort I held down the hatred that

surged within me. I longed to storm and rage at this creature whose magnetism and good looks concealed an inward monstrosity. My fingers itched to rake his face as Kate had done, but I remembered that Philippe was bargaining for Kate's freedom, and I knew I must say nothing, do nothing that might jeopardize the outcome. Moving forward, I looked down the length of the table and said, "Where is M'sieu Chatillon?"

"You mean the gentleman who accompanied you on your journey here?"

"Of course."

"Ah. That M'sieu Chatillon. Well, he has gone to see my wife."

I stared. "But I have just left her, and I did not pass him."

He waved a hand in a vague gesture. "Perhaps he went by a different way. These old castles have many passages."

I was sure he lied, but could not imagine what his purpose might be. After a moment or two I said warily, "I take it you have discussed the matter which brought us here?"

"Yes. He explained what he wanted very concisely. A most articulate gentleman, don't you think?"

"And he has told you what we discovered from the letter my father left, and the photographs I found?"

"To my great disappointment he refused to do so until I had entered into certain unbreakable agreements concerning my dear wife." He lifted his feet from the table and stood up, again with that smile of affection. "I believe the documents you speak of, the letter and photographs, are in your possession at this moment?"

I gripped my handbag tightly. "Yes, but I will show you nothing and tell you nothing until M'sieu Chatillon is satisfied that he has secured Kate's freedom from you."

He nodded, and gave a sorrowful shrug. "You have a hard heart, mam'selle, to speak so coldly of taking my new bride from me. Before we discuss it further, I would be grateful if you would allow me to show you something which I am sure you will find of interest, and then we will join M'sieu Chatillon and Madame Sarrazin."

I hesitated, but could see nothing to gain by refusal, and said impatiently, "Very well."

"Permit me to lead the way."

We went out of the room, along a passage, and through a large cluttered kitchen into a scullery. Here Sarrazin paused to light a lantern, then turned through an arched doorway into a small dark room with stone walls and a heavy iron bar set horizontally at waist height between two ancient stone blocks. At first I thought there was a circular pool of water beyond the barrier, but then realized there was no reflection from it, and I was in fact looking at a round black aperture set in the flags, some nine or ten feet in diameter.

Sarrazin stood by the protective bar and beckoned me to stand beside him, then pointed down. "The Valbrison Well," he said musingly. "Except that it is not really a well at all, but a natural shaft which drops sheer for eighty meters into a river that flows underground here for some twelve miles before emerging to join the Dordogne."

A sense of dreadful unease gripped me as we stood in semidarkness gazing at the great black hole. "Why do you think this might be of interest to me?" I said at last.

"Because you are a young lady of imagination, mam'selle. Consider now. Anything dropped down that shaft will emerge in a river gorge many miles from here after eight or nine days." He gave a little chuckle. "Even if a person were to fall down into the river below, then the body would reappear that same distance away and after the same time." He lifted the lamp and smiled at me politely. "This is not legend, you understand. It is an effect I have myself put to the test on two occasions, and what is most interesting is that the icy cold of the underground river causes the body to be preserved in such a manner that when it is found, usually well beyond the village of Domme, it appears that death occurred not more than a few hours ago. Thus, the impression is given that the unfortunate cadaver died by falling into one of the gorges far from Château Valbrison."

My unease had turned to dread and was now mounting to terror. I gripped the bar in front of me and said, "Why do you tell me this?"

"Simply as an exercise in imagination, mam'selle. Let us imagine, for example, that despite the fact that she had an ardent lover in the person of Philippe Chatillon, my wife married me because she believed I was a rich man. Let us imagine that when she discovered I was not rich, she decided to run away with her lover. I would be heartbroken, of course. I am sure I would go away to Paris, unable to remain here in the absence of the wife I love so dearly. And I would be in Paris eight or nine days later, when their two bodies were found in the river—*recently* dead, of course, from an accident that must have occurred during the preceding twelve hours."

In a voice that was an ugly whisper I managed to force out a few halting words. "Where . . . where is M'sieu Chatillon?"

"With your sister, as I have said."

My heart shriveled within me. Sarrazin had held me in conversation in the dining room more than long enough for Kate to have been brought here by his henchmen and—

I recoiled from the thought, and cried in a high fierce voice, "Where is my sister?"

"Quite safe, mam'selle." By the light of the lantern I could see in his eyes the deep pleasure he drew from my distress. "Let us go and join her now, together with your friend M'sieu Chatillon."

I felt lost and afraid as I followed Sarrazin out of the scullery. In the last few moments he had virtually laid claim to having killed at least two people. He might have intended merely to frighten me, and certainly he had succeeded in this, but I had a dreadful conviction that what he had said was quite simply true.

I knew now that he hated Kate and hated me because we were the daughters of Roger Chance, a man who had used and despised him, and whom he had envied to the point of obsession. I suspected, too, that Victor Sarrazin had now crossed the border of sanity in pursuit of his goal, which was to win the plunder he had coveted for so long.

I was so bemused by my muddled thoughts and fears that I scarcely noticed the route we took, but after two or

three minutes I found myself following him along a dark
passage with bare stone walls and into what appeared to be
a small, low-ceilinged cellar. Facing us were several ancient
iron-bound doors set side by side. Sarrazin lifted the lantern
he still carried, and I realized with a new spasm of shock
that this was not a cellar but a dungeon, and the doors were
the doors of cells. From a gap beneath one of the doors
came a faint light, and on a hook to one side of it hung a
great iron key.

Sarrazin walked up to the door, reached out, and pushed
a small square panel to one side. He looked into the cell
for a moment, then stepped back and motioned me to take
his place. The bottom of the peephole came just level with
my chin, and as I gazed down into the cell I felt not only
horror but also a return of that sudden and primitive ferocity
that had come to me as I held Kate in my arms. If I had
had the power or means to destroy Sarrazin in that moment,
I would have done so without scruple or hesitation.

There was no chair, table, or bed in the little cell, and
no window. On one side the stonework had been built out
to make a horizontal surface two feet from the ground,
presumably to offer a place for sleeping, and on this were
the rotting remains of a palliasse. An oil lamp stood on the
floor. Kate knelt beside it, cradling Philippe Chatillon's
head on her lap as he lay sprawled on his back, unconscious,
blood still running from a cut on the side of his head as
Kate tried to staunch it with a ragged piece of fine white
cambric.

No doubt she had looked up and seen Sarrazin when he
first opened the panel, but she was not looking up now. As
I stared numbly I saw her pluck her skirt aside, pull the
hem of her petticoat into view, and tear off another piece
to press against Philippe's wound. I had always loved Kate,
but in that moment I loved her as never before. God alone
knew how frightened she must be, but with bloodied skirt
and hands she was gently and carefully tending an unconscious man she had never seen before, and doing it as if
her own plight was of no consequence.

I whispered, "Kate."

She looked up, glaring defiance, then her face changed. "Bridie... are you all right?"

"Yes," I said shakily. "He's brought me to see you. I don't know why."

"He'll tell you when he's ready." She looked down, pressing the wad of cambric against Philippe's head. "Is this the man who came with you?"

"Yes. Philippe Chatillon. Is he... is he badly hurt?"

"I'm not sure. Didi brought me down here only two or three minutes ago, and I found him lying on the floor like this. His heart and his breathing are steady, though."

Leaning against the wall beside me, Sarrazin laughed. "It will take more than a crack on the head to kill Chatillon," he said. "Who knows, it might even bring him to his senses! The lovesick fool must have been out of his mind to come marching into Château Valbrison with you as he did, but I have no complaints. It has solved a difficult problem for me."

A look of contempt and loathing touched Kate's bruised face. "Don't trust him, Bridie," she said. "I'm not sure what he's planning now, but don't trust him for a second."

I stood trying to think, then suddenly turned away, dropping my handbag as I buried my face in my hands and leaned against the wall, weeping. Behind me, Sarrazin laughed again, and through my stifled sobs I heard the sound of the panel being closed, the click of a catch to hold it in place. "Come, mam'selle," he said briskly, "we have work to do."

I drew in a deep breath, turned, and bent to pick up my handbag. As I stood up again he lifted the lantern and smiled at me. "We shall now return to the dining room," he said, "and there, dear sister-in-law, we shall talk, you and I. There you will tell me everything you know, everything you have gleaned or deduced, and give me everything you possess that may throw light upon the whereabouts of Le Sorcier's treasure. If you are tempted to refuse, please remember the so-called Valbrison Well, and what may happen to a deceitful wife and her secret lover."

* * *

Ten minutes later I sat looking at Victor Sarrazin across the debris of food on the long table as he pored over the letter and photographs in front of him. I had told him everything, all that Philippe and I between us had worked out concerning the Capricorn Stone, the pointing shadow, and the crowbar . . . "*the waiting crow*." For two minutes now Sarrazin had sat gazing down at the photographs in brooding silence. Suddenly his head came up, and I saw that the hazel eyes were glinting with triumph.

"*Tête de Chèvre*," he said softly. "I knew it at once, but I have been trying to understand how . . ." His fist thumped down on the table. "By God, that cunning dog had me tricked for years! He would come from Paris with a locked attaché case. I had him followed everywhere there when he was about to come to Valbrison, but without result. We could never discover where and when he visited his hoard— and no wonder, because he did not visit it! The attaché case was empty! When he wanted me to sell a piece of jewelry for him, he always took the afternoon train and would stay overnight at the village of Charlet before coming here in the morning to do business with me. *And during that night he paid a visit to the hiding place . . .*"

Sarrazin sprang to his feet, almost ran to a sideboard, and opened a cupboard to drag out several maps and books. "Here!" He was back at the table, a map spread out, jabbing at it with his finger. "Here is *Tête de Chèvre*. I saw it once when I was a boy." His finger moved. "It lies between Charlet, here, and Château Valbrison, but nearer to us than to Charlet. And there is no road between, only high hills of barren rock." He looked up from the map with a wild glare. "That artful fox who was your father would go from the smithy at Charlet during the night, by horse or on foot, to select from his plunder or add to it. And through all the years that I handled the business of selling for him I never dreamed that the booty of Le Sorcier lay almost under my hand." He looked down at the map again. "No more than an hour's ride from the gates of this château!"

Sarrazin dropped into a chair, flung back his head and gave a shout of laughter. Shaking a fist at the grimy ceiling he cried, "But I win at last, my so-clever mocking colleague! Victor Sarrazin will have the spoils of Le Sorcier!" Jumping to his feet he strode to the door and jerked it open. "Alex! Didi! Here, quickly!"

He was folding the map when the two men arrived. "We have it, my friends," he said with a grin of triumph. "Didi, fetch a bull's-eye lantern, some rope, a short jimmy, and a pistol. Hurry, man. I want to be away in five minutes. Alex, go and saddle my horse. One for the girl, also. She can have the gray. I'm riding up into the hills with her, to make sure there's no mistake about Roger Chance's treasure being where it should be."

Alex stared. "Why take the girl?"

Sarrazin's eyes narrowed. He walked up to the man and held a menacing finger under his nose. "Never question me, Alex," he said softly. "I take her because I wish to." His face contorted in a brief spasm of pure hatred. "Because I wish to have with me one who is flesh and blood to that damned Englishman in the moment when I seize his spoils." He snapped his fingers. "Now be off and see to the horses. We have a fair way to go before sunset."

There was a hint of fear on Alex's bony face as he said, "But . . . excuse me, Victor, but we have no sidesaddle for the girl."

"You have a *knife*, idiot! She must ride astride, naturally. If you slit her skirt and petticoats front and back, then there is no problem. Get her some safety pins and she can make it a divided skirt for riding, heh? There is a box full of such things in the bedroom where I was romping with the dark girl earlier. Look on the dressing table there."

I sat with clasped hands resting in front of me, beyond shock now, trying to keep alive the hope that still flickered within me. It was a tiny hope, but at least it was not ground-less. As Alex reached the door I said without looking up and in a voice that was not too unsteady, "If you will please bring scissors and safety pins, I will see to my dress without assistance."

Sarrazin spoke from behind me now, his voice grim. "Very well. But let there be no delay, little sister. One minute's delay and by God I'll show you how quickly a dress can be altered."

I said, "I shall not delay you."

Somewhere a clock chimed once. Looking down at my hands I could see the watch on my wrist. The time was half past four o'clock. Unbelievably, it was less than an hour since Philippe and I had crossed the threshold of Château Valbrison.

⚡ sixteen ⚡

The horse beneath me was sweating. Sarrazin and I had been climbing for more than an hour now, starting our journey along the track that led directly north from Château Valbrison into a small wooded plateau. Beyond the woods there was no track, only a natural way leading up into hills, which quickly became barren except for the few hardy plants growing in crevices of rock.

I had cut my skirt and petticoats, as he had ordered, and pinned the cut edges to make crude breeches for riding. My wrists were bound, with perhaps fifteen inches of rope between them so that I could manage the reins. There was no reason for Sarrazin to have bound me, for I could attempt nothing against him, but I knew that it was all part of his craving to humiliate me. He rode ahead, with my horse on a long leading rein. One pocket of his jacket was weighed down by a heavy pistol. In his saddlebag was a coil of rope and a bull's-eye lantern. A short steel lever—a jimmy— projected from under the flap. Attached to his saddle by a strap on the left, below the pommel, was a cavalry saber in a sheath.

During the first hour of our journey he had talked eagerly from time to time. It was hard to recognize him as the man of such quiet yet potent charm I had first met in a country lane near Wynford, the man with a ready smile and frank eyes which made it almost impossible to mistrust him, or even to think of it.

As we climbed he had sometimes spoken out of sheer excitement and exuberance. "Observe the saber, dear sister Bridie. It belonged to my long-departed father, a great

313

gentleman and an even greater fool, who laid down his life fighting for *la belle* France. They brought the saber back from the field of battle and returned it to my mother, who placed it tenderly in my young hands, urging me ever to live up to his name, and expiring soon after from a broken heart. You will observe that she was as great a fool as he. One cannot help feeling ashamed of such parents, even though one can in no way be blamed for them, since one does not choose them."

He turned to look back at me, eyes alight with malevolent glee. "Why do I keep the saber, you ask? Why do I carry it now? In fact, you do not ask, but I ask for you, and now I will tell you, dear sister. I keep it as a constant reminder not to be a fool, as my parents were; to remind me that life is neither more nor less than an unending struggle between the living; therefore the welfare and happiness of Victor Sarrazin must ever be my first and only concern. This calls for duplicity, of course, which is an art to be practiced and nourished with unfailing attention. It also calls for the elimination of those foolish scruples we acquire in our childhood, which are so weakening to our purpose..." I stopped listening, and wondered if I would ever have the chance to seize the pistol from his pocket.

At other times he spoke in order to frighten me as intensely as possible, and in this he succeeded, for I knew that his words were not empty. "I have had an interesting thought, dear Bridie, which springs from my most satisfying hatred of your father. Hatred is a splendid passion. It has the virtue of actually existing, whereas its opposite, love so-called, is merely an illusion. But let me tell you my thought. It has occurred to me that in view of the fact that you left Paris so brazenly in the company of the bold Philippe Chatillon, it might be more suitable if *you* and he were found in due course in the waters of the Dordogne, rather than he and Kate. I mean, of course, in the event that you have deceived me"—he turned to look at me with a smile—"or in the event that I can think of nothing better to do with you. Naturally, I would then have to find another way of attending to my dear wife, but that should not be difficult for an affectionate husband such as myself. For example, since she no longer wishes to take me to her bed, and since I would not have her in any way deprived, I could pass her to a gentleman I know in Morocco. He runs an establishment with splendid beds and a variety of ladies, and I assure you that he would reimburse me most handsomely for the pain I should feel at giving up such a young and beautiful English girl . . ."

Somehow I held down my terror. I had never even seen a pistol close-to, but I supposed that if I had it in my hands I would only have to point it straight and pull the trigger. Deep within me I knew the moment would never come, but I still clung to a slender thread of hope for Kate. Whether or not Sarrazin found the spoils, I doubted that I would ever return alive from the high empty valleys, but there was still a chance for Kate and for Philippe, if only they were able to seize it.

The sun was low in the sky now, and we were moving north along a broad limestone valley with a series of smaller valleys running off at intervals on the eastern side, low chasms with steep walls, often sheer, and level bottoms heavily strewn with rocks and boulders. Sarrazin had not spoken for a long time now, and for the past ten minutes had been riding with head turned to look down each valley as we passed its mouth. Suddenly he gave a great wordless cry of triumph and reined in his horse, an arm lifted to point with a quivering finger.

"There, girl! There is *Tête de Chèvre!*"

We were looking along one of the valleys opening off the cliff on our right, and to me it seemed little different from any of the others. At first it ran roughly straight between sheer walls, veined and riven. Then, after a hundred paces, it bent in a dogleg so that the rest of the valley was hidden from us. Sarrazin was still pointing, and suddenly I saw it, the strange formation of the cliff face at the dogleg where the valley turned. There, beyond all question, was the giant head of a goat. It was in half profile, and the discoloration of various hollows and channels in the rock served as much as the freak of natural sculpture to make the features stand out clearly. The horns were black, where two curving furrows ran up from the bulge of the brow over a steep rounded slope. The eyes and the tip of the nose were in reality blackish-brown hollows. A slight undercut formed the lower jaw of the not quite symmetrical face, and some thin wavering cracks beneath gave the effect of a little beard.

Sarrazin glanced back at the red orb of the sun dropping toward the horizon, and gave a jerk on the leading rein. Sweat trickled down his face as he looked at me for a moment, eyes flaring, and I knew it was not the sweat of exertion but of raging greed.

"Come!" he said hoarsely, and we moved into the valley. As the horses picked their way between rocks and furrows, and we drew nearer to the point where the valley turned, the goat's head lost its form to some extent with the slight change of angle and viewpoint. Once round the sharp bend, the valley ran straight again for a good distance before twisting once more, narrowing still, and sloping very slightly down. For as far as I could see, the walls were scarred with cracks and holes, but I was only fleetingly aware of this, for my eyes were held instantly by the Capricorn Stone, and I heard Sarrazin give a gasp of delight.

It was just as I had seen it in the photographs, a weathered crag of hard rock, rising solitary from the softer limestone, and no more than a stone's throw from where we sat. Here, for a long stretch, the valley bottom was smooth and even, strangely clear of runnels and debris. But then, a hundred paces beyond the pillar and as if a line of demarcation had been drawn, the ground became an eruption of rock and boulder, a wild sea of twisted stone from wall to wall, as if there had once been rapids here in some bygone age before man walked on earth.

Our horses stepped onto smooth ground, and a few seconds later we were before the Capricorn Stone, with the setting sun throwing a great black finger of shadow at an angle across the valley bottom. Sarrazin was actually grunting with excitement, making a small ugly noise with each breath. It was hard to remember that I had ever seen him with the outward manner of a calm, urbane gentleman. He was an animal now.

Without a word he nudged his horse along the line of the shadow. My own horse followed, still on the leading rein. Where the shadow ended, Sarrazin continued in the same direction, constantly glancing back to ensure that he was not diverging from it. In another few seconds we came to the cliff of seamed and pockmarked rock that formed the southern wall of the valley. There we stopped, and Sarrazin snapped feverishly, "Get down, girl, get down!"

I swung down from the saddle. There was no stiffness, for my muscles were in perfect condition from the months of constant dancing, and I was fleetingly thankful for this. It was unlikely that I would be given the smallest chance to harm Sarrazin in any way, but if by some miracle a chance came, I wanted to be nimble enough to make the most of it.

He was on foot himself now, staring at the wall of rock. Suddenly he whirled round, face distorted, and swung his arm to hit my face with the back of his hand, lifting his voice in a shout of fury. "Where is it, you——?" He used a French word unknown to me. "Where is it?"

The quickness and timing learned with Alfie Perkin and Company had stood me in good stead, for I was able to duck to one side, taking most of the force from the blow. Even so, it made my face burn and my eyes water with shock. I cried frantically, "I don't know! I've never pretended to know! I've told you everything there is to tell!"

I was backing away from him slowly, along the wall of rock, and he was advancing like a cat about to spring, his eyes murderous. It was then I saw it, the vertical overlap of rock which even at a short distance would look like one of the hundreds of ancient channels blackened by rain and weather.

"*There!*" I cried, pointing past him with both my bound hands. "It's an opening! There!"

He stopped short, watching me suspiciously, then put a hand on the pistol in his pocket and flicked a glance over his shoulder. Almost at once he looked back, and now his sweating face was agleam with eagerness once again. "Not quite where the shadow pointed," he said, panting. "Different time of year . . . or day. Who cares?" He ran to his horse, took the lantern and the iron lever from the saddlebag, then crouched to light the lantern, fumbling with matches, cursing as he broke one in his haste. When he stood up he looked at me again and jerked his head toward the crevice. "You first, little sister, I don't want you behind me."

The gap was tall and narrow, and the random thought came to me that a broad-shouldered man like my father would have to pass through sideways. I wondered how many times he had done so over the years, and marveled that a man so clever could also be so stupid as to have thought my mother would ever have been able to come to such a place to find his spoils. The light from the lantern shone past me above my head as Sarrazin held it high. After I had moved three cautious paces, hands outstretched in front of me, the narrow passage turned abruptly and opened out. It was hard to judge the size of the cave, for parts of it were lost in shadow, but it was higher than a tall man, and at least as big as our little sewing room at Latchford Hall.

Sarrazin's hand thrust me against the wall. "Stand still," he growled, and strode past me, turning to shine the beam from the lantern steadily round. The cave was roughly oval in shape, with the roof at one end sloping steeply down until there was no more than a wide horizontal crevice between roof and floor. Sarrazin moved the light slowly across the ground. There was no debris, no scrap of paper, no man-made thing to indicate that any human foot had trodden here for centuries past. A few small rocks were scattered about amid limestone dust and rubble. The lantern beam fastened on the only rock of any size, a rather flat-topped piece of stone, shaped like a lozenge and perhaps as long as my arm from end to end, with a rounded underside which seemed to be resting snugly in a shallow natural hollow in the ground.

"It's under there," Sarrazin breathed in a croaking whisper. "Under there, by God!" The beam began to dart wildly about the cave. "Where is the crowbar? The waiting crow?

Where the devil has the fool hidden it?" His voice rose in fury and he moved quickly round the cave, crouching, peering, cursing again in his frustration. The light came to rest on my face, and I knew he was about to make me the whipping boy for his frenzied anger. Fear quickened my mind and I said, "He would have hidden it higher up. I'm sure that's what Papa would have done."

The black shadow behind the lantern grunted. The beam turned and began to move slowly round the walls, casting up and down as it moved. Twice it hesitated, then came suddenly to rest on a thin tapering crack at shoulder height. Sarrazin moved forward, peered closely with the lantern, then gave a gasp of triumph. Next moment I saw him reach in and draw out a heavy crowbar, almost losing his grip on it as the flattened end came clear and dropped with a metallic clang to the ground. He stood the lantern down so that the beam rested on the big lozenge-shaped stone, moved round to the far side, and began to work the tip of the crow under the edge.

At first he tried to turn the whole rock over sideways, grunting and straining, but there was no fulcrum high enough on which to rest the lever, and he then realized that the lozenge must be edged out of its recess little by little. It was a task that took a full two minutes, and as the movement of the flat rock gradually disclosed a cavity beneath it, Sarrazin's wild gasping made him sound ever more like some dreadful animal striving in the darkness beyond the pool of light.

At last the stone was clear of the cavity. Sarrazin flung the crowbar aside and went on one knee to reach down and lift from the hole something wrapped in oilskin and suspended from the end of a short chain. I think I had expected to see some sort of chest, and so had Sarrazin, for he had brought the short iron jimmy to pry it open, but as he tore the oilskin away I saw a cylinder of dull metal. When he put it down, it reached from the ground to his bent knee, and was wider than he could span with his hand. He peered at the flat top, grunted again, then hugged the cylinder against his chest and curved a hand round the top, dragging at it with an unscrewing movement. The lid turned easily, and seconds later he set it aside, tilting the cylinder so that the light shone into it.

There was no dramatic sparkle of massed jewelry, only something that looked like gray cloth, velvet perhaps. He lifted out the topmost object, quite a small thing wrapped in a piece of the cloth. Very carefully he set it down on the ground in the lantern's beam, and with shaking hands unfolded the corners of the cloth. Green, white, and red fire glittered from between his suddenly motionless hands. Emeralds, diamonds, rubies... a brooch, a pendant, I could not tell from where I stood, lay coruscating under the touch of the light. For long moments Sarrazin did not move, then a high-pitched laugh broke from his lips and he reached feverishly into the cylinder again.

I wrenched myself from the trance that had held me, and took a wary step backward. I was in the shadows, my back to the narrow entrance, and although Sarrazin faced me he was for the moment totally obsessed, almost mesmerized by the hoard of plunder that was now in his hands. I took another step back, and then another, my mind a fever of half-formed thoughts.

I could not hope to harm or disable him, even if I was able to reach the saber which still hung from his pommel and found the courage to use it, for he was quick and strong, and carried a pistol in his pocket. My best hope was to escape and hide in this great tangle of high valleys. If he failed to hunt me down, I would somehow find my way to Charlet, to the smithy perhaps, and to the police...

I could not think beyond that. I had turned the corner now and was backing out of the crevice and into the light. For a moment I was desperately tempted to mount his horse and take mine on the leading rein, but I was no horsewoman, and knew I could make but painfully slow speed over the seamed and rocky ground beyond the Capricorn Stone. If he realized in the next minute or two that I had gone, he would catch me easily enough on foot. He might very well be able to halt his horse by a shouted command. And then

I would have only seconds to live; of that I was now quite certain.

As I emerged blinking into the fading sunlight of the evening I turned at once and began to run, thankful now for my divided skirt. But I did not make for the valley mouth. I was running hard in the opposite direction, across the long stretch of smooth ground that led up into the valley and gave way abruptly to a jumble of huge boulders mingled with rocks of every shape and size spreading right across the valley bottom. There, if I reached it safely, I might with good fortune be able to hide like a beetle in a heap of pebbles till darkness fell. It was a stretch of ground over which no horse could move, and for a man to search it on foot would be a formidable task.

I knew there were no seconds to spare. Entranced as he was, Sarrazin would soon realize the folly of peering at his spoils in the darkness when he could carry them all into the light. In that moment he would discover that I had vanished from the cave, and . . .

I had never been more thankful for my hundreds of hours of training, for I was in no measure breathless when I reached the bank of cluttered rock. Fine balance and deftness of footwork were instinctive to me now as I leaped to a sloping surface, sprang across to the top of a rock beyond, then dropped down into a twisting path that ran for only a few steps before it was blocked by a boulder resting across a crevice. Even as I wriggled through the crevice beneath the boulder I heard a great shout from along the valley.

Sarrazin's voice.

Because of the echoes I could not make out the words, and perhaps I would not have known them, for he was screaming in French and it sounded like wild abuse, blasphemy, and threats. I hugged the ground, frozen with fear, then forced myself to wriggle on. Once through the crevice I looked about me for some point that would allow me to watch Sarrazin without being seen, and after another minute of crouching, crawling, and clambering I found the ideal place. Just in front of a flat outcrop, a rock with a tapering peak leaned against a crag, with only a hand's-breadth gap between them. I could lie flat on my stomach on the outcrop, and through the gap command an almost full view of the valley to the dogleg bend beyond the Capricorn Stone, but I could not myself be seen.

As I drew myself up warily onto the flat surface, every nerve aquiver, I thought of Kate and Philippe, and mumbled a half coherent prayer that they would not miss the one chance of escape that lay in their grasp. Then I was staring through the slender gap, just in time to see Sarrazin as he vanished from my view round the dogleg bend, urging his horse on at a pace that was wildly dangerous over such broken ground.

He had naturally thought I must have run that way, but would soon discover his mistake. The gray I had ridden from Château Valbrison was still standing by the cave, but there was no way that I could make use of it. In the west, only half the sun now showed above the ridge of rock beyond the main valley. I knew that if I did not escape I would die, and my best chance of escape, slim though it might be, was to do nothing for the moment and wait for darkness.

Soon Sarrazin would reappear. Unable to sight me in the valley mouth, he would know that I must have taken the other direction. He would return, and begin the task of hunting me through the endless jumble of rock on foot. I would have to leave my vantage point then, and find the most hidden cranny in which to tuck myself away. Or I could listen for his approach and try stealthily to evade him amid the maze of rocks in a game of hide-and-seek . . . with death as the penalty for being found.

I was trying to decide which course was better when Sarrazin reappeared, moving at a slow pace now, allowing his horse to pick its way along the treacherous ground. He came to the smooth stretch and moved on to halt by the Capricorn Stone, a hundred yards or more from where I lay. Then he dismounted, walked to the cave entrance and disappeared. I guessed that he was first going to secure the jewelry before starting the hunt for me. Awkwardly I began to use my teeth and left hand fingers to worry loose the knot securing my right wrist, lifting my head every two or three seconds to keep watch for Sarrazin.

A hand gripped my ankle gently, and the shock was like a physical blow. Every nerve within me seemed to give a silent scream, and my head snapped round as if on a spring.

Weather-brown face, bright blue eyes with crow's feet at the corners, moustache turning down at each end of the long upper lip, dark green shirt, no jacket, black gaucho hat pushed to the back of his head, a rope coiled over one shoulder... Nathan McFee. He lay prone on the same outcrop, his head near my left foot, and as I gazed in frozen wonder he wriggled forward to draw level with me. His hand touched my chin, drawing me toward him a little, and he kissed me gently on the lips. "That's my girl," he said quietly, and smiled. "That's my Bridie."

I wanted to say a dozen things at once, but all I could manage was a bewildered whisper. "Nathan?"

"In person, honey. Tell you everything later, but for the moment just know I really love you and never stopped. Now keep watching for Sarrazin." I turned my eyes back to the crevice, and through my body there surged a great golden tide of joy and relief. The danger remained, but I was no longer alone. Nathan was with me.

Nathan, Nathan, Nathan! My heart sang.

"Tell me what's happening," he said, and reached for my left wrist. Something cold touched the flesh briefly, then the rope fell away.

Struggling to hold my voice under control I said in a whisper, "He's still in the cave. He brought me up from his house, Château Valbrison, this afternoon—"

"I know, Bridie. I trailed you on foot the whole way. Does he have a pistol?"

"Yes."

"Figured he would, so I didn't dare get close. Once he saw me he'd just stick that gun against your head and give his orders."

Nathan's hand ran gently, lovingly over my hair and came to rest on my shoulder. I kept my eyes fixed on the point where I knew the cave entrance to be. Within, Sarrazin would be carefully packing away in the cylinder the pieces of jewelry he had taken out in his first frenzy of haste and greed. "He's married to Kate," I said, and marveled that my voice should sound so calm. "She's a prisoner in the château now."

"I know that too, Bridie. That's why I'm here."

"The man I came with, Philippe Chatillon, he's a prisoner with her, and Sarrazin has threatened dreadful things."

"I didn't know about Chatillon, but if he's with Kate I'm glad. He's a good man."

"But he's hurt, and I'm so frightened for them, Nathan. Do you have a pistol?"

"Never carry one, honey. Made a promise to Ma, way back, after they strung up Pa. Carry a Bowie, though." I glanced down for a second and saw in his hand the knife he had used to cut the rope from my wrist, a big knife with a blade partly straight and partly curved, the back of the blade very thick, almost as wide as my little finger, and covered by a strip of brass. "If I get to close quarters he's dead," Nathan was saying absently, "but there's no chance while he's got a pistol."

"He has a saber, too." Though my voice was steady, my feelings seesawed wildly. One second I could feel nothing but joy at having Nathan beside me, the next nothing but fear for Kate and for Philippe.

"A saber?" said Nathan.

"Yes. A cavalry saber. It was his father's, and he keeps it as a kind of horrible joke."

"He's the sort who'd like to use it, though," said Nathan reflectively.

"Can we . . . can we get out this way?" I pointed back over my shoulder without turning my head. "Work our way to the other end of the valley?"

"No good, honey. It's a box canyon."

I did not know the term, but could easily guess its meaning. "We could climb. You must have come in that way yourself, Nathan."

"Sure. Couldn't risk following you in here, so I came down the next valley and climbed the ridge between, but it's sheer this side, and I had to use the rope and shake it loose twice. Besides, we'd never have the time—"

"He's coming out, Nathan! Carrying a kind of cylinder we found, a container with all the jewelry."

"Right. Keep watching."

"Why wouldn't we have time?"

"Because Sarrazin holds Kate. That's like having a knife at your throat, and he's going to start using it any time now. Let me have some of your petticoat, honey. I'll need two pieces, each about two feet square." He laid down the knife. "Use this. I'll be back in under a minute."

He seemed to melt away from beside me without a sound. I saw that Sarrazin was moving toward the gray. As he began to tie the container securely to the saddle with his coil of rope I looked down at the knife wonderingly, then picked it up, rolled on my side, and began to unpin my skirt to reach the petticoat.

❧ seventeen ❧

I was still writhing about in a truly immodest state of undress when Nathan returned, but this did not trouble me, and seemed not to trouble him, either. He took the knife from me, completed a cut I had begun on the second "leg" of my petticoat, then pulled my skirt into place again for me and rolled on his back beside me. Now I saw that he had returned with two rocks, about the size of large coconuts and fairly regular in their rounded shape.

Working with strong deft hands he folded each rock into a square of white lawn from my petticoat and knotted it securely there, then sliced a six-foot length from his lasso and began to tie one end of it to the knotted cloth holding one of the rocks. As he did so, and as I finished pinning my skirt again, from a hundred yards and more down the valley Sarrazin lifted his voice in a penetrating call.

"Bridie! Bridie Chance!"

Nathan flicked a glance at me and said, "Here it comes, honey. Brace yourself."

Before I could ask what he meant, Sarrazin continued: *"Bridie Chance! I know you are hiding nearby. I know you can hear me. Listen well, now. If you do not come from hiding in three minutes, I will return to Château Valbrison. And with the help of my friends I shall begin to make your sister wish she had never been born! Do you understand, Bridie Chance?"*

I felt the blood drain from my face. Nathan finished tying the other end of the six-foot rope to the second rock, knotting it to the gathered linen. "That's what I figured," he said quietly. "And he means it, Bridie, believe me. Only one

327

way to save Kate, and that's to finish this business right now. You ready to take a gamble with me?"

I nodded mutely, but my eyes must have shown my trust, even in the poorer light of approaching dusk. He smiled, rolled on his side to face me, and kissed me again. "Just keep beside me. I guess he'll come at us fast, either with the pistol or the saber. Don't worry if it's the pistol, because it's twenty to one he'd miss even at five yards from a moving horse, no matter what the dime novels say. And he'll never get that close. When I say '*Now*,' you go down on one knee right beside me." Again he touched his lips to mine. "The rest is up to me. I love you, Bridie Chance, and I sure hope you're going to love me again."

I put my hand to his cheek and said, "I've never stopped, Nathan."

Sarrazin was calling again, repeating his message, but we lay looking into each other's eyes for long seconds, and in Nathan's eyes I found all I needed. Explanations would come, if we lived, but they no longer mattered.

He took my hand and said, "Let's go, Bridie." Next moment he had slithered from the outcrop, and was turning to help me down into the cleft where he stood between two boulders. The way we took from this point was different from the way I had entered the jumble of rock, and we did not have to crawl beneath the bridgelike boulder. Nathan led, holding my right hand in his left. The great knife he had called a Bowie was in a sheath attached to the back of his belt. In his right hand he gripped the center of the rope connecting the two rocks. These, tightly encased in the squares of lawn from my petticoat, hung down his back almost to his knees. I had no idea what was in his mind, and felt too empty to speculate. I had laid down my burden now, and Nathan had taken it upon his wide shoulders.

The sun had gone, and the western sky was red with its dying as we stepped from the maze of rocks hand in hand and began to walk slowly forward. I saw that Sarrazin had mounted his horse and was silhouetted against the sunset, staring with one hand lifted to shade his eyes. Suddenly a great shout burst from him. "*McFee!*"

Nathan halted, and I stopped beside him.

"McFee!" Sarrazin's voice throbbed with triumph as he called the name again. "By God, you have presented me with a clean sweep today, Yankee!" His arm swept suddenly high in the air, and for a moment something glinted blood-red in the reflected rays of the vanished sun. Then there was only the multiple echo of hoofbeats on smooth rock as he set his horse to a gallop, the bared saber held forward and up at arm's length, in the classic position I had once seen in a painting of a cavalry charge.

Beside me Nathan said pensively, "Crazy as a redskin with a bellyful of hooch. Right, Bridie . . . *now*."

I released his hand and dropped to one knee beside him. Suddenly I was trembling despite his easy confidence, for there was something truly blood-chilling about the sight of Sarrazin coming hard at us with the saber poised to strike. A single blow would cut a man almost in two, and no doubt he expected us to turn and run, so that he could take each of us in turn as his target.

Beside me Nathan lifted his right arm. I looked up to see that he still held the rope by the middle and was swinging the two weights round horizontally above his head, with a distance of perhaps twelve inches between them as one followed the other in a whirling circle. From the depths of childhood memory a word tried to reach my consciousness, a word associated with others . . . gaucho, Argentina, pampas . . . *bolas*! Now it came back to me. Bolas—two or sometimes three iron balls with a length of rope between, skillfully thrown to wrap round the legs of wild cattle or large game . . .

Sarrazin was thirty yards away when Nathan released the makeshift *bolas*. The two cloth-covered rocks flew through the air, gradually separating until the rope between them was fully extended and horizontal. But Nathan had not thrown for the horse's legs, he had thrown for the man. I think Sarrazin saw nothing of the rope in the fading light, only the bulk of the two weights at each end as they flew toward him on a path that would take one on each side of him.

He had opened his mouth in a wordless, whooping cry

of exultation, and I could see the white gleam of his teeth, when the rope passed inches above the horse's head and caught him across the chest, just below the raised right arm holding the saber aloft. The effect was instant and startling, for the flying rocks snapped viciously round behind him with the speed of a sprung trap, the rope tightening in a flash to pin his left arm to his chest so that he lost control of the reins. The twin weights whipped round again across his chest and his back, still full of impetus and spinning closer with the shortening of the rope, one weight finally thudding against his chest and the other catching the back of his head as he reeled sideways.

Limp as a sack of mud he fell from the saddle, head striking rock, saber clattering away across the limestone. The galloping horse veered slightly but came on at a furious pace, and Sarrazin's left foot was caught in the stirrup. I gave an instinctive cry of horror as I saw his body bumping and twisting across the unforgiving rock, head rolling loosely. Beside me Nathan crouched a little, and as the horse passed close on his right, with Sarrazin's body trailing on the far side, Nathan spun round and jumped. For a moment he clung with one hand on the pommel and one on the horse's mane, knees drawn up, then he touched his feet to the ground and came instantly up into the saddle with a single bound, crouched low, hands reaching forward.

I saw the shirt split down his back as he lifted himself from the knees and used all his strength to wrench the animal to a slithering, rearing halt. Then he slid to the ground, soothing the frightened creature with a quick word and gentle hands. As it quieted, he freed Sarrazin's foot from the stirrup and dropped on one knee beside him. I had to tell myself to stand up, for I was dazed by the speed with which it had all happened. As I walked toward Nathan I saw smears of blood on the rock. He looked up and gave a shake of his head. "He's dead, Bridie. I guess he died when he first hit the ground."

I stood still, keeping my eyes on Nathan, not looking at the sprawled figure of the man who would have murdered us, and I felt nothing but relief. Nathan rose to his feet.

"Will you go and bring the other mount, please, honey? I'll tie Sarrazin on that and we'll ride double on this one, it's stronger."

"Yes, Nathan." I turned and began to walk to where the gray I had ridden stood near the cave entrance, then suddenly I caught my breath in alarm and broke into a run. Kate . . . and Philippe. I had forgotten them in the last few moments. As I came hurrying back with the gray I called, "We must go to Kate, quickly, Nathan!"

"Sure, Bridie." He had brought his lasso from among the rocks, and tied one of the squares of petticoat over Sarrazin's face so that it was hidden. Now, with an easy movement, he lifted the body and hung it face down over the gray, in front of the dull metal cylinder tied across the back of the saddle. "Don't fret too much, honey," he said as he began to secure the limp figure with his rope. "Sarrazin's men won't touch your sister without his orders."

"But . . . but she and Philippe might be trying to escape," I said urgently. "They were in a cell, and Philippe had been hit on the head, but I don't think he was too badly hurt, and Kate was looking after him, and I saw a big key on the wall." I paused to draw breath, then plunged on. "There was a gap under the door, so I dropped my handbag and pretended to sob against the wall with my face in my hands, and that's when I took the key from the hook. And then, when I bent to pick up my handbag, I left the key on the ground and pushed it under the door with my foot when I stood up."

Nathan had finished his task and was looking at me with hands resting low on his hips, blue eyes wide with surprise. Then he gave a little laugh. "That's my girl," he said.

"But don't you see?" I cried. "If they find the key and try to escape, those men might hurt them! I'm so frightened for Kate. Sarrazin has four dreadful brutes there, Nathan."

"But Kate has the Frenchman with her, and Chatillon's good. I've only met him once, but I know his record, and I wouldn't mind having him alongside in a tough situation." He took my face between his hands and kissed me. "Anyway, we'll be down there in well under an hour." He picked me up and put me in the saddle of Sarrazin's horse as if I were a child, then swung up behind me, holding the gray's leading rein.

I said, "But there are four of them, Nathan."

He slid an arm round my body. "They've no leader, Bridie. And I have you back now, so I'm riding tall tonight."

Dusk became darkness before we were ten minutes on our way down from the high valleys, but then came a clear moon to ease our going. In that time we scarcely spoke except to murmur a loving word. I rode with Nathan's arms about me, my back against his chest. He held the reins loosely, allowing the horse to pick its way down the pathless slope, and his free hand was below my heart, holding me pressed to him. For a time I wanted nothing more than to be close to him in this manner, all anxiety shut away, mind empty of thought, simply feeling his presence, rejoicing in it, knowing a happiness and contentment beyond all telling. I sensed that for the moment Nathan, too, was glad simply to hold me in his arms, to murmur a loving word and touch his lips to my neck as we rode, to have me turn my head and kiss the corner of his mouth.

At last I gave a long sigh as if rousing from sleep, and pressed my hand over his. "Tell me, Nathan, dear."

He held me yet more tightly, and when he spoke his soft drawl was a little ragged. "That day, the day I left you, a man brought a message to me at the stage door between houses, Bridie. It was from Sarrazin. Said by the time I read it, he would be in France and married to your sister Kate. If I valued her welfare, and yours, I was to get out of England by the first possible boat. The message said I'd be under observation, and he'd be told by telegraph if I didn't act right away. I had to give the message back to the man, so I'd have no evidence of it. I guess reading those words was the worst moment of my life, Bridie."

I leaned my head back and pressed my cheek to his. "Oh, Nathan. Why didn't you tell me?"

"Because you're Bridie Chance, and a poor liar, and I knew Sarrazin was using Kate to get his hands on you. I took passage from Southampton to New York, but I quit the ship at Le Havre and headed down here to get Kate away from him. I didn't know how it would work out, especially with them being married, but the one thing I couldn't risk was having Sarrazin find out I was still in the field." I felt Nathan shrug. "I knew he had me figured as the biggest threat to his laying hands on the cache of jewelry. That's why I couldn't tell you, honey. I didn't dare. If I did, and somehow you came face to face with him, he'd soon find out I was still around, and then he'd go loco. I was scared of what he might do then."

I said, "Yes. He wasn't sane any longer." Then, after a little pause, "When you were in London, why did you ask Charlie if I was courting?"

"Wanted to know if Sarrazin was trying to get at you. I'd been warned by Philippe Chatillon that he could charm pretty well any girl, if he set his mind to it."

"Yes. He did try with me, but...I didn't want to be charmed." I pressed the broad strong hand that held me. "Nathan, was it very hard for you that day you went away—I mean, pretending you didn't love me and had only been trying to discover what I knew about the stolen jewelry?"

"I never had to do a harder thing in my life, Bridie," he said slowly, and leaned forward to touch his lips to my cheek. "I'd already quit Pinkertons when we were in Manchester, when I first knew I loved you. I sent a cable straight off, saying I resigned, and I guess they were mad as wet hens. No way they could put a new man in, because I told them I wouldn't have it. Anyway, they cabled back and said they'd be glad if I'd just stay on guard to keep any criminal parties away from you, and only report anything I considered to be to your benefit. That was fine with me."

"Whyever didn't you tell me then?"

"Tell you I'd struck up acquaintance under false pretenses? That I'd started out by working for a detective agency, trying to pry information out of you?" His voice was very soft, his lips almost touching my ear. "Bridie, I was afraid you'd hate the sight of me. Afraid you'd believe I was just trying a new line to find out what I wanted to know."

I shook my head. "No. I would have believed you, Nathan. I love you."

"Those are the best words I ever heard." He was silent for a moment or two, then, "Bridie... you know what nearly broke me? It was when I pretended I'd never loved you and was only doing a job. You could easily have cut me to pieces with words for being a low-down skunk, but you didn't. You just said good-bye and wished me well... and nearly tore my heart out." He bent his head to kiss the curve of my neck in the darkness.

As we rode steadily on I learned that he had come down from Le Havre to Brive by train, but without Lucifer, for there had been no time to arrange transport for his horse. From Brive he had traveled on foot through wooded valleys and over barren hills, moving by night when he had open ground to cover. The terrain was unfamiliar to him, but he was a seasoned lone traveler, well able to live off the land and fend for himself. He had been able to buy maps in Limoges, and if the ground was new to him the sky was not, and the stars were old familiar friends whose ways he knew.

It had not been difficult for him to reach Valbrison two days ago and make a small hidden camp for himself in the woods that lay just to the north of the château. It was through these woods that Sarrazin and I had passed little more than two hours ago. Nathan had missed seeing my arrival with Philippe, but had been watching the château from a vantage point in the woods when he had seen me leave with Sarrazin, and had then trailed us up into the high valleys where the Capricorn Stone stood.

"Wasn't easy figuring what to do when I first got here," he said as we came down toward the woods. "Seemed like Kate was here of her own free will, and all I could do was watch and wait. Then I saw them bring the women in, the saloon girls from Brive, so I decided Sarrazin must have stopped pretending, and I figured your poor sister would be real glad to get out now. I was going in tonight, Bridie, hoping they'd all be drunk and... busy. Kate was Sarrazin's wife, but I figured to hell with that. I knew you'd want her out, no matter about being married to that scum, so I aimed to fetch her out, head for Paris with her, cable you, and go straight to Philippe Chatillon. He's not official police, and I reckoned he was the best man to advise Kate how to get free from Sarrazin, even if it meant us taking her off to the States."

I rubbed the big sinewy hand that rested under my heart. "You couldn't have chosen better, Nathan. Philippe was watching Kate in London, and he's fallen completely in love with her."

Behind me Nathan laughed softly in astonishment. "I'll be damned. Isn't that something?"

There were lights burning in two or three upper windows of the château as we rode through the outer courtyard and dismounted under the archway leading to the small inner courtyard. In several other windows there was a paler glow, as if lamps had been lit in some of the passages and the light was filtering through to the windows of rooms where doors had been left open.

Nathan untied Sarrazin's body and heaved it over one shoulder without ceremony. "Stay close behind me, honey," he said, his voice calm and gentle. "They sent the women away, so there's no call for those lights upstairs. It makes me think your sister and Philippe Chatillon must have found that key, and now there's some kind of hide-and-seek game going on. Let's go and tell Sarrazin's friends the game's over."

He walked with long strides toward the porch on the far side of the inner courtyard, the body over his shoulder, and continued unhurriedly up the steps to the ancient door. I felt no fear now, for I had put my whole trust in him, and I did exactly as he had said, keeping a pace or two behind him all the way. Reaching out, he heaved on the bellpull, and we heard the loud jangling within. A full minute passed. We waited patiently in the darkness, not speaking, not needing to speak, close to each other in our minds. At last there came the rattle of a huge bolt being drawn and the voice of a man calling urgently beyond the door. The handle was turned from within, the door began to open, and the words became clear as the man shouted anxiously in French, "Victor! Thank God you are back! They have broken out—"

The door was open no more than six inches when Nathan smashed the flat of his foot against it at waist height in a tremendous kick. The timbers shuddered as they were hurled back, and I heard a cry of anguish. Nathan stepped into the poorly lit hall, and I followed him. The thickset man called Didi lay sprawled on his back half a dozen paces away, one hand clasped over a bloody face, the other groping for a pistol that lay where it had evidently fallen beside him as he was flung to the floor.

Without apparent haste Nathan stalked forward. The man found the pistol, raised it, then gave another scream of pain as Nathan casually kicked it from his hand and sent it slithering across the floor. Didi was still staring up in frozen terror when Nathan shrugged a shoulder and dropped Sarrazin's body across him. Next moment, to my surprise, Nathan spoke in French. *"Voilà votre maître,"* he said. *"Il est mort. Voulez-vous le suivre à l'enfer?"*

There is your master. He is dead. Do you wish to follow him to hell?

The words were spoken with the same drawling intonation that Nathan used in speaking English, and the accent was quite the most astonishing I had ever heard, the kind that makes a Frenchman wince or laugh. But I think no man alive could have looked into Nathan's face at that moment and laughed. Certainly Didi showed no inclination to do so. He gave a strange whimper and crawled frantically away from the body, gabbling incoherent pleas and excuses.

Nathan looked up, and I followed his gaze. Only two lamps were burning in the hall, but there were no lights at all on the gallery above, and the staircase rose into a pool of darkness. Nathan moved to the foot of the stairs and stood listening. A ray of light gleamed on the brown back showing through his ripped shirt, and I saw that the big knife was in his hand now. Lifting his voice he called, "Monsewer Chatillon?"

From above there came a sudden scuffling noise, a gasping cry, and then from behind the curtain of darkness a limp figure came tumbling into view, rolling with considerable impetus down the stairs. Nathan stepped aside as it finally sprawled to a halt on the dusty and unpolished floor at the foot of the stairs. The man Philippe had called André l'Apache lay face up, unconscious, a short black club attached to his wrist by a leather loop.

A voice from the darkness said, "There is surely only one man in the world with such an accent, and I am more than glad to hear it, Mr. McFee." Philippe Chatillon emerged from the gloom at the top of the stairs as he spoke. He was in shirt-sleeves, a stained bandage made from strips of white petticoat round his head, a heavy black poker hanging from his right hand.

Nathan sketched a mock bow and said, "Glad to see you, monsewer. Bridie tells me there were four men here."

"Thanks to Bridie providing the means of escape, I had already managed to surprise and disable two of them." He nodded down at the senseless form of André l'Apache. "And your most welcome arrival made a diversion which enabled me to do the same with that one. But I am most grateful to you for dealing with Didi. He was the one with a pistol—"

Philippe broke off and half turned, reaching out a hand. "Yes, come, *ma petite*," he said gently. "It is finished now." A shadowy figure appeared from the darkness of the gallery, moving toward the head of the stairs, and next moment Kate was there beside him, taking his outstretched hand, turning to gaze down at us, her eyes charcoal black in a face as white as bone.

"Where . . . where is he?" she said in a voice so low I could barely hear her.

Nathan took off his hat and gestured to where he had dropped the body. "Sarrazin is dead, ma'am," he said quietly. "He went loco and tried to kill us both with a saber. Came off his horse though, with a little help, and took a fall that killed him."

Kate nodded slowly, and the fierce tension seemed to drain out of her. She looked past Nathan to where I stood, and her voice broke as she said, "You were so kind before,

Bridie. Don't be cross with me now it's over. Oh, please don't."

I could not speak, but moved forward and opened my arms to her for the second time that night. I had learned from my own experience that this was a gesture which told far more than words. She gave a little sob, then caught up her skirts and came flying down the stairs, not looking at the sprawled bodies of the living and the dead, pausing only for a moment to catch Nathan's hand in both her own and to look up at him with wordless gratitude before turning to throw herself into my arms. She did not weep, but her teeth were chattering as she spoke haltingly, her face pressed into my shoulder.

"Bridie, you're safe. Oh, thank God you're safe. I was sure he meant to kill you. Oh Bridie, I've been so stupid, so wickedly stupid... caused so much trouble and pain. I'm so ashamed I wish I could die. And Philippe has been so good to me... I scarcely know who he is, just his name. But nobody could have been more gentle and comforting. And so brave, Bridie. We found the key you'd pushed under the door, and he said when he'd dealt with those awful men we'd come after you, but I was so frightened that we would be too late, I didn't dream there was anybody else to help you. That must be Nathan, the one you wrote to me about in your last letter. Oh Bridie, I'm too ashamed to face him, too ashamed to face Philippe now. Hold me tight, Bridie..."

I did not try to stem her outpouring of sorrow and humiliation. There would be time enough later to give comfort and reassurance, to try in every way possible to heal the deep and cruel wounds she bore within her. For the moment it was enough that she could turn to me and say all that was in her heart. I just kept gently patting her shoulder until at last her muffled, faltering voice trailed into the silence of exhaustion.

After a little while I lifted my head and was vaguely surprised to see that the hall was empty. The body of Sarrazin had disappeared, together with Didi and the unconscious André. Still holding Kate I said, "We have to wait a little while. Nathan and Philippe are busy. Come and sit down, darling."

She moved like a sleepwalker as I led her to a settle, and sank down beside me in the circle of my arm, her head pillowed on my shoulder. Nathan appeared from above, dragging the black-haired and barely conscious Felix down the stairs by his collar. "Just tidying up, honey," he said as he passed us. "Won't be too long now. This is the last one."

I nodded and closed my eyes. Time passed, and perhaps I dozed. When I roused again I saw Philippe standing watching us, his face pale and weary in the lamplight, but his eyes alert. Kate did not stir, and I wondered if she had fallen asleep. In a low voice I said, "Please can we go soon, Philippe? This is a place of horror for my sister. For us all, I think."

"In a very few minutes we will leave, Bridie." He turned his head to look toward the dining hall. "Sarrazin lies in there, and we have locked the others in the cell below. My good friend Nathan has ridden to fetch his belongings from where he was camped in the woods. He will bring the carriage from the coach-house, and we shall drive down to the station at Valbrison. I will speak to the local gendarme, telling him to take charge here for an hour or so until men can be sent from the police post in Brive. We ourselves will take the next train to Brive. There is one every hour at ten minutes past, so we shall catch the train soon after nine o'clock, and spend tonight at a hotel there."

My head ached, and it was an effort to make my mind bestir itself. After a moment or two I said, "The police won't ask questions of Kate tonight, will they? She's endured so much, Philippe."

He shook his head quickly. "Have no fear of that, Bridie, I will arrange everything. When we reach Brive I will telegraph a colleague in the Sûreté, a man of authority. This case is of great importance now, since it involves the recovery of Le Sorcier's spoils, so it will be dealt with by Paris, where I have much influence."

"Shall we be involved in . . . court proceedings?"

Again he shook his head. "The examining magistrate

will certainly find that Victor Sarrazin brought about his
own death. Beyond that, there is nothing to answer. The
newspapers will make something of the recovery of the
jewelry, of course, but you have both suffered more heavily
from that sort of thing before. And very soon . . ." he spread
his hands and smiled, "very soon it will all be past. Finished."

"I shall be truly glad then, Philippe."

"So shall we all. I must tell you that Miss Kate has been
splendid in these hours of severe trial. She cared for me
when I was hurt, and remained entirely calm throughout the
time of danger which followed."

"Yes. I'm very proud of the way she behaved."

"Tomorrow we shall go to Paris. I hope that you and she
and the good Nathan will be guests in my home. There is
ample room."

"Thank you, Philippe. You're very kind, and it would
be a great relief to be under your wing until this affair is
over."

"It will be my pleasure." We had been speaking almost
in whispers, and now he made a little gesture toward Kate.
"Is Miss Kate asleep?"

She stirred in my encircling arm, and pressed her face
more closely into my shoulder. In a barely audible voice
she said, "No . . . but I'm afraid to look at you, Philippe."

"Afraid?" he said wonderingly.

"Ashamed. I have brought you all close to death by what
I have done."

"No. That was Sarrazin's work. Do not blame yourself
for being deceived by him. That was his genius."

There was a little silence. I did not speak, for I sensed
that this was a moment of very great importance, and the
issue rested in Philippe's hands. He said reflectively, "The
bodice and skirt of your dress are smeared with blood, Miss
Kate. Blood from the cut on my head. When I was hurt,
you cared for me and held me in the comfort of your arms
until my senses returned. When we moved against our cap-
tors, you put your hand in mine and placed your trust in
me. Between those who have passed through the shadow

of death together, as we have, there is a bond which might otherwise take a thousand days to forge. Until three hours ago we had never spoken, but surely we are close friends now, you and I?"

Kate stirred, and I slid my arm away as she sat up. For a moment her head was bowed, then she lifted it and looked at Philippe. Her face was smeared with dirt, her hair in disorder, her eyes weary and older than her years now, yet still she was beautiful.

"I am a second-hand woman, Philippe," she said.

He smiled. "Rubbish, *ma petite*. You are a young, talented, and beautiful girl with more than enough intelligence to realize that you have been the victim of a monster, and that you have the whole of life before you. Let the past lie dead, and let the future begin tomorrow." He extended a hand. "Please. Will you take my hand in friendship, Kate?"

She closed her eyes for a moment. When she opened them again I saw tears run down her cheeks, then she stood up, moved slowly toward Philippe, and took his outstretched hand. A wave of thankfulness swept through me. He reached to gather her other hand and they stood facing each other. "All will be well," he said quietly. "All will be well, Kate."

I rose and moved to the open door. A carriage and pair stood in the starlit courtyard at the foot of the steps. From the outer courtyard came the sound of hooves, and next moment Nathan cantered through the archway. For a brief second I saw, as I had once seen long ago, a fiery pinpoint against the dark silhouette of his figure; then the small red glow curved through the air and fell to the ground, leaving a thin trail of sparks as he tossed the cigar away.

He reined in, slid to the ground, kissed me, and said, "Just went to fetch my gear, honey." He threw a rolled blanket and a knapsack into the carriage, then turned and slipped an arm round my waist. "Where's Kate?"

"In the hall, Nathan dear." I pressed a hand over his.

"How is she?"

"I think she'll be all right. Philippe is looking after her."

"Ah. That's good." He grinned, lifted his voice, and

called in his excruciating French, "*La voiture vous attend, monsewer!*"

I heard Philippe laugh and say, "*Mon Dieu!*" A few seconds later he came out with Kate, walking hand in hand. Nathan was holding the carriage door open for her, but she paused, turning to him.

"I have not thanked you yet, Mr. McFee."

He smiled. "My pleasure, ma'am. And you'd best call me Nathan, seeing that we'll soon be brother- and sister-in-law."

"I think you are a lucky man to have Bridie for a wife, Nathan."

"I think so too, Kate."

"And I count myself lucky to have you for a brother." She put her hands on his shoulders, went on tip-toe, and kissed his cheek, then turned and climbed into the coach. Nathan blinked, pushed his hat back on his head, and looked at Philippe. "There's something about these Chance girls," he said.

Philippe laughed, then extended his hand toward the open carriage door and made a little bow to me. "Please to ascend, Bridie, and then let us be away."

I shook my head. "You go with Kate, please." I took Nathan's arm and hugged it to me. "I'm going to ride with the driver."

⚡ eighteen ⚡

Early on a morning of golden weather in my second summer in New England, I rose from the splendid bath in the newly installed bathroom next to the nursery at Greenways, and reached for one of the big white towels. As I dried myself I smiled at the memory of the times I had sat in a battered hip bath in dressing rooms from Edinburgh to Birmingham, sponging paperhanger's paste from my body.

Excitement bubbled within me, for yesterday had brought two letters from England and there was much to look forward to, even beyond the everyday happiness that life had given me. When I had toweled myself dry I put on a clean shift, one of the short ones I wore in summer reaching not quite to my knees, then brushed out my hair and padded on bare feet through to the nursery where six-month old Philip Nathan McFee lay sound asleep in his cot. His wrath if woken up to be fed was terrible to behold, so I crept silently away, back through the bathroom and into our bedroom, where Philip Nathan McFee's father lay sprawled face down beneath a rumpled sheet.

Quietly I moved to the dressing table, picked up Kate's letter, moved to where a thin shaft of early morning sunlight squeezed between slats of the blind, and began to read the letter again. She wrote every month now, with the same unfailing regularity as Charlie Perkin, but this letter held special news.

Nathan said suddenly, "Morning, Mrs. McFee, ma'am."

I gave a start of surprise, then floated back across the room on wavering legs in a reverse Willow Strut, eyes wide and mouth round as I conjured up "Arnold" of Alfie Perkin and Company. Nathan, still in the same position, rolled one eye round to watch me, then came up on his elbow with a laugh that was full of delight. "Hey, it's better when you're just in a shift, Bridie. Your legs show more. Do the Crab Glide for me."

"Nathan, I'm always doing steps for you."

"Ah, come on, honey. Please."

"You're a great big baby, but I'll do it because I love you. And because you're always a wonderful audience." I had never felt the least bit shy with Nathan. Putting down the letter I hitched my shift up to my thighs, then went undulating across the room toward him in the first eccentric step I had ever learned, my face wearing an expression of wanton menace. I never worried nowadays about the way my face behaved, for Nathan loved what Nannie Foster had always called my "exaggerated expressions."

As I reached the bed with the final steps of the Crab Glide he gave a shout of laughter, and I flung myself upon him, kissing him hard and long. When at last I lifted my head he said a little breathlessly, "How's the young master?"

"Still asleep. Oh Nathan, isn't it wonderful news from Kate? Could we go to Paris after Christmas, so we could be there when she has her baby?"

"Sure, Bridie. Young Philip Nathan will be a year old by then. High time he started to see some of the world."

Kate had married Philippe Chatillon three months ago. We had been unable to go to the wedding, for our baby was then only twelve weeks old.

I looked down at Nathan and said, "It really will be so lovely to see her. And Philippe, too. I suppose in a way it's a pity she isn't going on seriously with her music, but I don't exactly feel sorry."

"You once said that if she wanted to be a concert pianist, she'd have to make that her life."

"Yes."

He gave me a little squeeze. "Well, I figure she's got something better. She can play for herself, her family, her friends. Let someone else be famous."

"Yes . . . I expect that's what I feel, Nathan."

He ran a finger along my lower lip. "And what about the other letter, Bridie?"

"Oh my darling, isn't it exciting?"

The other letter was from Charlie, and also carried special news. Alfie Perkin and Company had secured a booking to tour the major East Coast cities in burlesque—as music hall was called in America. They would be over here throughout autumn and winter, and had arranged for a break of two weeks before playing Boston, only forty miles from our home.

"May they stay with us while they're resting before Boston?" I asked. "I'm so fond of them, Nathan, I'll never forget all they did for me."

"Nor shall I, honey," he said soberly, and smoothed a hand over my brow. "Now listen, you write today and say they're to be our guests for those two weeks, but you also tell Alfie to get over here a couple of weeks before the whole tour starts."

"Oh, yes! But . . . why, Nathan?"

"Because there's work to be done. Folk in New York, Philadelphia, Baltimore, they'll have a little trouble with Alfie's accent, so we'll have to broaden it. Ethel's all right, and Charlie doesn't talk anyhow. I figure it might be best to cut down on dialogue and expand the action."

"Yes," I said thoughtfully. Nathan was right. Alfie would be almost as incomprehensible to some audiences in America as Jackie Blair, the Scottish comedian, had been to me on that dreadful night in Glasgow, but he could adapt his accent with a little instruction.

"And you can help build up the action, Bridie," Nathan went on. "You know the sketches, and you're good with ideas. You could start working out some fresh business right away, so you're ready for when they arrive."

I laughed. "All right. But I think it's just a plot, so you can watch me practice."

"No. That's a bonus, honey."

A faint wail found its way through from the nursery. We cocked our heads, listening, and the wail grew steadily more demanding. Nathan sighed, kissed me, and let me go. I rose from him reluctantly and moved to open the blinds so that bright sunshine lit the room. My husband sat up and followed me with his eyes, as he so often did. It gave me great pleasure that Nathan enjoyed watching me, for it made me feel loved and wanted.

"Fetch him in to feed him, Bridie, huh?" he urged softly.

"So you can just lie there watching, while we do all the work?"

"That's what I had in mind. Won't be much longer now, honey." He reached out his arms.

I went to him, ruffled his hair, and bent to be kissed again. Then, with my heart singing, I went through to the nursery to fetch our son.